"Magic has never felt so real. W. [...] -
sents an alternate world that feels [...]ory, even
when steeped in spellcraft and magic. It reminded me of the best of
Jim Butcher, but charts a path all its own."

—James Rollins, #1 *New York Times* bestselling author of
The Demon Crown

"*Breach* is a Cold War fantasy that nails the period flavor of a divided
Berlin haunted by the horrors of the past, with a great cast and plenty
of magic. Fans of Tim Powers's *Declare* or Charles Stross's *The Atrocity Archives* will like this one!"

—Django Wexler, author of *The Infernal Battalion*

"W. L. Goodwater delivers one surprise after another in his high-octane magical spy thriller *Breach*. It's like Lev Grossman's *The Magicians* meets John le Carré's classic *The Spy Who Came in from the Cold*, but with more action and better one-liners. Goodwater is a kick-ass new voice in the modern-fantasy arena!"

—David Mack, *New York Times* bestselling author of
the Dark Arts series

"*Breach* is a galloping, cutthroat thrill ride with characters you can
root for, even if you sometimes want to slap them."

—Lara Elena Donnelly, author of *Amberlough*

"With a vintage vibe and modern magic, *Breach* is a perfectly unique
spy thriller with an exceptional cast and a killer setting that's colder
than the Cold War ever dreamed of being. It's one hell of a mystery,
yes. But it's also a whole lot of fun."

—Cherie Priest, author of *Brimstone*

"Arcane magic meets Cold War intrigue in this alternate history series
opener. . . . Goodwater sprinkles powerful truths about the nature of
power into this entertaining tale of magic and espionage . . . [a] well-constructed world and thrilling vibe." —*Publishers Weekly*

"Goodwater's debut is a fantastic alternate version of the Cold War era. . . . Magic, espionage, and history combine in this thrilling, fast-paced fantasy." —*Booklist*

"Goodwater's debut novel is tightly wound in the way that only good suspense stories can be. . . . *Breach* combines the magical world building of *The City & the City* with the suspense of Cold War thrillers like *Bridge of Spies*, resulting in a cinematic suspense story that will keep readers on the edge of their seats until the very last page."

—*BookPage*

"John le Carré meets *The Magicians*. . . . Goodwater combines elements of spy noir with adult fantasy to create an entirely new magical world that remains very much grounded in our own. . . . A blend of fast-paced magical thrills and character-driven drama that also provides some much-needed catharsis based on the very real anxieties of the world that exists outside the pages of a book."   —Den of Geek

"Readers who enjoy slow-building action, spy thrillers, feisty hero-ines, and Cold War intrigue will love this book."

—Books, Bones & Buffy

"A fine thriller here, laced with just the right amount and balance of history, action, and magic."   —The Bibliosanctum

"Goodwater brings to life the Cold War setting in this entertaining spy fantasy/thriller . . . an excellent, entertaining debut. Spies and magic vie to maintain peace set against the background of the Cold War. Balancing pace, character development, plot points, and infor-mation reveals, *Breach* delivers a hell of a read."   —Primmlife

TITLES BY W. L. GOODWATER

Breach
Revolution

REVOLUTION

W. L. GOODWATER

ACE
NEW YORK

ACE
Published by Berkley
An imprint of Penguin Random House LLC
penguinrandomhouse.com

Copyright © 2019 by Walter Goodwater

Library of Congress Cataloging-in-Publication Data

Names: Goodwater, W. L., author.
Title: Revolution / W. L. Goodwater.
Description: First Edition. | New York : ACE, 2019. |
Series: A Cold War Magic novel ; 2
Identifiers: LCCN 2019012546 | ISBN 9780451491053 (pbk.) |
ISBN 9780451491060 (ebook)
Subjects: | GSAFD: Fantasy fiction.
Classification: LCC PS3607.O592258 R48 2019 | DDC 813/.6—dc23
LC record available at https://lccn.loc.gov/2019012546

First Edition: November 2019

Printed in the United States of America
1 3 5 7 9 10 8 6 4 2

Cover art: vintage cars in Cuba by taikrixel
Cover design by Pete Garceau
Book design by Kristin del Rosario

To my son. Thanks for sleeping occasionally so I could write this book.

ACKNOWLEDGMENTS

Two books in and I'm no less grateful to everyone who has aided, enabled, improved, supported, and cheered on my writing. Creating a novel is the work of a community. Thanks then to all, and especially:

To Jen Udden, agent extraordinaire, who turned my stand-alone spy fantasy novel into the Cold War Magic series.

To my editor, Rebecca Brewer, who fought from outline to final version to make this book better than I could have made it myself.

To my family, who let me write silly stories when I should have been sleeping.

To Aaron, for helping me break the story for this book over Cajun food.

To my early readers, who read this unpublished fantasy novel on a much tighter schedule than usual.

To the team at Ace, who are ace.*

And to everyone who picked up a copy of *Breach* and thought, *Sure, why not?* Bonus thanks to anyone who said something nice about it afterward. If you gave it out as a gift or got your book club to read it, you get a gold star.

And lastly to you, once again, for reading the Acknowledgments section when you know you aren't going to be in it. We've got to stop meeting like this, random reader who likes reading long lists of strangers' names. Or not. See you next time!

* *I'm a dad now; I'm allowed to make this joke.*

When the Soviets' magical wall bisecting Berlin starts to fail, the US sends Karen O'Neil, a young researcher with the Office of Magical Research and Deployment, to investigate. Her CIA minders hope she can fix the breach in the Wall before it creates an international crisis—and before she learns the Wall's true purpose. But that all changes when she meets Erwin Ehle, a German magician who helped create the Wall—and the one who caused it to fail.

The Berlin Wall was put in place to hide away Auttenberg, a district of Berlin corrupted by unspeakable Nazi magic. Deep inside those forgotten streets was a book with no name, written in many languages by many hands. It is known only by its opening lines:

Concerning that which must never come to pass . . .

This book has always existed, in one form or another. If it is destroyed, it will be rewritten.

Facing allies and enemies, ghosts of the past and illegal magic, Karen and Ehle enter Auttenberg and find that the book's magic has torn open a breach in reality. Beyond the breach is pure, raw magic. This power is so strong that anything that passes beyond the breach is destroyed so utterly that it is forgotten.

Karen defeats the Nazi magicians who opened the breach and destroys the book. Before the breach closes, Ehle steps through. Karen returns home and finds an unexpected book waiting in her desk drawer, written in her own hand, starting with the words:

Concerning that which must never come to pass . . .

ONE

Such a small thing, little more than a paperweight. Gerald held it up with delicate fingertips. It was heavy for its size, and warm to the touch. Under the harsh laboratory light, he could see his own reflection in the cube's glossy black surface: bespectacled and haggard. He must have aged a decade in the last year, the result of too many sleepless nights. When he first started with the company, he'd been too busy for sleep; with new breakthroughs discovered every day, rest had been an unwelcome distraction. But now he slept even less, for a different reason.

His coworker Ray's jarring voice brayed from across the room. "What's the ID number for that one, Gerry?"

ID number. An abstraction. Easier that way.

Gerald set the cube back down on his desk. "Number 26859-C."

Ray rolled over in his chair, the metal wheels whining on the tile floor. He never walked anywhere he could roll, a laziness that too often spilled over into his work.

"What's wrong with it?" Ray stopped his chair far too close to Gerald, who nearly choked on the ensuing cloud of aftershave.

"Nothing," Gerald said.

"Then why is it out of the security locker?"

Gerald had expected Ray's insufferable nosiness. Planned on it, in fact. "Routine testing," Gerald said. "Looking for storage bleed."

Ray leaned in and peered at the cube. It gave off a soft, subtle glow that hinted at what was contained within. "And?"

"No noticeable power loss," Gerald said. He quickly tucked the cube away into its cloth bag and turned to face Ray. "Don't you have enough on your plate without worrying about my work?"

"Well, forgive me for being curious." Ray rolled back a few rotations. The chair creaked underneath him. "Just trying to be friendly."

Gerald looked over the top rim of his glasses. "Have you finished everything for the product demonstration?"

"I'll get it done, Gerry. Don't you worry."

"I do worry, Raymond," Gerald said. "I worry because Mr. Magnus worries."

"Why? Did he say something?"

"You didn't see the memo?" Gerald raised an eyebrow. "He wants a full run-through of the presentation, with all required reports, tomorrow at ten a.m."

"Tomorrow?" Ray's face went pale. "I thought it was next week."

"Tomorrow," Gerald said. "Are your reports ready?"

"Ready?" Ray said, his pitch rising. "Hell no. I haven't even started."

"Then I guess you have a long night ahead of you."

"But the labs are closed for cleaning on Mondays." He was so anxious that he actually stood up and started pacing.

Gerald shrugged. "Take your documents home, work on it from there."

"I can't! I need too many proprietary documents. The security guys will never let me out of the building with them. They'll have me on a plane in half a minute. Or worse."

Gerald took off his glasses and began to clean the lenses with a corner of his lab coat. "What do you think will happen," he asked, "if you show up to the run-through with unfinished reports?"

That was all it took. Ray rushed around the lab, frantically filling his arms with folders and notebooks. Even a man like Ray could work hard given the proper motivation, and fear of Mr. Magnus's displeasure was more than sufficient. Ray was so concerned about the consequences of failure that he never noticed as Gerald switched out the bag containing #26859-C and placed it into his briefcase.

Gerald just wished he could stop sweating. Even though it was already December, it was still nearly ninety degrees outside. The humidity was even worse. But Gerald had other reasons to sweat as he walked down the main stairwell to the facility's exit; the security personnel at the Magnus Special Projects Laboratory trusted no one, not even Magnus employees. Perhaps especially Magnus employees. He was certain his shirt sticking to his back or the steam gathering on his glasses would be a dead giveaway.

Posters lined the primary hallway out of the facility. Each one depicted hardworking magicians and scientists making the world a better place.

MAGNUS INNOVATIONS—DISCOVER THE FUTURE, TODAY!
DO YOUR BEST! IT'S THE MAGNUS WAY!
LEAVING WORK EARLY? THEN YOU'RE HELPING
THE COMMUNISTS!

Near the end of the hall, prominently displayed, was one that Gerald stared at every day as he clocked in and out. It showed a devious set of slanted eyes floating over a rendering of their research facility, dark storm clouds glowering in the background. The words were written across the top in bold, bloodred script:

OUR ENEMIES ARE EVERYWHERE. BE VIGILANT! SPEAK UP!

Not for the first time, Gerald thought back on his days working at the Office of Magical Research and Deployment. The OMRD hadn't had much of a budget, and the research department produced only a few worthwhile innovations during his time there, but he had enjoyed the work. And more importantly, while working there, he'd never feared for his life. Or his soul.

When Gerald reached the exit, his stomach sank. Most days, a single bored-looking guard stood at the exit, watching over the mass exodus at six p.m. with a rifle and casual disinterest. But occasionally the head of security, a sour man named Alexander Sage, would decide to order a spot check. A spot check meant a dozen guards, heavy scrutiny, and random bag inspections. Today, of all days, Gerald counted at least sixteen grim-looking men flanking the doors, guns in hand. A few were armed with dowsing rods— tools for detecting magical energy—and were using them on the staff as they exited. The rods were calibrated to ignore low levels of power; the thing in Gerald's bag would make them glow like the star of Bethlehem. Sage himself was there, overlooking the procedure with his trademark scowl. The line of employees waiting to leave snaked around the corner.

Turn around, Gerald thought. *Put it back before anyone notices. Once you get in that line, it'll be too late.*

He sighed. It was already too late; it had been for a while now. He'd known that the moment he realized what was really going on at the facility. He got in line.

"I hate these inspections," the woman in front of him said under her breath. "What are they hoping to find anyway?"

"Traitors," said another man.

"Oh, don't be so dramatic."

"I'm serious," the man said. Gerald thought he recognized him: one of the marketing guys they'd brought on board in recent months to prepare for the product demonstration. "I heard they caught one a few weeks back. Someone trying to smuggle out secret formulas in his underwear."

"Please," the woman said with a laugh.

"Scout's honor," the marketing guy said, hand raised. "I heard they threw him down into the lower basement."

The woman scowled at this. "That's not funny." She shivered, despite the heat coming in from the outside doors. "Not funny at all."

The great secret of the Magnus Special Projects Laboratory's security was this: if the brutes with guns caught you putting the project at risk, the nicest thing they could do was shoot you, because they had other options.

Somewhere above them, they heard the rumble of thunder. Then again. And again, like footfalls. Exactly like footfalls.

"Ugh," the woman said, staring at the ceiling as the sound passed overhead. "Even the tame ones give me the creeps."

"That's good marketing copy," the man said with a chuckle. "Can I use that on one of our posters?"

Gerald wondered which one it was up there, not that it mattered; they were all unsettling. Unnatural. It was rare to hear them moving about. It wasn't like they wandered the halls where anyone could gawk at them. But they had to be tested, especially with the demonstration coming up. That was probably the real reason the labs were closed tonight.

They were approaching the front of the line. Gerald clung to his briefcase with clammy hands. He had contingencies for this; for all his mistakes, he wasn't a fool. But he was nearly at the guards and there was still no sign of—

Then he heard the sound of Ray's labored breathing. He appeared a moment later, his own bag bulging with documents he should not have. He too balked when he saw the guards, but Gerald waved him up.

"I don't have time for this," Ray whispered when he reached Gerald. "I've still got hours of work to do."

"It's fine," Gerald said. "Here, you can go ahead of me."

"Really?" Ray said. "Thanks, Gerry, that's great."

Gerald saw him tighten his grip on his bag. "Don't worry," Gerald said softly. "These guys don't care about documents. Just act natural."

"Right," Ray said. "Right."

The marketing guy made it through without an inspection. Then the woman, who just got a nod from the thick-necked guard at the door. Now the trickiest part . . .

As Ray stepped up to be inspected, Gerald put his free hand in his pocket. Inside, he felt the smooth grip of the bone-handled pocketknife his father had given him when he turned ten: his magical locus. He turned his head slightly, so he was facing away from the guards, and began to whisper the words to the spell. One of the guards waved the dowsing rod over Ray's bag; the thin stick of wood did not react. But then Gerald finished his incantation and the runes he'd traced inside Ray's bag while Ray was getting his lunch became charged with magical power.

"Wait a second . . . ," the guard said as the rod began to glow. Then spark.

The guard held up his burned-out dowsing rod. "Open your bag."

Ray nearly fainted. "What?" he asked, holding the bag to his chest. "I'm sure that was just a fluke or something. Those things break all the time."

The guard was joined by two others. Rifles appeared. Ray's bag was grabbed and its contents poured out onto a nearby table. Even from where he stood, Gerald could see the confidential and restricted stamps all over the pages. The guards looked at the documents, then one another, then Ray.

"I can explain," he said. "I needed to—"

"Take him," Sage, the head of security, said.

"No, no, no; you don't understand," Ray said. "I wasn't stealing anything! I just needed these to finish this report. I was going to bring them back, I promise!"

Everyone had stopped now and watched Ray plead his case with increasing volume as he was dragged toward a side door. Gerald felt a twinge of guilt. The punishment would be swift. Ray might keep his job, if he played nice. But it was necessary, regardless of the outcome. There was too much at stake.

"Keep moving," one of the guards said, all but pushing Gerald out the door. "Nothing to see here."

And then he was outside. Even in the evening, stepping out into the Cuban heat was an instant rebuke to whatever life choices had brought you to such a miserably hot place. But Gerald did not slow down; in truth he barely noticed the thick, sticky air or the lazy buzz of insects. As he moved away from the watchful eyes of Magnus security, he only noticed the weight of his briefcase and the thud of his heart drumming in his ears.

Gerald never felt safe in his cramped Havana apartment. There was only one window and it was covered with a threadbare curtain, but it still felt like anyone could be watching. Perhaps he'd been reading too many Magnus Innovations posters and now saw spies everywhere.

He would need to write a note. Even though he'd been planning this for weeks now, he still hadn't started it. He told himself that was in case the note was discovered, but that was a lie. The real reason was that he had no idea what to say. How could he explain what he'd seen, or the parts he could only guess at? How could he make her believe him? How could he make her forgive him?

No words were up to the task; that's why he'd stolen #26859-C. She'd have to see for herself.

He put the cloth bag and his quickly scrawled note into the box and folded it shut. Only then did he allow himself to breathe.

She would help him. She had to. There was no one else he could turn to, no one else he trusted. Not when lives were at risk. Not when lives had already been lost.

"I'm sorry for this," Gerald said. He started to write the shipping address:

> *Karen O'Neil*
> *Department of Theoretical Magic*
> *Office of Magical Research and Deployment*
> *Washington, DC*
> *USA*

He held the box up when he had finished. It fit in one hand. So much effort for such a small thing. He hoped it would be enough.

TWO

Karen had agonized over the wording for more than an hour already and had nothing to show for her effort. She'd written and then rewritten. She'd decided on an approach that she liked but then hated it before she finished the first sentence. Then she'd torn the page into little bits and started over. *Why is this so hard?* Finally, in a rush of frustration and exhaustion, she launched an assault on the typewriter with a flurry of clicks and clacks and then sat back to review the results.

Dear Director Whitacre,

Please accept my resignation from the Office of Magical Research and Deployment, effective immediately.

Sincerely,
Karen O'Neil
Head Researcher, Department of Theoretical Magic

What it lacked in eloquence, it made up for with brevity. Perhaps it was the starkness of the language, or maybe just seeing the words in black and white, but she felt untethered and more than a little frightened. The OMRD was more than her career; it was her life. Or it had been. She hurriedly folded the letter up and sealed it away in an envelope, where it couldn't hurt anyone. Not yet at least.

"Need me to mail that?" Her assistant's cheery voice startled Karen so suddenly that she nearly jumped out of her chair, banging her knee hard on her desk in the process. "Oh, that sounded like it hurt. Are you alright, Miss O'Neil?"

Karen rubbed her knee. "Yes, Madge," she said through tight teeth.

"Sorry, I didn't mean to—"

"It's fine," Karen said. She tucked the letter into a desk drawer. "And no, I don't need you to mail it. I need to think on it a bit first."

"You're the boss," Madge said in a grating singsong. Karen missed Allison, her former assistant who'd foolishly gone off and married some dummy from the third floor. After Allison had been Greta, then Muriel, and now Madge, each less competent than the last. She wasn't resigning to escape her litany of annoying assistants, but it was a small consolation to throwing away her dreams.

"Harry wanted me to ask you if you'd be joining them for the experiments tomorrow morning?" Madge said. "At least, I'm pretty sure that's what he said."

"No," Karen replied softly. "He can handle it without me." She didn't spend much time in the lab anymore. She used to all but live in the lab. Now, she felt uneasy. Too much magic had been cast there; the room hummed with it. It was a big reason for the letter she'd just written.

Madge dropped a pile of mail onto Karen's already overflowing desk with a thump.

"Anything worth reading?" Karen asked.

Madge shrugged. "I didn't really go through it."

"Isn't that part of your job?" Karen asked as nicely as she could.

Madge stared at her and blinked. "You want me to read your mail?" she asked slowly, as if sounding the words out phonetically.

Karen sighed to keep from screaming. "No," she said. "Of course not." She picked up the pile, fanned through it briefly, and then dropped the whole stack into the metal wastebin next to her desk. "Is there anything else?"

"Umm . . ." Madge chewed her lip a moment. Karen could only guess at the complex calculations taking place in order to come up with an answer. "Right, you also got a package." Madge produced a small cardboard box and handed it to Karen.

The box was a little roughed up from its journey through the mail and was covered in a multicolored parade of stamps and stickers from various customs agencies. It took her a moment to even find the return address.

"I didn't know you had friends in Cuba," Madge said as she eyed the box over Karen's shoulder.

Karen had to read the name a few times for it to sink in. *Gerald. What is Gerald doing in Havana of all places?* He had been her partner in the research labs at the OMRD for a number of years. Together they'd tried every spell, incantation, or ritual known to man that claimed to summon magic that could heal wounds. Many lab rats had bled under their watchful care, sadly to no avail. Magic, it seemed, had no interest in putting things back together, only taking them apart.

But now, after Auttenberg, Karen knew differently.

"He's an old colleague," Karen said, "who left the OMRD a few years ago to work for a private company." She'd even written his letter of recommendation. He was a good magician, meticulous and careful. He'd been nearly impossible to replace.

She'd had to rely on him more than ever after losing her locus in Berlin. Without the unique token magicians use to focus their spells, Karen had been unable to use her magic in the nearly three years since, which was something of a liability when you were employed as a magical researcher for the US government. So she stuck to writing about theory and compiling reports and directing other magicians to do the actual spellcasting, all the while enduring their patronizing glances and whispers. A magician without a locus was a pathetic creature indeed.

What would they think if they knew the truth?

"I've always wanted to visit Cuba," Madge said dreamily. "The beaches, the nightclubs, the casinos! I've heard that you can see movie stars just walking down the street in Havana."

That sounded far from idyllic to Karen, but she said nothing. The box was surprisingly heavy for being so small. She spun it around. There was something else too, a faint tingle in the back of her mind as she held it. Something magical was contained within.

Karen's skin started to crawl. She was used to sensing magic; she was surrounded by it every day at the OMRD. Before Berlin, the feeling carried a thrill. Now it left her cold, like someone unseen was watching her. Yet despite her misgivings, she couldn't deny her curiosity. She was reaching for a knife to cut the box open when she heard voices in the next room. "What's going on in there?" she asked.

"Oh, that must be the director and his guests," Madge said absently as she bit a fingernail.

"The director?" Karen asked. "What guests?"

"Director Whitacre is giving a tour of the site to some congressional aides," Madge said as if it were the most obvious thing in the world. "I told you about it this morning."

"No," Karen said, choosing her words very carefully. "No, you didn't."

"Oh," Madge said with a shrug. "Sorry?"

Karen had no interest in seeing the director and certainly no interest in seeing anyone from Capitol Hill. She loved the work of the OMRD; it was vital, now more than ever, but the politics of it all made her stomach churn. She would leave that to the director, who seemed far more interested in being a politician than a magician. Karen wasn't even sure she'd ever seen him cast a single spell. That thought made her wince. *No time for self-pity now,* she thought. Not if she was going to avoid the coming onslaught.

"I'm going home," Karen said as she shoved the package into her leather satchel and threw the strap over her shoulder.

Madge blinked. "But . . . what will I tell the director?"

The voices outside her office were growing louder. She hurried for the back door. "Tell him," Karen said, "that I went home."

I t was dark before Karen reached her apartment. Living within walking distance of her office was convenient, though the walk was probably better suited to early September than late December. The wind blew right through her jacket and left her cheeks red and her fingers numb. The air tasted of coming snow. Christmas lights hung from roof gutters and skeletal trees all along her street, a cheerful multicolored reminder that this was a season for peace and joy. Karen did her best not to notice.

"You have to come," her sister, Helen, had pleaded over the telephone a few days earlier. "It's Christmas."

"I'll try."

Helen had sighed. "We both know what that means."

"Would you rather I lie to you and say that I'm coming?"

"Martha asked if you're going to be there."

"Really? You're going to play the niece card on me?"

"Whatever it takes," Helen had answered.

"I'll try."

She should want to spend time with her family, even if her

mother and father were coming. She should be happy to see her niece, who was growing up so fast while Karen wasn't looking. She should be excited about twinkling lights and Christmas trees and presents wrapped with a bow, but she wasn't. Maybe she'd known how to play that expected role once, but not anymore.

Not since Auttenberg. Not since magic turned on her and almost destroyed everything.

Parked cars lined the street, but it was otherwise nearly empty. Someone was walking toward her, wrapped tight in a heavy jacket with hands plunged deep into the pockets. Across the street, a weary mother herded woolen-scarfed children inside for dinner. People were going about their busy lives, unaware of the truth Karen had learned on the other side of the collapsing Berlin Wall: that magic wasn't some indifferent force waiting to be wielded by the gifted and the skilled. Magic had its own agenda, and it could not be trusted.

She thought about the letter she had written to Director Whitacre; would she shred this one like all the others? Though she struggled to see a future at the OMRD, she could not imagine what she would do elsewhere. She had worked so hard to earn her position there and just couldn't—

Lost in her thoughts, Karen didn't move out of the way of the man walking toward her, and they collided, which knocked her off balance. She felt a strong hand grip her arm, steadying her, but before she could thank the man, there was a sudden flash of metal.

"Keep your mouth shut and you won't get stabbed," he whispered into her ear as he pressed the knife's tip into her stomach. His breath was hot on her neck. "Give me your money. Now."

Adrenaline was sharp in her mouth as Karen tried to breathe. Even through her winter clothing, the knife pricked her skin, and the mugger's fingers dug painfully into her bicep.

"Hurry up," he said, tightening his grip.

She tried to ignore him, tried to retain control. Her magic, usually little more than a dormant whisper, now roiled inside her. She could sense the fire desperate to ignite on her fingertips. Power surged against the boundaries of her will, searching for a crack or a weakness.

"It's in my bag," she said, each word spoken with terrified care.

"Get it out," the mugger demanded. "Now."

She could kill him. It wouldn't be hard. She'd done it before, in Auttenberg. She could do it now, with a thought, and he'd die before he realized what was happening.

She unclasped the satchel and reached inside. She felt the package, her keys, and yes, her wallet. But that's not what she grabbed. She had the pistol free and the barrel shoved into her assailant's face in an instant, the dexterity she'd gained from years of spellcasting hand exercises finally paying off.

Karen slowly cocked the hammer with a shaking thumb. "Let go of me," she said. "Now."

The man's hands fell away. The knife vanished. "There's no need for that," he said as he continued to move back the way he had come. "This is just a misunderstanding, that's all."

Karen said nothing; she didn't trust her words. It took all her focus to keep the gun steady and her bloodthirsty magic in check. Her assailant took advantage of her hesitation and fled up the street, the slap of his shoes echoing back to Karen as she watched him disappear into the night.

The mugger waited in the aching cold for almost an hour before his employer finally appeared. One moment, he was alone with his steaming breath and numb fingers, and the next, the peculiar man who'd hired him was there, his face lined in shadow.

"It's about time," the mugger said.

"You failed," his employer said with his weird European accent.

"She had a gun," the mugger said. "A gun. You didn't say anything about a gun."

His employer sighed. "My instructions could not have been clearer." His employer came a little closer, the streetlamps casting light down on him. He was a tall man, and thin, but it was his tattoos that drew the most attention. Strange script spun and whirled across every bit of exposed skin, words written in some unknown language all over his body like parchment. Black lines traced up his neck and twisted onto his gaunt cheeks, ending just below his bright blue eyes. "You were supposed to scare her so she would use her magic."

"Magic?" the mugger said. "The gun was bad enough. She was a magician? You sent me to mug a magician? That's nuts, man. Are you trying to get me killed?"

"Whether you live or die is of little consequence to me," his employer said.

"Well, it matters a lot to me." The mugger paused a moment in reflection. "And why would a magician even need a gun?"

"A surprisingly astute question."

"Double," the mugger said. "I want double."

The tattooed man raised a blond eyebrow. "You wish to be paid double for accomplishing nothing?"

"I want to get paid for doing what I was told and not getting my head blown off by some crazy woman magician." In a flash, his knife was in his hand, the blade low and pointed at his employer. "Is that going to be a problem?"

The mugger never really understood how it happened, but his knife was suddenly gone. No, not gone; it was in his employer's hands. The man hadn't moved a muscle, and even if he had, they were too far apart for him to have grabbed it. The mugger gaped while his employer carefully folded the knife and tucked it away in his heavy jacket.

"If you are afraid of her magic," his employer said, "then you should be terrified of mine."

For the second time that night, the mugger started to back away from a fight he knew he couldn't win. "Nice doing business with you," he muttered as he hurried away.

The tattooed man remained. Her apartment building was just down the street. The lights in her windows were off. Nothing moved. A gun. He hadn't expected that. What need would she have for such a thing? And why was it so hard to get her to use her magic? He knew her locus had been lost, just as he knew that would be no impediment, not for her. She wasn't like the others; there was still hope for her.

Or so he believed. The others doubted. Questioned his motives, his conclusions. This did not bother him. There were always doubters—even among the faithful—and he was a patient man. This woman was unique, they would see. As soon as she drew on her magic, all doubts would be silenced.

So he remained, and he watched, as a light snow began to fall.

THREE

K aren huddled in the corner of her cramped bedroom. She'd tried to sleep in her bed, but lying there in the dark left her feeling exposed, vulnerable. Wrapped in a wool blanket with her back pressed against the solid walls of her apartment so she could face the door, she felt somewhat protected. The gun on the carpet next to her also helped. She'd bought it on a whim almost a year ago. The weight of it in her satchel had been comforting, though in truth she never expected to need to use it. She just wanted to have it so that she knew if something terrible happened, she wouldn't have to rely on her magic.

That was her big secret, after all, the one she'd kept entirely to herself after the events in Berlin. No one doubted her story that she couldn't cast magic after her locus had been destroyed; magicians everywhere immediately understood the ramifications of losing a locus. But she wasn't like magicians everywhere and she didn't need a locus anymore. She didn't even need the complex incantations and arcane spells that filled every magician's library. Berlin had changed everything. When her life was on the line, she'd drawn on power she never knew she had. She'd tapped into something deep: pure will, pure magic.

REVOLUTION   19

And it terrified her.

In Berlin, the magic had taken control.

No, that was a lie. An easy, comforting fiction; she'd been in control the whole time.

She'd killed those Soviet soldiers. *She'd* almost doomed them all by feeding the breach. Because it had felt good to have power.

Her magic had changed since. Before, it had been like a part of her, a muscle she could flex at will. But now it felt like something trapped inside of her, biding its time. The mugger had almost set it loose. If she hadn't been armed . . .

Why am I bothering to watch the door? The thing she feared most was already in the room with her.

In that moment, aching from sitting on the hard floor, afraid of her attacker, afraid of herself, afraid of the gun glinting dully on her blanket, she made a decision. Tomorrow morning, she would go to the director's office and deliver her resignation in person.

The OMRD wasn't the place for her anymore. Her coworkers still believed magic was something they could control, something they could use for good. She knew better; she'd seen through the breach, to the nothingness beyond. She didn't know where she'd go or what she'd do, but she couldn't be around magic.

So resolved, she finally was able to sleep.

Until she heard the voice.

Karen bolted awake, skin tingling. A few hours had passed. Her room was quiet, dark, empty. But she'd definitely heard something.

There it was again. A voice, muffled, coming from her living room.

Ignoring cramped muscles, she unfolded from her huddle and hefted the pistol in both hands. Her bare feet hardly made a sound as she crossed her bedroom floor, the barrel of the gun leading the way. She didn't hear anything from the other room. Was it the mugger? Had he followed her back to her apartment? She tightened her grip on the gun and stepped out.

The living room was as she'd left it. She saw no strangers and no knives. The boards under the carpet groaned as she moved into the room; she froze. Still nothing. Her small kitchen was to the right, just out of her line of sight. Had the intruder ducked in there? She inched forward, a sliver of the kitchen coming into view with each step. When she couldn't take it anymore, she rushed the final distance and came around the corner with a yell.

The kitchen was empty.

Her apartment was empty.

Karen lowered the gun. It must have been a neighbor in the hallway outside her front door. The heat of adrenaline drained away, turning her sweat to ice. She let out a long-held breath. She hadn't used to live in fear. What was she doing, wandering around in the dark with a gun? She was more likely to hurt herself than do anything heroic.

Her fingers were drawn to the spot on her stomach where the mugger had put his knife. She'd been fearless before, yes, but also naïve. Ignorant. The world, she had learned, was full of things worth being afraid of.

Then the voice spoke again. It was in the same room.

The sound was coming . . . from her kitchen table. From her satchel.

She'd been given the bag in Berlin, that much she remembered, but little else. She had no memory of who had given it to her, like a part of her mind had been locked down for her own protection. From the outside, the bag appeared mostly plain, just battered leather and a few brass clasps. But when she'd investigated inside, it was full of remarkable enchanted items. Without the use of her magic, she could not activate the enchantments, though she had

asked her assistants to analyze a few of them over the years. Some
had obvious uses, for combat or defense. Others remained a mystery,
including a peculiarly shaped box sealed with a locking spell more
powerful than any Karen had seen before. Mysteries and secrets.

She wondered sometimes why she kept it. It could be dangerous, after all. But it felt important. It felt like the missing memories
were important. And a modern woman deserved a sensible hand-
bag that could explode at any moment.

Or start talking in the middle of the night.

Carefully, slowly, she opened the satchel. The enchanted items,
in all their neat little pockets and pouches, stared silently back at
her. None of them had spoken. But Gerald's package thrummed
with magical potential. Karen took it out of the bag and set it on
the table. She'd meant to open it when she got home, but a knife
pressed to her gut had distracted her somewhat. Her mouth was
dry; all thoughts of sleep had been exiled.

She found a pair of scissors and cut the box open and retrieved
two items: a folded piece of paper and a velvety pouch closed with
a drawstring.

Gerald's note read:

Karen,

*I am so sorry. I can't trust anyone else. You have to
understand that I didn't know what they were doing. I
would have never been a part of this if I had known.
You have no reason to help me, not after what I've done. I
should never have taken it. I didn't know what it was,
but . . . no, I should apologize in person.*

Taken it? Taken what? She read on.

*Handle the enclosed item with the greatest of care. I don't have
all the answers, but I know it is the key to all of this. It is—*

Karen stopped reading the letter; the velvet pouch was starting
to glow.

She pulled back the drawstring and reached inside. Her fingers
brushed something smooth and warm. She set it on the table next
to the letter. It was an inky black cube, maybe three inches on each
side, polished and glassy. It gave off a low, steady light—almost
like moonlight—that cast strange shadows across her tiny kitchen
table.

It was obviously magic, but it wasn't just another enchanted
artifact. Enchanted items were filled with enough magical energy
to complete their appointed task: illuminating a dark place, or
heating your water for tea, or even launching an attack on an enemy.
Karen knew what to expect from these items, knew how they felt,
what vibrations they gave off.

But this cube was something else entirely. If a standard enchanted item was like a flashlight, then the cube was the sun. It
had more stored magic than anything she'd ever seen. How had
she not noticed this before? *What is this thing even made out of?* No
material Karen knew of could safely contain this much magical
energy. *How do they keep it stable?*

Then another thought occurred to her: *Is it stable?*

She leaned away from it, as if a few more inches would keep her
safe if it decided to blow. She suspected the outcome would look
something like those grainy films of nuclear bomb tests in the Pa-
cific. *Why would Gerald send this to me? Why would he even have such
a thing?* Karen reached for the letter to finish reading it when her
hand froze in midair, hovering over the cube.

It spoke. A small voice, tinny, but unmistakably human and
clearly belonging to a young girl. Now out of the satchel, the words

weren't muffled and they weren't in English. Being a classically trained magician, she had bits and pieces from a dozen or more languages jumbled up in her head, but after a moment of concentration, she understood.

"Ayudame," it said in Spanish.

Help me.

FOUR

There was a reason the gray-haired man did not like to go outside during a Moscow winter: the people. A lifetime in Russia had left him indifferent to the inhospitable cold, but even after decades in the great city, he could not abide the stupidity of drivers splashing their automobiles through icy puddles and sliding through filthy snow. It was a wonder they did not all end up in smashed-steel graves every morning. People afoot were barely more tolerable: wrapped up in fur and wool like they had never felt a blizzard's sting before, they stomped carelessly along in their heavy boots and knocked one another aside without apology. It was inelegant and loud, wet and foul.

And yet, some conversations were best done face-to-face, where you could measure the man to see if he was up for the task.

He could not remember the last time he had come to this part of Moscow; he had not missed it. The city was not without its charms, but they were not well expressed in the faceless, soulless rank-and-file apartment buildings that rose up on either side of the road like tombstones. These endless housing blocks were the Soviet Union's great paean to necessity: the Party served the people, and the people needed somewhere to hide from the cold.

The gray-haired man did not double-check the address in his greatcoat or the one affixed to the concrete building; he knew he was where he needed to be. The sun, if there even was one in the colorless Russian sky, was dipping low already, but he did not expect this would take long. The man he had come to see had waited in silence long enough. He would be ready.

He knocked on the door twice, ignoring the arthritic jab in his knuckles. He had given up the luxury of acknowledging pain a long time ago. When the door opened, the two men did not exchange words. The man inside moved away, back into the shadowed room, and the gray-haired man entered.

"Your country is too cold," the man said. His Russian had improved during his time in exile. "Men are not meant to live here."

"Children and weaklings should not live here," the gray-haired man said. "Men find a way to survive."

His host laughed. The sound echoed in the sparsely furnished room. The man did not look well. His skin was too pale for his complexion, his eyes rimmed with darkness. But this could easily be remedied with a change in climate.

"Survival has not been my problem, comrade. I have not done much during these years," his host said, "but I have survived."

"And for good purpose," the gray-haired man said. He offered his host a cigarette. When he lit it, the room danced with brief orange life. "I have need of you, Ramón."

"You have need?" Ramón asked. "Or the Chairman has need?"

Despite Ramón's appearance, his mind had not dulled. This was good. "I do," the gray-haired man said. "The Chairman and the Party are . . . distracted. I seek to gather what is necessary to help them pay closer attention."

"If you want me to return to my home and kill that butchering fool Franco, I will do it, even if it costs me everything."

"I too look forward to such a day," the gray-haired man said, "but that is not our current purpose. For now, Spain is a lesser priority."

His host seemed to diminish before his eyes. Ramón would serve the will of the Party, but he was not without biases. He could not be blamed for that. Suffering has a way of commandeering one's perspective. "Then why are you here?" he asked.

"Cuba."

Ramón's dark eyebrows raised. "Why Cuba?"

"They are on the brink of revolution," the gray-haired man said. "Even now, rebels hide in the mountains and jungles, waiting for a chance to topple their corrupt capitalist government."

"And it is close to the United States."

The gray-haired man nodded. "That is a consideration, yes."

Ramón crushed his cigarette. "So what would you have me do?"

"The Chairman doubts the sincerity and tenacity of these rebels. He does not believe they will be successful. I have my concerns, but wish to know more. That is where you can be of assistance."

"You want me to take the measure of these men," Ramón said. "And then what?"

"If they have the necessary mettle, help them burn their enemies to the ground."

The gray-haired man handed him a parcel. Ramón opened it and spread its contents on the dusty floor: stacks of bills in multiple currencies, passports, lists of contacts. He lifted the passport marked ESPAÑA and ran his fingers over the embossing.

"There is one more thing," the gray-haired man said.

Ramón nodded, as if this was not unexpected.

"There is an American company outside Havana," the gray-haired man said, "called Magnus Innovations. They are executing magical research and we believe they may be approaching a breakthrough, one that we do not wish to see fall into the hands of our enemies."

"What sort of breakthrough?"

"A dangerous one. And a necessary one." The gray-haired man did not explain further. Information such as this required careful compartmentalization. It was enough that Ramón knew this research was vital; he did not need to know anything about First Lightning.

"Am I to infiltrate this place as well?"

The gray-haired man shook his head. "We already have an asset in place, but you will oversee the operation. If the situation in Cuba continues into instability, your support may be required."

Both men rose and moved toward the door. The outside cold seeped in through the wood. "My expectations are high, Ramón."

"I have not lived this life only to fail now."

"Other men have broken similar promises to me," the gray-haired man said.

Ramón shrugged. "I am not other men, and you are standing in my home for a reason."

"Yes," the gray-haired man said. "Yes, I am. Good luck on this difficult mission, comrade. I suspect I am sending you into an inferno, but see if you can recover some treasure from the ashes."

FIVE

The office of the director of the OMRD was open, airy, and inviting. Gone were the massive desk and the floor-to-ceiling bookshelves that had dominated the space when the organization was run by Karen's mentor, Dr. Max Haupt. In the years since his retirement, Karen had lost count of the number of replacements who had occupied this room. They never seemed to last long, each using the post as a political stepping-stone to some more prestigious placement. The latest director had been in place for three months, and Karen had only met him a few times. He did not come to staff meetings; he did not concern himself with detail.

I see my role as a cheerleader, he'd said to the assembled staff on his first day, his hair perfectly coiffed, his smile perfectly bright. *I'm here to make sure you all know you have the support you need. Though I'm not about to run out onto the field myself and try to catch a pass.*

On the wall opposite the window, where Dr. Haupt had kept a priceless library of Germanic magical texts, Director Whitacre had hung a series of oil paintings of famous American magicians: Ambrose Cabott, advisor to George Washington during the Revolutionary War; Henry Baker Fielding, the lion-maned, wild-eyed founder of St. Cyprian's University of the Arcane; and granite-faced Luther Cunningham, the US attorney general who had brought to justice the Boston coven responsible for the Somerville Massacre. The weight of their august scowls fell heavy on her; she scowled right back.

"Sorry if I kept you waiting, Karen," Director Whitacre said as he sat down across from her. They were in plush leather armchairs that flanked the paintings. The room felt more like a smoking lounge at a country club than the office of the leader of the US government's experts on magic. "I had a breakfast appointment with President Eisenhower, and you know how Ike can go on and on."

She didn't, but chose not to correct him. "Thank you for meeting with me, sir. Allow me to explain why I asked to speak to you."

He listened patiently and without interruption as she spoke. She could read nothing of his reaction behind his kindly and placid eyes. "Karen," Director Whitacre said when she was done, his hands raised in a semi-shrug, "I guess I just don't know what to say."

Karen shifted in her chair. "Sir, you can say—"

"Please, you must call me Vernon."

"Vernon," Karen said, the forced familiarity an unpleasant taste on her tongue, "I was about to suggest that you can authorize me to investigate this matter fully."

"I can appreciate that suggestion, Karen, I really can," Director Whitacre said. He slapped a hand on his knee. "But it just isn't that simple."

The cube sat on a table between them, next to two empty glass tumblers and a bottle of bourbon. The cube's light had faded, as had its voice, but she could still feel the raw energy trapped within.

"How so?" she asked as diplomatically as she was able.

"Well, for starters, what are we really investigating here?"

"An object imbued with a level of stored magical power previously thought impossible," Karen said. She paused a moment, then added, "And an object that spoke to me, in Spanish, in the voice of a little girl."

The director had managed a smile up until this point. "Do you think you can make it talk again?"

"I have no idea how it works, sir," she said. "That's why I need to investigate."

"And that's another issue, Karen," he said. She had some trouble placing his accent, though it was definitely from somewhere in New England. She'd never heard of him before his appointment to this office, and the rumor was he didn't even remember how to do much magic himself. "One that I'm having trouble overcoming."

He leaned forward in his chair, elbows on knees. "From what I'm told, you've done some damn fine work with your department down in Theoretical Magic. But now you're asking for authorization for a field operation. That seems a bit out of your purview, don't you think?"

After reading Gerald's request at her kitchen table, Karen had decided she would come visit the director, not to resign as planned, but to get the support she needed to help an old friend. Sitting here now though, listening to the director's excuses, she wished she'd brought her letter of resignation along, just in case.

"Are you familiar with my file, sir?" she asked. Her tone was not as deferential as it probably should have been, but what use was formality between two pals as close as Karen and Vernon?

The question didn't seem to sit well with the director. "Why, yes, I am," he said after a moment's thought.

"Then you know I have field experience," she said. "Significant experience."

The director wet his lips and leaned back, the leather groaning as he settled into it. "That is true," he said.

Karen held up Gerald's note. "My contact says his company—Magnus Innovations—is hosting some sort of product demonstration in Florida. That's the only time we could meet before they all go back to Cuba. I just want approval to go there and speak to him, find out what he knows about this . . . thing, and what his company is doing with it."

The director sighed and looked uncomfortable. Holding up a hand, he began to rummage through his pocket and at last came up with a silver dollar. "My lucky coin," he said with a self-deprecating smile. "And my locus. Gift from my grandfather. Minted in 1904, in San Francisco. Forgive me, I don't have much call for casting magic these days."

She watched him fumble through a spell and resisted the urge to correct his pronunciation and a few of his chalk markings. Eventually he managed a passable version of Righetto's Silence and all sound from outside the room faded away. No one could overhear their conversation now.

"An interesting precaution to take inside our building," Karen noted. "Are you afraid your secretary is working for the Soviets?"

Whitacre did not laugh. "You of all people should know that the Soviets are not to be taken lightly. They have ears all over Washington, and they aren't even the only ones to consider here." He tucked his locus back into his pocket. "What do you know about John Magnus?"

"Magnus," she repeated. "I'm guessing he founded Magnus Innovations?" All magicians knew this company; in college, she'd used items they'd enchanted, and did so even now in her research. They made all sorts of magical knickknacks and then sold them to magicians at exorbitant rates. She'd been surprised when Gerald chose to go work for them, but she couldn't blame him. Working for the OMRD might fill one's soul with civic pride, but it did little to fill one's pocketbook with cash.

"Indeed he did," Director Whitacre said. "John Magnus owns the market on consumer enchantment. And even though he can only sell to magicians, it's still made him one of the richest men in America."

Karen's heart dropped a little. She hadn't really had time yet to measure the obstacles in her path. Gerald had asked for her help and that was enough for her. But now the battle ahead was starting to take shape. Rich men had power, resources, and connections. One of the richest men in the country, who surely provided any number of services to the OMRD, had influence right where he needed it the most.

"Vernon," Karen said, creaking forward in her chair, "this thing is dangerous. Power of this magnitude is difficult for anyone to control. If they aren't careful, it could cause a catastrophe. And that's even before we discuss where this magical energy came from and what they plan to use it for. And why it spoke to me last night and asked me for help."

The director stared at her and said nothing, joining the painted faces in their disapproval.

"I understand that we don't want to make enemies with John Magnus, but it is our mandate to investigate potentially unethical magic in this country," she continued. "We can't abandon that duty just because the person under investigation is rich."

Director Whitacre returned to his seat and interlaced his fingers. The wedding band on his left hand clacked gently against what appeared to be a class ring on his right. "I hope, Karen, that you are not suggesting my decision is being influenced by inappropriate factors."

"Sir, I—"

He held up a hand. "You can have your investigation on one condition."

Karen blinked at her sudden change of fortune. "Name it."

"You can go meet your friend, but you will be accompanied by a senior agent from the Department of Public Inquiry."

She felt whiplash. "Sir," she said, "Vernon, I don't need an inquisitor as a chaperone. I can take care of myself. And Gerald's note said that he's interested in meeting with me only."

"And that's why you're still going," the director said. "But despite your history, you are a researcher. The agents of Public Inquiry are trained to investigate and respond to dangerous magic in the field. It would be foolish to send you into an unknown situation without proper support, especially considering your current circumstances have left you without use of your own magic."

Ouch. So he had read her file. It was difficult to argue his point, and probably impossible to change his mind. The inquisitors were the prima donnas of the OMRD, always flaunting their battle scars—both real and invented—but they were also the best trained for magical combat and defense. Plus, unlike researchers like her, the magicians in Public Inquiry actually counted as law enforcement officers. She wasn't sure what resistance to expect trying to reach Gerald at this event, but having a skilled partner with a badge might not be the worst idea after all.

And yet, the idea still rankled her. She didn't need some smug, third-rate magician who knew how to summon a big fireball second-guessing her every decision. Gerald was her friend and the package had come to her.

"Sir, with all due respect, I—"

"And I know just the man for the job," Director Whitacre said. He leaned over and called through the door to his secretary. "Mrs. Shipley? Call downstairs and have Daniel Pierce sent up. I'd like a word with him."

Daniel Pierce? Inquisitors were known around the OMRD for telling fish stories, but not Daniel Pierce. Karen had met him a few times at office parties or during interdepartmental briefings, and he had always been a cool customer, never boasting, just stating the facts. If the rumors were true, most of what the other inquisitors only bragged about doing had actually been done by Daniel Pierce.

"Mrs. Shipley?"

Karen held up a hand. "Sir . . ."

"Trust me on this one, Karen. You'll see."

"But, sir . . ."

"Mrs. Shipley? Where is my blasted secretary?"

Karen gestured around the room. "Sir, the silence spell. She can't hear us."

"Oh, right," the director said with a chuckle. "I wasn't lying when I said I don't do a lot of magic anymore."

While the director dispelled the Righetto's Silence and summoned Mr. Pierce, Karen considered her options. She didn't need Whitacre's permission to meet with Gerald. She could pay for her own flight to Florida and figure out the rest once she knew more. But if things got messy—and something told her they were going to get messy—it would be preferable to have the official backing of the OMRD. She'd do anything to help Gerald, but preferred not to make an enemy of one of the richest men in the country without some support.

Lost in her thoughts, she hadn't noticed the new arrival. He and the director stood by the door, exchanging low whispers. When Whitacre saw Karen looking up, he smiled and ushered the newcomer over. "Daniel Pierce, please meet Karen O'Neil, from Theoretical Magic."

Pierce was a tall man, handsome, with jet-black hair and a strong jaw. He offered a hand and a token smile without much warmth. *Good*, Karen thought. *We don't have to pretend to like each other.*

"Oh, we've already met, sir," Pierce said. "I was at the meeting when Miss O'Neil briefed us on her department's investigations into methods for combating the effects of magical fatigue. Compelling, practical stuff. I passed it along to all our field agents."

"Um," Karen said. "Thank you. Nice to see our research being put to good use."

"That's the idea of the OMRD, right?" Pierce said. "Magicians in the labs and in the field, all working together for the common good."

Whitacre beamed. "I couldn't have said it better myself. Now, Daniel, let's get you up to speed on the situation we're looking at here."

The director explained about the cube and Magnus Innovations; Pierce nodded as he listened. Karen sat on her hands and tried not to look annoyed at the delay.

"Well," Pierce said when the story was done. "Sounds like a tricky spot, but—"

"Not really," Karen cut in. "I know where my contact is going to be and when. I can get in and find out what he knows without anyone from Magnus Innovations being the wiser. I appreciate your input, Agent Pierce, but I don't need a babysitter."

They were all quiet for a moment. Karen feared she might have overplayed her hand, but then Pierce's mouth twitched in amusement and he said, "I was going to say that it sounds tricky, but I know a bit about Miss O'Neil's experience, and I don't think it should be an issue for her."

Karen opened her mouth, but no sounds came out. Agent Pierce was . . . not what she'd expected.

"Be that as it may," Director Whitacre said, "even the most capable agents work best as a team, don't you think? As you said, that's the idea of the OMRD: a team, stronger than the sum of its parts. Trust me when I tell you that if something is rotten within Magnus Innovations, you'll need all the help you can get."

Pierce bowed his head in deference to the director. "An excellent point, sir." He then turned to Karen. "It looks to me like this is your show, Miss O'Neil. But if you think I can offer any assistance, I'm happy to be along for the ride."

Karen's eyes bounced between the two men. If Berlin had taught her anything, it was that trusting anybody—even friendly men in nice suits—was a fool's game. But Berlin had also taught her how easy it was to get in over her head. "Very well," Karen said, resigned to her fate. "When can we leave?"

SIX

The airplane's wheels hit the tarmac with a reassuring jolt, rattling the luggage and the passengers alike. Outside the window, Miami looked reassuringly sunny, though rain clouds lurked in the distance. Palm trees wrapped in Christmas ribbon waved at the plane as it taxied. Even if their mission to reach Gerald proved a waste, at least she'd gotten away from the winter in DC.

Agent Pierce stirred awake when the plane came to a stop. It hadn't been a long flight, but Karen was still impressed by how he'd slept the entire way, hands folded across his stomach. Even when the smiling stewardesses, in bright blue hats and skirts, had come by offering free drinks and cigarettes, he'd remained still. *Is he actually sleeping or just trying to avoid conversation?* Either was fine with her. It struck her, however, that even with his eyes closed, he didn't for a moment appear vulnerable. She had no doubt that if something had gone amiss, he'd have been on his feet in an instant.

"We're running behind schedule," Pierce said as he checked his chunky gold watch, the first communication he'd offered since takeoff.

"You know, while you were napping I went up to the cockpit and asked the pilot if he could fly any faster, but he just ignored me," Karen said.

Pierce let her comment go without a reply; probably for the best. He had supported her with the director, so she ought to be nicer to him, but that wasn't as easy as flipping a switch to "Friendly Mode." She'd give him a chance. If he proved to be helpful, maybe she'd cut him some slack.

As the other passengers filed by, he rose and donned his navy jacket, somehow still wrinkle-free, and set his fedora on just so. He looked about ten years older than Karen, which meant he would have fought in the war, but he looked too dapper in his tailored suit and tie to remind Karen of a soldier. "Your contact's letter asked us to meet him at eleven a.m.?"

"He asked to meet *me* at eleven," Karen answered. "I'm not sure how he'll feel about you being there as well."

"The hotel is probably twenty minutes from here," he said. "We should still have time."

"You come to Miami often, Agent Pierce?" Karen asked.

He did not respond.

The lobby of the Miami Gardens Resort Hotel was enormous, full of leafy palm trees, breezy white linen, and humidity. A massive gaudy Christmas tree loomed over everything, the pine needles nearly invisible behind the layers of flashy tinsel. The room was crowded too, though Karen saw few overt signs of the impending Magnus Innovations product demonstration. According to Gerald's letter, the demonstration was not open to the public, but rather to key potential investors and shareholders. She did, however, see plenty of hard-looking men loitering around the perimeter of the room, watching. Between their dark suits and darker scowls, they did not look much like tourists trying to beat the cold with a quick trip to the beach.

"Do you see him?" Pierce asked without looking at her. His face revealed nothing, but she noted his hand tightly gripping a set of dark-wood rosary beads: his locus, she assumed. She hoped he would not have cause to use it.

"Not yet," she said. Pierce replied, but it was hard to hear anything over the murmur of voices and the clack of shoes on the Spanish tile. *Okay, Gerald. We're here. Don't let me down.*

Karen tightened the strap on her satchel and held it close to her body as she pushed through the hotel crowd. The cube—and her pistol—were tucked safely within. It may not have been wise to bring the cube along on the mission, but it didn't feel right leaving it behind either. The director had offered to store it in the vault at the OMRD, where they kept all the rare magical artifacts they didn't want to disappear, but she'd declined. It would be safe there, but if Gerald could show her more about how it worked or what it was, it was worth the risk. She hoped.

They found him sitting alone at a small table near the hotel bar, shrouded by large palm fronds. She almost didn't recognize him; though it had only been a couple of years since their last meeting, in the meantime his hair had gone thin and gray. He'd never been a heavy man, but now he was gaunt, his eyes sunken behind his thick glasses. His skin was pale and dotted with sweat, his fingers twisted in a nervous knot.

"Karen!" His too-loud voice echoed on the hard floor, and he immediately put a hand to his mouth.

"Gerald," Karen said, her voice much lower. She embraced him; his suit felt hollow under her arms, like the man she'd known was made of air.

Gerald's eyes narrowed as Pierce approached. "I thought you would come alone," he said to Karen.

"I tried."

Pierce extended a hand. "I'm here to help," he said. "I'm an—"

"I remember you. You're an inquisitor," Gerald finished, shaking his head.

Pierce bristled at the slang. "I was going to say an agent of Public Inquiry. My department is very concerned by the information you sent to Miss O'Neil. We'd like to know more about what you know."

"Karen," Gerald said, a hand on her arm, "I told you I can't trust anyone. Magnus has eyes everywhere. If he knew I was talking to you . . . if he knew I stole one of the storage containers . . ."

Karen closed her hand over his. "It's okay, Gerald. We're here now. Should we go outside? Somewhere less . . . crowded?"

Gerald shook his head vigorously. "They have men watching the exits. I'd never make it five feet out those doors."

She'd never seen him like this, afraid of his own shadow. "Fine, Gerald. Just tell me what's going on."

He glanced around the lobby. Everyone bustled about, oblivious to their meeting. He ushered them to his table, where he cowered behind the biggest leaves.

"They recruited me to work on improving the storage capacity of enchantments," Gerald said, his voice barely audible above the busy din. "I thought it was the chance of a lifetime, that I could make a difference. My team worked a long time without any real success, but that didn't seem to bother them. Mr. Magnus himself came down to our labs and thanked us for our hard work. So we worked even harder."

"That cube is remarkable," Karen said. *And obviously dangerous,* she chose not to add. There would be time for that later. Gerald looked ready to break under the strain as it was. Even in their toughest days at the OMRD, she'd never seen him like this. He'd always been the resolute one.

"I wish I could be proud of what we accomplished," Gerald said. He stared down at his hands. "For a while, I was. Too proud. Didn't ask questions. Didn't see what was happening. Didn't want to know."

Pierce leaned across the small table. "That cube is bursting with stored energy. What did they want to do with it?"

Gerald moved back in his chair, away from Pierce. He shook his head. "You're asking the wrong question," he said. "It doesn't matter what they wanted to do with that magic; it matters where they got it from."

A meaty hand clamped down on Gerald's shoulder from behind. Another grabbed his upper arm and yanked him to his feet.

"There you are," said the well-dressed man holding Gerald in place. "We thought we'd lost you."

Karen and Pierce stood. There were six men in total, appearing out of nowhere, all dressed in suits and ties, though they looked more like bouncers than businessmen. The man holding Gerald smiled at Karen, flashing a gold tooth.

"What is this about?" Karen demanded.

"You'll have to excuse our friend here," the gold-toothed man said. "He's needed upstairs for an urgent consultation."

"You aren't taking him anywhere," Karen said, her voice flat.

The gold tooth vanished along with the smile. "Girlie," he said, "I suggest you learn to mind your tone." She saw his fingers press down hard into Gerald's flesh. "And to avoid matters that are none of your concern."

"Gerald is leaving with me," she said as calmly as she could.

She felt a hand on her arm; Pierce leaned into her ear and whispered, "Now is not the time."

Karen pulled her arm free but held her tongue. Pierce wasn't wrong; she didn't have the slightest idea how they were going to overpower all five well-dressed thugs and escape with Gerald, but that didn't mean she had to be happy about it.

Gold Tooth chuckled. "Got to keep this one on a tight leash, I see," he said to Pierce.

Go to hell, you fat—

"Karen," Gerald said softly, deflating the heat of her anger, "I'm sorry."

They dragged Gerald away toward the back of the hotel, disappearing behind some double doors labeled EMPLOYEES ONLY. Karen glared at the backs of their thick heads as they went, wishing she could summon some hellfire down on them, or at least knock that gold tooth out of the man's dumb face.

"Karen, we need to—" Pierce began.

"Don't touch me again," she said, refusing to look at him. "And don't tell me the right time to fight. I don't answer to you."

He didn't reply. A silence, punctuated with echoing laughter and distant Christmas carols, settled between them. Karen felt paralyzed and foolish. Gerald had asked for her help, and what had she accomplished? She still had the cube, but was no closer to understanding it or to saving him. But she hadn't come all this way to turn around now. She was about to head for the hotel entrance when a woman approached them, her high heels heralding her arrival like drums.

"Excuse me," she said. She was pretty except for her caked-on makeup and gravity-defying blond bouffant. Her nail polish was bright enough to help direct Santa's sleigh, and when she smiled at them, Karen was immediately impressed by how utterly insincere the expression was. The woman motioned toward a nearby bank of elevators. "If you'd like to follow me . . . ," she said.

Karen and Pierce exchanged a glance. "Follow you where?" Karen said, not bothering to hide her annoyance. "Who are you?"

The woman's rictus smile stared blankly back at them. If Karen had spoken to her in Latin, she might have given the same response. After a long delay, the woman blinked her too-long eye-lashes and said with feigned sweetness, "I'm so sorry, I thought you knew."

"Knew what?"

"Mr. Magnus would like to see you."

SEVEN

They entered the hotel's penthouse through double mahogany doors heavy enough to repel a siege. White marble floors greeted them. A gold chandelier bristling with light hung overhead. Beyond the entryway was a sitting room filled with garish artwork, plush chairs that clearly had never been sat upon, and a six-foot-tall fountain burbling clear water from a fat cherub's mouth. Karen wondered if a room like this came with its own harem of loincloth-wearing slaves, or if you were expected to bring your own from home. Against one wall, a poster propped against an easel boldly proclaimed: WELCOME MAGNUS INVESTORS. THE FUTURE BEGINS TODAY.

"You can wait here," the blond woman said without looking at them, before disappearing into the gilded sprawl.

"We're wasting time," Karen said to Pierce when they were alone. She glared at a nearby painting, wondering if its eyes were following her. "We need to find Gerald before they whisk him back to Cuba. Or worse."

"We'll find him," Pierce said. He, too, eyed their surroundings suspiciously. "But this is an investigation into what Magnus's company is up to. What better place to start than at the top?"

Karen was not reassured. Mr. Magnus was certain to have the answers they were after, but she doubted he would be forthcoming. He had no reason to help them and plenty of reasons to throw them off the trail. The fountain cherub seemed to be laughing at her.

"Welcome!" The voice broke like an explosion in the marble-floored room, echoing from all sides like a divine proclamation. John Magnus appeared in a doorway, arms wide as if he were greeting old friends. He was younger than Karen imagined, no more than forty, with tan skin and a full head of sandy hair. She guessed his suit—double-breasted with bulbous brass buttons—cost more than her parents' house. He was handsome, of course, with an unnervingly genuine smile and a crackle of energy behind expressive hazel eyes.

They made introductions and he shook each of their hands with both of his, ushering them deeper into the suite. "Meredith," he said to the blond woman hovering nearby, "some champagne for our guests." He inclined his head toward them conspiratorially, adding, "Truly excellent stuff. Just came off the ship from France this morning. It's meant for our little shareholders' meeting later, but I doubt they'll miss a bottle."

"We appreciate you meeting with us, sir," Pierce said.

"Of course, of course," Magnus said. He motioned for them to sit and he took his place across from them. "I'm never too busy for employees of the Office of Magical Research and Deployment."

Karen shifted in her puffy chair. "You know who we are?"

"Not personally, no. But I'm a details man, and I can add two and two and get four. You are both magicians, that much is obvious. Well dressed, with that official air about you. And if memory serves, there's a 7:45 A.M. flight from DC that would have put you in Miami . . . well, in enough time to arrive right about now."

Magnus seemed quite pleased with his observations; Karen found it off-putting. "How did you know we were magicians?"

"Like I said, I'm a details man. I always like to know who or what I'm dealing with, so I make sure to have magic detectors available whenever I hold an event. Magnus Innovations' dowsing rods are quite helpful in this regard. But enough formality, please," he said cheerily. "I'm happy to have the OMRD here. We've done quite a bit of business with your organization. If only your budgets were bigger, but alas, it is always difficult to get Congress to pay for anything to do with magic. Shortsighted old windbags, the lot of them. Someday they'll change their tune, I guarantee. It isn't always easy, convincing—"

"Mr. Magnus," Karen said, cutting in, "we came here to meet with an old colleague of mine, a man who now works for you. However, our conversation was cut short by some thugs I can only assume are also Magnus employees."

Somehow Magnus nodded gravely while still smiling. "Subcontractors, in fact, but yes, they were acting in an official capacity."

"I would like to speak to my friend," Karen said.

"Time is money, Miss O'Neil," Magnus said. "And even more so when you are in the research phase of new product development. Your friend—Gerald, I believe?—is working on an important project for us and was needed urgently back at our facility. I trust you understand."

"I trust that you understand," Karen said, "that your explanation is extremely difficult to believe."

"Karen . . . ," Pierce said softly.

"No, it's fine," Magnus said. Still, his smile remained. Nothing seemed to faze him. "I know that our security team can be a bit overzealous. I apologize for any unpleasant impressions they may have made. Ah, our champagne."

Meredith delivered a silver tray with three crystal glasses, each fizzing with a rose-gold liquid. Magnus raised his and Pierce joined him, but Karen left hers where it sat.

"Mr. Magnus," she said, "my friend has left us with some disturbing questions about the work going on at your magical research facility. Perhaps you'd like to enlighten us on what exactly you are researching there."

Magnus sipped his champagne and sighed in delight. "Are you sure you won't try some?" he said. "I don't know how these Frenchmen do it, but it is a magic all its own." He placed his glass on an adjacent table and steepled his fingers. "The details of our research are proprietary, I'm afraid. It would be impossible for me to divulge them without a warrant."

Karen pressed. "Why Cuba, Mr. Magnus?"

Now there was a glimmer in those hazel eyes; she'd caught him off guard. The location of his facility was probably meant to be secret. "We have an arrangement with the Cuban government," he said after the briefest of pauses. "Our research laboratory is state-of-the-art, in large part thanks to their support. I'm sure we could even arrange a tour. Have Director Whitacre contact our PR department and we'll set something up. Vernon and I are old friends."

Magnus stood. Their audience was complete.

"Thank you for your time," Pierce said, shaking the man's hand.

Karen should be pleased; she wanted to get out of there and see if she could find Gerald. But this snake in a business suit had smiled and twisted his way out of providing any useful information to them. He'd just wasted their time, which is probably exactly what he meant to do. They were in his element, and a man as rich as John Magnus never had to answer any questions he did not want to.

Don't worry, Gerald. I'll find you and then we'll figure out what's really going on here.

As they neared the door, Magnus called out after them. "Actually, there was just one more thing. I think you might have something that belongs to me."

The cube. He knew about the cube. Of course he did; he had magical detectors in place around the hotel, and the cube was so charged that it would light up like a Christmas tree. *How could I be so stupid?* No wonder Magnus's goons had descended on them so quickly; Karen had given him up. "I'm afraid we don't know what you mean, Mr. Magnus," Pierce said calmly.

Karen appreciated Pierce's effort, but there was no use trying to hide what Magnus already knew. Maybe there was a chance to get him to answer a question after all. She pulled the cube from her satchel and held it out. The chandelier's light danced on its dark faces like a constellation. "Do you know why this cube spoke to me, Mr. Magnus? Do you know why it asked me for help?"

Magnus's effortless charm slipped a little. He knew they had the cube, but hadn't expected it had started talking to them. *And you probably don't like surprises, do you, Mr. Magnus?*

Then the salesman smile was back, like the sun coming out from behind a cloud. "We still have some time before my meetings," Magnus said, checking his watch. "Perhaps you'd be interested in seeing a small product demonstration."

Magnus ushered them into the penthouse's conference area, a long carpeted room that had been cleared of all furniture. The room was dim; the windows had been covered with heavy drapes. Posters, similar to the one in the entryway, lined the room on both sides like billboards on the highway. Karen approached one. It depicted a happy family around the dinner table: smiling parents, laughing children, steaming food. A perfectly normal domestic scene, except for the inhumanly tall figure that hovered in the background near the kitchen. It was pale, almost colorless, and its face was free of all features or expression. It wore a red checkered apron and held a perfectly baked pie in one upheld hand. Wavy white lines of steam rose above the golden crust. The poster's header announced:

WITH MAGNUS INNOVATIONS, HOUSEHOLD CHORES ARE A THING OF THE PAST!

The next poster showed a line of US soldiers dressed in olive green as they charged up a drab hill. Alongside them and a good few feet taller, two of the same pale figures strode like demigods, impervious to oncoming enemy fire. This one read: HELP US KEEP OUR BOYS SAFE FROM HARM!

Karen glanced down toward the end of the room. In the gloom, it was hard to make out any details of what she saw: a large shape, covered with a cloth.

"I'm not a magician myself," Magnus said. His voice carried in the nearly empty room. "Failed the tests in spectacular fashion. No, my destiny lay elsewhere."

The rest of the posters showed similar tableaux: faceless giants escorting small children, directing traffic, carrying heavy freight. Their headlines varied but all came back to the same theme: we can change the world, if you'll give us some of your money.

"Selling enchanted items has been good for me," Magnus went on. "But I always felt like we could do more, that we could create a product that helped not just magicians, but every hardworking American man, woman, and child."

"So you are a patriot then?" Karen asked as they approached the covered shape at the end of the room. "And here I assumed you were just interested in profit."

Magnus waggled a finger. "Facing a war with Communism, the most patriotic thing a man can do is make a profit."

Karen was about to ask what any of this had to do with the cube that Gerald had sent her when Magnus stepped up to the tarp. "There's someone I'd like you to meet," he said, grabbing a handful of canvas. With a flourish, he ripped the covering away. "This is Solomon."

Karen fought to keep her jaw from dropping open. The figure stood at least eight feet tall; its head nearly brushed the ceiling. It was humanlike, or at least human-shaped, with long limbs and massive hands. Its pale white skin reminded Karen of modeling clay. Its face was blank, no eyes, nose, or mouth, just an empty expanse, like the sculptor hadn't quite finished his work. In its chest, where a heart might be, she could see a faint rectangular glow.

"Solomon is our prototype construct," Magnus said. His voice had the proud air of an eager parent. "A magical semiautonomous servant, able to respond to commands even from someone without magic. Solomon, please greet our guests."

The claylike figure moved with a fluid grace, like a dancer underwater. It raised its right hand, extended the fingers, and waved. Magical energy radiated off the construct; it must take an immense amount of power to animate such a thing, power like what Karen had sensed in Gerald's cube.

"We've built a few more constructs, but there are always issues to be worked out, and then of course there are the complications of mass production," Magnus said. "But after we show Solomon off to our investors, I'm sure we'll have the capital necessary to continue development."

There were records in magical history of artificial creatures like this: golems, constructs, homunculi. But none were substantiated

and all were considered to be apocryphal at best. Modern enchantments, while useful in a myriad of ways, were mostly straight-
forward, simple things created for a single purpose. Nothing
like this.

"I'll take your awed expressions as a good sign for my upcoming
meeting," Magnus said cheerily.

"This is unprecedented," Karen said, because she felt she should
say something.

"Can my marketing team use that quote?"

Karen turned to Pierce. "Is this legal?"

The inquisitor seemed as jarred by Solomon as Karen was.
Without taking his eyes from the construct, Pierce answered,
"There are no specific laws governing magic like this. Because it
shouldn't be possible."

"That is what makes it an innovation," Magnus said.

"It is powered by one of these?" Karen held up her cube.

"Precisely," Magnus said. "Your friend Gerald helped us immensely with breakthroughs on the storage of magical energy.
Solomon here requires its fair share of it. But these enchanted
items are not limited to power supplies; they also provide the magic
instructions that allow them to process and execute orders. They
really are their heart and soul, which is why we've come to call that
object you have there an 'anima.'" He smiled. "That's Latin for
'soul.'"

"I know what it means," Karen said. She felt dizzy. Staring up
at the larger-than-life construct wasn't helping. "And the voice I
heard?"

"Solomon does not have a voice of its own, sadly," Magnus
said, patting the creature's arm. "But we are working on improve-
ments to the design to allow for back-and-forth communication.
Magically simulated personality, quite remarkable. We believe

it will help people accept these creatures into their homes. We want them to feel like part of the family." Magnus shrugged. "Our research teams are very focused. One group isn't always informed of what other teams are developing. So when your friend Gerald heard voices coming from one of our anima, I fear he may have jumped to some inappropriate conclusions."

Magically simulated personality. *Is that what I heard? Is that all this is?*

"I hope this has cleared up our little misunderstanding," Magnus said, clapping his hands.

"I would still like to talk to Gerald," Karen said.

"As I said," Magnus replied, "he was needed urgently back at our facility. Perhaps he'll be available for a consultation when you visit for your official tour, if you are still interested?"

"Of course," Pierce said as he shook Magnus's hand.

Magnus turned to Karen. "If you are now satisfied, perhaps you'd be willing to return our wayward anima?"

Karen swallowed, and tightened her grip on her bag. She wasn't about to give up something Gerald had risked so much to send her, but if it truly was just another consumer enchantment, what reason did she have to keep it? But before she could answer, Pierce stepped in and said, "Unfortunately the object is still part of an active OMRD investigation. It would be inappropriate for us to return it until that investigation is concluded."

Magnus nodded slowly. "Of course," he said. "Solomon, please show our guests to the door."

Right, Karen thought. *Now that the man has spoken, Magnus listens. Typical.*

The construct crossed the long room in a few liquid strides and then bent to delicately open the far doors. It bowed and extended an arm, directing them out. Even though the construct had no eyes in its featureless face, Karen felt like it was watching her.

"Thank you for your visit," Magnus said as they exited. "I hope you found it informative."

O utside the hotel, a light rain started to fall from the darkening sky. Pierce grabbed a newspaper from a nearby stand and held it over their heads to block the drops. With the sounds of the busy street flooding over them, Karen stopped and stared up toward the top of the massive structure.

"Before you start," she said when she saw Pierce watching her, "I realize now I shouldn't have brought the cube."

"Actually," Pierce said, "I was going to say that I thought you did remarkably well in there. He'd never have summoned us upstairs if we didn't have the cube, and if you hadn't kept the pressure on him, he wouldn't have shown us any of that."

"Did you believe anything he said?"

"Not a word. You?"

"Solomon seemed real enough," she said. The image of the pale figure was burned into her thoughts. "I believe that he needs more money." She pulled out the anima. *A soul, he called it.* "And that he wants this back. I wonder why he didn't just sic his goons on us too."

Pierce laughed.

"What?" Karen asked.

"He's not that stupid. If his goons tried to stop us, I'd have killed them." The words were spoken so casually, so matter-of-factly, that Karen's skin went cold, despite the oppressive Miami humidity.

"Killed them," Karen repeated.

"Stopped them," Pierce corrected.

"They had guns."

Pierce shrugged. "I'm good at this job, Miss O'Neil. That's why the director asked me to help you. So what now?"

Karen wasn't sure what part of the inquisitor's job involved using magic to subdue half a dozen armed thugs, but she didn't press for details. "Now," she said, "we need to talk to Gerald."

Pierce rubbed his chin. "How are we going to find him?"

Karen tucked the anima away. "I think I know someone who can help with that."

EIGHT

Karen held up the envelope and compared the address.

"Are you sure this is the place?" Pierce asked as he turned off the engine of their rented sedan.

The house in front of them was probably better described as a shack. The paint was peeling, the roof sagging, and the stairs tilting. It stood on narrow stilts, presumably to keep the nearby Atlantic Ocean from rushing in the front door at the first sign of a Caribbean storm. The front lawn was sandy, weedy, and overgrown. It didn't look like the kind of place they'd find much help, but the address matched and they were out of time.

"Why do you even have that with you?" Pierce asked, nodding at the envelope.

"I thought we might need a little extra help down here," Karen said. "And oh, look, I was right. Let's go," she said as she swung open her heavy car door.

Sea gulls squawked overhead as they climbed the stairs. The air tasted of salt and decaying seaweed. "How do you know this person again?" Pierce asked.

"We worked together briefly," Karen said. *But memorably.*

She knocked and waited for an answer. No sounds came from within.

"Maybe he's not home?" Pierce offered.

Karen knocked again, louder, and was rewarded with a thump and some muted swearing. A moment later, locks clunked and the door slowly swung open. In the doorway was a bleary-eyed man whose thick gut was barely contained by his smudged robe. His puffy, waxy cheeks were flushed, and his nose was traversed by a road map of red veins. The air that escaped around his broad body smelled of gin.

The man looked at Karen, then at Pierce, then back at Karen. "Huh," he said.

"Hello, Arthur," Karen said.

The former chief of the CIA's Berlin Operating Base dragged a hand across his mouth and cinched his robe a little tighter. "How did you find me?"

Karen held up the Christmas card.

"Ah," Arthur said. "No good deed . . ."

"Can we come in?"

Arthur looked again at Pierce. "Is this a social visit?"

"We need your help."

He grunted at that, but then turned and let them inside. Karen noticed the bottles first: whiskey, rum, beer, and a few she didn't even recognize. The whole house, which seemed to be little more than a living room, tiny kitchen, and small bathroom, stank like a distillery. Karen wondered what would happen if someone lit a match.

"Enjoying retirement?" she asked.

"Best decision of my life," he said. He picked up a bottle and held it up for inspection: empty. "Leaves me with plenty of time to pursue my hobbies."

"Such as?"

Arthur slumped onto a deflated sofa. "I'm between hobbies at the moment," he said. "Don't like to get pinned down for too long. Things start to lose their spark. Now, what can I do for an old friend?"

"I need your help, Arthur," Karen said. She noticed an armchair across from the sofa, but decided it was probably better to stay standing. "I have a friend who is in a lot of trouble."

Arthur stuck his unshaven chin out at Pierce. "I know Miss O'Neil, but who are you supposed to be?"

"I'm Agent Daniel Pierce," he answered, extending his hand.

Arthur ignored it. "And what do you do for a living, Agent Pierce?"

"I work for the OMRD Department of Public Inquiry."

Arthur raised his eyebrows. "You're going to have to do something about that title," he said, shaking his head. "Takes too long. You're boring people before you even get halfway through. How about 'Magic Police'?"

"I'll pass your suggestions along to my superiors," Pierce replied humorlessly.

Arthur looked back at Karen. "I don't like him," he said. "I hope he's not the friend that needs help."

Karen quickly explained about Gerald and Magnus. "We don't know where those goons are taking him, but my guess is back to Havana. Once he's there, we'll never get him back."

"And how am I supposed to help?"

"We need information, and I thought you might still have contacts."

"Contacts," Arthur said, the word like a bad taste in his mouth. He found another bottle on the floor, this one with an inch of amber liquid waiting at the bottom. He drained it. "I burned a lot of bridges on my way out the door, Karen," he said. "Went out with a bang, you might say."

"Please, Arthur," Karen said. "Anything you can do."

Arthur pulled himself up on wobbly pale legs. "I need a piss." A moment later, he disappeared into the bathroom at the back of the building.

"What are we doing here?" Pierce asked in a low, sharp whisper.

"We need his help," Karen said firmly.

"That old drunk can't help us. We're wasting time."

"Show some respect. That 'old drunk' used to be the CIA's top man in West Berlin," Karen said, though that did seem like a long time ago now. Had the intervening years changed her as much as they had Arthur? She might *look* cleaner, but that meant little.

"Whatever he used to be," Pierce said, "he's washed-up now."

In Berlin, Arthur had seemed invincible, like he secretly ran the whole place. He probably did. But maybe it had all been an illusion, like so much in that gray city. She should have known better; she'd been warned not to trust spies.

They waited in silence, hope pulling away like the tide.

"I don't know where else to go," she said eventually, to herself as much as to Pierce. She never should have let those men take Gerald. She could have stopped them. Deep within, she felt her caged magic shift, just enough so that she knew it was there. *We could have saved him,* it seemed to say. *Those goons were nothing. We've killed stronger men than that.*

"Let's go," Pierce said. "I can contact the local police, see if they can—"

They were interrupted by a loud flush from the rear of the house. Water pipes gurgled lazily in the walls. Arthur appeared a moment later, his robe replaced with a pair of dark slacks and a white shirt he was unsuccessfully trying to tuck in.

"They're moving your pal tonight," he said, his voice still slightly slurred by the booze. "Out of Miami International Airport, Flight 149, departs at 4:50 P.M. for Havana, Cuba."

Karen stared at Arthur. "What?"

"You heard me," he said, tightening his belt, then thinking better of it and leaving it a little looser. "What, you don't keep a telephone in your toilet? Only place I use mine."

"You learned all that," Pierce said, "while using your bathroom?"

"Like she said," Arthur replied, "I have contacts. There are only so many airports in Miami, and Magnus Innovations has a corporate account with Pan Am that they just used to book three tickets to Havana. Two round-trip, and one one-way."

He squatted down by his sofa and pulled out a dusty cardboard shoebox. He lifted the lid and hefted a Colt .45.

"What's that for?" Pierce asked warily.

"I'm not a fancy magician like you lot," Arthur said as he slid the gun into his belt. "So I have to protect myself with more conventional means."

"Arthur," Karen said, "you don't have to come with us."

"I didn't have to find out where your friend was either," he said. "That's the one good thing about retirement, Miss O'Neil: you don't have to do much of anything if you don't want to."

He still looked a mess, with his thinning hair too long and his cheeks rough with a neglected beard, not to mention the bloodshot eyes and alcoholic mush to his words. At the same time, he looked ten years younger than the man who'd stumbled into the bathroom.

"So why are you helping us?" she asked.

"Boredom mostly," he said with a shrug. "And curiosity." He stood up a little taller, and for the first time, he reminded Karen of the man who'd run Berlin Operating Base with an iron fist. "If this is anything like our last adventure, it's bound to at least be interesting."

Karen ignored Pierce's questioning look. She hoped whatever happened next, it was nothing at all like Auttenberg. "Then let's go save Gerald."

NINE

Gerald was fairly certain they were going to kill him.

When he first started working for Magnus Innovations, he'd ignored the rumors about people disappearing overnight—their lockers cleaned out and the names erased. They'd seemed like the kind of stories that are bound to circulate among bored, overworked researchers with overactive imaginations. Magnus Innovations was a big, important company, a household name among magicians, not some nefarious criminal organization. John Magnus was an intense man, driven toward success and profit, but not murder.

Or at least Gerald had thought, before he was grabbed by a gang of goons with loaded pistols hanging inside their suit jackets.

He'd actually been surprised when the car pulled up to Miami International Airport. They were still going to kill him, but they wanted to wait until they were back in Cuba first. Maybe they wanted to ensure he had all his research notes in order. Nothing could jeopardize the project, after all.

"Keep walking," the goon on his left said into his ear. "We don't want to be late for our flight." Would they shoot him in the airport lobby if he tried to run? Not that they'd give him the chance.

His escort was down to just two men, but either of them looked like they could break his neck with their bare hands, if the need arose.

He briefly considered using magic. What good were all those years in school and working as a professional magician if he couldn't summon some cosmic power to aid him in his darkest hour? But no matter how hard he tried, he couldn't recall the words to a single useful spell. He knew a hundred archaic incantations that claimed to restore life to wounded flesh, but in fact did essentially nothing. He knew which runes carved into which material could maximize energy transfer and retention. He knew how to warm a tepid cup of coffee with a few words in ancient Greek, but he couldn't think of a single way to smite his enemies.

But Gerald had no regrets about contacting Karen. He wasn't ready to die, but he couldn't have lived knowing that he'd done nothing to prevent the unspeakable. He just hoped Karen would bring everything to light.

He didn't see the man coming the opposite way until they collided. Torn between this unsuspecting tourist and the goon's hand forcing him forward, Gerald was pulled off his feet and collapsed to the polished white floor in a heap next to the man he'd run into.

"I'm so sorry—" Gerald tried to say. His captors were on him in an instant, yanking him up. They ignored the other man, who seemed to be struggling to stand. He was older, with graying hair and an expanding waistline. Sweat beaded his brow, and Gerald had caught a whiff of whiskey when they went down.

Without thinking, Gerald reached down and helped the man up. The two dark clouds following him glowered, but said nothing. Better to not make a scene, any more than they already had.

"Thank you," the older man said as he squeezed Gerald's hand tightly. "Sorry about the little bump there. I get so turned around in this airport that I forget to watch where I'm going."

"Scram," one of Gerald's escorts said as he clamped down on Gerald's shoulder. The older man just nodded and stepped aside.

Gerald felt the piece of paper the older man had pressed into his palm. His heart began to thud. When the two goons stopped a moment later to check the terminal map, he glanced down.

Bathroom. Now.

"Umm . . . ," Gerald said. His tongue stuck to the roof of his mouth.

"Shut it," the taller of the two—a square-headed brute called Duke—said.

"I need to go to the bathroom," Gerald said, his voice a dry squeak.

"Hold it," the other one said without looking at him. He was bull necked with a cracked front tooth. He was called Chip.

"Through the whole flight?" Gerald said. He could barely hear himself over the sound of his blood thumping in his ears. He didn't know what was going on, but whatever this was, he knew it was the last chance he was going to get. "I can't. I need to go now."

Duke and Chip exchanged glances. All around them, passengers dressed in their best hurried toward their airplanes. Their plane would be boarding soon. And then it would be too late.

"Fine," Duke said. He pointed at a nearby sign. "Let's make this quick."

Gerald didn't know what to expect. His hands were shaking, his breath coming in shallow wheezes. He wasn't cut out for this sort of life, with shoulder-holstered guns and secretly delivered messages. He was almost relieved when the bathroom appeared empty, then realized what a foolish thought that was. *They are going to kill you, Gerald. And you don't want to make a scene.*

"Hurry it up," Chip said, pointing at a stall. "We don't got all day."

No one is coming to save you. Gerald swallowed. "No," he said.

Duke laughed. Chip did not. "What did you say, little man?"

Sweat steamed Gerald's glasses. He planted his feet, facing his captors, and repeated, "No. If you're going to kill me, you can do it here, but I'm not going anywhere with you."

Chip reached into his jacket and slid out a pistol that looked like it fit very comfortably in his huge hand. "Boss won't like it," he said with a shrug of his ham-hock shoulders, "but if you insist."

The metal door on one of the stalls Gerald had thought was empty suddenly ripped free of its hinges and flew through the air in a blur, crashing hard into Chip and smashing him into the sinks. Porcelain and goon alike crumbled. The air tingled with the sense of spent magic.

For a second, nothing else happened. The only sound was the spray of water from a broken sink pipe. Then Duke was moving, drawing his gun, closing in on the offending stall. But as he neared, another man stepped out to face him. Gerald recognized him as the agent of Public Inquiry who had come to the hotel with Karen.

Duke's gun came up, but the inquisitor batted it aside with one hand while driving the heel of his other into Duke's nose. There was a crunch, and then blood. *Are all inquisitors trained to fight like that?* But Duke didn't go down. Instead he charged, swinging his gun like a club. The butt caught the inquisitor hard on the shoulder. The blow stunned him, allowing Duke to press in with a low kick that threw him back, off balance.

He's going to shoot him, Gerald realized. The barrel of Duke's gun was coming up. The inquisitor couldn't react in time, and had nowhere to go for cover. In that instant, ancient words came unbidden to Gerald's lips. A lifetime of training for this moment: when he spoke, magic leapt to his command.

The water spraying into the air suddenly hardened, the air puffing like clouds around it. The newly formed chunks of ice obeyed

Gerald instead of gravity and snapped through the air at Duke. There wasn't enough to hurt him, or even knock him down, but it got his attention. Gerald shouted the spell now, and more ice slashed down at Duke, shattering on his chest and face.

Duke swung his gun around and leveled it at Gerald. *Too late now.*

But the inquisitor was ready. With a hand outstretched, unstoppable magical force reached across the distance between him and Duke and knocked the gun aside just as he squeezed the trigger.

The sound of the gunshot in the bathroom was deafening, but the bullet flew wide, shattering a mirror instead of Gerald. Duke swore and brought the gun back into line, but this time, the inquisitor recited a few quick lines in Japanese, and then a flare of lightning arced through the room and crashed into Duke. The goon went rigid. His suit smoldered and then he fell, splashing face-first into the puddle at his feet.

"That was . . . incredible," Gerald said, his voice so soft he wasn't sure anyone but himself heard him.

"The gunshot will have drawn attention," the inquisitor said. "Did Magnus send any other thugs with you, or just these two?"

"There were more, a few more," Gerald said. He couldn't stop looking at Duke. He'd never actually seen anyone defeated with magic before. Sure, there had been drills and such in school, and he'd watched the St. Cyprian spell fencing team compete a few times, but nothing like this. Was Duke dead?

"Where are they?"

"Waiting with the car," Gerald said. His voice sounded weird in his head. "Where's Karen?"

"We don't have much time," the inquisitor said. He grabbed Gerald's arm. "I need you to focus. Tell me exactly what part you played in all this. What work have you done for Magnus?"

"I worked in Containment," Gerald stammered. "Maximizing storage efficiency, making sure the power stored in the animas was stable, that sort of thing. Why?"

"John Magnus is not a good man," Pierce said. "He must be stopped."

But just as Gerald was about to reply, they heard shouts outside the door.

TEN

When Pierce told Karen to stay with the car, she'd nearly punched him. She doubted she could have done much damage, but it would have felt good.

"This is *my* investigation," she had said instead. "Gerald is *my* friend."

"And you'll help him best by waiting here," Pierce said. "We need to play it safe. If they see you, they'll recognize you from the hotel."

"You were there too."

"I can blend in," he said. "And unlike you, I have my magic."

She knew the inquisitor was right. How was she going to disarm two hired goons, even if they could catch them by surprise? They'd shoot her in an instant. After her run-in with the mugger, she knew better than to trust her hidden magic; it was far too eager to get free. Hopefully, Pierce was better prepared for such a confrontation; he certainly seemed confident in himself, though such confidence was rarely in short supply with men like Pierce. Arthur had been reassuring, but she'd ignored him. Her friend was in danger and she was waiting in the car, helpless. She had flashed back to her apartment after the mugging, when she'd been so paralyzed with fear that all she could do was stare at the door and wait.

But then she saw the black sedan loitering a little ways down from the terminal entrance. The car itself did not draw her attention, but one of its occupants stood outside, leaning against the hood, his cigarette sending plumes into the sky. When his mouth opened, the late-afternoon light glinted off a gold tooth. Karen ducked behind a support pillar. She could make out three more silhouettes in the car. A small goon army. *Backup, in case something goes wrong?*

She needed to warn the others. They'd hoped Magnus wouldn't bother sending so many men on escort duty. But she was supposed to wait, stay out of harm's way. Maybe she should. Maybe it would still work out fine. Her fingers drummed on the car door handle and then on the metal bulk of the pistol in her bag. *To hell with that.*

Karen reached the front of the airport terminal where she'd watched Arthur and Pierce enter. Holiday travelers in hats and dresses burbled all around her, ushering luggage and children with equal care. Overhead, airplanes roared like metal dragons, their bellies full of well-dressed patrons on their way to Chicago or New York or parts beyond. Karen held her satchel close to her body. So many people, so much noise. It reminded her of the crowds around the failing Berlin Wall, chanting their demands for freedom only to be silenced with gunfire and magic smoke. The memory chilled her. Her hands were trembling; sweat trickled down her back. *Maybe I should go back to the car,* she thought.

She heard the gunshot a moment later. At first, she wondered if it was another echo of Berlin, a memory made solid by her own untrustworthy brain, but then she heard shouting, screaming. And saw travelers running.

Oh, look. Something went wrong.

The black car emptied in an instant, the goons it carried charging the terminal like bulldozers. Karen slipped aside just as they passed; they did not notice her. She'd hoped Pierce would be a little more discreet with the extraction, but it was too late for that. Now she just hoped everyone made it out unharmed.

Karen ducked through the fleeing populace and into the terminal. She expected to see security guards or police, but she only saw confused passengers and the backs of the goons as they vanished around a corner. She didn't know what she could do, but she wasn't about to wait around and hope. She pressed on, following the noise.

But as she rounded the corner, she walked right into a gold-toothed smile. "Why am I not surprised to see you again, girlie?"

Karen moved back and reached for her satchel, but she was surrounded. Rough hands pinned her arms to her body. A chill raced down her spine. Deep inside, her magic twitched.

"You two," the gold-toothed goon said to his companions, "go check on Duke and Chip. We'll be there in a second." Two of them ran off. Karen was shoved through a side door labeled AIRPORT STAFF ONLY. It emptied into a gray, echoing stairwell that led up and down.

"Let's see that little purse of yours," Gold Tooth said. Before Karen could stop him, he ripped the satchel from her grasp and tossed it to his remaining companion. "While we wait, you want to tell me what's going on here? You and your buddy launching a rescue mission?"

Karen's eyes never left her satchel. "Don't open that," she said in a low voice.

"Ooh," Gold Tooth said with a laugh. "Girlie has secret things in her bag."

The magic inside her was waking up. Her fingers tingled. The goon pulled her satchel open and tossed out a few of the enchanted items before pulling out her gun. "She's packing heat," he said, spinning the chamber to check each of the rounds.

"You got a little fire in you after all," Gold Tooth said, taking the pistol. "Now, why don't you tell me what's going on here before I decide to test your little popgun on your kneecap?"

The other goon continued rummaging. Karen's hands clenched.

"She's got something locked in here," the goon said. "One of the pockets. Looks big. Something's inside. Could be important."

"Then open it, you moron," Gold Tooth said. "It's just a purse lock. Break it."

Kill them, her magic said. *Before it is too late.*

The goon strained as he tried to pull open the locked pouch. And then a moment later, he was screaming.

Karen hadn't applied the runes herself; she would have needed to use magic to do so. But she'd been very explicit with the magician she'd hired: no one but her was allowed to open this pouch. If anyone else tried . . .

I'll make them regret it, the rune expert had said. Karen had paid him a lot of money for his work; apparently, it was well spent.

The goon dropped the satchel and writhed. White-hot magical energy crawled lazily up his arm, causing his muscles to spasm and contort in its wake. His eyes were wild with panic. Then he thrashed like a wounded animal, falling to his knees before finally collapsing to the concrete floor.

Karen did not wait for him to lie still. She crossed the distance between her and Gold Tooth and used that momentum to drive her knee as hard as she could into his groin. He let out a groan and dropped her gun. She scooped it up and then retrieved her satchel. The lock was unharmed, though it still shone with a faint glittering light from the magic's aftereffects. Though some of the energy had been expended, the warding runes were still in place and potent.

She ran for the door but Gold Tooth was up, growling. He grabbed her arm and twisted it. She swung the pistol but couldn't get enough of an arc to land any heavy blows. Then her center of gravity shifted as Gold Tooth pulled her arm so hard she stumbled off balance. She tried to reach out a hand to steady herself, but she wasn't fast enough. Her skull cracked against the metal stairwell railing.

The world around Karen blurred. Metal filled her mouth and her ears. Her vision narrowed and she felt numb all over, except for a rising, searing pain in her head. She had fallen to her knees, but had barely noted the scrape of concrete when she fell. She tried to focus, but everything was slipping through her fingers. Through the haze, she saw the dark shape of Gold Tooth looming over her.

Her muddled brain formed a single thought: *Now.*

For the first time since Auttenberg, Karen reached for her magic. Through the pain, the doubt, and the fear, she grabbed at it like a lifeboat. She felt it stir in response, a familiar yet now also foreign feeling.

But then it slipped away again.

Blood trickled down her cheek from a cut on her scalp. Her ears still rang. *Focus,* she told herself as her thoughts cleared. Had she forgotten how to do this? Or had she overestimated her abilities without a locus?

"Good-bye, girlie," Gold Tooth said. "Nobody's going to miss you."

Karen slid back on the cold, hard floor, but escape wasn't an option. Where was her gun?

Where was her magic?

Then the door leading into the stairwell burst open. Gold Tooth spun but wasn't fast enough. Pierce hit him hard and threw him against the railing. The goon swung, but Pierce ducked the blow and hit him again. And again. He was so fast, impossibly fast. Karen sensed magic in the room.

Her vision cleared. Gold Tooth threw one last wild punch that hit only air, and then Pierce pushed him over the railing. The goon gave out a yelp, and then Karen heard a distant smack as he hit the ground, two stories down.

Pierce had killed him. Only it wasn't Pierce. Whoever this was, she'd never seen him before. Her savior had a similar build to Pierce, but was dressed not in a suit but in tattered dark clothing. He had a hood up that covered his blond hair and obscured some of his pale face. He knelt down a few feet from Karen.

"Ah, that was too close," he said, his voice turned by a vaguely European accent Karen couldn't identify. "I would have never forgiven myself."

The words jumbled in Karen's ears. "Who—"

"They've taken so much from you," he said softly. He shook his head. "You mustn't doubt yourself, Karen O'Neil. You are too important. Your magic is too important."

The cloud of pain still hung over Karen's brain, but she felt her every instinct quicken. She stared at him anew, a burst of adrenaline stimulating clarity of thought. She didn't see any weapons, or an obvious locus, if he was indeed a magician. The skin of his long-fingered hands was covered in black ink, tattoos of runes, strange words, and other symbols whose origin she couldn't even guess at.

"Who are you?" she asked. "How did you know my name?"

"Because I have been watching you. I know how that must sound. But I see such potential in you. You probably cannot see it yourself. Not yet."

"You don't know me."

His pale lips smiled at that. "I know you have learned how to control your magic without spells or a locus. That alone sets you apart from so many of our kind who settle for repetition instead of revolution. And I know you saw something in Berlin. You saw beyond the veil, to the Power Beyond."

Muffled shouting came through the stairwell door. And then bangs. Gunshots.

"You are needed elsewhere. I won't keep you," he said. His voice was kind, almost paternal. He stood. "You need to trust your power. It is the only thing you can trust. Everything else in this tainted world is a lie, but not your magic."

Then he was through the door and gone.

Karen forced herself to her feet. She ignored the fresh wave of nauseating pain in her head and steadied herself on the wall. She had to find Gerald and the others. The rest of this madness could wait. She gathered up her satchel and gun and found the door.

Back out in the main terminal, she heard more gunshots. The sound rattled around in her head; she couldn't make out where it was coming from. Then, a moment later, she saw Arthur coming toward her. Then Pierce.

"We have to go," Pierce said. Sweat covered his forehead. "Now."

"Go?" Karen said. "Where's Gerald?"

"I'm sorry, Karen," Pierce said. "They got him."

"Got him? What are you saying?"

Pierce's face was grim. "He's dead."

ELEVEN

The spy took one last look at the exhibition hall before turning off the lights. Fliers were strewn on the ground. The table of refreshments had been picked clean. A few hours earlier, the room was full of noise as potential Magnus investors watched the demonstration. They had been impressed, as expected; Solomon was remarkable, groundbreaking. Mr. Magnus had them right where he wanted them.

But then the questions started. *What do they cost? How long do they take to produce? Are they safe?* In the end, many promises were made but no checks were written. Mr. Magnus had labeled the entire exercise a disaster, and that was before they received the call about the airport.

She had much to report. The gray-haired man would be pleased.

Mr. Magnus's voice drifted through the walls: ". . . these are your men. You promised me that—" A pause. "How am I supposed to conduct business when—" Another pause, longer this time. "I understand. Spend whatever you have to, just make this go away."

The spy had no sympathy for men like Mr. Magnus, cold, ravenous capitalists who saw the world as plunder to be hoarded. They were loathsome, a plague on humanity that should be washed away. And yet, on a day like this, with all his great plans crumbling around him, she almost felt sorry for him.

"Meredith!"

The spy closed the door to the exhibition hall and found Mr. Magnus in an adjoining room. His jacket and tie had long been removed. A half-empty bottle of bourbon sat on the desk next to the telephone he had just slammed down.

"Sir?" the spy asked. She had never liked the sound of English, but relished the challenge of mastering another language so well that native speakers never questioned her accent. She had even started to dream in English. "How can I be of assistance?"

"I need my flight back to Havana moved up to tomorrow morning," Mr. Magnus said. He leaned back on the desk and stared up at the ceiling.

"I'll take care of it, sir," Meredith said. Her voice sounded bright and clear, despite the events of the day and the late hour. When it was always an act, it was easier to maintain a positive attitude in adversity.

"What a mess," Mr. Magnus said, picking up the bourbon. "This was supposed to be my chance to get myself free of Rabin and the others. All I needed was some new capital. But now . . ." He took a swig straight from the bottle. "Now I have even less money, the OMRD is sniffing around, and on top of all that, one of my researchers gets shot in a major airport."

The arrival of the OMRD agents had been a surprise. Magnus Innovations was many things, but it was not sloppy. It had taken Meredith many months to work her way into a position to learn any details about the company's research initiatives; the OMRD never should have had the first clue that there was something worth investigating. The gray-haired man would be very interested in this development.

"The investments will come, sir," the spy said. She wasn't sure

why she bothered; part of her wished she could put a bullet in this
fool's head and be done with it. But those were not her orders . . .
not yet. For now, she was Meredith, dutiful personal secretary.
"Solomon's value is obvious."

"To you and me, perhaps," Mr. Magnus said. "But it is the same
story, every time. I could roll out a product that turned garbage
into gold, and these damn investors would only talk about how
magic just isn't marketable. 'Americans trust things they can understand, and they just don't understand magic.' Ignorant, penny-
pinching fools, the whole lot of them."

Americans, so easily influenced by their irrational prejudices.
The spy did not pretend that the Soviet Union was without its own
blind spots, but America seemed to make a sport of it. How had
they managed to win the last war without trusting their own magicians? Just another reason the global prominence of the USA was
both baffling and concerning.

"Is there anything else you need tonight, sir?"

"No, no," he said, running his hands over his face. "I just need
to wallow in my misery a little while."

"Very good, sir," she said and headed for the door.

"Meredith." Mr. Magnus's voice reached her just as she was
about to leave. "What do you have there?"

She stopped. He was not usually so attentive; it made her job
easier. If he was going to start paying closer attention to her ac-
tivities, she might have to adjust her tactics.

"Oh, these?" She held up the stack of postcards in her hand.
"Just some notes to send to the family back home. Most of them
have never been to Miami before."

"Of course," he said, nodding. "Sorry. Never can be too careful."

"Definitely, sir," she said. The postcards would go to various
addresses in various small American towns, nondescript places
with white picket fences and maple trees in their front yards. And

once their neighborhood mailman delivered the glossy pictures of Miami Beach, her friendly notes would be decoded, translated, encrypted anew, and delivered to the gray-haired man's desk. "Good night, Mr. Magnus."

"Good night, Meredith."

She closed the door quietly on her way out.

TWELVE

Karen stared at the ceiling, but instead of its rough white texture, she saw badly lit stairwells with metal railings and a leering gold-toothed smile. And Pierce telling her Gerald was gone. And the sound of her own heart, thumping away in the dark.

They'd found a motel not far from the airport to lick their wounds. The rooms were small and the bed was lumpy, but Karen didn't care. She needed calm; she needed quiet. What she got instead was the steady drone of the air conditioner and unwelcome memories. Maybe solitude wasn't such a good idea after all.

"I'll call the director and explain what happened," Pierce had told her. "We'll get the first flight back to DC in the morning and decide where we go from here."

Karen knew what waited for them back at the OMRD. There would be meetings and paperwork, a discussion of reassigned priorities. She could already see the pained look on Director Whitacre's face: going for sincerity, but falling closer to dyspepsia. Regrets would be shared; losses would be cut. This investigation would be over.

She couldn't help but think of Dennis, the young CIA agent

who had been killed in the tunnel under the Berlin Wall. An entire life—and all its potential—gone in an instant. And for what? Had his death mattered? Years later, who remembered him? Who would remember Gerald?

The OMRD wasn't an old agency, founded a few years after the war. When Karen was recruited right out of school, the whole place had been full of noise and chaos and uncertainty. Why were they here? What was the OMRD supposed to be? Gerald had actually started a few months before her. There was no Department of Theoretical Magic yet, just some vague ideas about how to implement the "R" in OMRD. Some of those early meetings had been contentious, but Karen had reveled in all of it.

After about a year or so, it was obvious someone needed to head this new department. Karen knew her connection with Dr. Haupt would get her the interview, but she'd have to earn the job herself. She studied and prepared more than she ever did at St. Cyprian's. She could still picture the dour faces of the senior magicians conducting the interviews. She knew she'd impressed them, no matter how hard they'd tried to hide it.

When she finished, she went down to the lab she shared with Gerald. "When is your interview?" she had asked him.

He took off his thick glasses and began to clean them with a corner of his lab coat. "I removed my name from the list."

"You did what? That's nuts. You'd be great at the job."

"I think I'd do okay," Gerald had said. "But I think you'd be amazing, and I don't want to give those old men upstairs another mediocre male name to consider when they should be giving the job to you."

Karen rolled off the bed and poured herself a glass of tepid water. It tasted like old pipes and chemicals. Outside, a light patter of rain hissed on the gravel parking lot.

Gerald was gone, and it was her fault.

There was a question that her mind kept bending toward. Despite her grief, the question lingered patiently, glowing in the periphery like the neon signs outside her window.

How had the tattooed man known her name?

He had used magic, of that she was all but certain, though it hadn't been any spell she was familiar with. And moreover, he'd been there just as she needed him. Which meant he'd been watching her. For how long? And for what purpose?

Karen picked up her leather satchel and held it to her chest. Its weight comforted her; the scent of magic within, an exotic spice to which she could put no words, helped calm her turbulent thoughts.

She opened it up and inspected the inner lock one more time. It held. Her gun was there as well, but it offered her no real sense of protection tonight. It felt oddly inert, disappointingly nonmagical.

Trust your magic, the tattooed stranger had said. How could she, when it had failed her when she needed it the most? What good was a weapon if she couldn't use it when her life was on the line? If the tattooed man hadn't arrived, she'd be the one broken at the bottom of the stairwell. How long had she feared her magic would break free, beyond her control? She needn't have bothered. Apparently its bark was worse than its bite.

She took out the cube, the source of all their trouble. An anima, Magnus had called it. Gerald lost his life over this thing. Had it been worth it, or was it all just a misunderstanding? A magically simulated personality?

Its black faces were still, but Karen could sense the latent energy inside the anima, waiting. It warmed her hands, working into bone and tendon. She didn't trust her magic, couldn't trust it. But she had needed it and might need it again. She had to know if it would be there if she called on it.

Okay. This doesn't have to be terrifying. Just don't think about Auttenberg. Or the breach. Or what lay beyond it.

Karen sat on the bed, cross-legged, the cube held out in front of her. Someone shouted outside, a distant, muffled sound. Cars drove by the motel on wet tires. A door slammed down the hall. Karen heard all this but set it aside. She tried to remember the excitement of her first days learning magic, or the thrill when she started to tap into something beyond spellbooks and incantations and loci. And she tried to forget what it felt like to kill someone with that magic.

She breathed out. It was there, just beyond her reach. No, not beyond, not if she wanted it. Karen focused, stilled her thoughts. Her magic whispered to her, a vapor of sound in her mind. She felt a familiar quickening in her blood, power that she long coveted and then shunned, the power that changed the course of her life and then changed it again.

This time, she grabbed hold.

The magic roared. It filled her thoughts, her vision. It flooded the motel room. The alarm clock on the bedside table began to float in midair, and then the table itself joined in. Static began to rush out of the radio, a sudden sharp hiss of white noise. The air around her snapped with potentiality.

Oh, God. It felt right; it felt like coming home. A tear ran down her face. Why had she waited so long? How could she deny herself this feeling?

A moment before she gave herself over to it, she felt a hint of an old memory, like scar tissue that tugged at the surrounding skin: the terrible, inexorable pull of the breach, of that raw, nullifying magic that threatened to rip open the sky.

Calm down, she told herself. *You are still in control here. Do what you need to do.*

Almost regretfully, Karen asserted her will and the magic reluctantly responded. She stared into the anima. Something moved inside, little more than a trick of the light. Was it safe to go probing around inside a strange magical energy source of untold capacity? It was too late for such concerns.

There was resistance when her magic met the magic in the anima, so she pressed down harder, wrapping it on all sides. *Come on,* she thought. *I need answers here. I need you to—*

The anima flared to life as blinding light filled the room. Karen steadied herself, her magic responding to her need and dimming the glare. The cube began to shake in her hands, a faint tremor at first but then more violently.

What will Pierce think when he comes to my room and finds a smoking crater instead? She realized she was assuming she'd only blow *herself* up, but she had no reason to be so optimistic; she might take out the whole motel. Or all of Florida.

"Por favor." The voice broke through. Images flashed in Karen's mind, too fast to see. "Por favor. Ayudame." Help me, please. Was this the personality Magnus claimed they had created? Another burst of light and motion, not in the room but in Karen's brain. What was it?

"Mi nombre es Maria," the voice inside the anima said. "Maria Perez Zamanillo. Ayudame."

The pictures in Karen's mind slowed and sharpened. A girl, twelve or thirteen years old, with long braided black hair. She reminded Karen of Martha, her niece. Green eyes. A dimple in her right cheek. Smiling. No, she was running. Running away from something unseen; running, but never really moving.

"Maria," Karen said. "Maria, can you hear me?" She fumbled for the Spanish. "¿Puedes escucharme? Me llamo Karen."

A silence. Then: "Sí. Karen." Another pause. "Karen, tengo miedo." I'm scared.

"Maria, it's okay," Karen said. She couldn't remember the right words in Spanish, could barely get them out in English as tears ran down her face. "Don't be afraid."

"Karen . . ." Maria's voice was fading.

"No, stay with me, Maria. I can help you. I will help you."

"Por favor . . . ," Maria said again, but then the cube and the room darkened. Karen's magic slipped away; everything crashed back to the ground. She lay on the bed for a moment, her skin covered in a fine sweat that was already causing her to shiver.

Gerald had come to her for help, but she'd only gotten him killed. A beautiful, gentle life, gone, just like that. It was too late to save him, but maybe it wasn't too late to help him. Something terrible was unfolding; some foul magic was at play. Since Berlin, Karen had waited. No, she'd *hidden*. But maybe that wasn't an option anymore.

In a deep place in Karen's gut, a fire sparked. And began to smolder.

She rolled over and grabbed for the telephone.

Arthur sounded a little groggy and a little drunk when he answered. "You're calling late, Miss O'Neil."

"How did you know it was me?"

"I'm a spy, I know things," he said. "Also I haven't given my number to anyone else."

"I need your help again."

The connection to the anima was long gone, but the face of that little girl was seared into Karen's mind like a brand. And now she had a name: Maria Perez Zamanillo. It wasn't much, but maybe it was enough. It would have to be.

"Arthur, how would you like to take a vacation to Havana?"

THIRTEEN

Karen and Arthur arrived in Havana under a bright sun that turned the ocean sapphire and the city gold. Though they were met in the airport by incongruous pine trees bristling with ribbons and lights, welcoming the flurry of American snowbirds coming to celebrate Christmas in style, the air reminded Karen of summertime. A large colorful mural covered an entire wall of the terminal and proclaimed in English: WELCOME TO CUBA: LAND OF ROMANCE! Karen cocked an eyebrow at the smiling, sunglassed couples depicted on the scene frolicking on the sand, but Arthur just kept walking.

Outside the terminal, a large wooden nativity scene had been set up with the words *FELIZ NAVIDAD* hanging overhead. As they waited for a taxi, Karen couldn't help but feel sorry for the sculpted wise men; she imagined they'd be a lot more comfortable in shorts and sunglasses than robes and crowns.

Havana itself sparked like a live wire. Tourists trailing luggage clogged the walkways. Cars of every shape and color blared their horns and screeched their brakes in a peculiar smoggy song and dance. Music, bold and hot, filled every remaining crevice, though

Karen could never spot where it was coming from. Old men with eyes wreathed with sun-deepened lines gathered on street corners in white short sleeves, tossing dice from a cup and blowing pungent cigar smoke high into the Cuban sky. Signs hung over their heads hawking coffee and Pepsi-Cola in every store.

As their taxicab, rank with the deep smell of old tobacco, pulled alongside the water, Karen marveled at the sight of sunbathers sprawled along the yellow sand. A few even wore red Santa hats with their swimsuits, dramatically underscoring the oddity of this Caribbean yuletide display.

"It's probably snowing back in DC," Arthur said when he saw Karen gaping at the weather. He'd shaved and combed what was left of his hair; with a clean shirt on, he looked a little less like a drunk and a little more like the spymaster of Berlin she remembered.

"Don't remind me," Karen said.

Tall buildings lined the beach, towering modern skyscrapers alongside preserved Spanish domes and columns. A medieval-looking fortress, pale stone darkened by sea spray and lichen, kept vigil along the water's edge, not far from the neon bustle of hotel-casinos. White-spired cathedrals overlooked the large inviting windows of department stores and glittering marquees announcing upcoming performances by Frank Sinatra and Dean Martin. The past and present seemed to hold an uneasy truce in Havana, each side staking out their territory along the valuable and crowded beachfront.

Farther down, the traffic slowed. Karen leaned out the window to look ahead. Men in dark military uniforms and mirrored sunglasses huddled on the sidewalk around a couple of men in handcuffs. The prisoners stared blankly into the gutter while passersby on the street gave them a wide berth.

"Policía," their taxi driver said, crossing himself. He kept his eyes forward even as they drove past the commotion.

"What did they do?" Karen asked. "Those young men?"

"Communists," came the reply.

They drove by and the Havana noise soon swallowed them.

"Have you been to Cuba before?" Karen asked Arthur as they drove.

"Never had the pleasure," Arthur replied. "Though I think my wife would have liked it here." He glanced out the window. "Pity your friend Mr. Pierce couldn't join us."

Karen gave Arthur a dirty look, which he pointedly ignored. When she'd told Pierce she wasn't going to go back to DC with him, the inquisitor hadn't been exactly supportive of Karen's travel plans.

"What do you think you'll be able to accomplish?" he had demanded. He seemed angry. It was the first time Karen had seen him upset. "There's a process for this."

"That process is going to let Magnus get away with whatever it is he's doing down there," she'd shot back. "Men like Magnus own the process."

"So what are you going to do? Break down his front door and demand the truth?"

She had expected questions like these, but even still she hadn't been able to come up with any answers she liked.

Pierce mistook her silence as uncertainty and had pressed on. "Dealing with Magnus in the US would be hard enough," he said, "but down there, he's invincible. He can afford a few senators here, but he's got the entire Cuban government on his side, and Batista doesn't play by the rules. If they think you are meddling with Magnus's business, they'll deport you if you're lucky. Or you may just disappear."

"You seem to have the mistaken impression I was asking you for permission."

That had drawn a smirk from Pierce, a look Karen had endured a thousand times. She was suddenly glad he wouldn't be coming along. "The director might have something to say about that," Pierce had said, not bothering to hide the condescension. He'd been supportive of her up to this point, but now that she was going off book, his patience with her had apparently worn thin.

"You can tell Whitacre," Karen replied, choosing her words ever so carefully, "that I've decided to take a vacation for the holidays."

Pierce had sighed. "Magnus isn't worth it, Karen."

Karen's face burned a little. She knew he wasn't going to help her, but she had hoped he would at least understand. "I'm not going for Magnus," she had replied. "I'm going for Maria."

She stared out the dirty cab window at the sprawl and opulence of Havana; had it been a mistake to come here, hoping she could make a difference? How would she find the trail of one little girl in all this? And what would she do even if she could?

"I'm sure we'll manage without him," Karen said. Arthur didn't argue. She motioned to the elegant cafés and shops whipping past them. "I don't mind the sightseeing, but shouldn't we have the driver take us to our hotel soon?"

"Oh, he is," Arthur said. He leaned forward and pointed out the front window at a huge building gleaming bone white in the sunlight. Fronds from spindle-legged palm trees wafted across the main entrance. Endless rows of windows lined the facade; Karen felt dizzy trying to count the number of floors. The building was crowned with columns and arches blending Spanish and art deco styles. Across the front hung a huge bright sign, with letters almost a story high: EL PARAÍSO.

"We're staying there?" Karen gaped as the taxi pulled up under the gold awning. The uniforms of the valets waiting there were nicer than anything in her closet back home.

"Nothing but the best."

"We can afford it?"

"My treat," Arthur said. "Or Uncle Sam's. I have a generous pension."

Karen stared at him with a raised eyebrow.

"What?" he asked with feigned innocence. "You doubt my intentions?"

"I believe you once told me not to trust anyone."

Arthur shouldered open the car door and held out a hand. "I don't get out much, Miss O'Neil," he said, "so I want to enjoy myself."

Karen didn't move. "And?"

He smiled. "You'll see."

After they checked in, they retired to their rooms before dinner. Karen pulled back the heavy drapes and let the late-afternoon light spill onto the brightly patterned carpet. A few hundred feet below, pale forms in swim trunks and bathing suits lounged around the brilliantly blue pool. A few brave souls mounted the trilevel diving board and splashed spectacularly into the water. Echoes of laughter rose up like incense. Beyond the striped parasols was the main seaside road, and then the endless expanse of ocean.

I don't know where you are, Maria, or what they've done to you. But I'll find you, even if I have to burn this whole city down.

Karen's vehemence surprised her, but something inside her had bent when she heard the girl's name. She thought of her niece, Martha, and what it would do to her sister if anything happened to her.

She changed clothes and checked the clock. Arthur had been

adamant about meeting precisely at five p.m. for dinner. She grabbed her satchel, but realized it would likely be out of place in a fancy restaurant. Reluctantly, she stored it in her room's safe. She felt exposed without it.

Arthur met her downstairs. He'd even put on a tie.

"You don't seem the sort to crave fine dining," Karen said as a tuxedoed waiter showed them to their table. Crystal chandeliers hung overhead. Candlelight danced on heavy white tablecloths.

Arthur held out her chair. "A meat-and-potatoes man, myself," he said.

"I doubt we'll find a good pot roast in Havana," Karen said. She eyed the other patrons. There was far too much money in this room. Diamonds sparkled from necks and ears; gold glinted on wrists and fingers. Gray cigar smoke shrouded everything.

"Maybe we both need to learn to appreciate the finer things in life, Miss O'Neil."

"And maybe you need to tell me what's really going on."

Arthur subtly nodded toward the entrance. Karen followed his gaze. A man and woman entered the restaurant, and the waitstaff flew into a sudden flurry of activity. The new arrivals were shown to an empty table near the back, with a view of the pool and gardens outside. The man was older, late fifties, with thick silver hair, an expensive suit, and careful eyes. His far-younger companion was a stunning woman with deep brown skin and a dress of green satin. Even in a crowd as wealthy as this, they stood out.

"His name is Morris Rabin," Arthur said, his voice almost too low to be heard over the noise of silverware on dinner plates. "He owns El Paraíso. In fact, he owns a number of hotels, including the one your friend Mr. Magnus used to host his little demonstration back in Miami."

Karen had thought some of the Christmas decorations in the lobby had a familiar look about them. "So?"

"He is also the primary investor in Magnus's operation here in Cuba," Arthur said, "though there are others, President Batista among them."

"What does a hotel operator want from Magnus Innovations?"

"I have no idea," Arthur replied as he unfolded his napkin and laid it on his lap. "But Morris Rabin is far more than a hotelier; he all but runs the Havana Mob."

"The Mob?" Karen said, her voice too loud. Heads briefly turned in their direction.

"He started off running the Jewish Mob in Jersey, but his operation has steadily grown since the war. Other bosses have come and gone, but Rabin just keeps getting bigger. Among his fellow gangsters, he's known as 'the Quiet Man.' Quietly taking over and eliminating the competition," Arthur said. "Those goons back at the airport were known associates of Rabin's crime syndicate."

Karen's fingers flexed on the stem of her wineglass. Rabin's men killed Gerald. Maybe Magnus gave the order, but this mobster had given him the means. She forced her hand to relax and ignored the eagerness for violence she felt twitching inside. "So he's providing money and manpower," Karen said.

Arthur nodded. "He wants something from Magnus. Something valuable."

Karen risked another glance toward Rabin's table. He didn't look much different than the other patrons in the restaurant, just another paunchy middle-aged man in a nice suit enjoying the Havana nightlife. What would a mobster want from Magnus? Her mind flashed to Solomon, the massive pale construct in Magnus's hotel room. Was that what Rabin wanted? An army of mindless magical slaves? That didn't seem right.

"By all reports," Arthur was saying, "Rabin is quite the fan of the magical arts."

Karen turned back. "A magician?"

"Not as far as anyone can tell," Arthur said. "Just a connoisseur. A collector."

"How refreshing," Karen said. "Most nonmagical people find us terrifying. I don't recall you being all that keen on magic yourself."

"I look at magic the same way I did my wife," Arthur said. "As long as we stayed in separate rooms, we got along just fine."

Karen wasn't sure if she should laugh at that; it sounded like a joke, but something in Arthur's eyes warned her off. She was about to explain all the ways that magic could improve Americans' quality of life if they would all stop acting like cavemen seeing fire for the first time, when someone from a nearby table turned around and spoke.

"Excuse me," the woman said, looking at Karen, "but I couldn't help overhearing. Are you a magician?"

The woman was a little younger than Karen and was dressed in shimmering silk. Ruby earrings caught and scattered the room's warm light. Her blond curls were pinned up and styled with more care than Karen had ever bothered with in her life. She was beautiful, but she was more than that: she was glamorous.

"Yes," Karen answered warily. "I am."

"Oh, marvelous," the woman said. She extended her arm, gloved to the elbow and graceful as a swan's neck. "My name is Sandra. Sandra Saint. I'm an actress; maybe you've heard of me? *The Princess of the Amazon? Oriental Moon?*"

Karen looked to Arthur but he was no help. "Sorry, no," she said. "I don't get out to the movies that often."

Sandra waved that away with a flick of her bejeweled wrist. "Those were awful anyway. I don't know where they even find these writers, I truly don't." She leaned in closer and lowered her voice. "But my next movie is going to be a real crackerjack. It's called *The*

Magician's Curse. I can't say much about it—it's all very hush-hush—but I'm going to be playing a lady magician, just like you!"

Karen raised an eyebrow. "Sounds . . . intriguing."

Sandra continued as if Karen had said nothing. "But I just know these idiot writers will botch the whole thing, as they always do. They know nothing about magic and less about women, but I want to get this right. If you're the real deal, maybe I can pick your brain for a bit?" She flapped her hands in a crude approximation of a magic spell. "Just to make sure I get the details right, you know?"

"Umm . . ." Karen wasn't certain how to respond to such an unexpected request. "Sure."

"Marvelous!" Sandra said, clapping. "Are you in Havana long? We're here through New Year's. Sure beats Christmastime in Los Angeles. So dreary. You're staying here at the hotel?"

Karen nodded. She wasn't sure why she was agreeing to help this stranger, though she doubted she was the first person Sandra Saint had recruited in this manner.

"Perfect. We'll meet for drinks in the bar. Or maybe you can show me some of your magic in the casino!"

"Sandy!" Her dinner companions had risen and found their coats and waved to her from the doorway. "Let's go!"

Sandra touched the back of Karen's hand; Karen had to fight hard not to flinch. "I can't wait to hear all your stories! A real magician, and a pretty girl one at that. What are the odds? A Christmas miracle!"

And then she and her entourage swept out of the restaurant in a cloud of mink and perfume. The other patrons barely even glanced up from their hors d'oeuvres; the sight of Hollywood starlets in evening wear was apparently commonplace under the glitzy lights of Havana.

"Look at you," Arthur said with a grin, "making friends already."

"Can it," Karen said. "How did you know Rabin would be here tonight?"

"He eats here every night."

"And how did you know that?"

"I have friends too," Arthur said. He shrugged. "Or at least people who owe me favors, which is better than having friends, in my experience."

Karen leaned across the table. She felt the heat of the center-piece candle on her cheeks. "What are we doing here, Arthur? You bring us here, to this hotel, to this restaurant, to show me this Mob boss working with Magnus; are you trying to scare me? Convince me to go home?"

"I tried convincing you to behave back in Berlin, and we saw how effective that was," Arthur said. He sighed and looked a little deflated, a little older. "Look, I'm here, aren't I? I'm on your side."

"But?"

"But you need to know what you are getting yourself into." He stabbed the air with a breadstick. "John Magnus is a dangerous man. He has money and connections, here and in DC. He's a bad man to have as an enemy." Arthur turned his eyes across the room, to where Rabin sat. The waiter was pouring wine. Nearby, a dark-skinned musician in a white tuxedo gently massaged the keys of a magnificent grand piano. "But Morris Rabin? He's just a bad man. Magnus will make your life miserable; Rabin will just kill you."

Karen thought about the gold-toothed goon, and about Gerald's body lying alone in some Miami morgue, waiting for his family to come and claim him. These were not the sort of stakes she had expected when she started her work at the OMRD, and part of her knew she was in over her head. But the rest of her knew that for the first time since Auttenberg, she felt something other than numbness or dread: she felt like she was doing something that mattered, something that might actually help someone.

"Don't worry, Arthur," Karen said. "It's okay to be afraid. I'll protect you."

Arthur snorted. "Glad that's cleared up then. Now, where's our waiter? Do you have to run the Havana Mob in order to get service around here?"

FOURTEEN

The next morning, Karen found Arthur waiting in the hotel lobby with another man. The stranger was about Arthur's height and thin to the point of gauntness. He seemed ill at ease in El Paraíso, like a jackrabbit ready to bolt for the tall grass at the first sign of a predator. He held a faded hat in front of his body with both hands and couldn't seem to stop glancing out the massive front windows at the cars lazily driving by outside.

"Karen," Arthur said as she approached, "I'd like you to meet an old friend of mine, Joaquin. He's offered to do a bit of driving and translating for us."

"Thank you," Karen said, taking Joaquin's callous hand. A record player filled the echoing lobby with Bing Crosby's saccharine Christmas merriment, certain not to alienate the American vacationers.

"Of course," Joaquin said. His voice was soft, his accent strong. "I could not trust Arthur to be a proper guide, especially not after his last visit to my beloved Cuba."

Karen narrowed her eyes at Arthur. "You said you'd never been to Cuba before."

"I've been to lots of places I've never been to," Arthur replied with a shrug.

The cracked blue leather creaked as Karen slid into the back seat of Joaquin's car. She rolled down the window and smelled the sea spray. Gulls complained overhead. And then she heard just the low rumble of the engine as they pulled out onto the road.

Arthur twisted awkwardly in the front seat to face Karen. "Joaquin has been digging up some leads for us."

"It has not been easy," Joaquin said, his voice nearly lost under the road noise. "If our Maria's family were wealthy, we would find them easily. But the poor are easily forgotten, and sadly, a missing child is not an uncommon occurrence in Havana in recent months. The investigations go nowhere. Our leaders do not seem to have an interest in a few lost children. Too many other issues on their mind."

"Such as?" Karen asked.

Joaquin jerked a thumb toward the southeast. "La revolución."

"The government isn't popular?"

"Government?" Joaquin said with a sharp laugh. "We had a government in Cuba once. Now we just have a military. Batista realized he could not get reelected, and then realized he did not have to."

"So do you trust these rebels then?"

Joaquin spat out the window. "Filthy socialist teenagers, hiding in the jungle, armed with guns and bombs and Marx. They know nothing about running a country. They think their outrage makes them righteous." Karen had no trouble hearing him now. "All they have brought to Cuba is death."

"And Batista?"

"He is a coward and a thug. But he is a capitalist, so America loves him, is that not so, old friend?" Joaquin said, jabbing Arthur in the ribs with a bony elbow.

"I can only take credit for so much of American foreign policy," Arthur said. "And most of that is on the other side of the Atlantic."

"You are too modest," Joaquin said. "There are no such things as local problems anymore, only global ones. Or do you think the games you play with the USSR in Europe have no impact on us here in Cuba? You think there are no Soviets driving around Havana on this sunny day, just like us?"

"If there are Soviets in Havana today," Arthur said, "I hope they are getting a similar lecture."

As they traveled east, the towering hotels and palaces gave way to blocky apartments crammed in on each other, every building painted a different color: yellow and pink and blue and green, some vibrant, some long faded. Kids kicked a tattered ball in the street while women in white dresses fanned themselves under the shade of old ceiba trees.

They stopped at a few of these buildings. Karen and Arthur received wary looks, but Joaquin was welcomed easily. He spoke in rapid Spanish to the people they encountered, and while Karen's grasp of Spanish was limited, she clearly understood the shaking heads and downcast eyes.

So they kept going. Maria's family was here, somewhere. They might have even more questions than Karen did, but it was a place to start. Having been warned about pickpockets, she'd left her satchel back in the safe in her hotel room and felt uneasy without it. She wasn't sure what she'd do if they found themselves facing armed mobsters, but she didn't like feeling unarmed.

With the sun starting to hang low in the sky, they drove off the paved roads into a shantytown on the eastern outskirts of Havana. Karen saw homes no bigger than sheds, made with corrugated metal and scrap wood. Others had thatched roofs that looked like they hadn't changed in two hundred years. There were kids at play here as well, though fewer, and Karen also noted more young men, often shirtless, with deep brown skin and empty faces. They glared at Joaquin's car as it kicked up dust.

"They are macheteros," Joaquin said. "Sugarcane cutters. They work day and night during the harvest. But for the rest of the year? They wait. They watch. They wonder how much of Cuba is for them, and how much is for the American tourists and criminals." He pulled down the brim of his hat against the sun's glare. "If someone comes here and tells these men about the benefits of socialism, they will listen."

He parked his car near a cluster of homes that looked like they might be leaning and probably wouldn't survive long in a light breeze. "Even with a name, finding someone in Cuba is difficult," Joaquin said before they got out. "But I have been told that the Zamanillo family lives here. And that they have a missing daughter."

They were met by a balding man with a drooping mustache whose ears stuck out perpendicular to his head. Sweat made his shirt cling to his chest. He didn't make eye contact with Karen, but answered Joaquin's questions in a whisper.

"Their Maria vanished six months ago," Joaquin said. "Only thirteen years old."

"Ask him if they have any suspicions about who took her," Karen said.

When her question was translated, the man just shook his head. Karen thought she saw tears forming at the corners of his eyes. A woman approached them then. Her hair was pulled back in a bun and her floral-print dress was stained around her midsection, for want of an apron. Two young kids with dirty knees hovered behind her, waiting in the shadows of the doorway. Joaquin greeted her and asked the same questions. The woman's response was long and sharp.

"This is Maria's mother. She says Maria wasn't taken; she left them on her own," Joaquin said, trying to work translations in between the woman's sentences. "She ran off to Havana, because . . ." He seemed to struggle with the translation for a moment. "She was maldita."

"What does that mean?" Karen asked. The balding man had covered his face with his hand, but his wife just kept talking, her voice rising, her cheeks flushing.

"Literally, it means cursed," Joaquin said. "In this case, it means she had magical ability."

Maria had the talent. Karen wondered how they tested children for magical aptitude in Cuba. In the US, every schoolchild went through the same process, administered by trained examiners: some bizarre questions that the kids rarely understood, a few detection spells cast by the examiners to check for any latent magical presence, and finally walking the child through casting their first spell. Karen had wanted it so badly that she'd fumbled the instructions three times before she finally got it right.

"What else is she saying?" Karen asked. "Anything about Magnus?"

"No, no," Joaquin said. He spoke in Spanish, listened, then spoke again. "She says her daughter ran away because they would not let her learn how to use her magic. Someone told her about a place in Havana that would teach her—corrupt her, to use her mother's word—and so she left. At first, she wrote them a few letters and sent them with friends, but then that stopped too. They haven't heard from her in months."

Karen felt her elation at finding Maria's parents turn to despair. "Does she know anything about where she went in Havana? Where she was going to learn about magic?"

Maria's mother gave a hard, quick reply even before Joaquin could translate Karen's question. "She says," Joaquin said, "that if you want to know what happened to Maria, you will need to find La Bruja."

FIFTEEN

The phone jangled. Meredith swallowed and snatched up the receiver. "Magnus Innovations, Mr. Magnus's office," she said in her sweetest voice. "May I ask who's calling?"

The voice on the other end was soft but unmistakable: "I want to speak to him."

"Of course," she said. "One moment please."

She stood up from her desk and straightened her skirt. Mr. Magnus would not be pleased, but that was not her problem. Her boss may have a fierce bark, but when his master yanked on his chain, he always came to heel. She crossed the room and pulled open the double doors that led into Mr. Magnus's private office.

"What is it?" Mr. Magnus demanded when she entered. He looked haggard, as he had ever since their return from Miami. His hair was barely combed and his tie hung off the edge of his massive oak desk like a fallen flag.

"Mr. Rabin is on the line for you, sir," she said.

He nodded grimly. The call was not welcome, but not unexpected. "Very well," he said, running a hand over his face. "Put it through. Oh, and tell Jenkins downstairs that if I don't have a positive status report on my desk by the end of the day, he should just drown himself in the ocean." For emphasis, he pointed out the giant windows behind his desk, where the blue water stretched forever in all directions.

"Of course, sir."

Meredith returned to her desk and informed Mr. Rabin he was being transferred. As she clicked the necessary buttons to route his call into Mr. Magnus's office, she also activated the small recorder she had installed shortly after arriving. The recorder made no sound and looked like a stapler, just another innocuous piece of office detritus. The teams in Moscow needn't have bothered; no one ever paid enough attention to her for any questions to be asked. She was, after all, just the secretary.

Typically she recorded important calls like these and listened to them later in her apartment, after which she would encrypt the transcriptions onto various postcards to be mailed the following day. It was dreary work, but safe. But today, she let her curiosity get the better of her and decided to listen in live.

". . . they are fools, that's what I'm saying. They can't see the opportunity in front of them, even if I make Solomon dance a waltz or bake a meatloaf." Mr. Magnus's voice was strained; he was trying too hard. Men like him only knew how to handle victory, never setback.

"So you got no new money." It was a statement, not a question. Mr. Rabin rarely spoke above a whisper; the file Meredith had read on him before coming to Cuba had said that in the criminal underworld, he was known as "the Quiet Man."

Magnus paused a long moment before replying. "No."

"Tell me again, John," Rabin said, "why my substantial investments were insufficient."

"This is research, Morris," Magnus said, though he sounded

very uncertain about using Rabin's first name. "Uncharted territory. We can't know how much time and money it will take; we just keep at it until we've made our breakthrough."

"I've funded you through several breakthroughs," Rabin said. "How many more are required before you produce something useful?"

"And those have been remarkable, as I've told you," Magnus replied. "Solomon wouldn't have been possible without—"

"I am not paying you for a magic slave," Rabin cut in. "I have plenty of men who do what I tell them. What I need is for you to give me what you promised me."

"My people are working on it, I swear," Magnus said. "Day and night. I'm working them like dogs, Morris. We want the same thing. If we can make this work, I'll never have to beg investors for capital again. I'll have enough money to run my own country. I'll let you join my cabinet. How's minister of finance sound? Or secretary of booze and gambling?"

The telephone was silent. Meredith thought maybe Rabin had hung up; it wouldn't have been the first time. But then his small voice came through, just before the line clicked dead: "Don't disappoint me."

Meredith licked her lips, a bad habit; her lipstick tasted like wax. Another small indignity she weathered for the sake of this disguise. But perhaps not forever. Now the pressure was mounting. Magnus could not keep this going for much longer. Men like Rabin could be patient when necessary, but not if they felt like they were being conned. Criminals were usually rather intolerant of such things. Then it would be time to move to the next phase of her mission.

The gray-haired man would be pleased to get her report.

SIXTEEN

a Bruja probably does not exist."

They were driving back into Havana. Karen was tired, hungry, and frustrated, but not without hope. They had a lead.

"Humor me," she said to Joaquin. "If she exists, who is she?"

Joaquin sighed. "Magic has a complicated place in Cuban culture," he said eventually. "For some, like the Santería, it is sacred. It is the only true way to commune with the saints."

Something about that name jogged Karen's memory. "I've read about that," she said. "They speak Lucumí, right?" It was an African language known for particular magical potency. She was fairly certain they'd even tried a few Lucumí spells back in the lab at the OMRD.

Joaquin nodded. "But they are a small minority in Cuba. For the rest, magic is at best dangerous, and at worst, heretical. If a child is found to have magical ability, they may just be ostracized. Or they may be banished, or worse."

Karen's dad had always hated her magic and even now never missed a chance to make her feel unwelcome, but at least he hadn't kicked her out of their home.

"So, a few years ago," Joaquin went on, "a rumor started spreading about a magician in Havana who would take in children with magical talent and teach them how to use their abilities. To some, she became a bit of a folk hero, and to others, an evil kidnapper."

"La Bruja?"

"If Maria went looking for her, there's no telling where she ended up."

So much for their lead. But it was, after all, their first day in Cuba. Not a bad start.

Joaquin dropped them off at the hotel, declining to come inside and promising to meet them again following the holiday. "Be careful," he said before he pulled away. He tipped his hat toward El Paraíso. "Do not forget you are sleeping in the beast's lair. Cuba is a beautiful place, but unforgiving to the unprepared."

"Delightful company as always, Joaquin," Arthur said. When he had gone, Arthur told Karen, "He was always a bit of a worrier, that one."

"Remind me how you two met?"

"I don't remember," Arthur said as they went inside.

When the elevator spat them out near their rooms, Arthur's stomach grumbled. "It's past my dinnertime," he said, "and I'm not sure what it was we ate last night. Let's find someplace to eat that doesn't serve salad, shall we?"

Karen laughed but didn't argue. "Let me just wash the dust off my face," she said as she reached her room. "I'll meet you back out here in ten—"

The door to her room was ajar. Not far, just a little. The cleaning crew? She nudged the door a little farther. Her suitcase was on the floor, cut open. Her clothes had been thrown across the room, scattered in a dozen little piles. Everything else in her luggage had been tossed into a corner of the bathroom.

Karen only hesitated a second before running to the closet. She yanked the door open so hard it slammed against the wall. The safe where she had stored her satchel was open. And empty.

Arthur stood in the doorway. "Mine too," he said. "Luckily we didn't have anything valuable in—" Karen was already pushing past him, back toward the elevator.

They took it. They took it. Distantly, a small part of her told her to calm down, not to do anything rash. *They couldn't have known what was in the satchel. No one knows.*

"Karen," Arthur called. "Karen!"

It didn't matter if they knew. It only mattered that she got it back. She pressed the button for the ground floor, and the doors closed before Arthur could catch up.

At the entrance to El Paraíso's restaurant, the maître d'hôtel smiled at her and started to open his mouth to speak, when Karen shoved him out of her way. She ignored his startled yelp and more than a few gasps and headed for the table by the windows.

You are about to get yourself killed, she thought. She dug her nails into her palms but barely registered the pain. This was reckless, dangerous, stupid. But she had no other choice.

"You took something of mine," she said when she reached the table. "And I want it back."

Morris Rabin looked up from his soup. His dispassionate eyes met hers and held. He wasn't a big man, but the weight of that gaze made her legs suddenly freeze. A moment later, she was grabbed from behind as Rabin's goons materialized all around her. *Stupid, stupid.*

The boss of the Havana Mob set his spoon down gently on the table. "That's alright," he said softly. "She was just about to join us for dinner."

Karen was released and another chair was brought. She rubbed her arm where the goon had held her. She could still feel his grip. As she sat down, she looked from Rabin to his date. She could not read the woman's expression any more than she could his. Karen's heart raced and her mouth went sour.

"My name is Morris," Rabin said, offering a smile so slight Karen wasn't sure it could possibly be intentional. He motioned across the table, saying, "And this is Isabel."

"And you already know my name, don't you?" Karen asked.

"I do," Rabin said, "but why don't you introduce yourself anyway, to be polite."

"Is it polite to break into someone's room and steal their things?"

Rabin's eyes betrayed nothing. "I own all these rooms," he said. "You are my guest."

"A paying guest."

Rabin held up a finger in gentle protest. "Your friend is paying," he corrected. "From his account funded by his CIA pension, I believe."

Karen paused a moment. She had jumped into this headfirst, thinking she knew how deep it went, but suddenly she was finding it a little hard to breathe. "You are well informed, Mr. Rabin," she said. "If you know so much already, why did you feel the need to rummage around in my suitcase?"

A waiter appeared at Rabin's shoulder, tentatively offering more wine. As his glass was refilled, Rabin ignored her question and instead asked, "And how did you like Miami, Miss O'Neil? I lived there for many years, but don't miss it too much."

"I ran into some unpleasantries in the airport."

Rabin nodded knowingly. "That can happen. In fact, a few of my associates experienced something similar very recently. One of whom, in fact, ended up with a broken neck for his trouble. Thrown down a flight of stairs." Rabin's cheek twitched, a small motion but noteworthy on so immobile a face. "During an altercation with a young female magician from the OMRD."

Karen felt her fingers tighten, her jaw muscles flex. *Don't get angry now,* she thought. *Or at least not any angrier. This is unsteady ground we're walking on here.* "They were going to put a bullet in my head. Someone else threw your thug down the stairs, while the rest of your men killed a good friend of mine."

"That's not how they remember it."

"I'm sure it isn't," Karen replied.

They stared at each other over congealing soup. Rabin's appetite seemed to have diminished since her arrival. His bodyguards loomed just behind her; retreat was no longer an option. Instead she had to hope there was a way out on the other side.

Karen leaned her elbows onto the tablecloth; her jacket left small dusty smudges on the white cotton. "Do you know what Magnus Innovations is doing with children like Maria Perez Zamanillo, Mr. Rabin?"

He coughed slightly. His date, Isabel, suddenly fixed her eyes on him. "I've never heard that name before," he said.

"That wasn't an answer to my question."

"John Magnus is a business partner," Rabin said. "But his business is his business."

"That is a convenient perspective," Karen said.

Rabin motioned to the nearest bodyguard. "Ezra, go check the lost and found. I think Miss O'Neil may have misplaced something." When he left, Rabin grabbed his spoon and stirred his soup, but then thought better of it and let it drop with a clang of silver on china. A drop of red splattered onto the tablecloth. "You seem like a committed young woman. I admire that. To a point."

Karen made no reply.

"Now that we've had this pleasant chat, I'll leave you to your business, Miss O'Neil," he said. "As long as it doesn't get in the way of mine."

"I'm here for a little girl," Karen said, "and some answers. If that meddles with your business, then you've made some poor choices."

Another twitch marred Rabin's face. Was that anger? Had she cracked his armor? To Isabel, he said, "She speaks to me like you do. No respect. Women think they can walk all over me. Must be my gentlemanly nature."

Ezra reappeared. He held Karen's satchel.

"I do hope you enjoy your stay at El Paraíso, Miss O'Neil," Rabin said. "Until next time."

Arthur met her just outside the restaurant. She ignored him until they were down the hall, by the elevators.

"What in the blue hell were you thinking?" Arthur demanded. "Did you not hear me last night? Rabin kills people. Makes them disappear. You think just because you work for the damn OMRD that he'd hesitate for a moment to bury you in a shallow grave in the Cuban jungle?"

Karen said nothing. She held the satchel close to her chest and waited for the elevator doors to open.

Arthur sighed and ran a hand over what was left of his hair. He looked tired. And old. "What could be so important in that bag that you'd risk your life like that?"

She spun on him. "What do you remember about Auttenberg?"

He took a step back. His brow crinkled. "Not much," he said slowly. "I remember getting captured by some Soviets who shouldn't have been there, getting saved by Jim, and then some magic nonsense inside of a church. I think maybe you tried to destroy all life as we know it?"

"Do you remember why we all went into Auttenberg?"

"Everybody wanted some Nazi trinket," Arthur said, "but by the end of the night, we'd all forgotten most of the details. My superiors weren't too pleased with that part of my report, except they couldn't complain too loudly, since they'd forgotten too. Like the thing had never really existed."

"Trust me," Karen said, "it's best we all forget." The elevator opened and she hurried on. Arthur didn't move.

"Karen," he said as the elevator doors closed, "merry Christmas Eve."

When she got to her room, she bolted the door and sat on the bed. Inside the satchel, she found her gun and the velvet bag containing the anima. She set those aside and inspected the runes on the inner pocket. Still intact. Its contents were still safe. She exhaled, slowly and deeply, and touched the lock. It was attuned to her, and only her. The lock clicked. She opened the flap and drew out what was inside.

A notebook, identical to the ones they used in the labs at the office. She flipped the pages. They were full of words, diagrams, shapes, symbols, and incantations. Strange, unknowable spells, and something more: descriptions of another world, another plane of existence. The raving of madmen, across continents and generations. A book full of magic . . . and death.

She stopped on the first page, the first line: *Concerning that which must never come to pass* . . .

Karen closed the notebook, shoved it back into the pocket, and reengaged the lock and wards. Then she threw the bag across the room.

Suddenly cold, she wrapped herself in a blanket, pressed her trembling hands to her body to stop them from shaking, and wept.

SEVENTEEN

Christmas dawned on Havana with church bells and music. Karen had barely slept the night before. As she lay for endless hours staring into nothing, it made her think of Christmases as a kid, willing her sleepy eyes to stay open to catch a glimpse of reindeer. Though unlike bygone childhood days huddled under shared blankets with her sister, she didn't look to this morning with great anticipation. Cuba would turn inward on Christmas, Joaquin had explained, to spend time with ritual and with family. Not a great opportunity to canvass the streets looking for Maria or La Bruja.

"Do you still have people we can talk to?" Karen had asked. "Or have we already burned through your contacts in Havana?" She'd feared the answer.

"We will find her," Joaquin had said. His indirect answer had not been inspiring. "You will see."

There were presents, still unwrapped, piled in a corner of Karen's apartment. She'd bought them all in one mad rush. She'd hoped finding the perfect gifts for her sister and niece would summon some latent Christmas cheer and help her through the rest of the dreary year. It hadn't; she'd written her latest letter of resignation from the OMRD the next day.

Arthur knocked on her door twice, but she didn't answer. Instead she sat in the ruins of her hotel room, her satchel close, and wondered when she'd feel safe again.

As the sun was setting, she finally got up her nerve and picked up her telephone.

"Hello?"

"Hey, Helen," Karen said.

"Karen!" her sister replied, too loud. "Merry Christmas! Are you coming over?"

Karen looked out the window at the beach. "No, Helen. I'm stuck at work."

"Work? On Christmas?"

"You know how it is."

"Actually, no, I don't," Helen said. Her voice sounded very far away. "Are you okay? You sound like you've been crying."

Ugh, older sisters; how do they always know? "I'm fine."

"Fine," Helen repeated skeptically. "I'm not sure which is worse: working on Christmas, or lying to your sister on Christmas."

"I'm trying to do something important," Karen said. "I'm trying to help somebody. A little girl is missing. She's vanished, and her family . . . I think I can find her."

"That's awful," Helen said. Karen didn't tell her that Maria was probably about Martha's age. "I can't even imagine. I hope you find her."

"Me too."

Silence on the line. Then Helen said, "Okay, Karen. Okay. Do what you have to do. We just miss you. Maybe you can come by on New Year's Eve?"

"We'll see."

Another silence. "Don't work too hard, little sister."

Karen wiped a tear away and swallowed hard before responding. "I'll do my best. Give Martha my love. And Merry Christmas."

Her room suddenly felt very empty. She rubbed her red eyes and went out into the hall and found Arthur's room. She knocked, but there was no answer. "Arthur," she said. "I'm sorry. Arthur? You there?"

She found him downstairs in the casino. Even on Christmas, nearly every table was full. A fog of cigarette smoke cast the room in gray but could do little to mute the garish decorations in red, gold, and green. Every man wore a suit and tie, his hair shiny with Brylcreem. Their ladies hovered at their shoulders in polka dots and pearls. Chips clacked, roulette wheels clicked, and chrome-plated slot machines rattled. Arthur sat at a blackjack table, a drink in his hand, his tie loosened around his thick neck. His pile of chips dwindled.

"Hit me," he said to the dealer, who flipped over the jack of spades. It was not the card he was hoping for. "Merry Christmas to me," Arthur said in disgust as he drained the glass.

"Bad luck?" Karen asked.

Arthur pushed away from the table. "*My* luck." He staggered toward the bar and Karen followed. The bartender had a rum waiting for Arthur when he slumped onto a red leather stool.

"I'm sorry about yesterday," Karen said.

Arthur shrugged. "I can handle it if you've got secrets," he said, slurring the last word. "A death wish, though, might be a little harder to manage."

"Don't worry about me. I'm not sure what my life really looks like these days," Karen said, "but I'm not looking to lose it anytime soon."

He raised his rum in a salute. "Good. You're too young to die anyway. Leave that to old men like me." He threw back the glass. "Tired, old, washed-up men like me."

"Arthur . . ."

"They fired me," he said, staring into the empty glass. "I didn't retire. After a few decades serving our fine country working for more than a few different acronyms, they showed me the door and shoved me out. Left me with my pension and the clothes on my back. Didn't even get a handshake."

"I'm sorry, Arthur."

"Me too," he said. "Only thing I ever loved was that damn job. Well, maybe the wife too, but I liked the job more. Though I guess they both stabbed me in the back."

"What happened?"

He laughed at this; too loud, a drunkard's laugh. "You should know, since you were there."

"Auttenberg."

He waved the glass across the expanse of the chattering casino floor. "The whole damn thing. I let the Soviets nab one of our boys. I let the Wall come down. And then I let the bloody Nightingale and that traitor Alec go free. Of course nobody remembers how that little bit of goodwill helped convince Moscow to deescalate a potential catastrophe. It was a 'violation of protocol,' which is akin to blasphemy in DC. Adherence to protocol, after all, is what separates us from the apes."

Karen wasn't the only one to have lost something of herself in that strange place. "I'm sorry you got dragged into my mess."

"Oh, you can't take full credit. There was plenty of mess to go around."

They'd all lost so much to end Auttenberg's curse, but she didn't regret her actions. When everything was at stake, anything could be sacrificed. When she told Arthur as much, he snorted. "Good. Then maybe it was worth it."

"I hope so," Karen said. She helped him to his feet. "Come on. Let's get out of here before you lose any more money."

"You're probably right," he said, wobbling toward the exit. "If a man's going to be sick on Christmas, it should be in the comfort of his own hotel bathroom, not some gaudy casino."

"Right," Karen said. "The true spirit of the holiday."

"Amen," Arthur said. As they waited for the elevator, his watery eyes struggled to focus on her. "Why are we here, Karen? What's this really about?"

"Finding a little girl," she said.

"Lots of little girls we could be chasing," he said. "Lots of other good to be done."

"This one landed in my lap," Karen said. "Gerald asked for my help. Since Berlin, I haven't felt like I've been much help to anybody. Maybe I'm just trying to remember how."

Arthur somehow nodded solemnly while letting out a cataclysmic burp. "Good enough for me." He started to go pale as the elevator doors opened. "Now, let's hope this thing moves fast but very gentle."

Meredith saw the mark when she returned to her apartment. She almost missed it; no one had tried to make direct contact with her during her entire time on mission in Havana. But there it was, written in chalk on the side of her apartment building, a symbol only she could recognize: someone was waiting for her.

Her door was still locked, the windows shut. And yet he was there, sitting at her desk, when she entered. She closed the door without a word. Her contact was a gaunt man with deep-set eyes and brown skin. He did not look Russian, but that was not surprising. If they had sent a Russian to find her, it might have drawn attention. Luckily for them, there were Communists in every people on earth.

"Why are you here?" she asked. She kept her voice low, but did not hide her annoyance. She filed her reports on time. She had already completed many of her objectives. There was no reason for Moscow to check up on her.

Her contact did not immediately respond. Instead he stared at her like she was a curiosity in a zoo. He was measuring her, deciding what he thought of her. She did not care what he thought, what any of them thought.

"The gray-haired man sends his regards," her contact said eventually. "My name is Ramón."

"I don't care what your name is," she said. Her apartment felt too small with another person in it, and the fact that the gray-haired man himself had sent him did not make her any more comfortable.

Ramón did not seem to notice her rudeness. "I am here to make contact with the revolutionaries and see if they might become our allies. But the gray-haired man is also very interested in your mission and wants to ensure its eventual success."

"My mission is not at risk."

Ramón studied his fingernails. "You've been in the field for some time now. Have you enjoyed your time wallowing in capitalist excess?"

"Look around you. Does it look like I am living in luxury?"

He stared at her. "I am from Madrid, but have been forced to live in Moscow these long years. Do not pretend there is no difference. It is December; how many women do you think are walking in Red Square dressed as you are now?"

"You miss the sun on your face, comrade?"

"I heard a joke recently," Ramón said. "A man goes into a shop in Moscow and asks, 'You don't have any meat?' The woman behind the counter says, 'No, we don't have any fish. It's the shop across the street that doesn't have any meat.'"

Meredith did not laugh. "It is you who sounds unhappy with

living conditions in the Soviet Union, comrade, and yet you come here to question my loyalty?"

"I am satisfied with the choices I have made and the sacrifices they have required." Ramón tilted his head as he continued to stare. "Are you?"

Her face revealed nothing; she willed every muscle to remain still. "Life is not about comfort," she replied. The words came easily; she had been trained to speak them her entire life. "Life is about service and purpose."

Ramón considered her response. He drummed his fingers against her desk; the sound was thunderous in the otherwise silent apartment. "The gray-haired man trusts you will acquire the information we seek, but wonders if you will be able to properly disrupt Magnus's operation, when the time comes."

Meredith could not suppress a sneer. "I will put a bullet in his head."

"But that is not the same thing, is it?"

She said nothing. Magnus Innovations was a large and well-funded company, and the research facility in Cuba was well guarded. She could steal documents and record telephone calls, but bringing down the entire place would be a challenge. Not one she was willing to admit, however.

"There is an American here in Havana," Ramón went on. "A woman from their Office of Magical Research and Deployment, Karen O'Neil. She's come to Cuba to search for a missing girl. We believe this will put her in conflict with Mr. Magnus."

"I met her in Miami," Meredith said. *How does this man know about me and my purpose in Cuba?*

Ramón raised an eyebrow. "Then she is already making a nuisance of herself. Good. We think she can be valuable to your mission, if properly aided."

"I require no assistance."

Her contact stood. His expression was blank: no warmth, no rancor. "You will be judged on your results, not means. Do what must be done. I need not remind you that Moscow can be . . . unforgiving."

She locked the door behind him when he left. Her hands trembled as she fumbled in her desk. At last she found what she was looking for, what she desperately needed. The box of cigarettes danced in her unsteady grip, but her nerves began to settle the moment she pulled the smooth smoke into her mouth. She remembered the first time she had a Cuban cigarette, like a lover's caress on her cheek, soft and inviting. So different from what she had smoked in Moscow. She had smelled it on Ramón: the harsh cardboard tang of Belomorkanal cigarettes, straight from Leningrad. Odd, how a smell could conjure up such vivid memories, even ones she had buried so deep. A chill ran up her arms, an echo of a distant Russian winter.

She would do the mission. Of course she would. What other choice did she have? But she would miss moments like this, wrapped in the night and Havana smoke. More memories to bury.

EIGHTEEN

The following day, they drove around the Havana outskirts again with Joaquin, this time seeking information on La Bruja. They spoke with shopkeepers standing guard over mounds of produce, barbers polishing silver steel blades against leather straps, serious-looking men whose fedoras were wreathed in cigar smoke, and even children playing with chalk on the street, but no one would speak of La Bruja. Some laughed; others made the sign of the cross. One man, the owner of a small corner store, complained how urchins had come in and set a small fire using their magic, so they could steal candy from behind the counter while he was distracted. An older woman with her hair wrapped in a colorful headdress said La Bruja was a Santería priestess; another said she wasn't even human, but rather the goddess Ayao in disguise.

"I am sorry," Joaquin said near the end of the day. "We will find her."

It seemed to Karen that the people Joaquin approached now watched them more warily, even before he spoke, as though they knew what he would ask. Word was spreading, but their notoriety wasn't helping their cause.

Karen had a dull headache when Joaquin dropped them off that evening. She wasn't sure how long they could keep this search up. At what point did it become foolish to keep looking for Maria? Magnus had all the time and money in the world, and eventually Karen would have to return to reality, whether they were successful or not.

"Excuse me. Sir?" Karen almost didn't register the voice, but Arthur suddenly stopped. A well-dressed man with a serious face at the registration desk was waving Arthur over.

"What's this about?" Arthur grumbled to himself, but changed direction and headed to the desk.

Karen crossed her arms as she waited. Smiling tourists filed by, oblivious to her, as if a little road dust made her invisible to the sort of clientele who could afford El Paraíso. Signs hung on silver easels on either side of the walkway advertising the upcoming New Year's Eve Gala: a night of dancing, champagne, and celebration. On the sign, a woman in a black dress and pearls clung tightly to a man in a pristine tuxedo. Fireworks exploded over their heads. It didn't look like Karen's kind of party.

Karen was considering whether or not to keep waiting for Arthur when she noticed someone approaching. She hadn't seen him when they first arrived; he must have been standing behind one of the palatial columns lining both sides of the lobby. He was a big man with a round gut that preceded him by some distance. He was completely bald; the winking Christmas lights reflected clearly off his polished scalp. He had a bushy mustache, high red cheeks, and disconcertingly large hands.

"Howdy," he said as he neared. "Enjoying your vacation here in Cuba?"

Karen's grip tightened around her satchel's strap. She didn't like how close the man was standing or how intently he was staring at her. "Sadly I'm here for business," she said. "Not pleasure."

The bald man nodded knowingly. "And what line of work are you in, sweetheart, if you don't mind my asking?"

Karen glanced over. Arthur was carrying on an animated conversation with the man behind the desk that neither looked particularly happy to be having.

"Actually, I'd prefer not to say," she said, inching her way back.

"That's smart, sweetheart," the bald man said. "Never can be too careful when traveling abroad, especially a young woman like yourself. All sorts of trouble you might get in."

Other tourists milled about the lobby; their laughter echoed across the marble floor. The jangle of the casino reached them from down an adjoining hallway. Outside, the sun was setting on another perfect Havana day, but all Karen felt was a chill.

"If you'll excuse me—" Karen started to say as she saw Arthur approaching, a scowl creasing his face.

"Arthur!" the bald man said as he reached out to take his hand; Arthur did not return the gesture. "Fancy running into you in Havana. Of all the gin joints, am I right?"

"Lloyd," Arthur said. "What are you doing here, besides ruining my vacation?"

"Is that any way to treat an old pal like me? Aren't you going to introduce me to your pretty little lady friend?"

"Karen, this is Lloyd Ellis," Arthur said. "CIA Cuba Station chief."

CIA? Karen's head began to spin. Why was the CIA getting involved with their investigation?

"I have to tell you, Arthur," Ellis said as he pushed his hands into his pockets, "I was disappointed when I heard you'd been in Cuba a few days and hadn't given me a call. I'd almost wonder if you were trying to avoid me."

"No more than I'm trying to avoid the stomach flu," Arthur said. "I trust you're responsible for freezing my bank accounts?"

Ellis's grin revealed a row of square teeth with a wide gap at the front. "No, Arthur," he said. "I wouldn't know a thing about that."

"Cut the crap, Lloyd. What do you want?"

"In general, I want to be left alone," Ellis said. "I want a nice, peaceful Cuba because that makes my job and my life easier." The gap-toothed smile faded; so did the mock camaraderie. "So when I hear about a couple of Americans—one a former CIA man, to boot—wandering around Havana, asking troubling questions, agitating the local populace, well, that makes my job and my life harder. And that I cannot tolerate."

"You must have us confused with someone else," Arthur said. His voice was low and cold. "We're on vacation."

"See, now your little sweetheart here just told me it was a business trip."

"You misheard her. That wouldn't be the first mistake you've made in your professional career, would it, Lloyd?"

Anger narrowed the bald man's eyes and tugged at his upper lip. "You want to be cute, Arthur? You want to screw with me? I'll see you marched out of here with a bag over your head. You might not mind, but you think your pretty little friend here would like that?"

"Arthur's pretty little friend," Karen said sweetly, "thinks you should go to hell."

Ellis snorted. He looked back and forth between Karen and Arthur, as if trying to decide which of them was worthier of his disdain. "You don't get it, do you?" he said. He patted his chest with the flats of his hands. "I'm the nice option. The not-nice option is waiting outside. Have you heard of Buró para Represión de las Actividades Comunistas? Batista's secret police. Quite brutal, I'm told. Usually they go after suspected revolutionaries, but they seem to be making an exception in your case."

Karen couldn't resist glancing out the big main windows, but she only saw the usual parade of glossy town cars and taxis.

"Now," Ellis said when Karen and Arthur didn't reply, "let's get you two enemies of the state on a plane back to the mainland before I have to cancel Miss O'Neil's passport and invalidate Arthur's government pension, shall we?"

The magic twitched. Since she'd summoned it in Miami, she felt it moving more often, old instincts waking up and asserting themselves. Ellis probably had no idea what her magic could do to him; Karen didn't want to think about it, how easy it would be to break him in half. But as he stood there and mocked them with a snide grin, a primal urge for violence grew inside her chest.

"We're trying to find a missing girl," Karen said, trying to distract herself, "and I have to wonder why the CIA doesn't want her found."

"There are lots of missing girls in the world, sweetheart," Ellis said. He pointed to the door. "Now let's all walk out of here together, before you become one yourself."

That part of her she didn't recognize, the part that had metastasized since Auttenberg, the part that wanted blood and fire, grumbled inside like a distant but approaching storm. *What are you going to do?* she asked herself. *Incinerate a CIA agent in the middle of a hotel lobby?* It was insane to even consider, but when the alternative was just giving up, she wasn't sure how many other choices she had left.

"Karen," Arthur said. His voice brought her back to herself; the magic simmered but waited. "Go out front, see if Joaquin is still there. If not, find a taxi. Go anywhere, just don't look back."

"Arthur, what are you talking—" Karen started to say before she saw he had drawn his gun and had it leveled at Ellis.

Ellis noticed it as well. "Arthur, please," he said, though Karen thought she noticed a hitch of uncertainty under the condescension. "You aren't going to shoot me."

"You're right," Arthur said calmly. "I'd never do that on purpose. But I'm an old man, frail. My finger might slip. Accidents happen. And however you want to spin it, you're the one who'll be on the floor, bleeding."

"Arthur, what are you doing?" Karen asked.

"Just go," he said. "Find the girl. Figure out what Magnus is up to and maybe put a bullet in him while you're at it." He pressed down some wrinkles in his shirt with his free hand. "Don't worry about me. My old pal Lloyd and I have some catching up to do."

Karen needed only a brief look in his eyes to make up her mind. Without another word, she turned and moved quickly toward the exit. Behind her, she heard Ellis start to say something, but then Arthur cut him off. A moment later, she was out the door, greeted by the last of the day's warmth and the smell of the ocean.

Joaquin was still there. His car was parked a little ways down from the main entrance, and he stood beside it. He was not alone. Half a dozen men in military-style uniforms surrounded him and his car. They had guns on their hips and in their hands. The dying sunlight reflected off their mirrored sunglasses.

Karen froze. There were more BRAC agents off to her left, leaning against the building and smoking. Their rifles hung loosely from their shoulders. Ellis wasn't bluffing.

She ducked behind a potted palm tree. It wouldn't hide her long, especially since they were here looking for her and Arthur. She surveyed the area. There were no taxis waiting, only a few cars off-loading their weary and wealthy passengers. A limousine, sleek in black and chrome, rumbled to a stop just beyond the BRAC agents. A gaggle of women in dresses and heels waited for the driver to come open the door. Karen almost ignored them, but then realized she recognized one of them.

Careful to keep as many obstacles as possible between her and the soldiers, Karen moved from her hiding place and approached the waiting women. She immediately felt out of place with her dusty jeans and battered leather satchel next to their silken finery and gaudy handbags, but there was little time for that now.

"Excuse me," she said, her voice low. "Your name is Sandra, right? We met the other night, in the restaurant."

The head of blond curls turned to face her. For a moment Karen was afraid the actress wouldn't remember her, but her eyes lit up as soon as she saw Karen. "The magician!" she said, clapping her hands in delight. "Girls, this is that lady magician I told you about."

The group let out a brief chirp of excitement; Karen stole a glance toward the soldiers to see if they noticed. A few of them were staring. One threw down his cigarette and crushed it under his boot.

"You said you wanted some details on how magic works, right?" Karen said quickly.

"Oh, do I! That would be marvelous!"

"How about now?" Karen said. The soldiers were starting their way. "Where are you ladies headed? I can tag along and we can chat on the way."

Something changed in Sandra's perfectly blue eyes. With a toss of her hair, she looked behind her, where the BRAC soldiers approached, and then back at Karen. In that moment, a mask slipped and Karen wasn't staring at some vapid actress anymore, but at a sober, streetwise woman who knew what danger looked like.

"That sounds marvelous," Sandra Saint said. Her smile returned in full radiance, though she held Karen's eyes a moment longer than necessary. "Driver, get us out of here right now. Let's start the party!"

They piled into the limo, and the driver pulled away onto El

Malecón just as the BRAC soldiers reached them. Karen twisted around to watch them through the tinted windows: they retreated to their waiting jeeps and were soon following closely. Her stomach fell. Escape wasn't going to be that easy.

Sandra's friends had already found a bottle of champagne and were toasting one another with high-pitched glee. Karen sank down into her seat. First the CIA and now the Cuban government. *What a fool,* she thought. You don't get to ruin Morris Rabin's soup course without consequences. It had been a few years since she had last considered herself naïve, but now Agent Pierce's words of warning echoed mockingly in her mind. She looked back again. There were three jeeps now, keeping their distance but not letting them out of their sight. She hoped Arthur and Joaquin would be okay.

"Do all magicians live such dramatic lives?" Sandra asked quietly.

"No," Karen admitted. "I'm one of the lucky ones."

"Are you a spy or something?"

Karen shook her head. "I'm just here trying to find a missing girl. Her name is Maria."

She nodded toward the jeeps. "Did those bastards take her?"

"I don't know," Karen said. "Actually, I think it might be something worse than that."

That seemed to be enough for her. She didn't know—couldn't know—the details, but didn't need to. Like Ellis had said: there are a lot of missing girls in the world.

"Ooh," one of Sandra's entourage said as she suddenly remembered Karen was in the limo with them, "show us some magic!"

"Can you light something on fire?" another asked over the rim of her champagne glass.

"Or make a man fall madly in love with you?"

"Or better yet, light a man on fire?"

They all laughed, all but Karen. And Sandra. "You don't need to perform," she said softly.

Karen was reminded of her little niece and all the times she had begged her to do magic for her. To Martha, magic wasn't scary; it was just magic. Back then, Karen had felt the same way. Though she'd also had her locus and fewer memories of what her magic could really do.

The magic had come when she called for it in the motel in Miami. Even without her locus, she had been able to connect to the anima; more importantly, she hadn't lost control. No one had died. But did that mean she was ready to put on a little show for these eager Hollywood socialites?

"That's alright," Karen said. She had to know. If her magic could be relied upon, she had to know she could use it when and how she needed. Was she like every other magician who lost their locus, sad and powerless, like a bird with clipped wings? Or was she the power-crazed monster who tore through Auttenberg with eyes of white fire? Or was she something else entirely? She had to know.

She held out her hand, palm up. It wasn't necessary, but it helped her to focus. She knew the magic was there, eager, but she had to let it out on her terms. This was a little like squeezing a drop of water out of a vengeful fire hose, but she knew her will was strong enough.

Small embers of colored light winked to life above her palm. It was familiar magic, but usually done with a litany of Latin, not just the power of thought. But as she had come to learn, magic followed its own set of rules.

The limo was silent. These girls must have heard about magic all their lives, but had probably never seen it. The magic lights reflected back at Karen in their eyes. She lifted them, spun them. How long had it been since she'd used her magic for something so frivolous, so beautiful?

Karen smiled, something she hadn't done in a while. She'd become a magician to do great things and change the world, but she'd also become a magician because of this very feeling, a calm assurance in her own power. She'd almost forgotten that.

But in that moment of repose, her will faltered. And the magic sensed it and struck.

The embers of light flared bright, too bright, and scattered around the limo. One burst through a champagne flute, spraying amber light and broken glass. Another scored the leather seat like a falling meteor. The rest cut through windows and metal as they exploded out of the car and extinguished themselves in the night air.

No one spoke. Luckily, no one was hurt.

"Wow," one of the girls said, her long-lashed eyes huge. "That was amazing."

Magic isn't your toy, Karen thought as the wind whistled in through the limo's newly formed pinprick holes. *It's a feral snake you think you've tamed, but it's just waiting for your hand to get too close.*

But it did give her an idea. She ignored the hushed murmurs that were starting up and lifted her palm again. The lights reappeared, hotter and brighter this time. The other passengers shrank back a little. Karen felt sweat on her lip, and then realized it was blood dripping from her nose. Her outstretched hand was shaking; it was taking every ounce of will in her body to keep the magic in check.

Then she let it go. The lights shot out through the holes their siblings had already created, out and back, down the street, and into the tires of the trailing jeeps.

Karen heard screeching. Without its front tires, one of the jeeps had spun out of control and slammed into a guardrail, blocking the road. The other jeeps piled up behind. All traffic stopped. The soldiers scrambled out of the upturned vehicle, but could do nothing but watch the limo glide away into the Havana night.

NINETEEN

Karen had them drop her off on a busy street lined with bars and nightclubs. Light and music spilled out onto the sidewalk in equal measure. The air thrummed with muffled laughter and drumbeats. Sandra offered to take Karen back to El Paraíso, or the airport, or anywhere else, but Karen just shook her head.

"You've done enough already," she said. "No need to get you into more trouble."

"Don't you worry about that," Sandra said. "I've missed getting into trouble."

"Thank you," Karen said.

Sandra nodded. She smiled, sadly, wistfully, and then the starlet mask slipped back into place. "Good luck," she said. Then she got into the limo and they drove off down the street.

When they were gone, Karen slumped against the closest building. The magic was thrashing around inside of her, clawing up her insides. Now that she'd stirred it from slumber, it wasn't ready to go back to its cage. Karen squeezed her eyes shut and clamped her hands over her ears. She must have looked crazy, but she needed to focus, needed to center herself. A fire was burning in her gut, and it was growing.

You are in control of this.

It didn't feel much like she was in control.

Magic may have all the power in the universe, but it can't do a damn thing on its own. It needs you, which means you're still in charge.

Focus.

With astonishing effort, the fire began to recede. A few moments later, it was gone.

Magic had been so easy, once. And so freeing. Now it was terrifying.

She wiped a drop of blood from her nose and straightened herself. She might have her magic under control, but her situation was still far from settled. The BRAC soldiers would still be coming and she had nowhere to go. But she had to keep moving.

Down the street, she wandered into a nightclub and ordered a drink. She sat alone at a tiny table in the corner and watched the door. A live band played jazz on a narrow stage: a ticking high hat and thumping upright bass. A woman in a bright blue dress sang; her wide white smile lit up the room. Couples danced. Glasses clinked. The door opened and closed; people came and went. Karen sipped at her drink and felt like the walls had eyes.

One man near the bar whispered to his companion and they both looked her way.

The bartender took a telephone call, eyes downcast, spoke a few words, then hung up. Did he glance at her in the mirror?

Not everyone in Cuba works for the secret police, she reminded herself. Or at least she hoped that was true. But she couldn't overcome the weight of stolen glances, so she slipped out as a large group of revelers entered.

It was getting colder outside, enough to remind her that it was December after all. The sky overhead was clear, but the stars hid behind the glow of Havana's nightlife. Karen walked quickly along the street, casting sideways glances at every passing car. She needed a place to hide and figure out a plan. She wished she knew how to get in touch with Joaquin, but she didn't even know his last name. She had no friends, nowhere to sleep, didn't speak Spanish, and was pretty sure that pale yellow sedan had circled past her at least three times already.

Karen ducked down a side street. Maybe they should have just gone with Ellis. She could have continued her investigation from back in Washington, but somehow she doubted they would have let her back into Cuba. And while she had a home to return to, what did Maria have? A broken family and a cold trail.

Headlights illuminated the street behind her. Was it that same yellow car? Around her, she saw closed businesses and more sparkling nightclubs. She was about to pick one at random and disappear into the crowds when she saw an OPEN sign on what appeared to be a bookstore. She pushed open the glass door; a bell rang. The air inside was warm and dry and smelled of old paper. Ancient-looking maps of Cuba, curled and turned orange with age, hung on the wall opposite the door. The shop was narrow, with only a few rows in the stacks, and filled with far more books than it could reasonably display. They cascaded off the shelves and onto the floor. Literary stalagmites dotted the landscape. Dust covered most of them.

A man with a white beard greeted Karen in Spanish from behind a counter as she entered. When he looked up over the wire rims of his glasses and saw her, he switched to English.

"I didn't expect to find a bookstore open so late," Karen replied.

"My home is cold," the bookseller said. "My wife is dead, and my cats hate me." The line sounded well-worn, like he'd delivered it a few hundred times and had the cadence down perfectly. "I do not mind staying late."

"Do you get a lot of business from drunk nightclub patrons?"

"Enough," the bookseller said. "Sometimes they are sick on my floors. But sometimes, they decide to immediately buy two dozen books. Alcohol leads to fascinating choices."

A car drove by outside; Karen shot a glance that she hoped didn't appear suspicious, but she didn't get a good look.

"Are you shopping for something in particular?"

The accumulated mass of pages surrounding her was overwhelming. Too many words, too many stories. She hadn't realized it before this moment, but she hadn't read anything other than lab reports since Auttenberg.

"Do you have any magic books?" she asked.

The bookseller carefully folded up his glasses. "Una maga then? I always wondered what it would be like to command power like that," he said. "But then again, I get lost in my own shop and trip over my own feet, so perhaps magic is best left to the young. But I do have a small collection."

He came out from behind the counter and led Karen to the rear of the shop with shuffling steps. There was barely enough room for his bone-thin frame to fit between the stacks. How long had it been since he'd sold a book from this far back in his inventory? The bookseller took out a heavy iron key and clicked open a tall cedar wardrobe. A few books toppled over as he swung the door out, but he just kicked at them absently, like misbehaving pets.

"Take a look," the bookseller said. "They may all be nonsense, for all I know. Though if they are fake, you do not have to tell me. I think I would rather keep pretending they have some value."

Karen thanked him and he worked his way back through the maze toward the front of the store. She ran a finger along the spines of the books in the wardrobe. Most were old, as magic books often were; too few modern magicians bothered to publish new works, content instead to proffer tradition over innovation. She recognized some. One had been a textbook she'd used during her sophomore year at St. Cyprian's; she smiled slightly as she remembered how much she'd hated that class. She slid another one from the shelf: *Majik ak Mistè*, a book she'd last seen in the subbasement of the CIA base in Berlin. She flipped through the whispering pages. Unlike the CIA's copy, this one hadn't been censored with a sharp knife to the point of uselessness.

She picked up another one. Not a book of spells, but a biography of Chester Halloway, credited in the subtitle as "one of the greatest magical minds in American history." Karen rolled her eyes. Halloway had been an actual magician in the nineteenth century, but he was mostly just a con artist. Karen had personally researched and debunked half a dozen of his healing tinctures and incantations during her time at the OMRD. Another of his outlandish claims had been that he could grant magical ability to nonmagical people. He'd been run out of a number of towns when that claim didn't pan out. His tale had come to an abrupt ending during the Grand Magical Exposition of 1895, when he attempted to demonstrate the complex feat of passing through a solid brick wall. It was difficult magic; few magicians in history had ever been able to manage it, much to the relief of bank vault owners. In front of a crowd of hundreds, Halloway had cast his spell and phased into the wall, but never came out the other side. It was said that when the wall was knocked down, the bricks had bled.

Karen was reaching for a book with a filigreed spine when she heard the bell. Boots scuffed on the hardwood floor. A man's voice, speaking Spanish. The bookseller responded. Karen inched toward the front of the store, just until she could see a sliver of the counter. Two men were there, rifles slung over their shoulders. One of the soldiers was thrusting a finger into the bookseller's face, his angry Spanish shattering the store's calm.

She was trapped. The only way out was through the door she had come in by, through the soldiers. She moved back, hidden among the books, and hoped they wouldn't be thorough. As she stepped, her foot caught on a low stack of world atlases. The sound was slight, barely there, but the voices at the front of the store suddenly stopped.

What could she do? She could let herself be captured, or she could fight. Both seemed impossible, stupid, suicidal. Footsteps on the wood floor; someone was approaching.

Come on, Karen. Magic is more than a cudgel. Get creative.

Light-bending magic was hard. It worked best in low light and when you stood completely still. The effect was never perfect; a magician who knew what to look for could usually spot the telltale distortions. But in the right situation, you could be invisible.

That is, if you knew the correct spells and had a strong locus. What Karen had instead was about two seconds before a gun was shoved into her face plus an unshakable desire to survive the night.

She reached for her magic once again and directed it, shaped it, willed it.

The soldier appeared. His hand was on his pistol, still in a holster. He was younger than Karen had expected, but already had a dead-eyed stare. Those eyes probed the stacks, passing over her once, and then again. He took another step. He was only feet from her now; she could smell his sweat. She tried to make herself as small as possible, but it wouldn't matter in the narrow aisle. If he kept going, his shoulder would brush hers and the illusion would fail.

The soldier swallowed; she saw his Adam's apple rise and fall. He started forward. Karen held her breath.

"¿Que ves?" asked the other man from the front of the store.

The soldier stopped and sighed. "Libros," he said, then turned away. A moment later, he was gone. Karen exhaled as silently as she could.

But they did not leave. The soldier's voice became louder, angrier. The bookseller tried to respond, but the soldier did not let him speak.

They must have known I came in here, Karen realized. *And now they think he helped me escape.*

She heard a scuffle. The boots fell harder on the wood. The bookseller gave a shout of protest that was cut abruptly short. Something hit the floor. Karen moved closer; the magic blurred around her as the illusion faltered, but she had to see.

The bookseller was on his knees. His glasses had been crushed, now little more than a pile of shards and bent wire. He was bleeding from a cut on his scalp. One of the soldiers stood over him, his rifle raised with the butt poised to strike again.

Karen did not think; she did not feel. She just acted.

She clenched her magic like a fist and struck the soldier next to the bookseller square in the chest. The magical blow slammed him back against the wall, rattling books from their shelves. The other soldier turned toward her as Karen reappeared, his hand reaching for his pistol. Karen reached for it as well and locked his hand in place. The man struggled against her; his face twisted with exertion. Karen's magic was strong, but the source of her magical energy was limited. So as he pushed even harder, she released his hand. As the gun flew wildly out of its holster, she grabbed it again with tendrils of force and ripped it from his grip and sent it sailing over the stacks.

Without his gun, the soldier decided to attack her barehanded. He made it two steps before Karen's magic hurled a thick dictionary through the air at him, smashing it into his throat. The soldier gasped and clutched at his neck. Another blow knocked him flat on his back.

Karen ran to the bookseller and was about to help him up when a burst of pain exploded inside her skull. The first soldier had recovered and had brought his rifle down hard on the back of her head. She fell to her knees.

The bookstore was hazy, the lights too bright.

The second soldier was getting to his feet.

The man with the rifle was turning it around, leveling the barrel at her.

The room slowed.

And then exploded.

Karen did not feel the blast until afterward. Her magic was tired of its constraints; she didn't even have a moment to hold it back. Suddenly her mouth and eyes were full of smoke and she was watching charred pages of books as they fluttered through the air like burning moths. The floorboards beneath her were blackened and blasted apart. The shelves had been knocked aside like fallen monuments.

One of the soldiers had been thrown back through the glass door; he now lay unmoving in the street outside. She saw no sign of the other, or of the bookseller. As she stood on shaking legs, she thought she heard a moan somewhere behind her, but it was difficult to be sure. She started to move that way to see if there was a survivor, but then she heard the unmistakable sound of sirens approaching.

This little store had been an oasis, cramped and crowded and overgrown with books no one would ever buy. And now it smoldered, fated to become a ruin the moment she walked in the front door. Her eyes burned. Her ears rang. Everything smelled of blood and burning paper.

Run, the last coherent part of her mind whispered. *If you get caught, this was all for nothing.*

She pushed through the cracked bookshelves, the shattered door, and the growing crowd outside. She had no strength left, every bit of herself lost in that arcane tantrum, but she had to keep moving. One step, then another. A few people tried to ask if she was alright, but she ignored them. Moving was what mattered; it was the only thing that mattered.

She reached another street and turned down it just as the spinning red lights began to descend on the former bookstore. *Just keep moving.* Her shoes scuffed on the sidewalk as her legs rebelled against lifting her feet, but she didn't stop. *Just keep moving.* She tried not to think about the bookseller's kindly eyes or his cold apartment or his waiting cats.

Just keep moving.

She barely even saw the headlights as they slowed alongside her. There was just enough time for her to register the sedan's pale yellow paint before a rough canvas bag was forced over her head and her world went black.

TWENTY

MEMORANDUM

Subject: Transcription of Magnus Innovations Staff Meeting
Location: Magnus Special Projects Laboratory, Havana
Date: 27 December 1958
Present:
  John Magnus, CEO
  Harvey Fish, Director, Legal and Compliance
  Duane Kellogg, Chief Magical Researcher, Transference
  Oliver Green, Chief Magical Researcher, Containment
  Alexander Sage, Head of Security
  Meredith Johnston, Personal Assistant to CEO
  (transcribing)

[Begin Transcript]

Magnus: Thank you all for coming. I hope you have good
         news to share. Before we get started on the
         status reports, Alex, any security concerns we
         need to know about?

Sage: No, sir. A few minor infractions, as usual.
         Nothing my team can't handle.

Magnus: No sign of any outside intrusion?

Sage: None. The Commies will have to try a lot harder if they want to infiltrate this facility.

Magnus: And the seals on the lower basement?

Sage: Intact. My men just checked them this morning. That thing's not getting out.

Magnus: Excellent. Alright, gentlemen, give me the good news.

Green: Yes, sir. We completed work on two more constructs. The power sources have been installed and are completely stable. We can—

Magnus: I don't give a damn about the constructs, Oliver. Our investors don't give a damn about the constructs. We tried, and they didn't sell. I need status on our primary objective. Duane, that's you.

Kellogg: Our last batch of tests were all negative. But we have a new approach we'd like to try out.

Magnus: A new approach?

Kellogg: One of my guys was cleaning out the desk for that guy over in Containment that we lost.

Green: Gerald.

Kellogg: Right. Well, we found some notes he'd taken. At first it looked like gibberish, some real weird magic, but we think he might have been onto something.

Magnus: Something that can help?

Kellogg: We think so. We'd like to give it a try.

Magnus: What's stopping you? Make your team work all

night if you have to. I need results, Duane. I
needed them six months ago.

Kellogg: There's a bit of a problem, sir.

Magnus: Out with it.

Kellogg: We need more test subjects.

Fish: We've been over this, Duane.

Kellogg: I know, I know, but with this new approach, we
want to start fresh. The remaining subjects are
taxed to their limits. Who knows what effect
that will have on the tests? We might be seeing
false negatives.

Magnus: Fine. Alex, what can your team provide?

Sage: One of my guys thinks we might have a lead.
Not just one kid, either. A whole school of them.

Kellogg: Multiple subjects would be ideal.

Fish: You want to send Magnus security personnel
into a school? Our Cuban hosts can overlook a
lot, but that might be asking too much.

Magnus: Don't worry about it, Harvey.

Fish: You pay me to worry about these things, sir.

Magnus: I think I have another idea. Alex, confirm that
location for us.

Sage: It might take a couple days.

Magnus: As quickly as possible. Spend whatever you have
to. The rest of you, get back to work. Oliver, hang
back a minute. I want to talk about these new
constructs. I think I might have a job for them.

[End Transcript]

TWENTY-ONE

"W hy are you in Cuba?"
    "What is your job with the CIA?"
    "Why does BRAC want you?"
"¿Por qué estás en Cuba?"
The questions pummeled her. Some of the hits, she just took. Some, she tried to return. But still they came. Sometimes in Spanish, sometimes in English. Over and again, the same questions, the same disembodied voice with the thick Cuban accent. Her hands were bound behind her back, her legs tied to a chair. They hung a spotlight in front of her face; all she saw of her captors were gray-black blurs.

"What is the CIA's mission in Cuba?"
"What is your mission in Cuba?"
"Who do you work for?"
She told them about Maria, though not about the anima or Magnus. She told them about La Bruja, but did not mention Arthur or Joaquin. Still, the questions came.

"How long have you worked for the CIA?"
"What does the United States want here?"
"Why are you in Cuba?"

Restraining her hands did nothing to stop her from using her magic, but she wasn't sure if her captors knew that or not. She doubted it. But despite the blinding light and the unending questions, they weren't hurting her. After they grabbed her, the car ride had taken hours; she could be anywhere now. Escape was possible, but maybe not wise. At least not yet.

That was not the only reason she didn't want to use her magic; she could still smell the burning books on her clothes.

"Why are you in Cuba?"

After answering that question a dozen times, she started to doubt her own answers. Why had she come so eagerly? Did she think she could save Maria? Or was it more about what she was running from: her sister's invitation, for one; or the resignation letter waiting in her desk at the OMRD; or the dread that had shadowed her since Auttenberg? But this is where running away got you: lost in the wilds, tied to a chair in a dark, damp room.

Eventually, they took the light away. A few hours after that, they brought her some water. An hour after that, the door behind her squawked and a girl came in. She had a tray of food. She set the tray down and then untied Karen's hands and legs. Karen thanked her, but she said nothing. She smiled though, a welcome pleasantry. She couldn't be more than sixteen, with dark hair and eyes and an unsearchable face. A pink scar a few inches long tugged at one cheek.

"Thank you," Karen said with a scratchy voice.

The girl gave her a wink and then was gone.

Freed from her bonds, Karen explored her tiny room. The walls were metal, but thin. It felt like a shed of some kind. The floor was hard-packed dirt. The door was heavy and locked from the outside, but Karen could get it open, if she needed to. If she trusted herself to.

When her next visitor came, she briefly saw the hint of early dawn behind him. He was a tall man, dressed in faded military green, but with no insignia. He wore a belt, but carried no weapon. He had a similarly careworn canvas hat, but instead of wearing it he clenched it in one hand, absently slapping it against the palm of the other. His tanned face was darkened further by a neglected beard and streaks of grime.

"Please," he said, motioning to the chair, "sit."

"Are you going to tie me down again?"

"Would it do me any good?"

Karen paused a moment before answering. "No."

"I thought not." He produced a small stool, which he placed on the dirt floor across from her chair. He sat and waited for her.

She pulled the chair back against the shed's far wall and sat. Her captor had dark circles under his eyes, almost like bruises. They made him look unwell.

"You can call me Ramón," he told her.

"Are you going to ask me if I work for the CIA?" she asked.

"No," he said, smiling faintly. "I know that you do not."

Karen shifted in the chair. She hadn't slept in more than a day and her head had been pounding ever since the bookstore, but she didn't want this man to know how weak, how utterly spent she felt. "And how do you know that?"

"Because you work for the American Office of Magical Research and Deployment," Ramón said casually. He slapped his leg with his folded hat and waited for her response.

Fatigue sapped at her. Her thoughts came in clumps, mushed together and indistinct. She blinked and forced her mind to sharpen. "And who do you work for, Ramón?" she asked. She looked around the shed. "I'm guessing based on the quality of my lodgings that I'm not a prisoner of the Cuban government. So that leaves the rebels, who I imagine would be very keen to know more about what the CIA is up to in Cuba."

"No doubt," Ramón said.

"But you just told me where I work," Karen said. "And I'm guessing that means you also know my name, but you were saving that reveal to try to maximize my disorientation and break down my resolve. I don't know much about the Cuban rebels, but I hear they are students and farmers. How would they know my name and where I work? And why would they try to use that information against me?"

If he betrayed any emotion, it was a slight bemusement. But he did not interrupt her.

"So then who exactly are you? I'm guessing a spy, but the question is who are you spying for? Spain? That doesn't seem right." She cocked her head. "But who would possibly benefit from a Communist revolution on an island just off the coast of Florida? Or, asked another way: Are there a lot of Spanish-speaking Russians?"

Ramón did not reply. He merely sat and stared, his sallow face impassive. Had it been a mistake to confront him? She was still a prisoner after all; maybe she should have been more diplomatic. But she was exhausted, and not just from the lack of sleep. She had no energy to waste feigning respect.

"They know of you," Ramón said softly after a long silence. "In Moscow. They speak of you. 'The American girl who bested the Nightingale.' I should not say that many speak about these things; there are not many who are allowed to know about the Nightingale, or about Auttenberg. But in some hushed rooms, they do wonder about the girl whose magic was so powerful it nearly destroyed the world."

Ugh, spies. No matter their country of origin, they all had that cheery smugness in their eyes when they told you something they weren't supposed to know.

"They don't know anything about me," she said. She tried to clear her mind, flush out the memories of Berlin and the bookstore, but instead she could hear cracking pavement and smell charred paper. "Or my magic."

Ramón shrugged. "Personally, I know nothing about magic," he said. "And I have never been to Berlin. I only know what the whispers say." He slapped his leg with his hat again, a solid thwack. "And they tell me something else about you. They tell me you are trying to bring down John Magnus."

"He a friend of yours?"

"He is a capitalist parasite," Ramón said. "I hope they hang him in La Plaza Vieja, where women and children can spit on his corpse." He delivered these words with conviction, but little passion. "Though I wonder why *you* are after him."

"I think he had my friend killed," Karen said. "And he's somehow involved with a girl who's gone missing."

"So?"

"So?" Karen repeated. "So he needs to be stopped."

"By you?"

"By anyone, but I'm more than willing."

"And what are you willing to do to stop a man such as John Magnus?"

Karen considered the question. *What* does *this man want from me?* "I'll burn his world down if I have to." The heat of her answer surprised her, unnerved her. If Magnus was hurting people like Maria, then she would stop him, no matter what. But the violence in her words, was that who she was now? Or was that the bloodthirsty magic, working its way to the surface?

Ramón nodded. "Tell me: Do you know what he is really doing in that facility?"

"Do you?"

"Sí."

"Will you tell me?"

"I think not."

Of course not. Spies don't share information; they hoard it. So why was he here, speaking to her? Certainly not to help her in her mission. No, he was here because he wanted to learn something from her, something he considered valuable.

"How do you know what Magnus is really doing?" Karen asked.

"I am, as you say, a spy," he said. "And my benefactors have eyes in every dark corner."

"If we're both against Magnus, you should just let me go."

"If it were up to me, perhaps," he said casually. "But, like you, I am a guest here and our hosts do not trust you."

"Do they trust you?"

"They are not very trusting. They are idealistic. It is difficult to be both."

"You sound like you know from experience," Karen said. "I mean, before you sold out whatever ideals you had and started working for the Soviets."

Ramón shook his head and pointed his hat at her. "This is why everyone hates Americans, Miss O'Neil. You think the world is a battle of good and evil, and you are the heroes. Perhaps things were so simple when Hitler was marching across Europe, but he is dead and the real world is far more complicated." He stood up, dusted off his pants. "It is easy for you to think you work for the angels and I work for the devils, but this is a child's reasoning. You will see. And you will be disappointed that your American ideals are just noise. And you will be disappointed in yourself for ever believing otherwise."

Karen tried to stop herself—it didn't seem wise to provoke him further—but she could not hold back her laughter. "I'm sorry," she said, still chuckling. "It's just that for a moment there, I believed all that nonsense you spouted earlier about Auttenberg. Now I know it was just posturing." She forced the mirth from her voice; her eyes—

hard, unblinking—locked onto Ramón's. "Because if you knew anything about what happened in Auttenberg, you wouldn't stand there and lecture me about devils. But you don't have a damn clue."

Ramón pounded on the shed door, and an outside bolt was slid. "It has been a pleasure," he said. "Good luck in your quest." And then he was gone.

A temporary barricade had been erected around the blasted-out storefront. Most of the shattered glass had been swept clear, but some small pieces still crunched under the feet of the mixture of people who slowly passed, necks craned to catch a glimpse inside the ruined building. There was not much to see beyond the ropes and Havana police cars, just toppled bookshelves surrounded by charred books. Luckily the fire hadn't spread; soon this relic would be boarded up and then eventually subsumed by the nightclubs and restaurants that surrounded it on all sides. Tragic, yes, but also progress.

The American tourists floating by whispered the various rumors that had sprung up since the blast, the most convincing of which was that the revolutionaries had come down from the mountains and torched the old man's shop as a warning to the rest of Havana about the troubles to come. It was a bold new move for the Communists, but what did you expect from these unwashed savages? Didn't they like to burn books after all? It would have been far too easy for one of them to toss a firebomb through the window of a fine upstanding business. What a shame.

But the tattooed man knew no firebomb had done this. Even now, the air was rank with uncontrolled magic. It had drawn him unerringly across the city, a beacon in the dark. She had eluded her would-be captors at the hotel, and she had eluded him as well, but she could not escape what was inside her.

As the evening drew long and the onlookers dwindled, the tattooed man found his way to the rear of the building, beyond the view of the lingering police. The bookstore's backdoor was locked, but no one bothered warding such doors against magic. Too many spell variants to consider, too few magicians skilled enough to counter each. It wouldn't have mattered; magic like his couldn't be countered. He spoke no words, traced no runes on the door or in the air. He simply willed the door to open and it complied.

Inside he had to navigate a storeroom piled with unwanted books. The room was utter chaos, but the tattooed man doubted that had anything to do with the explosion. He slid through the piles until he found the curtain that led to the front. It was dark enough in the store that he could move about inside without drawing attention from the nearly deserted street. Blackened pages crinkled as he walked.

It was stronger here, the echo of her magic. He could feel the shape of it. It was more than he expected.

He felt vindicated. The costs of finding her name, the months of watching, the failed attempts to draw her out: they had not been in vain. He breathed in the smoky air of the bookstore, satisfied.

The tattooed man shrugged out of his jacket and set it aside. He unbuttoned his right shirtsleeve and rolled the fabric up to his elbow. The skin underneath was pale and crisscrossed with black ink. He had a brief but intense memory of when those marks were made: the sharp sting of the needle was nothing compared to the feeling of the magic binding to his blood. He banished the memory and instead focused on the image of someone far away.

The tattoos quivered. An observer might have mistaken it for a trick of the light, or a tremor in his arm. But he knew better. The ink embedded in his skin became liquid again and swirled and churned. A moment later, the ink came together to form a crude outline of a face.

"Have you found her?" The voice was soft, and between the long distance and the distortions of magic, it sounded barely human.

"Yes," the tattooed man said. "She is in Cuba, as expected. But there is more."

The ink face frowned. "Tell me."

"Her magic is strong," he said. "I can feel the influence of the Power Beyond."

"As you predicted."

"This is more than I predicted. I think she could be a conduit."

The eyes widened. There was a long silence in the ruined bookstore. It was a bold claim he was making, but he felt sure of it. The traces of the beyond in Karen's magic were too strong to be dismissed. Finally, the strange voice said, "Do you think the book has already returned?"

"I cannot say," the tattooed man said. *But I can hope.* "I have lost her for now, but I will find her again. And if she has been chosen by the Power Beyond to rewrite the book, I am certain she will have it with her."

"Do what you must," said the voice.

The man dismissed the magic, and his tattoos returned to their normal place. He wondered what the others would think of this news. Some would dismiss it, surely. But others would believe. And when he returned to their ranks with the blessed book in his hand, they would all believe.

Her trail was gone, but he did not despair. She had come to Cuba for a purpose and she would not be denied, not with her power. So all he had to do was wait, and watch, and plan. He smiled, a rare gesture. He could bide his time. He was nothing if not a patient man.

Then he stepped over the broken doorway and disappeared into the Havana night.

She waited. The hours were unkind: her body hurt, her thoughts ran rampant across every subject she wanted them to avoid, and still the door remained firmly shut. She tried to sleep but abandoned the effort as futile. She considered her options, formulated and dismissed plans of escape, of vengeance, and waited.

It was completely dark outside when the shed door opened again. In the distance, stars burned above a black wall of indistinct trees. A single figure, too small for a man, stood in the open doorway. Her visitor slipped into the shed on perfectly silent feet.

"Come," the girl whispered. Even in the darkness of midnight, Karen could make out the scar on her face. "Follow me." The girl pressed Karen's satchel into her hands.

"Where are we going?" Karen asked, though she didn't truly care much about the answer; any place was better than continuing to rot away in some forgotten hole.

"Come," the girl said again. "Tengo una jeep. Puedo llevarte a la Habana." Karen could guess at the meaning: she had a jeep and was going to take her back to Havana.

They paused at the door. The girl scanned the night, crouched and still, like a mouse watching for any signs of the cat. The shed smelled of motor oil and sweat; the outside smelled like dirt and wet moss. The cool air felt restorative on Karen's skin.

When she was convinced it was safe, the girl waved Karen forward and they moved into the night. Karen could make out some squat buildings off to their left; yellow light filled a few clouded windows and drifted out from open tent flaps. The ground beneath her shoes was damp, like after a rainstorm. She heard voices—men's voices—but they were far-off.

The girl suddenly stopped and Karen nearly ran into her. They huddled in the gloom, not even breathing. Footsteps in the mud, a soft sucking sound. Coming nearer. A man, backlit by the rest of the camp. He pulled on a cigarette, and his face lit up in orange and red. He looked young and unwashed, his beard a black tangle.

He'll see us if he comes any closer, Karen thought. How far away was the jeep the girl claimed to have? Could they reach it before he sounded the alarm?

She heard something. A voice. The rebel heard it too; his head turned in their direction. Karen realized it was the girl. One of her hands clutched the beads she wore around her neck: brightly colored, like polished glass. The other hand she had pushed deep into the soft earth. And she was whispering. Karen didn't know the language, but she knew the purpose. The necklace was a locus; the words were magic.

The rebel threw down his cigarette. He took a step toward them. And then Karen felt the spell complete; magic rustled in the air on hidden wings, its breath quick and cool on Karen's face. The rebel stumbled; his legs buckled. Then he fell to the mud with a quiet splat.

"Asleep," the girl said with a stifled giggle. "He okay."

"You are a magician?" Karen asked quietly. A few feet away, the rebel started to snore.

"Sí, magic." Her eyes were deep unbroken pools whose depths Karen couldn't hope to investigate. "Come. We go to La Bruja."

TWENTY-TWO

The drive from the rebel compound back to Havana might have been more harrowing than her captivity. The road—it was generous to even call it a road—wound down into the darkness like a tailspin. They didn't use the headlights, but the girl didn't seem to need to see where she was going. After a while, Karen decided it was best to just close her eyes and try not to think about how fast they were going or how close their tires were coming to the edge of the road. The girl—who introduced herself as Elisa—talked nonstop. Karen caught a few scattered words: "America," "capitalism," "magic," "Havana." Her Spanish came in rapid bursts punctuated by a wildly waving hand that seemed under control only when she had to use it to grind the jeep through its reluctant gears. Elisa didn't seem to mind that Karen had no idea what she was saying.

When the road leveled out a bit, Elisa pointed excitedly under the seat. Karen understood enough and fished around in the dark. She came up with a half-empty bottle of whiskey, but Elisa grabbed it and tossed it out her window, spitting in disgust after it.

"Asqueroso," she said with an exaggerated shudder. Karen inquired with a raised eyebrow and Elisa explained, "Sometimes drink, sometimes piss."

Karen took her meaning that the jeep's other, male drivers might use old bottles to relieve themselves, and carefully wiped her hands on her pants.

"Doesn't matter the country, men are disgusting," she said, mostly to herself, but it drew a big laugh from her companion.

"Disgusting!" Elisa repeated, slapping the steering wheel. "Men!" She spat again.

Warily, but with Elisa's urging, Karen rummaged around until she found something else: a brown paper bag. Inside, she found hard sugar candies wrapped in colorful paper. Elisa whooped in triumph. Karen could not help but grin at the girl; her animated, chattering savior was certainly not what she'd expected to find in a rebel camp. She dropped a few of the candies into Elisa's eager hand and took one for herself.

And so they made their escape, with flavored sugar dissolving on their tongues and Elisa continuing her cheerful rant about the universal uselessness of men.

With Elisa's voice a consistent raindrop patter in the background, eventually Karen slept. Her dreams were indistinct and vaporous, but for the first time in what felt like days, she had a moment of rest.

She was instantly awake when the jeep came to a stop. When the engine puttered and went still, the whole world seemed to roar in silence. They were in a gravel driveway. Ahead of them was a khaki building crowned with clay tiles the color of rust. Nearby, the sprawl of Havana had begun to encroach on this old place, but for the moment it was held off by stucco walls heavily laden with bougainvillea. In the gray light of dawn, a carved wooden sign was barely visible: EL ORFANATO DE NUESTRA SEÑORA DE LA CARIDAD DEL COBRE.

Elisa hopped out of the jeep. Karen followed, though her cramped legs moved much slower. The sound of the rocks crunching under her shoes roared in the early morning quiet. They approached the heavy door, but it swung open before they could knock. A stern-faced nun wearing a starched, winglike cornette stuck her head out to greet them. Her unyielding eyes fell questioningly on Karen, but when she saw Elisa, she slammed the door shut. The tap-tap-tap of hurrying feet echoed back to them from the far side of the wall.

Karen looked to Elisa, who just rolled her eyes, popped the last of her candy into her mouth, and leaned against the doorframe to wait. A few minutes later, the door opened again, revealing another nun accompanying the first. The newcomer was stooped, and her lined face looked to be as old as the building crumbling around them. She carried herself with an authority that Karen knew was seldom questioned.

"Por favor," the older nun said, "entre."

Within the outer wall was a wide courtyard made of irregular red brick. In the center stood a massive ceiba tree with thick gray branches denuded of leaves. It must have stood in that spot for hundreds of years, its bulbous roots now beginning to dislodge the nearest bricks. The base of the tree was spotted with fruit along with other strange items: unlit wax candles, a scattering of coins, and small cloth bags of unknown contents.

The nuns led them past the tree and away from the main building, toward a clutch of small huts built against one of the outer walls. Lights shone in the windows. Elisa walked ahead as if she knew the way, but as she ducked inside, the older nun caught Karen's arm and held her back.

She spoke in slow, measured Spanish. The first nun offered a translation. "She says that this is a sacred place," the nun said in lightly accented English. "The work we do for these children is sacred. They have nowhere else in the world to go."

"This is an orphanage?" Karen asked.

The older nun nodded when Karen's question had been translated; her wide headdress gave a little flap. "Our duty is to the children God has given into our care," the nun said curtly and with conviction. "The girl you come with and the woman you are here to see carry trouble wherever they go. Do you bring trouble into our home as well?"

I'm on the run from the Havana Mob, the Cuban government, Soviet-backed revolutionaries, and possibly even the CIA, not to mention I've picked a fight with one of the richest men in the world who has a whole army of magicians working for him. Me, trouble? Of course not, ma'am. Karen did not share these thoughts. Instead, she said, "I've come to Cuba only to help."

When Karen's reply had been translated, the old nun sighed and clucked her tongue. "She says, 'If fewer Americans came to Cuba to help, we would need far less help.'" When Karen tried to respond, the old woman held up a hand and waved her to silence. Her companion translated: "All who seek justice and love mercy are welcome within these walls. But do not forget that there is only one Savior here, and he is not from the United States."

The two nuns retreated to the main building, their black robes softly rustling in the otherwise quiet courtyard.

"They are mostly a joyless bunch, but they mean well," said a voice from behind. Karen turned back toward the huts. Elisa was there with another woman. The woman had dark skin and long black hair pulled back from her face. Her clothes were plain; she wore no makeup. Yet even in the gloom of the courtyard, Karen recognized her.

"Isabel, isn't it?" she asked.

The other woman's lip twitched: a subtle smile. "I wasn't sure you'd remember me," Morris Rabin's mistress said.

Karen motioned to the orphanage around them. "This is a far cry from El Paraíso."

"True," Isabel said. "I like it here much better. Come inside. We should talk."

They sat in Isabel's tiny kitchen at a small wooden table that had been worn smooth by the touch of countless hands. Brightly colored cups of tea steamed between them. A cluster of fresh-cut yellow bells sat in a vase on the table's edge. Elisa did not join them, but rather hid in the corner, leaning against the wall in an old chair and doing her best to appear to ignore them.

"So," Isabel said, "I hear you have been looking for me."

In the better light of the kitchen, Karen studied the woman across from her. The flawless beauty she had noted in the hotel had been no illusion. Isabel looked young, though far from naïve, and Karen did now note a few lines in the dark skin around her eyes. She wore a collection of necklaces like Elisa's, with beads of every color carefully intertwined. Her eyes betrayed nothing, though they hinted at a dangerous lack of predictability, a feigned calm that hid whatever waited beneath. Her home smelled of spice and mint, and the heat of the teacup in Karen's hand was the best thing she had felt in days.

"I am actually looking for a little girl," Karen said. "Her name is Maria Perez Zamanillo."

Isabel's face did not react, but Elisa's chair creaked a little too loudly.

"Her family told me that she disappeared," Karen went on, her eyes flicking between Isabel and Elisa. "And that La Bruja was to blame."

Isabel let out a mirthless laugh and whispered something under her breath in Spanish. "Maria left her village because of su madre, not because of me. When I met her, she still had the welts on her face and arms where her mother hit her. That crazy woman thought she could beat magic out of her daughter like dust from a rug."

"So you know Maria?"

"Of course I know Maria," Isabel said. Her voice had taken on a sudden sharpness. "She lives here, or she did until she went missing." Isabel set her mug of tea—otherwise untouched—aside and leaned across the table. In the small room, they were suddenly very close. "What I want to know is why some strange white woman from America is sitting in my home asking me about one of my students like I owe her an explanation."

Karen's back was against the kitchen wall; there was no retreat. "I am just trying to help."

"I heard you tell the nuns that," Isabel said, "and I don't believe you either."

And why should she? Karen had no obvious reason to be here and had given them no reason to trust her. They would be fools not to doubt her, and Isabel did not appear to be a fool. Which meant Karen had to decide if she was willing to trust her. She was also a stranger, but worse, she was the mistress of Magnus's chief financial backer. She might have just walked into the beast's mouth.

But she was exhausted, on her own, and out of good options. Maybe it was time to trust someone.

Karen pulled her satchel onto her lap. After getting her host's nonverbal approval to reach inside—she did have a gun in there, after all—Karen opened the flap and retrieved the velvet bag that contained the anima. "This is why I'm here."

Karen explained how the cube had come into her possession and the events that had taken place since. If Isabel was an enemy, then this was not new information for her. And if she was an ally . . . having made an enemy of nearly everyone else she had met on this island, Karen could desperately do with an ally at this point.

The kitchen was silent when she finished. Karen had told Isabel everything—that is, everything except the nature of her own magic. Instead she just said that she was a magical researcher who had lost her locus. It was the truth, of a sort. She was giving away enough secrets; she did not feel compelled to tell all.

In the stillness, Isabel stared at the anima. Its dark shape felt profane in the warmth of her home. Her face proved inscrutable.

"Thank you," Isabel said eventually.

"I know I don't belong here," Karen said softly. "But if I'm going to make this right, I think I'm going to need your help."

"I appreciate you sharing with me," Isabel said. She waved the cube away, and Karen put it back into her satchel. "And I will be willing to help you on one condition."

"Name it."

"The next words out of your mouth are whatever you left out of that little story. Whatever small detail or hidden sin you don't want me to know. Otherwise you can get the hell out of my house and get the hell out of Cuba."

Karen forced her face to remain still, willed her breathing not to change. It was possible that Isabel wasn't an enemy, but ally or no, this woman was not safe. But Karen had no other choice. She had to convince Isabel to help, and if she knew that Karen's magic could explode and kill everyone around her at any moment, Karen doubted she would be willing to. Maybe she had heard about the incident at the bookstore, or maybe she could sense the chaos twisting inside of her. Or maybe she was just guessing.

"I've told you everything," Karen said.

Isabel's clear eyes burned into her, unblinking. Karen stared back. "Very well," Isabel said. She stood up from the table and cleared the dishes. "My children will be getting up soon. Let me show you what we do here."

TWENTY-THREE

They met a gaggle of children in a small classroom in the back of the main orphanage building just as the sun started to come through the windows and slash the room with dusty haze. When Isabel entered, a cheer rose in one high voice from the assembled students. Karen counted a dozen children, boys and girls from a wide spectrum of ages. They sat expectantly at wooden desks piled with crumbling books facing a green chalkboard rimed with white powder. The nun who had been supervising them until this point rose and left in a bristling silence without even a glance toward Karen or Isabel.

"The sisters tolerate my work," Isabel said when she saw Karen watching the nun, "but they don't all approve."

Before they could speak further, a few of the smaller children escaped their rickety desks and wrapped themselves around Isabel's legs. "Yeye Isabel!" they cried.

"What did they call you?"

Isabel bent down and kissed each of them on the tops of their heads, then shooed them back into place. "They call me Mama," she said. "In Lucumí. They have no parents, no family who will acknowledge them, no one to teach them how to use their remarkable gifts. So they are my family, my children."

The sincerity in her voice vanished as she switched to Spanish and demanded order from the teenagers whispering in the back of the room. Karen glanced around and realized that Elisa had slipped away at some point. She hadn't been comfortable in the orphanage since the moment they arrived, so Karen was not surprised.

". . . a chance to impress our guest," Isabel was saying, having changed to English. "Come now, who wants to show señorita Karen what they've learned?" A sea of blank faces stared back at them. Isabel clucked her tongue and said something in Spanish that sounded mildly threatening. Still no movement. Isabel sighed and said, "Rogelio."

A rail-thin boy with a mane of black hair shrank down in his chair, but soon all eyes turned on him. So he stood up, resigned to his fate.

"Have you been practicing, Rogelio?"

The boy nodded, but Isabel rapped her knuckles on the chalkboard and he replied, "Yes, Mama Isabel."

"Good," she said. "Then you can show us all El Oso Bailando." The other students laughed; Rogelio looked like he wanted to crawl under his desk and cry. Karen remembered days like this in school, but unlike many of her classmates, she had always wanted to be the first to demonstrate a new spell. She never had the answer in math class or knew the right dates in history, but once she had been tested and found to have magical ability, the magic classes became her life. However, she could not remember a spell called El Oso Bailando.

"Come up here, mijo," Isabel said. She motioned for him to come stand behind a large table in front of the chalkboard. He complied with the same enthusiasm he would have shown if he were facing down a firing squad. "Now, ¿donde está el osito? ¿Donde está Ishu?"

As if part of a planned performance, one of the girls in the back immediately launched a brown projectile over her peers' heads. Isabel caught it out of the air with a practiced hand and set it on the table in front of Rogelio. Ishu, it turned out, was a stuffed toy bear the color of a yam. The stitching on one arm was starting to fail; curds of white fluff poked through. One of his glassy eyes was missing, replaced with a black threaded "X." Despite his rough state, he was adorable, except to Rogelio, who seemed to be staring at the poor bear with a mixture of fear and loathing.

"Está bien," Isabel said, clapping her hands. The room fell silent. "Now, Rogelio, can you make Ishu dance?"

Rogelio sighed. He took up a piece of chalk and began to draw a few symbols on the table, looping circles around where Ishu sat in expectant silence. A few times, he made a mistake and quickly wiped the chalk away. Isabel stood over him, nodding and whispering soft encouragement. When he'd finished with the chalk, he stood behind Ishu and began to chant the words to the spell. The language was strange and tonal; more Lucumí, Karen assumed. After he finished reciting the words, he tapped Ishu on the head.

Nothing happened.

Giggles filtered in from the back, but Isabel cut them off with a hard stare that would have made Karen's blood freeze.

"Otra vez," she said, and Rogelio tried again. The stubborn bear refused to move. More laughter tormented Rogelio; a tear quivered on his cheek, and more threatened to fall in short order. Isabel touched his shoulders, told him to try again, and then turned to the other students.

"Ishu can't dance," she said sternly, "because he has no music. Marisol, get the tambourine." There were groans. "Come on, you want Ishu to dance or not?" She tapped out a beat on the table and then Marisol—a girl of eight or nine with a long braid down her back—started shaking a tambourine to match.

As Isabel led them in a song they all knew, Karen knelt down next to Rogelio and studied the chalk work on the table. It was a simple spell, really, though she hadn't seen this particular variant before. She relished this magic, children's magic: how to make pretty lights in the air, or change the color of sand, or get a toy bear to dance. None of it was powerful; harder magic required the forging of a locus to channel the magician's will, and children were not ready for such a task. But Karen wondered if the world would be a better place if they stopped teaching spells at this age, before they introduced magic that could burn and hurt and kill.

"Hi," she said quietly to Rogelio over the music.

He sniffed but said nothing.

Karen surveyed the chalk again. The writing was clearly to direct the magic into the bear and across the table. She could see which lines must be for determining Ishu's movements and which were to focus the limited energy so it didn't just dissipate as soon as it was cast. But if that was the case, then these two lines were transposed . . . and that line needed to cross here . . .

She touched Rogelio's arm and then casually nodded to the mistakes she had noted. He looked at her, then down at his work, then smiled. He cleared his cheeks of tears, leaving a few white smudges in their place, and then picked up the chalk again. A few marks later, and Ishu suddenly hopped to his stubby feet.

The students cheered as the little bear danced to their song across the table. The song got louder as he went. His jerky motions were hardly elegant but to Karen's eye, they were pure artistry. Rogelio beamed.

As the magic faded, Ishu sat down on the opposite side of the table and the song became applause and Rogelio returned to his seat. Isabel turned back toward the front of the room. Her eyes met

Karen's and something inside of Karen shifted. Magic had brought so much ugliness into her life in the last years, but now she was reminded it was capable of more than that. Sometimes it could make a toy bear dance and a little boy smile.

"Está bien," Isabel said sharply. "Who is next?"

When they finally were able to dislodge themselves from the students with the help of a pair of unfriendly and uncompromising nuns, Karen and Isabel wandered out of the stuffy building and sat underneath the heavy branches of the courtyard's ceiba tree. There were a few dark clouds in the evening sky, the first Karen had seen since arriving in Cuba. Beyond the walls, she could hear car horns and distant music, but within the compound, there was an undeniable peace she hadn't felt in too long.

"I came here," Isabel said, "when I was a girl. My parents . . ." She waved them away with a dramatic hand. "The sisters took me in. First they gave me food and shelter, and then when they discovered I had magic, they had to decide what to do. Some voted to send me away. Some voted to ignore it. But the woman in charge, bless her soul, sent for a local Yoruba woman who was known as a worker of magic. She taught me everything she knew, and then the sisters bought me books, and then when I was strong enough, I used my magic to make my own money and bought even more."

"I'm surprised members of the church were so supportive."

"The church is just people," Isabel said absently. "Some good, some terrible. I got lucky. And now I help these kids to be lucky as well."

"And the orphanage doesn't mind keeping a room for La Bruja?"

"Cuba has its orphans, just like any other place. Children that no one knows what to do with. If those children have magic? No, no. There are no options, not for these kids. So the orphanages like having an option. Now they send them here, from all across Cuba, because we know what to do with them. It is our little secret."

A few of the children burst out into the courtyard, free for the moment from their overseers. Karen didn't recognize some of them, likely the orphans who lacked magical ability. They clustered by the gate and tossed a ball against the wall or played jump rope with a frayed rope. Closer, Karen saw Rogelio and Marisol shepherding some of Isabel's youngest students. They had chalk and Ishu with them and were trying to help the younger magicians figure out how to make the bear move. When the bear's legs started to twitch for the first time, laughter filled the echoing courtyard.

Isabel's youngest student, a wisp of a girl called Aleja with huge brown eyes too big for her tiny face, ran up to them, a small purple flower in her hand. She held it out to Karen, murmured something in Spanish, and then ran off with a squeal.

"She says you are pretty," Isabel said with a laugh.

"Your students seem very happy here."

"This place is an escape for them," Isabel said. "An escape from pain, hunger, fear. They don't mind a little scolding from the sisters, not if there is a roof over their heads."

Watching the children, Karen asked, "Elisa was one of your students?"

"Ah, Elisa," Isabel said, a touch of sadness in her voice. "Such a strong will for such a young girl. What am I saying? I was twice as stubborn as her when I was that young. I bet you were as well. She is a powerful magician, but distracted."

"By what?"

"By idealistic young men who should shave their smelly beards and who have filled her head with dreams of revolution. So she plots with them in the mountains, who knows to what end."

"Where did she go?"

"Back to them, I'm sure." When she saw the concern on Karen's face, she waved it away. "She told me there would be no trouble. The revolutionaries picked you up but then had no idea what to do with you. They knew Batista wanted you so they decided they wanted you too. They are children and make decisions like children. She did them a favor getting rid of you."

Karen stared up through the tree's branches. A few stars were starting to come out, though they were faded by Havana's glow.

"And Maria?"

"Sí," Isabel said. "She came here to learn from me. She had potential—has potential," she corrected herself. "But also great fear. Fear of herself, instilled by her mother." Isabel laughed into the evening air. "Men are a plague, but nothing can break a woman apart like another woman."

"How long has she been missing?"

"Months," Isabel said. "Orphans come and they go. I've learned not to count absences. But sometimes they go and do not come back."

"More recently?"

Isabel nodded. There was something else, one of those secrets that danced provocatively in her guarded eyes. Karen thought better than to press, but then Isabel continued. "We've lost more than Maria. Nine children in the last year, all magically gifted. And one . . . was my sister."

The words rested heavily on Karen's heart. Isabel clearly loved the children in her care like they were her own, but there was no one in the world like a sister, your own blood.

"Graciela," Isabel said like a sigh. "She is thirteen years old. She was a baby when I came here, couldn't even walk, so I carried her. I promised I would always protect her. If she was hungry, I would smash a window and rob a shop to feed her. If a boy pushed her down in the street, I would set his hair on fire."

"She is a magician too?"

"Yes," she said. "Our family was blessed, or cursed. Both, perhaps."

"Isabel," Karen said, "I'm so sorry."

"There is nothing to be sorry for," Isabel said. "She is out there. I will find her. And then I will make someone suffer. I teach these kids trifles, dancing bears." She laughed. "But the old Yoruba woman taught me some terrible magic, magic I swore never to use. And I won't, not until I find the bastard who took Graciela."

A chill ran down Karen's back, only partially from the dropping temperature.

"And you think that man is this American, this Magnus?" Isabel asked.

"I wish I knew more," Karen said. "It is all mostly guesses at this point. The cube is from his research facility and is clearly connected to Maria. But now that I've found you, her trail is cold."

"We just need to find this facility," Isabel said. Her voice was harder than Karen had heard it. "Blow the doors off and get answers. Find Graciela."

"They killed my friend," Karen said. "I'd like nothing more. But they have security, not to mention whatever his researcher magicians have concocted. We need to know more or it would be suicide."

Talk of Magnus's security reminded Karen of a subject she did not wish to bring up. She liked Isabel and was growing to trust her, but couldn't guess at how she would react and did not want to lose this timid lifeline. And yet it seemed unavoidable, especially as their other options dwindled.

"Isabel . . . ," Karen began, "what—"

"You want to know about Morris."

Karen exhaled. At least it was out there now. "His men provide security for Magnus. According to my contacts, he is Magnus's primary donor."

Isabel did not look at her. She looked instead down at the rough bricks under their feet. "I don't have to justify who I share my bed with to anyone. But," she said after a while, "he is a kind man. I know how that sounds. I'm not a fool; I know what he does, who he is. But he is kind to me, and that is rare, in my experience."

"Does he know you are a magician?"

"Por supuesto. He collects magical things. I'm his greatest prize."

"Could he be involved in your missing students?"

"Never."

"Are you sure?"

Isabel stood up and walked a few steps away. "Here you are, asking me questions again like you've earned answers. You haven't even earned the questions."

Karen said nothing. What good were words? She didn't know these people. It was not her family who had been taken. She hadn't even spoken to Gerald in years before his package had arrived. She didn't live here; she was here in hiding, hiding from invitations to Christmas parties she wanted to avoid, and from memories she wanted to forget, and from realities she wanted to change but was powerless against.

"He knows Graciela," Isabel said into the silence. "He would buy her flowers on her birthday. Morris is bad for Cuba, probably bad for me, but I cannot believe he would help this bastard Magnus take my children away. I just cannot."

Karen stood. "That's good," she said. "If he's trustworthy, maybe he can help. Even if he doesn't know what Magnus is really doing, he has leverage on him. He can be our way in."

Isabel turned back. "Yes," she said. "He can . . . what was that?"

Karen had heard it too. A thumping sound. The hairs on the back of her neck stood up as she turned toward the heavy doors that led outside of the orphanage's walls. The sound came again, and when it did, Karen saw the doors jump.

"Isabel, something's—"

"I know," Isabel said. One hand reached reflexively up to the jumble of beads around her throat. Karen's hand settled on her satchel.

The doors suddenly exploded inward. Through the cloud of dust that followed, dark silhouettes appeared. Two—no, three. Tall, too tall to be human, they had to stoop to fit through the hole they had made. The ground shook as they moved closer, and by then Karen could make out their alien, featureless faces, their pale, claylike skin, and the soft glowing outline of the magical cubes implanted in their chests.

TWENTY-FOUR

The constructs crossed the courtyard in eerie precision, humanlike but also unmistakably artificial: their limbs floated more than moved, seemingly weightless despite their massive bulk. Karen recognized the construct in front as Solomon, the prototype Magnus took to Miami for the product demonstration. Solomon looked the most like a man, though much larger. The other two were slightly smaller with more exaggerated features: one with long, spindly arms that hung down below its knees, the other broad as a boulder with a bulbous head slung low between two massive shoulders.

Their violent entrance was so strange and unexpected that Karen was sluggish to respond, but Isabel did not hesitate. She screamed at the children playing near the gate, but they were paralyzed by the otherworldly visitors. With a few shouted words, Isabel summoned a nearly invisible wall between the constructs and the children. Solomon approached the shimmering barrier and with a motion that was so fast it registered mostly as a pale white blur, shattered it with the palm of one of its great hands.

Isabel spat more angry words into the air. Her fingertips ignited in green fire, which she sent spinning at Solomon in a churning burst. The flames roared and then were spent; Solomon was unscathed.

Karen finally forced her body to move. She bolted across the courtyard toward Rogelio and Marisol and placed herself between them and the long-limbed construct. She'd acted on instinct, without considering how she would stop something so strong and nearly twice her height. The children were just behind her. If she used her magic now, she couldn't be sure they'd be safe. She couldn't get images of the bookseller out of her mind. Not again.

Frantically, she flung open her satchel and pulled out her pistol.

You know that won't do anything.

Karen leveled the gun at the creature. "Don't come any closer!"

Behind her, she heard Isabel shouting and felt the crackle of more magic.

Long Arms did not slow as it approached.

Karen pulled the trigger. Once, then again. And again until every chamber was empty. The bullets sparked against the construct's claylike skin; it didn't even react. Closer, and closer, and her gun was just deadweight in her hand.

You know what you have to do!

The smell of burning books. The shattering of glass.

Use your magic!

Then the construct was on her. She watched in slow horror as one of its heavy arms cut through the air. She opened her mouth to scream, but then the blow landed and the world was spinning and the ground jumped up at her.

Karen lay on the bricks, the side of her face pressed into a sharp corner, vaguely aware of the cold seeping into her exposed skin. There was no air in her lungs. Her vision swam; she tasted the sharp tang of blood. From her slanted view, she watched Long Arms reach for one of the children. It picked Marisol up like a doll.

It produced something else in its other hand, some strange knobby wand. It held the wand up to Marisol's forehead. A moment later, a faint white light began to shine on the wand's tip.

Something distant and detached in Karen's mind knew the wand was an enchantment called a dowsing rod, a simple tool for detecting magic. They had half a dozen in a closet back in her lab; she realized now that they had probably all been produced by Magnus Innovations. The constructs were using them to determine which children in the orphanage had magical ability. So they knew which children to take.

Karen pushed herself up. Her whole body burned in sudden pain but she ignored it. The construct still had Marisol and was reaching for the cowering form of Rogelio. There was no time for pain. She reached into her satchel. The bag was full of enchantments made by its previous owner, and while many were still mysteries to her, she'd figured out a few of them. Her hand closed around a flat metal disc inlaid with hard-lined symbols.

"Hey!" she shouted at the construct. "Leave him alone!" She released just enough of her own magic to activate the enchantment and then threw it at the creature's feet. As it clattered to a stop, it flared to life.

When she was investigating the strange enchantments she found in the old bag, Karen had thought this one had been faulty, as all it did was emit unfocused magic. Eventually she'd realized that was its purpose, to release so much magical interference that it disrupted all other nearby magic. That chaotic din enveloped the construct in an instant. The dowsing rod sparked and smoked. The construct's arms flailed for a moment, then hung limp.

Karen wasted no time. She ripped Marisol from the creature's grasp and pulled Rogelio to his feet. "Run!" she said, pointing at the main building. "Run!"

Magic energy ripped through the night; Karen heard Isabel shouting spells and swear words in equal measure. The boulder-shaped construct was trying to pin her down, but the Cuban magician was too fast, too determined. However, the magic she was able to conjure did nothing to even slow the hulking thing.

Rogelio and Marisol were about to reach the safety of the other building. The distortion enchantment still had the long-armed construct tangled in its web. But where was . . .

Solomon smashed through the main doors of the orphanage building. It had two unconscious children dangling from the crook of one of its arms. Another was thrown over its shoulder. How had it gotten inside so fast?

Karen pulled a small leather pouch out of the satchel. It was closed with two separate straps, both knotted tight. This was dangerous stuff, deadly stuff, but the situation called for nothing less. She pulled one of the straps as she moved to intercept Solomon as it lumbered toward the shattered gates, but she only made it a few steps before something grabbed her and yanked her off her feet.

The distortion spell must have failed; Long Arms had a handful of her jacket and held her ten feet off the ground. She kicked at the creature's arm but it was like kicking a brick wall. Though she twisted and turned, its grip didn't loosen. Behind her, Solomon was nearly out of the courtyard, now holding both Rogelio and Marisol as well.

Karen screamed and pulled at the second strap on the pouch. Long Arms hesitated a moment, then seemed to make up its inanimate mind and started to swing Karen's body toward the unyielding courtyard bricks. She pulled the strap free and threw the pouch's entire contents into the construct's featureless face.

The night turned suddenly and brutally cold. The silver powder hung in the air like a cloud, then turned to ice, which raced along the construct's skin. Its motions slowed as the frost expanded and hardened and locked the creature in a white-blue prison. As the fingers of ice reached up to the hand holding Karen, she pulled her own arms free from her jacket and fell the rest of the way to the ground.

She hit the bricks and rolled. It hurt, but she was free.

But Solomon had vanished, and the children with it.

Isabel had her back pinned to the ceiba tree. Boulder loomed over her. Its massive hands were open, and reaching.

Karen realized then that her satchel was still with her jacket, suspended in the frozen hand of the long-limbed construct. No more enchantments.

You don't need them. You can end all this.

A crack ran down the ice holding Long Arms; it wouldn't hold for long. She had to get those kids back and keep the rest of them safe, no matter the risk. There were no options left.

Her magic rushed out of her like a flood. Without spells or incantations, she was only limited by her own creativity. She reached down, down into the bricks of the courtyard: hard, solid, sharp. And pulled. The bricks snapped and cracked. And then ripped free from the ground.

The first bricks crashed against Boulder in puffs of rust-colored dust but barely slowed its advance on Isabel. So Karen knotted the bricks together into a studded boulder and brought it down on the construct's head. The construct swayed, and Karen pulled up the broken bricks and hit it again. And again. And again, until the bricks were ruined.

"I thought you couldn't do magic anymore," Isabel shouted at Karen.

"Later," Karen shouted back. Now wasn't the time for words.

Brick fragments scattered as Boulder broke itself free of the pile.

"Keep them busy," Isabel said. She turned toward the tree and dropped to her knees, one hand against the wood. She was preparing more complex magic, something that would take time. Time Karen wasn't sure they had.

Boulder charged. And Karen's magic met it, lashing out at the creature's knees. It stumbled, fell, and plowed a row in the dirt where the bricks had been. Karen focused and gathered her will, burying Boulder with dirt and broken bricks. Magic had little effect on these things, but maybe if she could—

Long Arms hit her hard from behind. Pain blinded her, but somehow she knew another blow was coming and she threw up a wall of energy just in time. Each hit cracked like thunder; her magic held in place, but at a cost. She may not be beholden to incantations, but still only had so much of her own energy she could draw on, while these damn constructs seemed tireless.

"Isabel!" Karen shouted.

The response was a burst of profane-sounding Spanish, which Karen chose to interpret as Isabel asking for more time.

Karen's ragged breathing filled her ears. She wasn't ready for this; it was too much magic, too much power. Long Arms hit the barrier again, and Karen felt it like a blow across her chest. She didn't think she could hold it through much more abuse like that. Which gave her an idea.

The construct lifted both arms over its head and threw all its weight forward. At the last moment, Karen dropped the barrier and rolled to the side. All resistance suddenly gone, Long Arms lurched and fell headlong into the outer courtyard wall. Karen's magic reached out into the crumbling wall; she found the weaknesses and she pressed. As the construct began to stand, the wall collapsed on top of it. Dust billowed out in a white cloud.

Karen exhaled and fell back, her legs too unsteady to hold her. She'd expected Magnus's constructs to be strong, but they seemed nearly unstoppable. What would it take to exhaust their animas' power?

She was about to turn her attention back to Boulder when the rubble began to shift. Chunks of broken stone clattered to the ground. Something was moving underneath.

Hell, Karen thought.

The construct reached out its long arms and shrugged off the rubble. Karen scrambled back as she heard Isabel's voice, loud and strong, a chant Karen did not recognize. The construct heard it too—however these creatures heard anything—and turned toward her. Isabel's voice fell silent.

And then the ground erupted.

The roots of the great ceiba tree broke free of the earth and snaked skyward, propelled by Isabel's Yoruba magic. They wrapped around Long Arms' legs with a woody groan and tightened. The construct struck out at its bonds, but only more roots appeared. Now they had reached its arms and chest: more and more of the twisted bonds, moving in a jerky, halting, inescapable way. Long Arms began to thrash, but the roots only closed in tighter. They reached the creature's head, vining around its thick neck, and then stopped.

Karen looked to Isabel just as she collapsed. Karen reached her side in a few steps and turned her over. Blood trickled from her nose and one of her ears, but she was still breathing.

A scream pierced the courtyard. It was the little girl Aleja, the girl who had given Karen a flower and called her pretty. That moment seemed so long ago now. Aleja looked even smaller as Boulder nearly engulfed her with its grasping hand.

Enough. The word exploded in Karen's head in a voice she barely recognized as her own. The world around her blurred; her skin sizzled. She heard a roar—no, she felt it, a roar like water through a broken dam.

The following moments came to Karen in bursts: Aleja, crying, pulled from the construct's path. The construct turning toward Karen. A rush of light and heat. The crack of stone and clay. Blood in her mouth, fire in her blood. A throb, like a headache, like a heartbeat. Dirt spraying. A groan like metal failing.

In Auttenberg, Karen had become lost to her magic. In a moment of danger, of panic, she had reached too deep, summoned power she was not prepared or meant for. And she had just wanted more. And more. She was reminded of that hunger now: a black hole inside of her, limitless and desperate, ravenous like the breach the Nazi magicians had torn in the world. She was only vaguely aware of her battle with the construct, of its indestructible body breaking under her will. Such things didn't matter, not in the face of oblivion.

The only thing that saved her was her own weakness. In Berlin, she'd been able to draw on the inexhaustible power on the other side of the breach; in this shattered Havana orphanage, she only had herself. The flame burned hot, but then it went out.

She fell to her knees. Her vision returned to normal, though a haze filled the courtyard. Ahead of her, the ruins of the broad-shouldered construct smoldered in a shallow crater. It had taken everything—more than that—but she had stopped it. She turned toward Isabel. Even turning her head felt beyond her strength. Isabel was still down, though one of the nuns was with her. Another crouched nearby, holding Aleja. The girl was weeping. Karen's eyes met hers, and she looked away, but not before Karen saw the fear that had taken root there.

What did I do? Karen thought. The reply came back to her like an echo: *What you had to do.*

With the last ounce of energy left in her body, Karen pushed herself to her feet. Had they won? In the smoke and rubble, it was hard to tell. Where was Rogelio? And Marisol? She'd come looking for Maria, but had lost more children instead. Maybe it wasn't too late. Maybe if they hurried after, they could—

Something moved in the smoke. Graceful. Inexorable. The last thing Karen saw was Solomon's blank face as the creature's hand wrapped around her.

TWENTY-FIVE

Sound returned first. A clatter of metal on metal. The squeak of a wheel. Chalk rasping on concrete. And voices. Indistinct, a smeared watercolor of sound. Behind her. Above her. Then she heard her name, and a deep but ever-vigilant part of her brain came awake. Nerves fired. She kept her eyes shut and focused. The air was cold and sharp with the tang of bleach. She was on her back on a hard cot. Distantly, she could hear the murmur of machinery. Much closer, the sound of someone's nasal breathing. And magic.

There were spells at work around her, she knew. She could only guess at their purpose; she recognized some elements but not enough. But it was sophisticated, the work of multiple magicians. And it was growing.

Karen opened her eyes. The overhead lights were blinding. She tried to reach up to shield her eyes, but discovered that her hands were bound to her sides. But the effort made a noise, and the nearby nasal whine stopped. Her vision cleared just in time to see a rotund man in a white lab coat jump to his feet. He was staring at her in evident surprise. A bit of his lunch had fallen on his shirt.

As she noticed the crumbs, she also noticed what was embroidered on his coat: MAGNUS INNOVATIONS.

She reached for her magic as the fat man started to turn. She knocked him flat on his back with the barest flick of her will and was shifting her attention to the leather straps holding her wrists when pain like she had never before felt erupted behind her eyes. It was like her sinuses had filled with molten lava. The pain lanced out, jagged and hard edged, to her fingertips, her toes; muscles seized, bones cracked. Her teeth felt like lightning rods.

And then it was over, an eternity that somehow lasted a moment. She gasped for breath and wanted desperately to throw up.

"Nothing quite as effective as a live demonstration." She knew that voice. A handsome face swam into view; a moment later, she remembered who it was.

"Go to hell, Magnus," Karen said; her voice sounded like it belonged to someone else.

Magnus smiled and ignored her comment. He reached up and touched something around her neck, something she hadn't noticed before, a necklace made of iron plates and wire. Now that she knew it was there, its weight felt alien and unwelcome.

"I'll admit, it isn't a best seller," Magnus went on. "An enchantment that causes pain when the wearer attempts to use magic is a bit . . . medieval, but I will say that in certain practical cases, it can be a lifesaver."

"Where are the children?" Karen's mouth tasted like bile.

Magnus motioned to someone Karen couldn't see, and then more people in white coats appeared and propped up her cot until she was halfway to standing. As she expected, she was in a lab of some sort, not unlike her own. Flasks filled with magical reagents lined the walls, flanked by musty tomes and stacks of clipboards. The ground around her had been nearly covered in chalk lines:

intricate spellwork she didn't immediately understand. Magnus, dressed in an impeccable blue suit, was careful to stand just beyond the edge of the runes.

"I really must thank you for volunteering to be part of the important work we are doing here, Miss O'Neil," Magnus said. "Your contribution might be just what we need to overcome our recent setbacks."

"I didn't volunteer for anything," Karen said. Her dry voice sounded like a growl. "Where did your pet monsters take those kids?"

Magnus blinked. His face wore that same salesman look of banal affability Karen remembered from Miami, though it was far more disturbing in her present circumstances. He tugged absently on the sleeves of his suit jacket and said, "Miss O'Neil, I'm sorry, but I just don't know what you're talking about."

Karen pulled hard against the leather straps. The cot rattled but held her tight. "Tell me where they are. Where is Maria? Where is Graciela?"

One of the men in a white coat came and whispered something in Magnus's ear, and he nodded before returning his magnanimous countenance back to Karen. "I think you must be confused, my dear. Magnus Innovations is an upstanding company. A pillar of the Cuban community. Our research is always conducted under the strictest of ethical guidelines."

"So why am I tied to this bed with this illegal collar around my neck?"

Magnus blinked at her again. Maintained his unyielding smile. "We really cannot thank you enough, Miss O'Neil. Your willingness to help further Magnus Innovations' cause will not go unrecorded, I assure you. But now, my team tells me that they are ready to begin the procedure."

More men in coats. A few were checking the chalk lines against diagrams sketched out on their clipboards. One started mixing several ingredients together in a stone bowl: copper filings, sea salt, and three colors of earth from separate jars. Another began a low, rhythmic chant. And the last one, the fat man who had first noticed Karen waking, rolled a table into place in front of her. On top of the table, he placed a smooth black cube.

The room began to hum. The swelling magic pressed down on Karen's bones. She pulled again on the straps holding her down, but they didn't move. The lab bustled with activity like a disturbed anthill, but her eyes were fixed solely on the anima. It stared back at her with inert malice. *Is this what you saw, Maria? Did they bring you to this room? Did they have to tie you down too? Or was the fear of this strange place enough to keep you still?*

She breathed in the antiseptic air and pushed it out, then focused on the brutal metal wrapped around her neck. Its magic was a dull throb, waiting like a crouched predator. The memory of the pain magic still burned in the back of her throat. But lying still and hoping for the best would be worse. How much magic did she have left after the battle with the constructs? Would it be enough?

It had to be.

Karen unleashed all her remaining power on the collar. The pain hit her instantly; she suddenly couldn't breathe, couldn't think, couldn't see. But she held on to the magic, even as her body spasmed, and bore down. The enchantment sparked and hissed under her assault. The metal grew hot but she barely felt it against the agony that tore through her like a dull blade.

". . . fighting the collar. Can she do that?"

". . . won't matter."

"It's breaking!"

"That's not possible."

Go to hell, you bastards. I'll show you what's possible. She pushed harder. The enchantment pushed back, flooding her skull with rusty nails and fire.

"Start the procedure! Now!"

The iron collar cracked. Its magic, stupid and cruel, died with it. Relief hit Karen like a punch. In that first instant, it was almost worse than the pain. Then her vision cleared. She'd done it. Dumbfounded faces blinked bovine eyes back at her. Sweat crawled down her cheek, and for a moment, no one moved.

Karen disintegrated the leather strap holding her wrists and reached up to remove the smoking collar. Her magic writhed inside her, furious and hungry. She dropped the collar to the floor with a loud clang.

"Where," she said, her voice hollow in her own ears, "are the—"

One of the research magicians had enough sense to finish the final step in the incantation they had prepared. Suddenly the black cube's faces were traced in violently white lines, drawing patterns like frost. The room darkened; the candles they had stationed around her flickered and waned. The anima went dark. Then it shot a light straight at her.

It felt like someone had shoved a hand through her rib cage.

Karen tried to focus her magic on the anima, but couldn't. It was there, strong and desperate, but just out of reach, like her magic was being pulled in the opposite direction.

"What are you doing?" she demanded. No one answered her. It felt like someone was scraping out her insides, sucking her dry.

Come on. You smashed their damn construct, you broke that ugly thing they put around your neck. You can break this too. But she couldn't; she couldn't do anything. The cube pulled and pulled and she was stuck in the wind, screaming silently into a void opening up in her chest.

The fat man was saying something; she could see his jowls bobbing. "It's too much! It wasn't designed for this. Cut it off."

But then Magnus reappeared. "No. This is what we need. Don't stop it."

"Sir, if the anima can't contain all the power, then—"

"I said don't stop."

The lab was shaking now. The anima jostled on the table; glass jars rattled. And still the void expanded. Karen held her free hand up, tried to block the connection, but it ignored her. She wasn't involved; this was a transaction between magic, hers and the anima's. She was just a bystander. Collateral damage.

Lightbulbs overhead began to pop, sending fine mists of powdered glass raining down. The air was hot and charged, like after a lightning strike. She saw panic spread among her captors' pale faces. This was not going as they expected.

"Sir . . ."

She could see Magnus scowling, the lines on his face shadowed by the anima's burning light. Some of the jars behind him exploded. Reagents sprayed across the floor, but he did not react. "Fine," he said as the concrete floor began to crack. "Cut the connection."

One of the other magicians looked up in a panic. "I can't! The spell has already been cast."

"Then disrupt it," Magnus said, annoyed.

The magician reached for the anima, but jerked his hand back and clutched it in pain. Smoke rose from his fingertips.

The lab was full of wild magic now. Karen could sense it thrashing around the room like a cornered animal. The anima was full, beyond full, but the connection still pulled at her, tore into her, and the chaotic energy that had infected her since Auttenberg came rushing out like tainted blood.

"What are you waiting for?" Magnus's voice sounded far away. More activity as the researchers scurried around like lab rats stuck in a maze. And still the cube burned hotter and brighter.

Something familiar fluttered in the back of Karen's mind like a whisper. The circumstances were different; there was no German church, no ghosts of the Reich, no breach in the sky. But the raw magic ripping the room apart hinted at what she had seen beyond that breach, rhymed with it. The emptiness, the vast insatiable nothing from where all magic came; it was here, breaking into the world like blasphemy, summoned by arrogance and stupidity.

You have to stop this. They have no idea the danger they're in.

Karen's limbs felt like they were full of mud. Her vision was a blur. She felt weak, drained, exsanguinated.

Do something.

What could she do? It was their damn spell. She couldn't even draw on her own magic; how was she supposed to stop it? Her eyes fell on the chalk circles that spun out from her cot. If she could erase enough . . . but she couldn't reach the writing, even with one hand free.

Now!

Karen threw her weight to the side. The cot wobbled, but stayed upright. The room was mostly dark now, all lights snuffed out except the anima, which flared like the sun. She could see faint outlines of Magnus and his worthless researchers beyond the cube's corona, frozen in ignorant terror.

She jerked again. Her hands were free, but her legs were still pinned down. The tight straps dug into her skin but she barely felt them. Again. Again. The cot tipped. Karen pushed. And fell. Her shoulder hit the concrete hard. She heard distant shouting, saw movement, but she ignored it all. She reached out with her free hand and smeared the chalk writing closest to her. Immediately the connection was cut.

And then the anima exploded.

TWENTY-SIX

All at once, the magic in the Magnus Special Projects Laboratory turned feral.

Fires erupted in the Flammables lab. They had been using magical fire starters to test a new fabric that was laced with enchanted silver to resist heat; it burned, just like everything else in the lab.

In the Housewares lab on the ground floor, where Magnus researchers were working on an enchanted broom that could sweep all by itself, two researchers received concussions, and a third suffered a broken arm when the brooms became suddenly and brutally violent.

In the cafeteria kitchen, kettles for tea and coffee spewed superheated steam and scalding liquids until the metal turned molten and caught fire.

Magically reinforced glass windows exploded into knifelike shards. An enchanted marble fountain in the front of the building shot water a hundred feet into the air and then split in half. Typewriters that could take dictation clattered out the word "end" over and over until the paper fell out the back.

And the latticework of lethal barriers sealing off the lower basement went out.

Karen saw the moments after the explosion in flashes like snapshots. She saw the lab's doors and two of its walls blow apart. She saw white coats buried under rubble. She saw fire that the overhead sprinklers would never be able to extinguish. And she saw her way out.

With her free hand, she tore off the remaining straps and crawled through the wreckage toward one of the failed doorways. Once in the hallway, she scrambled to her feet and ran. She did not care which way she ran, as long as it was away from that room and the shouts that were descending upon it. She turned a corner, then another, then finally stopped, desperate for breath, aching, terrified.

That spell had been designed to drain a magician's energy and store it in that cube. Karen had never heard of anything like it. Stealing another magician's power was profane. *Gerald was involved in all this?* But that wasn't the worst of it. The spell had tapped into something in her, something unexpected. Something familiar. The breach that the Nazis had torn exposed another world, a darkness that wanted only to consume. And now she recognized that same darkness inside her, within her own magic.

Forget it for now. First you've got to find those kids and get out of this hellhole. Then we'll think about what comes next.

Footsteps. Coming fast. She didn't have time to run or hide. She made a fist instead.

The fat researcher from the lab came puffing around the corner. His eyes went wide when he saw who was waiting for him, and his feet slid out from under him before he toppled over. Karen was on him in an instant. She pressed a knee into his chest.

"Where are they keeping the kids?" she demanded.

"I . . . I don't know!" he said.

Karen leaned more of her weight into him. "If you think I won't hurt you to save them, you're wrong."

"I just work in Containment," he said quickly. "They don't tell me anything."

Her magic was drained; she felt like a hollow shell. But he didn't have to know that. "You saw what I did back there, even with that collar on," she said, her voice low and hard. "I can do far worse. Now tell me."

"He doesn't know, Miss O'Neil."

The voice came from behind; Karen rose and spun and found herself staring into the black hole of a pistol barrel.

Karen swallowed. "You seem awfully comfortable holding that gun," she said carefully, "for a secretary."

Magnus's secretary smiled. Her look was the same as in Miami: a pouf of blond hair, bright lipstick, starched dress. The gun was new, and there was something else, a knowingness in her subtle grin, an intelligence in her eyes.

"But something tells me," Karen went on, "that you might be more than that."

"Don't worry about what I am," Meredith said. "Worry about what the Magnus security team will do when they find you. Seems like you caused a damn fine mess here tonight."

"And I'll cause an even bigger one until I get back the kids they took."

"They aren't here," Meredith said quickly. "They are kept off-site and brought in only when the researchers want to run a test. And before you ask, I don't know where. Only Magnus knows."

Hell. "Are they safe? All the ones they took? Maria, Graciela, the others."

Meredith laughed bitterly. "I forgot that you don't know what's really going on here."

The laughter made Karen bristle. She thought about the leather straps biting into her skin and the blinding anima light. "Actually, I think I have some firsthand experience of what is really going on here."

"Fair enough," Meredith said. "Though I think you are still missing a few key details. That fat pig at your feet knows all about it, but he won't tell you. Luckily I know where to find them."

"And what do you want?" Karen asked.

Her grin turned a little, sharpened. "Let's say I've been making a personal collection of Magnus Innovations' research notes, and that some of what I'm after has been . . . off-limits. Until you came, that is. I'm going with or without you and we have very little time, so come along now or wander around until they find you. Decide."

"Let's go," Karen said without hesitation.

Meredith seemed pleased. "Bring the pig. We'll need him."

You're insane," the fat magician, who was apparently called Ray, said when Meredith stopped in front of an unmarked gray door at the end of a dark hallway.

"Why?" Karen demanded.

"No one goes down there," Ray said.

"What's down there?"

"The answers you want," Meredith said, "and the notes I need."

"What else?"

"The Lamb," Ray whispered.

Karen looked at Meredith, then back at Ray. "What are you talking about?"

"We have no time." Meredith jabbed Ray in the back with her gun.

"Then give me the short version," Karen said, arms crossed.

"The lower levels of the facility were sealed off due to some rogue enchantments," Meredith said, sounding annoyed. She pushed the door open. Stairs led downward. "Nothing a magician of your remarkable talents can't handle."

Ray wiped a handful of sweat from his forehead. "It'll kill us."

Meredith cocked her pistol. "Start walking or I'll kill you now."

Ray led the way down the stairs. Meredith followed, and Karen came last. She ran her hand along the doorway as they passed through. Layers and layers of protective runes had been inscribed around this door to seal it shut, but they were all faded now, powerless.

The lower basement was black and damp. Pipes ran overhead. Something dripped softly in the dark. The light switches on the wall did nothing, but Meredith had brought a pair of flashlights. She handed one to Karen and led them quickly but quietly down another hallway. They passed a number of padlocked doors: Weapons Lab A. Weapons Lab B. Storage. Testing Chambers A and B. Holding Chamber. At last they reached one marked RECORDS.

"Open it," Meredith said to Ray. For all her bravado in the light, she spoke very softly now. "I know you worked down here. I know you know the combination. Open it or the Lamb will be the least of your worries."

Karen glanced down the hall. More doors. Another set of stairs leading down. The floor was coated in dust. *How long has this place been abandoned? And why?*

Ray knelt by the door and worked the lock with clumsy fingers. When it clicked open, the sound seemed to echo all around them.

"Good little piggy." Meredith shoved him inside the room. Karen followed and closed the door. It was bigger inside than she expected. Lifeless lightbulbs hung over rows of brown filing cabinets standing at attention.

"Now what?" Karen whispered.

"Show her," Meredith said to Ray. "Show her your dirty little secrets."

Ray hung his head, but moved down the nearest row of cabinets like he was walking to his execution. He stopped at one marked PATIENTS but didn't open it. Karen pushed him aside and yanked the drawer open. It was crammed with yellow folders, each labeled with a name. She thumbed through them and then stopped.

ZAMANILLO, MARIA PEREZ. The name was like a punch to the gut. Karen realized that despite everything, some small but persistent part of her had hoped that Maria had never been involved with Magnus Innovations, that she had run away from Havana and was living her life somewhere warm and peaceful, away from the horrors Karen had seen and felt in the laboratory upstairs. But here she was.

"This one," Karen said, pointing, "has a red mark next to the name. So does this one. What does that mean?"

Ray said nothing.

"Tell her," Meredith said in the dark.

"The procedure," Ray began, "is supposed to take some magical energy from the donor and transfer it to the anima. It's supposed to be harmless, like giving a blood donation."

"Supposed to?"

"There have been . . . complications. No one really understands it, but sometimes the spell works too well, takes too much."

"It takes everything," Meredith said.

Karen's skin felt cold. "It kills the donor?"

Ray tapped the document in Karen's hand. "That's the date her body was autopsied and then cremated." He sighed. "When it happens, no one survives. And it draws something else out. A deeper magic. Maybe . . . a soul."

Ayudame, the anima had said to her. *Mi nombre es Maria.* Help me. This is what Gerald had suspected. This is what he had died for.

"Something of the donor is still in there," Karen said. "That's how you can animate the constructs."

He nodded reluctantly. "After the Conditioning team spends a while with the anima and breaks down the personality, it becomes pliant for commands."

Karen pulled out one of the red-marked files. The first page listed vital statistics for the donor: age, height, weight, blood pressure. Then a list of dates and procedures. Reports with details she didn't understand followed. She pointed at a section on the first page that contained a list of dates followed by the word "failure" and a notation. "What is 'TR'?"

She heard Meredith's low chuckle somewhere nearby. "Now you've come to it."

Ray glanced around nervously. His eyes kept darting to the door, but Karen wasn't sure if he was planning an escape or willing it to stay closed. "The constructs were an unexpected by-product of our work," he said. "The original goal was always transference."

Karen lowered the file and stared at Ray's dimly lit face. "Transference? You mean taking magic from one person and giving it to another?"

"Mr. Magnus wanted to expand his market," Ray said lamely. "Our enchantments are great, but can only be used by magicians."

"He needed more customers, so he needed more magicians," Karen said. The thought of it made her mind spin. Magical talent was statistically rare and unevenly granted. It didn't seem to follow familial or racial bloodlines, despite many claims to the contrary. It followed no known set of rules other than scarcity. If Magnus could give nonmagical people the ability to use magic, he would fundamentally rewrite the reality of humanity.

All for a profit.

"This says 'failure,'" Karen said. "Have they ever successfully transferred magical ability?"

Ray shook his head. "Not even once. There are rumors that we're running out of money. That's why we developed the constructs, to get more funding for the project. Though I heard some of the guys in Transference talking about a possible breakthrough they found in Gerald's old notes."

"Gerald?" Karen grabbed Ray's shirt. "You knew him?"

"Yeah," Ray said, surprised at the question. "We work together. In the same office. Or at least we did. I think he's on vacation or something. I don't know why he had anything that would help the Transference team though."

"He's dead," Karen said, letting him go. "They killed him." Morris Rabin's men, working for Magnus Innovations. Morris Rabin, the mobster obsessed with magic but with no abilities of his own. No wonder he was funding Magnus's operation. "Meredith, why did you want me to—"

Meredith was gone. A few cabinets were open, some folders scattered on the floor. But there was no sign of the secretary.

"Dammit," Karen whispered. "Ray. Ray." The researcher had gone pale. A bead of sweat dangled on the end of his nose, but he didn't seem to notice.

"Oh, God," he murmured.

Karen slapped him with the folder. "Ray, focus." She snapped her fingers in front of his face. "This thing down here you are so afraid of, what is it?"

"I . . . I . . ." He swallowed hard and regained his composure, what little of it was left. "One of the donors, a little girl. The staff took to her, especially the locals. She was . . . sweet, even during the tests. They called her corderita, little lamb."

His lips twisted closed and Karen had to prod him again to continue. "The constructs haven't always worked," he said. "A few would never respond to commands or would just stare off into nothing. Others just crumbled, not enough magic to hold them together. But one . . . down here, in the Weapons department, they made one designed for warfare. Unlike the others, it wasn't human-oid. Afterward, some of us speculated that's why it went wild: too foreign a body, too monstrous."

"They put that little girl's soul into a monster?"

Ray nodded and Karen wanted to throw up. "They thought we could sell it to the military, but as soon as they animated it, it went crazy. It couldn't be stopped, couldn't be controlled. They just sealed off the lower basements and stopped that part of the project. We had no other choice."

You could have decided not to steal innocent lives to fuel your greed, Karen thought, but kept that to herself. Instead, she began flipping through the remaining folders, looking for any sign of where the children were being kept or how many children they'd been experimenting on, but there was nothing. And no folder for Graciela.

Then Ray bolted. He moved surprisingly fast, propelled by rank fear. Karen didn't try to stop him. His shoes slid on the dusty floor as he reached the end of the row of cabinets and tried to make the turn toward the door. He regained his balance and disappeared.

Karen did not see clearly what happened next. She thought she sensed movement above her. She swung the flashlight up, but it caught only the old corroded pipes. The room was still.

Then she heard Ray scream.

Instinctively—and perhaps foolishly—she ran toward him. The flashlight revealed only moldy cabinets and Ray's footprints in the dust. Then the cabinets ahead of her rocked back violently, like something heavy had been thrown against them.

"Please, no! No—" Ray's screams cut off.

Karen stopped, crouched, and willed herself not to breathe. She heard a strange clicking sound, then the groan of bending metal. She turned off the flashlight and pressed herself against the wall of filing cabinets. An instant later, a dark shadow loomed above her on top of the cabinets opposite. She could barely make out the faint glow of the anima pulsing at the shadow's center.

For a long, terrible moment, nothing moved other than Karen's pounding heart. A sour fear spread in her gut, crawling up her throat and into her thoughts. *Don't move, don't move.* Then the dark thing uncoiled itself and expanded. Long limbs, like spider's legs, but each tipped with a sharp blade, reached down along the drawers, probing. The cabinets buckled under its weight, but it did not seem to notice. The bladed limbs clicked again on the concrete, this time only inches from where Karen was huddled.

She had no magic left, no enchantments, and fighting a humanlike construct had taken everything she had and more.

Click. Click.

Click.

I'm going to die down here.

No, no. Not yet. Her hand tightened around the flashlight. And then she threw it as hard as she could down the row of cabinets, away from the door. It clattered and broke in a burst of noise. The thing in the dark lunged toward the sound, rending metal and knocking cabinets over as it went. Karen ran.

She hit the door with a bang and was through. *Which way were the stairs?* She should have paid better attention. She just kept running. There was barely any light but she didn't care. Behind her, the records room door was ripped from its hinges.

Karen nearly ran into a wall. As she turned the corner, she stared into the glare of bright white flashlights.

"She's here!" someone shouted. She could only see silhouettes, but that was enough to see them swing rifles to shoulders.

There was a door to her right, slightly ajar. She threw herself at it as the bullets started to kick up around her. She fell into the room hard, spinning and dazed. Boots on concrete. More voices. Orders being given. And then that clicking sound, coming closer and closer and closer.

After that, it was screaming and gunfire.

Karen was on her back, staring out the open door into the hallway. Through muzzle flashes and the beams of haphazard flashlights, she saw glimpses of the alien form of the Lamb as it struck. Its skin was pale, like Solomon's, but the similarities ended there. The Lamb was all spindly limbs and curved blades and death, and it moved like a viper's strike.

Get up, her thoughts shouted at her. *Get up and run.*

She braved the ricocheting bullets and the Lamb's churning talons and ran. Though it was dark and she was lost, she ran. More than once, she hit a corner or tripped and fell, but despite scraped palms and aching legs, she ran.

And then she found the stairs. She took them three at a time. Behind her, the screaming had stopped.

She burst through a door and into the light. There had to be a way out, and she was going to find it. But all these hallways looked the same and led nowhere. Had she seen that motivational poster before? Something about working hard to stick it to the Communists. Was that the sound of footsteps? Or voices?

She hadn't gone far before she ran right into Meredith.

"You," Karen said despite burning lungs. "You left us to die."

"So you saw it then," Meredith said, impressed. "What did it look like? Oh, don't look at me like that, Karen. I sent those nice security guards down there to distract that thing for you, and this is the thanks I get?"

"This was your plan?"

"The piggy had to die," Meredith said with a shrug. "My collection isn't quite complete, so my job here isn't done. Couldn't have him jeopardizing my cover."

"And if the Lamb didn't get him?"

"That's what the gun was for," she said simply. "Now, do you want to get out of here or not?"

TWENTY-SEVEN

Karen had never seen the stars like this: brilliant and multitudinous, a cascade of faraway light that filled the night. Yet even as she stared at the cosmic beauty, all she saw were red marks next to forgotten names. Her cheeks and hands were numb with the cold; her eyes watered. But she did not stop. She'd been walking for about an hour and had put a few miles between her and the Magnus Special Projects Laboratory, but it didn't feel like enough. It might not ever be enough, not until she went back there and burned the whole place to the ground. Some stains could only be purged with fire.

Meredith had shown her a rear exit. There had been people running everywhere; the whole facility was on alert. But Meredith had just given her a white coat to wear and told her to follow. No one questioned them.

"Why are you helping me?" Karen had asked when she stepped out into the cold.

Meredith had laughed. "I'm not," she said. "I'm helping me." She'd pointed south. "Havana is about fifteen miles from here, but the main highway isn't that far. Maybe if you smile sweetly, you can hitch a ride back to town." Then she had slammed the door shut.

Maria, she thought, when she was finally too tired to keep forcing the words from her head. *I'm sorry. I'm so sorry.*

She'd come to Cuba with grand delusions: she couldn't save Gerald, but maybe she could save Maria. Maybe her life after Auttenberg could mean something, something other than fear and regret.

She knew better now. She'd seen the red mark on Maria's file. Her mission had been a failure before Gerald had even mailed the anima to her. Maria was already just a memory, an echo.

I'm sorry. I'm so, so sorry. The words continued, over and over, in her head, until she no longer could say whom she was apologizing to.

As she crested a hill, there was a deep crimson glow ahead. She was still too far from Havana for it to be the city lights, and it was too vast to be lights from the road. She continued onward, her path lit by the stars and an empty moon, on legs nearly too tired to carry her anywhere.

A mile farther, she saw the source of the glow: the sugarcane fields were burning. The harvest was coming soon, Joaquin had told her on one of their drives. The macheteros were waiting for it to start so they could feed their families and survive another year. *The rebels know this,* he had said. *They will use it.* And now they had, setting fires in the fields, using disaster to force the people from their complacency, ignite a war. At this distance, the flames moved lazily, belying their greed. The smoke curled high into the night sky and obscured the stars.

Karen walked on.

Meredith, there you are! Thank God," Magnus said, wrapping her in a tight embrace. "Sage here told me you had been taken captive."

Meredith dabbed a tear from the corner of her eye. The chaos from Karen's visit was beginning to settle down now, but it had given her enough time to hide away the documents she'd stolen from the lower basement. "That woman," she said, her voice catching. "She was mad. Simply mad."

"You're safe now, my dear," Magnus said. "Sage, report."

Alexander Sage looked at Meredith, then back at Magnus. "Still no sign of the intruder, sir," he said. He spoke in short declarative jabs, like many former soldiers. "But we're on lockdown now. We'll find her."

"And what about the rest of this mess?"

"Crews are still working on the cafeteria fire," Sage said. "Shouldn't take much longer."

"I don't give a damn about the cafeteria," Magnus snapped. "What about the lower basement?"

"Confirmed six dead, sir," Sage replied, his voice tight. "The rest of the security team broke engagement."

"You mean they ran."

Sage coughed, a habit he had when he needed a moment to compose his response. "You've seen this thing, sir," he said. "What would you want them to do?"

Magnus sighed. "Yes, yes, of course. And the seals?"

"I've got men placed at every stairwell. Locks are reengaged. Staff magicians are working on the barriers now."

"It took us a month to get those seals right the first time."

"The team is working as fast as they can, sir."

"Yes, yes. Good." Magnus ran a hand through his hair. His eyes were bloodshot and his complexion waxy; the long night was taking its toll. "We might just survive this disaster after all."

Sage stood at attention. "I'll take my leave, sir."

Magnus shoved a finger into his security chief's face. "You let me know the instant you find that magician."

Sage nodded and was gone.

"Sir," Meredith said as she touched his arm, "can I get you anything? Some coffee?"

"Yes, that would be wonderful. Thank you."

Meredith smiled and made for the door. It might have been a disastrous night for most at the Special Projects Laboratory, but not for her. She'd been trying to figure out a way into the lower basement for months. And then Karen O'Neil arrived.

On her way out of Magnus's office, she passed Oliver Green, the lead researcher on the Containment team. Never a particularly healthy-looking man, tonight he looked like he was standing in his own grave. As usual, he did not even glance in her direction. Meredith stopped just beyond the doorway and listened.

"What the hell was that, Oliver?" Magnus asked. "I thought you said the spell was safe, that we had all the kinks worked out. That was one hell of a kink."

"The spell *is* safe," Oliver said. "But that girl magician isn't."

"That is hardly reassuring," Magnus said. "Have you been down to the lab? The whole place is a wreck. Never seen anything like it. Is any of it salvageable?"

"Might be more than salvageable, sir," Oliver replied. Meredith held her breath. "The anima is intact."

"What?" Magnus said. "I saw it explode."

"The excess magic exploded," Oliver said. He sounded surprisingly confident about the details of a disaster none of these fools predicted. "But the rest of her magic is still contained within."

"I don't need another anima, Oliver."

"This one isn't like the others, sir."

"What do you mean?"

"We have only started examining it, but that girl's magic is . . . unique," Oliver said. "And potent. Duane believes it could be a prime candidate for another transference trial."

"Really? Finally some good news. Let's make it happen."

"We'll need some test subjects."

"I'll get you some volunteers."

Meredith slipped away to find the coffee before her absence was noted. After all these long months of planning and waiting, what an unexpected evening. If she was ever able to go home and file a report, she would have much to say.

When Karen's legs finally gave out, she figured she was less than a mile from the main road. It might as well have been a hundred. She'd never been so exhausted. The sleepless nights in the rebel camp, the battle in the courtyard, and the damn transference spell left her with nothing, left her as nothing. She was like that smoke clouding over the cane fields, burned up and tossed in the air, cold ash on a night breeze.

She was vaguely aware of the gravel biting into her knees and of the bruises she'd received from the constructs' fists. The agony of the magic suppression collar still lingered in her thoughts, a scar that would not soon fade. But none of that seemed to matter anymore. She could push past the pain; she'd done it many times in her life. But to what end? Havana was out there somewhere ahead of her, but did that even matter?

She'd failed. Whatever it was she'd come to Cuba to do, she had failed. Maria was gone. Gerald was gone. Ehle was gone. Why should she even—

Ehle? Who was that? The name had flashed in her mind for a moment and then was gone, like a shooting star. She didn't know anyone named Ehle. Did she? The name sounded German. She turned it over in her thoughts, and as she did, she felt a twinge deep inside, like an old injury reacting to the chill, down in the void where her magic had been. And it reminded her of what she'd felt back there in that lab, just before she broke the spell, which had reminded her of the breach in Auttenberg.

Ehle.

The gravel crunched as she got to her feet.

She hadn't walked far when headlights came around a bend in the road. Who would be driving toward the Magnus facility at this hour? Probably not someone she wanted to meet. But there was nowhere to hide even if she'd had the energy, so she stood her ground as the car slowed and stopped.

When she heard the door open, hope surged unexpectedly in her chest. *Could that be Joaquin's car?* She squinted but couldn't tell. A man stepped out of the driver's side. *Is he too tall to be Joaquin?* The passenger door opened as well. *Joaquin and Arthur, come to rescue me. Thank God.* Then she saw a third figure. Behind the lights, she only saw hints of movement. Dust curled in the headlight beams.

The figures came closer and their shapes became clearer: broad shoulders broadened by suit jackets, polished leather shoes that reflected the headlights back at her, pale, expressionless faces she did not recognize. She caught a whiff of expensive aftershave in the chilly air.

"Miss O'Neil," the driver said; it wasn't a question. Probably not many other bedraggled white women wandering rural Cuban roads at this time of night. "We're here to give you a ride. Mr. Rabin would like a word."

TWENTY-EIGHT

She sat in the back seat between two of Rabin's men. With the gentle swaying of the car and the heat seeping off their arms, Karen had to fight to stay awake. Despite her efforts, the drive took on a dreamlike quality. *None of this is real,* she thought. This wasn't her life, it was just a story of some stupid girl who'd run off to Cuba chasing ghosts and found herself riding to God knows where surrounded by goons in the back seat of a mobster's car. *Who could be so foolish? Where is her mother?*

The dream ended when they pulled into an underground parking garage beneath the familiar tower of El Paraíso. The car's tires squeaked as they stopped in a parking spot near a service elevator. There were no other cars in the lot.

"Not a lot of witnesses around," Karen said when she got out and saw the empty lot.

"Hoping for someone in particular?" asked the driver. In the yellow light of the garage, she could see him better: he had a square head, a square jaw, and a boxer's blunt nose. He looked chiseled from granite.

Karen smiled with faux sweetness. "Just a friendly face."

"We're real friendly," the driver said as they all piled into the service elevator and clanged the doors shut.

The elevator jolted and began its slow upward climb. Karen glanced at the other men. Thick necks all around, a few mustaches, a gold ring or two. They did not bother to conceal the pistols tucked into holsters under their jackets.

"One of you the guy who ransacked my hotel room?" she asked in the humming quiet. No answer. "Did they tell you I'm a magician? You know, I put a hex on my luggage. A nasty little spell for anyone who touches my stuff without my permission. Has your skin started itching yet?" She noted a few subtly exchanged glances. "You'll know it when it starts," she added with a dark chuckle. "But don't worry, it isn't permanent. Usually."

The elevator rumbled to a stop. Karen was surprised to be met by a blast of chill morning air when the doors were pulled open. No wonder the ride seemed to last forever; it had taken them all the way to the roof of the hotel. Havana in twilight stretched out before her, a world in miniature pricked with stars. The endless black ocean loomed beyond. This high up, the wind numbed her face and tugged hard at her jacket. Karen hugged her arms to her chest.

Morris Rabin approached from the far side of the roof. "Thank you for meeting me," he said when he was close enough to be heard. Even so, his voice was nearly lost among the gusts.

"How did you know I'd be on that road?"

"I like to come up here in the mornings," he said, nodding toward the edge of the roof and the city waiting below. "The quiet helps me to think."

After the night she'd had, Karen was too tired for this nonsense. "You brought me here for a reason," she said. "If you just want to chat, great. I can be a charming conversationalist. But if you need something from me, then I need some answers from you."

That brought the hint of a smile to Rabin's thin lips. "If you ask interesting questions, I'll answer them," he said. "As a token of my generosity, I'll answer your first question. Let's just say I got an interesting telephone call tonight. I spend a lot of money on Magnus Innovations. Some of it takes an indirect route."

Everyone has their spies, Karen thought. Is that who Meredith was working for? Karen doubted it.

"He's never going to deliver what you're paying him for," Karen said. They'd walked a little ways away from the elevator. The bulky henchmen had waited behind. A few of them scratched worriedly at their hands or necks. "It can't be done."

"Maybe, maybe not."

Anger flushed Karen's cheeks. "Did you know they were kidnapping children for their experiments?" Karen demanded. She moved in on him until her finger was shoved in his face; she heard a shuffle of feet behind her, but Rabin waved his men off. "Did you know they were killing them?"

Rabin brushed an imagined bit of lint from his lapel. "I've done a lot of things to get where I am. Not pretty things, but things that needed to be done. But I don't hurt kids."

"That's not an answer," Karen said. She didn't bother hiding her disgust. "I guess that question wasn't interesting enough. How about this one: Did you know they kidnapped Isabel's sister?"

"I love Isabel."

"Again, that's no answer," Karen replied. "Or maybe it is." The wind picked up and blew into her eyes, whipping her hair around her head. "You know where I've just been, what I've seen. What do you think Isabel is going to say when I tell her? You think she'll believe you when you try to convince her you knew nothing about it?"

Rabin showed his teeth when he smiled; they were brilliantly white and too big for his mouth. "Finally," he said, "an interesting question."

Now we come to it, Karen thought.

"Whatever you think of me," Rabin said, "I do love her."

"You have a strange way of showing it."

Rabin didn't respond. Instead he stared out at the waking Havana lights with tightly pressed lips. Karen remembered what Arthur had called him: the Quiet Man. Just a soft-spoken, taciturn Jewish man from New Jersey, more likely to be someone's stern grandfather than a Mob boss. But she also remembered the goons loitering behind them and the guns tucked overtly into their jackets. And she remembered Gerald.

"You can't understand," Rabin said eventually. He wasn't looking at her; she had to crane her neck to hear him. "You were born with magic. You'll never understand what it's like not to have it. Tell me, now that you've tasted what real power feels like, what would you do to keep it?"

"I know what I wouldn't do."

"You think you do," Rabin replied. "Everyone thinks they know, until the moment comes, and then people surprise themselves." He turned back to face her; she preferred when he was looking away, so she didn't have to stare into those eyes. "You want to save those kids Magnus took?"

Like everything else in this place, the question seemed like a trap, but there was only one way she could answer. "Yes."

"Good," he said. "Then we can do business."

"You know where they are?"

"No," he said. "I don't like to see how the sausage is made, if I can help it."

Meredith had told her that only Magnus knew. Ever the savvy businessman, John Magnus wasn't about to give up proprietary information. Unless he was forced.

"But you can get Magnus."

"That I can," he said.

Karen shifted her weight back onto her heels. "And in return?"

"This whole thing with Magnus is a lousy deal," Rabin said. "He takes my money and comes back to me with nothing except his creepy faceless men. Now that you've shown up and started turning over rocks, I see the whole mess is about to come crashing down, and soon." He tucked his hands into his pockets, the first outward sign that the cold had any effect on him. "When it does, I want you to convince Isabel I had no part in it."

What a thing: a mobster in love, worried about his reputation. "She already knows you're involved, that you fund Magnus."

"But that's all she knows," he said. "And all she needs to know. I help you get your hands on Magnus, get those kids back, get her sister back. Then Isabel's new magician pal who's seen everything sings my praises to the rafters. Everyone gets what he wants. Well, except Magnus, but he can go to hell."

Karen felt sick. As soon as he'd started describing his offer, she knew she had to take it. They couldn't storm the gates of the Magnus Special Projects facility any more than they could rely on help from the Cuban or American government. There were no good options, not if she wanted to save those kids; there were only the options in front of her.

"And if I refuse?" she asked.

Rabin's terrible eyes blinked once as he glanced over the roof's edge. "You think you and your magic can survive a fourteen-story fall?"

Karen didn't miss a beat. "You think your goons could stop me and my magic before I throw you off this roof?"

There were his blinding teeth again. "Your questions are improving," he said. "So do we have a deal?" He stuck out his hand.

"Your men killed a good friend of mine," she said icily.

Rabin gave the same answer he gave before. "That's not how they remember it."

"I'm sure it's not." She stared at the offered hand. She'd be a fool to trust him, maybe even a dead fool. Even if their interests had partially aligned, she knew it would be temporary. But for all its music and sand and glitter, Havana had proven an unfriendly place, and she needed someone in her corner.

Karen shook his hand.

"Smart girl," Rabin said. He waved toward his waiting men. "Tomorrow night is our big New Year's Eve Gala here at the hotel. Best party in Havana. Magnus will be there. My team is providing security for the event; no outside security allowed. If something were to befall Mr. Magnus as he left the party, well, we'd do our best to investigate, but these things happen."

"How do you know he'll be there?"

"Because I told him to."

Is this what she'd come to? Working with a criminal to conspire to kidnap a respected American entrepreneur? She could lose her job or be sent to prison. But when she closed her eyes, she saw all those folders in that drawer: so many names, filed away to be forgotten. And more to come.

"Isabel can never know we spoke," Karen said. "So I'll need another way back to the orphanage. I'll convince her we need to get Magnus, so naturally she'll want to lean on you. Act furious when she tells you the truth about him, then tell her about the gala. As long as she thinks this is all her idea, she won't be suspicious."

"A solid plan. People always surprise themselves," Rabin said as his men surrounded them. "I thought you seemed like the kind of person I could do business with. My boys will take you downstairs; your means of transportation awaits you. Until next time."

Rabin turned his back on them while they returned to the elevator. Karen caught one last glimpse of him staring at the sunrise as the doors slammed shut.

There was another car in the underground garage when the elevator reached the bottom. She recognized it immediately. When she stepped into view, Joaquin got out and smiled faintly. When the passenger door opened, her peripheral vision noted something wrong: Joaquin's passenger was the wrong shape to match Arthur's heavy frame. Her eyes struggled for a moment to settle on his face, his presence too incongruous to accept so quickly.

"Karen," Agent Daniel Pierce said cheerily as he tilted back his fedora. The inquisitor offered a bright and welcoming smile that was very out of place in the dim garage. "I think we're your ride."

TWENTY-NINE

They drove straight to the orphanage of Nuestra Señora de la Caridad del Cobre. Joaquin knew the way. They didn't speak much on the drive; there were many questions—and some answers—on either side, but Karen was content with silence for now. There would be more noise to come, she knew, and likely pain. But for now she could pretend the road ahead of them would stretch on and that Havana would stay drenched in the cool of early morning forever. She wrapped herself in Pierce's offered coat, leaned her head against the side of Joaquin's rumbling car, and finally, blissfully slept.

When she opened her eyes, the car was filled with the pink light of dawn. Pierce took one look out the window at the ruined gate and smashed wall and said drily, "This must be the place."

Karen winced as she got out of the car. Her abused muscles had constricted as she slept, and they protested being put to use again so soon. She surveyed the battered orphanage. Some repairs had been started, but the work would take time. A handful of winged nuns met them as they neared the gap in the wall that had once been a gate. Joaquin spoke to them in a low, respectful voice, but their eyes never left Karen. Her last visit had been brief perhaps, but memorable.

She stepped inside the walls and surveyed the battlefield. Most of the courtyard's grounds had been torn up. Bricks lay smashed all over. Near the old tree, she saw the tangle of Isabel's magical roots. The long-armed construct within had apparently succumbed to the crushing pressure; all that was left was a fine white powder. To one side, there was a small crater, still full of the remains of the construct Karen had unleashed her fury upon. It looked like a poorly managed archeological dig, all dirt and shattered pottery.

Karen reached down and pushed some of the ruined clay aside. At the center of the crater was the construct's black heart. The anima stared dully back at her, empty as a corpse. *Who were you? What was your name before they took even that from you?*

When she looked up, Isabel stood on the far side of the crater, arms crossed over her chest. She had a large cut over one eye. A deep scowl tightened her face.

"¿Donde están los niños?" she demanded.

Karen shivered in the cold. Her eyes ached; a few stolen moments of sleep hadn't been enough to prepare her for this. "I don't know," she said softly.

"They took you," Isabel said. Her voice was ice. "They took my children. But then you come back and they do not. What am I supposed to make of that?"

"Isabel, I—"

She held up a hand, cutting Karen off. "We need to talk. Tell your friends to wait out here until I decide if I like what you have to say." She retreated into her hut, and after a glance at Joaquin and Pierce, Karen followed.

Isabel's home was much as it had been when Karen visited it last, though without Elisa's silent presence, it felt emptier. She found Isabel in the tiny kitchen, banging drawers shut while preparing tea. On the kitchen table was Karen's satchel. She'd lost it in the fight with the constructs. It was open, its contents spread out across the surface: rings, stones, carvings, and assorted bags including the pouch that held Maria's anima—all the enchantments left to her by its former owner. *By Ehle*. The name echoed in her thoughts like a swear word her mother had forbidden, something she could think but wasn't supposed to give voice to.

As she stepped closer, she saw the book. At first, it did not register as strange; it was familiar to her after all, ever present, like a sharp rock in her shoe. But then the wrongness assailed her and turned her skin frigid. *No, no, no. Not now.* She'd spent every moment of the last few years protecting this book from prying eyes, but now there it was, out in the open.

Karen snatched the notebook from the table. "How did you get this?" she shouted at Isabel's back. *No one should be able to get through those runes.*

Isabel turned languidly, placed two cups of tea wherever she could find a place, and sat down. "I should ask you the same thing," she said. "Though I suspect you will just lie to me again."

Karen sat. She shoved the minor enchantments back into the satchel, but did not return the book to its place. Instead she set it down between them, careful not to let it fall open even a sliver, though she knew by heart every unspeakable phrase and impenetrable diagram contained within. She had written them all—though she had no memory of any of it—starting with the opening line: *Concerning that which must never come to pass . . .*

"You broke the seals, my protection spells," she said. "Those were strong magic."

"I know what I am doing," Isabel said simply. She turned her head to the side, as if studying a curiosity. "But I think maybe my abilities are nothing compared to yours. You put on quite the display, for a magician who has lost her magic."

"I wasn't trying to deceive you," Karen said. "What I told you was true, just not all the truth. It was just simpler."

"Simpler," Isabel repeated. "We have time now. Tell me the complicated version."

Karen stared into the dark tea. In its murky depths, she saw her many old lives: Learning magic as a young girl, bristling at the confines of pre-built, pre-imagined incantations, experimenting with another sort of magic, driven by her will rather than recipes, finding new paths within that magic, finding meaning in it, purpose. She saw a naïve but eager magician land at Tempelhof Airport, met by two equally naïve CIA agents on escort duty. She saw an endless black tunnel under the Berlin Wall and the death that waited for them there. There was a glimpse of a face, someone she knew but had forgotten, or maybe someone she just imagined. She saw a foolish child hell-bent on tearing down the Wall—but why? How had she known how to bring it down?—to get at the secrets that lay beyond. And she saw what became of that child when limitless power was offered to her. She saw the dead, the lost, and the void beyond the breach. The power she had craved as that young girl, the freedom she had coveted and won, never considering the price.

She told Isabel what she saw, described the details she could remember. She said things she had never spoken aloud, never dared to put into words.

"Magic isn't what it seems," she said into the silence that followed. "We think it is ours to command, that it is a gift some of us have been given by God or fate or whatever. But I think it is something else. And I think it can't be trusted."

Isabel sighed. It was not what Karen expected; the other magician sounded disappointed, or even annoyed.

"When those things came for my kids, you held yourself back," Isabel said. "You tried your gun, your little trinkets. You had fire inside of you, but you were afraid, so you covered it up." She leaned forward on the table; Karen could see dark bruises livid across her arms. "If you had used your magic when they first appeared, you could have stopped them from taking Rogelio. You could have stopped them from taking Marisol and all the others."

Her eyes burned, and Karen thought she might throw her out of her home and slam the door. But after a moment, the heat went out of her, and her hands settled in her lap.

"You didn't see what I was like in Auttenberg, or even what I was like when I destroyed that construct," Karen said. "I can't control it. It is dangerous. You think I could have saved those kids, but I could have just as easily killed them."

"You just told me you've spent the last few years hiding from it," Isabel replied. "You can't control it because you haven't learned how. With the power you've got, if you had been training since Berlin, nothing could stop you."

Karen had no reply.

"You've seen darkness, I don't doubt that," Isabel said. "But deciding if you can trust magic is a luxury I don't have time for." She pointed toward the main orphanage buildings. "Not when someone else needs you. Not when you can't just fly back to the United States when this is done."

Karen cringed; the words landed hard.

Isabel went on. "Where does magic come from? God, the saints, the orisha? Who knows. But what I know is that it is power. And no one is going to make me give that up, no matter the cost, not when it could save Graciela or any of those kids in there."

They sat in silence for a while. Their tea steamed, then cooled. Outside, the sun rose higher and began to peek through the small curtained window over the sink. Parakeets chirped. Down the road a ways, someone was playing music; in Havana, someone was always playing music. It drifted up to them, a tinny, uneven sound, probably an old record, warped by age. A woman sang. Karen couldn't make out the words, probably couldn't understand them even if she could, but she could tell it was a song of sorrow and loss. An odd choice for the early morning, or maybe not. Maybe it was always appropriate.

Isabel placed the tip of a finger on the book. "Tell me about this."

"I'd rather not," Karen replied.

"Should I get someone else to tell me?"

Karen pulled it out from under Isabel's finger. She was struck, as she always was, by how ordinary it felt; just like any of her laboratory notebooks, just paper and ink. Just a regular notebook, and also her darkest secret. Did she dare to share it with Isabel? Did she have a choice?

"The breach in Auttenberg," Karen said, "was caused by the magic described in this book. The Nazis took it and discovered a way to uncreate things, make it like they never existed. They used that magic on people in their death camps, then they tried to use it on their enemies, but something went wrong. Very wrong. After the war, the occupiers of Berlin covered it up, until we went in to stop it." *We? Who is* we?

"Someone told me once that this book has always existed, in one form or another," Karen went on. "Time and again, it appears, always sowing ruin. Whenever it is destroyed, it is always rewritten. But we did more than destroy it this time; we threw it into the breach. We unmade it. Everyone who came into Auttenberg after it just forgot it ever existed. It should have been gone forever."

"But you remember it," Isabel said quietly, "because you rewrote it."

Karen nodded. She explained how she had no memory of the writing, only of long nights of fitful sleep and unknown arcane symbols burned into the back of her eyelids. "It can't be unmade. The cycle can't be broken. I can't tell you how many times I've thought about destroying it," she said. "I even held a lighter up to it once. You can see the scorch mark on the cover here. But if I did, it would just come back somewhere else. It is going to keep returning until it finally destroys us all. So I kept it. I paid a small fortune to have my bag protected against thieves and rarely let it out of my sight."

Isabel turned and stared out the sunlit window. Now Karen could hear the voices of children echoing in the broken courtyard. "The old woman who trained me," Isabel said, "always told me that there was magic I must never do, but rarely said much beyond that. Except for one night, not long before she died. We were both drunk, celebrating something. Then she got very serious and told me, 'Isabel, my child, there are bad people in this world and so there is bad magic also. But don't fear bad magic, because bad magic can be stopped. Fear the rotten magic. Nothing can stop it. It eats and eats until the world dies.'

"'What is the rotten magic?' I asked her. But she seemed afraid of her own words. 'I'll say no more of it; never ask me again.' And I never did." Isabel pointed across the table at the book in Karen's hands. "I think that might be the rotten magic she was so terrified of. That is a dangerous thing to carry around with you."

It is a dangerous thing to carry around inside you, Karen thought, but did not say. Instead she shoved the book back into her satchel. "I'll worry about this book," she said. "*We* need to think about getting your sister and those kids back."

Grateful to pivot away from the nameless book that had wormed its way into her magic, Karen eagerly described the events at the Magnus Special Projects Laboratory. She told it all: the procedure, the disaster that followed, the horrible thing lurking in the basement, and her escape aided by the duplicitous Meredith. She excluded only the nature of her return to Havana, saying instead that she waved down a car on the main road.

"So those things," Isabel said when Karen was done, "that attacked us. They were . . . my children?" There was a different fire in her eyes now, a white-hot, cleansing flame. "They ripped out their souls and made them into slaves?"

"I didn't find Graciela's file," Karen put in quickly. "There were many that weren't marked like that. Most of them weren't."

Isabel said nothing. She sat perfectly still, spine straight, chin up, hands folded. But something in the room had changed, like a cloud had smothered the sun. This woman had a fearsome power in her. No one should have been able to break the seals Karen had placed on her satchel, and yet Isabel had. And in the fight with the constructs, her magic had been impressive even before she summoned the tree roots. Isabel was a shockingly talented magician, and a dangerous woman to cross.

"Los mataré a todos," she whispered. Her voice was so soft, Karen was fairly certain she was not speaking to her. "Todos."

Now it is time to decide where your loyalties lie: with this unpredictable witch who is likely your match in magical power, or with the crime boss who runs Havana and has promised to help you find the missing kids.

"Isabel," Karen said, leaning onto the wobbling table, "there'll be time for that, I promise you. But now we need to focus on getting your sister back. We need to get Graciela." At the sound of her sister's name, Isabel refocused her eyes. The fire wasn't gone—Karen didn't expect it would be until it had burned down Magnus's world—but she was at least listening again. "And to do that, we need to get Magnus."

Karen found Joaquin and Pierce outside Isabel's house. A gaggle of kids had them surrounded, some asking for candy, others for a piggyback ride. A pair of small boys with wide-mouthed grins were trying to pick Pierce's pocket. Karen tried to ignore the wary looks the children sent her way as she approached; how much of the fight in the courtyard had they seen? What did they think of her now?

"What's the plan?" Pierce asked.

"We need a place to stay," she said. "The orphanage has been through enough. They sent the other magically talented kids elsewhere, but still, Magnus's people could come back at any time."

"I know a place," Joaquin said. "We will be safe there."

"Good."

"Safe to do what?" Pierce asked.

Karen smiled. "Plan a kidnapping."

THIRTY

'm not really sure how long he expects to be occupied," Meredith said apologetically.

"That's fine," the bald man said. He offered a gap-toothed grin that was mostly obscured by his overgrown mustache. He had white medical tape across the bridge of his nose, and the purpling remains of two black eyes. Meredith did not inquire about the injury. He settled his impressive bulk into one of the leather armchairs that sat across from Meredith's desk. "I'll wait."

"It's just that we've had a very busy time in the last day," Meredith continued.

"I saw on my way up," he said. "Looks like a bit of a mess. If you don't mind my asking, what happened? One of your little toys get out?"

Meredith summoned a false smile of her own. "I'm sure Mr. Magnus will be happy to answer any of your questions once he is available. Are you sure I can't reschedule you?"

He crossed his expansive hands over his chest. "I've got all day."

She could feel the forced friendliness in her voice turning to ice. She picked up a pen and tried not to imagine jumping over the desk and jamming it into his sagging jowl. "Can I at least take your name down?"

"Lloyd Ellis," the bald man said. "Two 'L's in each name."

She wrote the name on her notepad as Ellis began to whistle. The tune had no discernable melody or rhythm; it was noise rather than music. It echoed off the polished floors and rattled in Meredith's ears. She underlined his name with a rasp of her pen, imagining the curving black line as a slash across the fat man's throat.

Calm yourself. Remember the mission. Remember why you are here.

She breathed out as Ellis hit a high note. It wouldn't be long now. After her trip to the lower basement the previous night, she had most of what she required. It was too complex to deliver via postcard; she would have to hand carry these documents herself. But the gray-haired man wanted more than just research notes, and so she remained at her post, wrapped in bright lipstick, a scratchy skirt, and a smile.

"And who do you work for, Mr. Ellis?" She blinked her long eyelashes at him.

"Oh, I'm not a professional man. This is a social visit," he said casually. "I'm an old friend of Johnny's. I've helped him out a time or two, so I just thought I'd stop by and see how he's doing."

Ellis, Lloyd. Forty-seven years old. Born in Grand Rapids, Michigan. Parents deceased. Divorced twice. No children. Served without distinction as military intelligence officer in European theater during the war. Current CIA station chief based in Havana, Cuba. The dossier Meredith had memorized before beginning this mission hadn't come with a photograph, but the description had proven accurate enough: *Tall, overweight, bald. Disliked by peers. Possible target for bribes.*

"I'm sure he'll be happy to see you then," Meredith replied. The CIA's involvement with Magnus Innovations was not news to her, not after all the time she'd spent reviewing their accounting documents. Though most of the funds for the Cuban facility had come from Morris Rabin, the US government had always been a willing but silent partner. But why was he here now? Had word of their recent disaster spread so quickly?

Meredith was spared another verse of Ellis's atonal performance by the sudden opening of the outer doors. Mr. Magnus strode into the room, arms outstretched. There was no evidence of his sleepless night. His suit was spotless, his smile effusive. Not one hair was out of place.

"Lloyd!" he said as his guest rose to pump his outstretched hand. "What a pleasant surprise! I hope you haven't been waiting long."

"Oh no," Ellis said cheerily. "I was just enjoying the delightful company of your secretary here."

"Isn't she great?"

Meredith's eyes flicked between the men. All smiles and friendly handshakes, all lies. These two hated each other, she could see. Now that was worth noting.

"What happened to your nose?"

Ellis's face momentarily darkened. "I walked into a door," he growled.

"Really," Magnus said. "I hope you gave the 'door' an equal thrashing. Anyway, I'm glad you've come by just now."

"Is that so?" Ellis asked. He jerked a thumb over his shoulder toward the hallway. "Because it seems like things have gone a bit to hell out there. I'd hate to have to report to our mutual friends that your operation is in disarray."

Magnus placed a hand over his heart. "If you'd asked me an hour ago, Lloyd, I would be singing a different tune. A mournful one at that. But we've had a breakthrough that I think our mutual friends will be delighted to hear about."

"A breakthrough, really," Ellis said. "How conveniently timed, just as patience was running a bit thin on the ground."

"It really is remarkable," Magnus said. "But I've learned that is often the case with projects like this. Epiphanies come when you least expect them. The night is darkest just before the dawn, as they say."

Ellis frowned. Deep lines segmented his ample forehead. All comradery dropped out of his voice. "We don't need fancy words, Magnus. We need results."

"Trust me, Lloyd, I understand," Magnus said. "It can be frustrating when your friends make promises and then fail to keep them. Like just the other day, when I asked you to find a certain female magician and send her back where she came from."

Bright red splotches blossomed on Ellis's cheeks. He looked like a bull about to charge. "I don't work for you."

"Not yet," Magnus replied cheerily. He put a hand on Ellis's thick shoulder and turned him toward the door. "But come now, let's put disappointments behind us. As it turns out, that particular magician proved to be most useful to us, so all's well that ends well. Come, I feel a demonstration is due."

Meredith stood suddenly. "Mr. Magnus," she said quickly. "There's a whole pile of papers here that need your signature, so they can get started on the repairs." She held the stack up with both hands.

"Fine, fine," Magnus said. "Bring them; I'll sign on the way. You've been with us through all this, Meredith, so you should get to see our moment of triumph!"

The two men headed for the door, Magnus in the lead. With their back to her, Meredith felt her ever-present smile falter. This was unexpected. Was it a ploy to distract Magnus's many patrons? That didn't seem right. Magnus was not above lying, even to the CIA, but he sounded sincere. Had Karen's magic really led to a breakthrough in their transference research? She snatched up a pen and tucked the documents under her arm and hurried after them, her heels clicking furiously on the marble floor.

The Transference labs had all been shut down following the previous night's disaster, so the team had commandeered some of the few rooms in the facility that remained mostly intact. Meredith had seen some of the previous transference tests—it hadn't been hard to manufacture reasons to attend—so she knew something of what to expect, but as they entered what had once been a lab dedicated to unsuccessfully developing magically driven automobiles, she detected something new: excitement.

They were intercepted immediately by Duane Kellogg, the head of the Transference team. Oliver Green, the glowering leader of Containment, hovered nearby. "Sir," Kellogg said, "you must come and see. The transference fields have remained stable this entire time. We've detected no energy bleed and no drop in intensity with the anima from Miss O'Neil."

"Please." Magnus put an arm around the man. "Explain it for those of us without advanced degrees in magical theory, like my good friend here, Mr. Ellis."

The researcher was so excited that he barely noticed the company's CEO's embrace. He pointed toward the center of the room, where they had cleared a wide space and positioned a single anima on a pedestal. The cube was not black as usual, but white-hot; those standing nearest were wearing dark sunglasses to ward off the intense light. "It means that we think we're ready to try, sir. And I think it'll work."

Magnus clapped his hands together. "Perfect timing, Lloyd," he said to the CIA man, who was not yet ready to share Magnus's enthusiasm. The anima's glow cast dark shadows on Ellis's lined face. "Do we have our volunteer?"

The researchers produced a bony, bespectacled man in his late forties. His forehead was dotted with sweat, and his glasses had begun to fog up around his nose. His eyes moved around the room but never seemed to settle on anything for very long, though they conspicuously avoided looking toward the burning anima.

"This is Norman Baker, from Accounting," Kellogg said. "We weren't expecting to be conducting transference tests this week so we didn't have anyone lined up, but Norman here was eager to volunteer, weren't you, Norman?"

"You said something about stock options?" Norman said in a reedy voice.

Magnus disengaged from Kellogg and latched onto the frail-looking accountant. "Norman, my dear boy, if this goes the way we think it will, we'll all be rich men and we'll have you to thank."

"Thank you, sir," Norman said with a bit of a stammer. "It's not going to hurt, is it?"

"We're on the edge of a new era for humanity, Norman," Magnus said, tracing his outstretched hand across an imaginary horizon and ignoring Norman's question. "For too long magic has been handed out on a whim. That's an injustice, Norman, and frankly un-American. If we can right that wrong, then it will be our names in the history books. Statues in our honor, Norman. Parades!"

Norman swallowed hard. "That sounds wonderful, sir. But are there any risks?"

Magnus had directed the poor man to his place on an "X" taped on the floor across from the anima. He faced him, a hand on each shoulder, and said, "Norman, there's absolutely nothing to worry about. The worst thing that can happen now is nothing. Now, let's get on with it!"

The accountant trembled in place while the rest of the Magnus Innovations team scrambled around the room in a flurry of unco-ordinated activity. Meredith found a corner out of the way and silently watched the magicians, their ever-gracious CEO, and his visitor from the CIA.

Cuba is a powder keg, the gray-haired man had told her before she came to Havana. *The Party does not see it, and the Americans do not know it, but it will explode in their faces. We must take what we can, while we can.*

She had taken much already; her return to Moscow would be a certain triumph. But if this capitalist dog Magnus actually succeeded here, then everything would change. Like a typically blind American, Magnus only saw the effect on his shareholders and his debts, which were many. But whether he understood it or not, he was on the verge of upsetting the balance of power in the world. And that could not be allowed.

"Norman, can you please follow the instructions on the card we gave you?" Kellogg asked from a safe distance.

Norman took out a folded piece of paper from his pocket. He raised his right hand, palm up, fingers curled like he was clutching an invisible grapefruit. He blinked at the instructions and held the paper closer.

"Et erit lux," he began in Latin, speaking very slowly to be sure to get the correct pronunciation. He read the rest of the spell carefully, his voice the only sound in the room packed with people. When he finished, nothing happened.

"Did I do it right?" he asked sheepishly.

"Perfect, Norman," Kellogg said reassuringly. "That's one of the spells examiners give to children to detect magical ability. You failed."

Norman managed a weak smile. "That's why I ended up working with numbers. Nothing magic about them." There was a polite chuckle from the assembled group.

"Quiet, everyone," Kellogg ordered. His magicians were completing their preparations. Their chants were a low drone. Magnus whispered something to Ellis, who continued to appear unimpressed. Then Kellogg raised his hands, and the final step of the incantation was complete.

Magic erupted from the anima and lunged for Norman Baker. It writhed like a mass of fiery tentacles as it enveloped the accountant. The ground around him sizzled. The paint on the wall behind him began to bubble and burn. Meredith could just make out the man's face behind the haze of light; he looked transfixed, like he was staring into the grille of an oncoming train.

The magic held him, consumed him, burrowed inside him. And then just as abruptly as it began, the spell ended, leaving the room in a crackling stillness. Norman was still there, still whole, and only slightly singed.

"Is it over?" he asked.

One of the researchers approached, carrying a thin stick of what appeared to be polished wood. He held it out toward Norman's face and spoke a word of magic. The dowsing rod began to glow.

"You'll have to do better than that," Ellis said to Magnus. "I know you guys manufacture those doodads by the crateful. It could be a trick, or maybe it's picking up magic left over from the spell."

"Patience, Lloyd," Magnus said soothingly. "You can't rush proper scientific protocols. Mr. Kellogg, please proceed."

After a moment's conference with his team, Kellogg addressed Norman. "Can you please repeat the spell on the card?"

Norman nodded and lifted his hand again. Meredith realized she was gripping the forgotten stack of unsigned documents so hard that her nails were leaving crescent marks. She forced herself to exhale as the accountant finished his incantation.

A tiny blue light appeared in the space just above Norman's raised palm. A collective gasp filled the laboratory.

"Is this right?" Norman asked, his voice a quaver.

Another hushed huddle among the researchers, then Kellogg reappeared, beaming. "Norman," he said, "you have cast your first magic spell."

The room burst into cheers and applause. Researchers hugged and slapped one another's backs. Magnus strode around the room shaking hands like a proud father at his son's birth. But Meredith watched Lloyd Ellis, whose face had gone very pale. The CIA man was doubtlessly considering the telephone calls he needed to make and reports he needed to write. His masters would not be prepared for this news. Neither would hers.

"Um, excuse me?" Norman's voice was almost inaudible over the congratulations. "I don't want to interrupt, but is . . . is it supposed to be doing that?"

The blue light that Karen's transplanted magic had summoned was growing. Norman seemed to be trying to lower his hand, but it was stuck in place.

"Norman, stay calm," Kellogg was saying. "I need you to repeat after me . . ." He grabbed the arm of a nearby researcher, but they just stared blankly back at him. "Just a second, Norman. We just need you to do another spell to counter this one . . . just a moment. Stay with us."

"It's so bright," Norman said.

"Close your eyes, Norman," Kellogg called out, but the accountant didn't seem to hear.

"Something's wrong," Norman said. His voice had fallen, like he was speaking only to himself now. "I can see something in the light. It's coming toward me."

"Do something, dammit," Magnus commanded.

"Norman, can you hear me?"

"It's dark," Norman said. "Can you see it? What is that?"

"Duane, that's enough," Magnus said to Kellogg.

"Oh, God . . . ," Norman said. "It's—"

Then there was a crackle of electricity and Norman collapsed to the floor like an empty sack. The blue light winked out of existence. Alexander Sage had appeared from the crowd. In his hand, he held a small carved figurine in the shape of Aktzin, god of lightning to the Totonac people of ancient Mexico. Such nonlethal enchantments were a popular item among Magnus Innovations' military clients and the magically gifted members of the facility's security team.

After a moment to catch his breath, Magnus thanked Sage for his quick thinking in incapacitating the panicking volunteer. "Everyone else," he said with a friendly flash of white teeth, "don't let a tiny hiccup like that dampen your mood. What we've accomplished today was extraordinary. Revolutionary. But the work is just beginning. Thank you all!"

The crowd clapped, but with slightly less enthusiasm than had overtaken them a minute earlier. Several members of the medical staff hurried over to Norman, who was groaning softly.

Magnus turned to Ellis, and Meredith slipped closer to listen in. "I hope you can appreciate the significance of what you just saw, Lloyd, despite a little complication there at the end."

"You can fry as many accountants as you'd like, John," Ellis said as he wiped a massive hand over his face. "As long as what I just saw was real, then you've just made some very important people very happy."

"We live to serve here at Magnus Innovations."

"What do you need from us?" Ellis asked.

Kellogg joined them. "Sir, the anima is still functional."

"Excellent. So we can run additional tests?"

"It appears so. Can we get more test subjects?"

Magnus nodded vigorously. "We've no shortage of volunteers."

"I would like some more samples of the donor magic, to help calibrate our approach."

"What does that mean?" Ellis said.

"It means," Magnus replied, "that we need that magician."

Ellis snorted. "The girl from the OMRD?"

"Yes," Magnus said. "That's what we need from you, Lloyd."

"Consider it done."

"Wonderful," Magnus said. "Ah, Meredith, can you escort Mr. Ellis here back to my office? I think he has some international calls to make. He can use my personal telephone."

"Of course, sir," Meredith said, grateful her recording equipment was already in place.

As they turned to go, the medical team pushed past them with a canvas stretcher. Meredith caught a glimpse of Norman's face as they hurried by. His skin was flushed and looked feverish. His glasses were gone. And his eyes, wide open and searching, were milky white and sightless.

THIRTY-ONE

Joaquin drove them to a small farm a few miles outside of Havana. He told them it was owned by a friend, or a cousin, or some other distant relation. He assured them that they didn't speak English and wouldn't ask questions. Loping gray mountains overlooked a wash of lush green trees beyond the carefully lined fields. Pairs of lumbering cows worked the rows ahead of sun-darkened men in straw hats and short-sleeved collared shirts open to their chests. Mottled clouds loitered above it all, threatening rain.

Karen and Pierce settled into a barn a half mile down the dirt road from the farmhouse where Joaquin said they could stay. The building was old, but the straw on the floor inside was dry. It smelled of animals, though they had been relocated for the duration of the Americans' visit. Isabel was gone, off to see if Rabin could help them in their quest. Karen had a feeling he'd be supportive.

"So," Pierce said as he took off his jacket and sat on a yellow hay bale, "you've been busy."

Karen had not yet decided if she was happy to see him. They needed the help, true, but Pierce struck her as the sort of man more interested in preserving the rules than achieving their goal. Still, he had helped her before and might be a valuable ally. "Does Director Whitacre know you're here?"

"Yes and no," Pierce answered. "Officially, I'm on vacation, like you."

"What changed your mind?"

He leaned forward, put his elbows on his knees. He was doing his best to appear comfortable in their rural setting, with limited success. "I wasn't against you, Karen," he said. "I know Magnus is dirty. But if you operate outside of approved channels, you limit your available resources."

Karen raised an eyebrow. "Really?" she asked. "That's your speech? You've had all this time, the flight down to Havana, even the drive out here, and that's the best you can do?"

"Fair enough," Pierce said with a slight smile. "I'll put it this way: I want to take Magnus down, but I'd like to still have a job waiting for me when I'm done."

"Then you'd better get back on a plane," Karen said. "My priority is a bunch of scared children that have been used like lab rats by a monster in a nice suit. If saving them costs me my job, then it wasn't a job worth having."

Pierce laughed. "Your speech was better. But you needn't worry," he added. "The director and I have an understanding. Daniel Pierce is currently enjoying a restful time in sunny Los Angeles. If anything untoward happens to John Magnus in Cuba, well, that can't be my problem, can it?"

"And where is Karen O'Neil?" she asked. "Officially speaking."

"I suspect she's visiting family in Colorado. You do have family in Colorado, don't you?"

"Sure," Karen said. "Why not."

"Good. Now that that is all sorted, can you tell me what on earth is going on down here? I'd like to know how I can help."

What did she really know about Daniel Pierce? He was a

talented inquisitor with a hard reputation. He was committed to
his work at the OMRD, that much was clear. So why would he risk
everything and come to Cuba after abandoning her in Miami?

"Tell me how you found me first."

Pierce chuckled. "What, don't trust me?"

"Should I?"

"Probably not," he said with a sigh. "It was a lonely flight back
to DC without you. Gave me time to evaluate my priorities. You
might not believe me, but I admire what you are trying to do here."

"Just not enough to help me."

"I'm here now, aren't I?"

"Remains to be seen if you're here to help."

"Very well," he said. "After I convinced Director Whitacre that
you might benefit from some support, he reached out to his contacts at the CIA. We hoped they'd know how to get in touch with
Arthur. As it turns out, they had him readily available, in a holding
cell at their compound in Havana."

"Those must be very good contacts," Karen said.

"I'm not at liberty to share any last names with you," Pierce
said. "But let's just say their first names are 'Senator.'"

So there are benefits to being political, Karen thought.

"I was granted the opportunity for a brief—very brief—audience
with Arthur, so I hopped on a flight first thing. Arthur is fine, by
the way, if a little upset at his confinement, but he was able to slip
me the contact information for his good friend Joaquin."

"Without the CIA noticing?"

Pierce chuckled at the memory. "Arthur is a clever old bird, I'll
give him that. And a mean one, when he wants to be. Let's just say
it involved a spilled cup of coffee, a lot of shouting, and a broken
nose. Not mine, thankfully."

"The CIA would have had you followed the moment you left
their site."

"They did try," Pierce said. "But while they might know Havana better than I do, they still tend to stand out in a crowd. Also someone should probably teach them about the many ways to use magic to become inconspicuous."

Karen felt a pang as she remembered Jim and Dennis, back in Berlin. She had no doubt that if they were given the job of tailing Daniel Pierce, they'd have lost him too.

"Joaquin was hesitant about meeting up at first, but I won him over. We drove around a bit, still looking for this La Bruja he said you were after. The man knows a lot of people, and he asked just about all of them about you. But it was going nowhere until we got a sudden and kind invitation from your new Mafia friends."

"They aren't my friends."

Pierce's smile fell. "I'm sorry. I didn't mean . . ." He sighed. "I'm sorry about Gerald, I really am. I wish I could have done more for him, but it was utter chaos in the airport and they were gunning for him. He just caught an unlucky bullet."

Karen almost laughed at Pierce's clumsy attempt to console her. Luckily, she didn't require any eloquent words from him to understand her own grief. She settled into a crook between two bales where she could stare out the barn doors over the fields below. A fleeting memory superimposed the burning sugarcane she'd seen as she fled Magnus's facility across the pastoral landscape ahead of her. She could almost still smell the smoke.

"Alright," she said. "Sounds like you put in enough legwork to get here. Let me tell you why someone needs to put a stop to John Magnus."

She laid out the tale as she had for Isabel, both in what she included and what she left out. Her anger rose as she recounted it again, but there was also a numbing effect to the repetition that she recoiled from immediately. This wasn't just a story to type down in some report or tell to an enraptured audience at an otherwise stuffy dinner party; this was life for those children and their families, the only life they'd ever get. She had a home to fly back to where corporations didn't steal kids off the street to experiment on, because those corporations came here, where willing governments were all too happy to sell their people to a decent bidder. And not without the tacit approval of the US government, considering Lloyd Ellis's arrival at their hotel.

"Well," Pierce said when she was done. "I don't know what to say."

"I'm going to stop him," Karen said, and Pierce was smart enough not to reply.

They sat in rustic, comfortable silence for a while before they heard the sound of a car. A few minutes later, Isabel appeared at the barn door.

"Morris says he'll help," she said.

The objective is Magnus," Karen said.

They had staged a miniature replica of El Paraíso's ballroom on the floor of the barn: traced lines in the dirt marked the outer boundaries; a few sticks demarked the dance floor, the kitchens, and the service corridors; rocks represented the expected security detail; an upturned bucket stood in for the parking garage; and lastly, at Isabel's insistence, a dried piece of cow dung took the place of John Magnus.

"Since he can't bring his own security with him, and hotel security will be told to turn a blind eye," Karen went on, "getting him won't be hard. But we need to get him out without drawing any unwanted attention."

The day had worn long; the sun was nearly set. Rain had come and gone, and come again. Three kerosene lanterns softly hissed and filled the barn with flickering light.

"Who cares if they see us?" Isabel said. "They can't stop us."

"Magnus won't have his goons, but he might have eyes in the crowd," Pierce said.

"And we can't have them follow us," Karen added.

Isabel scoffed. "We don't need to bring him back here. Give me two minutes with that snake, and I'll get him to tell me all his secrets."

"I'm sure you can make him suffer," Karen said. "But I'm not sure you can get him to talk, no matter how many minutes you have. That's why we need to get him off-site, so we can offer a trade."

"Tell me again why we can't blast open the gates to his fancy science facility and burn it all down?" Isabel demanded. "We've got three magicians now, and at least two of us have some talent."

"I can hold my own, don't you worry," Pierce added as he patted the pistol he had tucked in a leather shoulder holster.

Isabel threw up her hands. "Oh, yes, I forgot. An American with a gun can solve every problem."

"We can't just attack them," Karen interrupted. "We don't know how many more of those constructs they have. Even with Pierce, I don't like our odds against those things, do you?"

Isabel made no reply.

"You said that Rabin will summon Magnus to a meeting in his office in the hotel at nine p.m.," Karen said, tapping their crude diagram. "That means he'll be coming out of the elevator here. That's when we make our move."

"And we're certain he'll be alone?" Pierce asked.

"Nothing in life is certain, Daniel," Isabel replied coolly. "If you are afraid, you can stay here and wait for the women to do what must be done."

"So we'll be flexible," Pierce said. "Got it."

Karen drew their attention back to the diagram. "Once we've got him, we'll need to get him to the parking garage."

"Where I will be waiting," Joaquin added. He sat in the relative darkness near the barn door. Karen had been reluctant to include him in their plans, as he had the most to lose if things went awry. But in his quiet way, he had insisted on doing his part.

"Exactly," Karen replied. "To get there, we'll take him down this hallway here and then through these doors. Rabin says they'll be unlocked, but if not . . ."

"We'll be flexible," Pierce said.

Karen smiled. "I think you're getting the hang of it."

They reviewed the details again, and once more, covering the expected variables and possible contingencies until they were all satisfied. It was obvious that everything could fall apart at any number of points, but there was only so much they could account for.

"Do you want to discuss plan B?" Isabel asked as the night stretched on.

Karen rubbed her eyes. "Do you think we need to?"

"As Isabel so kindly pointed out," Pierce said, "nothing in life is certain."

When they'd finished, Joaquin and Pierce found places of relative comfort among the bales on the ground, while Karen and Isabel climbed an ancient ladder to a hayloft. Old wood creaked under them as they lay down on the straw.

"Do you think this will work?" Isabel asked into the darkness when the lanterns had been put out.

"It has to," Karen said. "We'll get her back, Isabel. I promise."

Isabel sighed. Insects buzzed softly outside. Somewhere down the road, a dog barked at shadows. "Don't worry," she said eventually. "I won't hold you to that promise."

It took Karen a long time to fall asleep.

THIRTY-TWO

Meredith straightened Mr. Magnus's black bow tie and offered him a mirror so he could inspect it himself.

"It looks perfect, Meredith," he said. "Thank you."

"Are you sure this is the best time to be attending a formal party, sir?"

"No," Magnus said. "It is a terrible time in fact. But Mr. Rabin was most insistent."

"I trust he was pleased to hear about the tests," she added as she held out his tuxedo jacket for him.

"Oh, yes," he said. "Quite pleased."

"And you didn't tell him about the . . . complications?"

Magnus frowned. The gesture always looked foreign on his face, like he'd never learned how to do it properly. "No," he said. "No use in upsetting anyone, not until we have more information. This is a triumph, for Magnus Innovations and for the world. There are always a few bumps on the road to glory."

There was a knock on the office door. A moment later, Sage entered.

"Good," Magnus said. "I was afraid it was Kellogg with more bad news."

"I saw him on the stairs," Sage said. "He wanted to see you. Told him I'd let you know."

"Oh, what is it now?" Magnus demanded of the heavens. To Sage, he asked, "Have there been any more incidents?"

"Yes, sir," the security chief admitted. "They're having issues with all the new test subjects."

"All of them?"

"I've ordered them confined to the containment units on the second floor."

Magnus sighed. He kept adjusting his lapels, cuffs, and cufflinks but never seemed satisfied with their placement. Finally, he gave up.

"I really must protest again, sir," Sage said. He stood with his feet slightly apart and his hands clasped behind his back, as if he were addressing a general. "I don't trust Mr. Rabin. Let me send some of my men with you."

"As I told you before," Magnus said, "I'll be fine. Besides, it would be unseemly to arrive at such a festive occasion with a small army at my side."

"We could blend in, sir."

Magnus laughed. "With those haircuts? Hardly. You and your men are needed here. Let me handle our criminal friends. You should enjoy your New Year's Eve."

"I'd enjoy it more if I knew you were secure, sir."

Magnus made eye contact with Meredith. "Now I'm getting it from him too. You are all such worriers. I didn't get where I am today by hiding behind armed guards and barbed wire fences." He flashed his patented smile. "I think I can survive one fancy party. And if all goes well, with Morris satisfactorily placated, we might be back in business."

Another knock. This time, it was Kellogg, who had apparently decided it was best not to wait for Mr. Magnus to come downstairs.

"What is it, Duane? I'm about to leave."

The last few days had taken a toll on all of them. Meredith couldn't even remember the last time she'd been home. Most of the researchers were working with only a few hours of sleep between them. Kellogg, whose spirits had been high as a kite after the initial transference tests, looked like he was taking the worst of it.

"Sir," he said in a hollow voice. "I'd like to suspend all new tests for now, at least until we can get a handle on what's going on with the current subjects. I know you wanted us to continue making progress, but now I think it is best for everyone if we slow down a bit here."

"Duane, what's happened to make you so worried? You've been with us a long time, you know these things are never clean right out of the gate. But we have to keep getting back up on that horse."

"I know, sir, but . . ." Kellogg's mouth hung open, but no sound was coming out. Meredith could not be certain if the researcher realized that or not. Finally, he managed to say, "It is getting worse down there."

"The volunteers knew the risks when they signed up," Magnus said. "That's why we offered them all an incentive. They can't expect us to give them something for nothing, can they? Now, you told me you had more calibration to do, maybe give the subjects a little smaller dose of that stuff inside the anima. How's that working out?"

"It isn't, sir. The stored magic isn't responding to our limits."

"Then fix your limits." Magnus put a hand on his shoulder. "I shouldn't have to tell you all this, Duane. This is your job, and you're good at it. We've been in the wilderness awhile on this project, but now is not the time for caution. It's the time for action. Right? Of course." He steered him toward the doors and motioned for Sage to escort him farther. "With any luck, by the stroke of midnight, our friends will come through for us as promised and we'll have our donor available once again, and then you'll be all set. How's that sound?"

He did not wait for Kellogg's reply before closing the door behind him.

A s much as Meredith wanted to get back to her Havana apartment so she could shower, eat, and sleep, those were secondary priorities. Her prolonged stay at the facility had meant she could not safely deliver any news of recent events to her handlers. She had to get it all down on postcards depicting various sandy Cuban beaches before it slipped out of her memory forever.

She trudged up the barely lit stairwell to her apartment door. After glancing down the hallway to make sure she wasn't being observed, she checked the tiny wedge of wood she had placed between the door and the frame: it was still there. Good. She'd never had any reason to suspect her neighbors knew anything about her true mission, but her instructors had always taught her that when you were in the field, only one thing would save your life: caution.

Meredith pushed the door open and was met by musty air. The door caught on a scattered pile of mail that had been shoved through the slot. She stooped and gathered it up, then shut and locked the door behind her. Beyond her thin walls, she could hear the rumblings of New Year's Eve parties all down the street. There would be music, singing, drinking, dancing. And then at midnight, parading in the streets while burning effigies of the previous year. It was a morbid tradition, but Meredith found it amusing to think the past could be disposed of so easily.

She tossed the stack of mail onto her desk next to the bed and retrieved her most recent acquisitions from her purse. She'd never had any trouble smuggling documents out of the Special Projects Laboratory. Maybe it was because she was Mr. Magnus's personal secretary, or maybe it was the way she smiled at the guards at the door. With their infernal dowsing rods, she could only take out documents, for now at least. She knelt beside her bed, felt along the floor for the loose board, and pried it up with her fingernails. The lockbox was waiting inside.

With these final research notes, her collection was nearly complete. Most of Magnus Innovations' inventions were trivial nonsense made to satisfy a lazy capitalist populace, but not everything. Some, especially those with a military application, would be of particular interest to certain magicians back in Moscow. She added the latest to the collection. In the light coming in from a window, she caught a glimpse of the paper's contents and noted the outline of a tall, humanoid figure with a square hole in its chest. Yes, Moscow would find this interesting indeed.

What would the gray-haired man do with an army of monstrous constructs? Or if Magnus ever successfully transferred magic ability, what would the USSR do with such an awesome responsibility? Though they preached redistribution of wealth to the masses, she doubted the Party would be so generous with cosmic magical power.

Once the stolen documents were secure, she set to work on her report. The format and cipher required her to be brief, so she would have to choose her words carefully. She clicked on the lamp over her desk and sat on the hard metal chair. For a moment, she allowed herself a brief indulgence and rested her head in her hands. Her instructors would not have approved, but she was tired; no, she was exhausted. She could sleep all night and still not recover.

Your duty is not to yourself; your duty is to the mission. She knew these words better than she knew her own name; her instructors had made certain of that. It was not a question of whether she believed them to be true. One might as well wonder if gravity were true.

So, slowly and reluctantly, she raised her head. To work.

But as she was about to start transcribing her messages so she could encode them onto the postcards, something in her pile of mail caught her eye. She slid it out from the rest: a postcard from Mount Rushmore National Monument in South Dakota. Her hands trembled as she flipped it over. It was dated from days ago, but she hadn't been here to receive it. It read:

Dearest Meredith,

Your uncle and I had the greatest time. You were missed. We saw 7 mountain goats. We won't be home until 2/13 if you are in need. Please send your love to your cousin in Florida. Hope to see you in the spring.

Yours truly,
Aunt Sally & Uncle Bob

How could she be so stupid? Fully awake now, she grabbed the specified book from her shelf, found the seventh line on the twenty-sixth page, and began the painstaking decoding.

When she'd finished, she sat back, the pen still clutched in her hand. She had a metallic taste in the back of her throat. There was no time for her long-delayed reports, no time for food or sleep. She looked at the clock. There was no time for anything.

Meredith pulled her single piece of luggage from her closet. She shoved a few items of clothing inside, just enough to look convincing. Under the clothes, she placed the documents from the lockbox. It wasn't an especially secure hiding place, but it would have to do. She gathered up the rest of her belongings, the notepad she used for decoding, the books used for the cipher, and the stack of unopened mail, and threw them all into a wire wastebasket. She found matches in the kitchen and struck one against the box and threw it into the wastebasket. It smoked against the paper for a moment, then caught.

She grabbed the suitcase and her purse and locked her apartment behind her. Smoke was already starting to seep under the door. She felt around in her purse until she found her pistol. She hoped she wouldn't need it, but the night was young and she had a great deal to do.

THIRTY-THREE

Spotlights stabbed the sky above El Paraíso. A line of limousines stretched down the street in a slow-moving procession toward the main entrance. Flashbulbs popped wildly as the famous, the wealthy, and the well-connected emerged in silk and ermine. The lesser mortals of Havana watched in muted awe from behind red velvet ropes and the scowling faces of hotel security. Beyond the front doors, the hotel was awash in music and champagne. Party guests laughed and drank and danced in golden chandelier light while tuxedoed waiters kept their glasses full and spirits high.

Karen felt absurd. The invitations Rabin had provided had allowed them easy access past the bruisers at the door, but despite the warm welcome, she had never felt so out of place.

"Relax," Pierce whispered in her ear as he led her into the crowd by his arm. "Haven't you ever been to a swanky party?"

Karen bristled at the question, but was forced to admit, "No, no I haven't. And having now seen one, I wasn't missing anything. It's loud and bright and these shoes are torture." Isabel had been kind enough to loan Karen appropriate attire for blending in at the gala.

The dress, while lovely, left her feeling exposed and frankly cold, despite the fur-lined shawl.

"You can't have a little fun while you're trying to save the world?"

Karen wanted to ask him if he'd be so full of good cheer if his disguise were as drafty as hers, but pressed her lips together instead. He seemed amused by her discomfort, so she wasn't going to give him the satisfaction.

"And what if Magnus recognizes me?"

"Trust me," Pierce said, "you look like a completely new woman in that dress."

He'd probably meant to offer her a compliment; he failed.

The music slowed as the band shifted effortlessly to their next song. The trumpet wailed out a lament over the partygoers' heads as dancing couples began to fill the floor.

"May I have this dance?" Pierce asked with a flourish of his hand.

"Oh," Karen said. "You're serious."

"We have to pass the time somehow," he said. "And we wouldn't want to stand out, would we?"

Karen gave him an unimpressed look, but took his hand. "I'm not much of a dancer," she warned.

"Just follow my lead."

He pulled her into the swaying throng, and they began moving to the steady beat. It took nearly all of Karen's concentration to keep from tripping over her own feet, which kept her from dwelling too long on Pierce's bemused smirk at her efforts.

Pierce squeezed her hand. "No wedding ring, Miss O'Neil? Haven't found the right guy to settle down with?"

"I don't like to settle," she replied icily. "And you? No Mrs. Agent Pierce?"

"Married to the work," he said with a shrug. "I'm guessing you understand."

She did. She didn't want to, but she did. It wasn't like she planned to give up her personal relationships when she joined the OMRD; that hadn't been included in her onboarding paperwork. But she'd never regretted the choice, no matter how many awkward conversations it forced with her mother. And she doubted any husband her mother would have approved of would let her run off to Havana with no warning.

"You know," Pierce said, "your talents are really wasted in research. With your experience, you should join Public Inquiry. There's a lot of bad magic out there that you could help us stop."

"In the director's office, you sang the praises of our research helping you in the field. That's what the OMRD is about, right?"

"And I meant it. But you could do much more if you were working with us directly."

Karen rolled her eyes. "Typical. You inquisitors always think yours is the only work that actually matters."

"We're also not too keen on that name."

"Why do you think the rest of us use it?"

"Fair enough," he said. "But I'm not wrong."

When she'd started with the OMRD, her research had felt like her life's calling, back when she could believe that magic's beneficent possibilities were endless and glorious. Part of her longed for those days again. Ignorance had been simpler.

"If magic is worth anything at all, it has to be used for something more than just stopping bad magic," she said. "Otherwise we're all just wasting our time."

"Let's say you spend the rest of your life in your laboratory, trying to find some spell that could change the world," he said. "What if you don't find it? What if, at the end of your career, all you have to show for it is failed experiments and unanswered questions?"

Karen laughed joylessly. "You really know how to sweet-talk a girl, don't you?" He tried to stammer an apology but she cut him off. "If you had asked me that a few years ago, you'd have hit a nerve. But today, I'm less concerned with unanswered questions than I am with unasked ones."

The song ended and was met with applause. Pierce released her hand and waist and offered her his arm. She took it and they made a silent circuit of the ballroom. A fat Cuban man in a medal-laden military uniform was entertaining a breathless audience of by-standers with bold proclamations and a few obscene gestures. Across from them was a buffet table dressed in its finest linen and arrayed with an endless supply of steaming silver dishes. A clump of arrogant-looking Americans huddled together near the door to blow inexpert mouthfuls of cigar smoke into the night.

"Is it nine o'clock yet?" she asked.

"Patience, my dear. We've still plenty of time to enjoy our-selves," Pierce said, patting her hand on his arm. She considered punching him. Or better yet, driving the heel of her ridiculous shoe into his foot. But then he offered to go and procure them some food from the besieged buffet, so she granted him a stay of execution.

As he slipped into the bustle, Karen was even more uneasy without him by her side. It wasn't just the revealing dress or the unfamiliar social choreography; it was the pressure of so many people. She couldn't feel comfortable around so many voices, so many faces, so many souls, not since Auttenberg. She felt a chill and wished she hadn't had to surrender her shawl at the coat check.

Then she heard it, a voice that cut through the rest of the noise. There, with the fat general with his medals. The fickle crowd had turned their attention away from the martial storyteller and now gave it fully to this newcomer with the spotless tuxedo and flawless smile. John Magnus.

Karen positioned herself just beyond the edge of his vision and scanned the room for Isabel. She was here somewhere, at Rabin's side, patiently waiting for the next phase of their plan, but Karen feared if she saw the man who had kidnapped her sister, La Bruja may decide not to wait before exacting her vengeance. Thankfully, Karen did not see her.

"You look lovely tonight," offered a man nearby with a brief salute of his champagne glass.

"Thank you," Karen said, barely looking in his direction. Another reason to despise parties like this: would-be suitors emboldened by a little drink and a little lipstick, plying their trade on any unaccompanied girl not fast enough to get away. It wasn't until she noted something familiar about his voice that she turned to face him more fully.

"Certainly quite the improvement over our last meeting," the man said with the soft purr of a Spanish accent. He was nearly unrecognizable. Gone were the dirt and the beard and the olive-green fatigues, replaced with carefully oiled hair, a smooth, angular face, and a crisp tuxedo that rivaled Magnus's. "But who am I to speak? Neither of us were in our finest dress."

"Ramón," she said. "I didn't think revolutionaries got invited to parties like this."

"It seems we both are skilled at getting in where we don't belong," he said. "And besides, as you so astutely pointed out last time we met, I am no revolutionary, at least not in Cuba. I am merely an interested observer."

Karen let her eyes flick past him for a moment, looking for Pierce, but he was lost in the mob around the food. Magnus too was missing. Had he been summoned to Rabin's office already?

"And what are you here to observe tonight?" she asked.

Ramón took a sip of his champagne. "You, of course."

Karen tried to keep her smile aloft but knew it was slipping. "And how did you know I would be here?"

"I've taken a special interest."

"I'm flattered."

"As you should be," he replied. "And how are you finding Cuba, Miss O'Neil? Is it everything you hoped for?"

"Cuba is lovely," she said, "though it appears to have imported a few unsavory elements."

Ramón laughed. "I hope that was not directed at me. Cuba has many problems, it is true, but they cannot be laid at our feet. You must look a little closer to home for that. Mr. Magnus, for example. He is a uniquely American cancer."

Karen had a hunch and decided to play it. "So that's why you let me go. Why the rebels didn't chase after us. I've seen what Magnus is really trying to do. If he succeeds, that would be a disaster for the USSR. So you thought I could stop him."

"I am just a humble servant," Ramón said with a slight bow of his head. "I cannot speak for the Soviet Union. If I did in fact intercede on your behalf, then it would have been on purely humanitarian grounds." He deftly placed his empty glass on a passing waiter's tray and snatched up two new ones, passing one to Karen. "Though if you were to ease the suffering of the noble Cuban people by disrupting Mr. Magnus's dangerous capitalistic conspiracy, well, then you would be thanked by compassionate people everywhere, including Moscow."

Where is Pierce? It shouldn't have taken him this long to get back. They needed to be ready when Magnus returned from his meeting, or they'd draw too much attention. Was it time yet? Of course the demands of womanly fashion had precluded her from wearing anything as practical as a watch.

"What I find most fascinating about Cuba," Ramón was saying, "is how it speaks to the future of all nations. It tries to grow in the shadow of the great United States while its government abuses its people and invites in American business to abuse them more efficiently. You can tempt a man with the promise of capitalism's wealth for a time, but when all he finds instead is the lash, he will only work your fields so long. Eventually, someone will remind him that his machete can cut down more than sugarcane."

"I suppose you're the one to do the reminding," Karen said. "And here I thought you were just an observer."

"Indeed I am," he replied. "For example, this very moment I am observing two CIA agents dressed as party guests working their way toward you so they can put an end to your challenge to Magnus."

She stole a glance over her shoulder. There were so many people dancing and flirting and toasting one another, but then she saw them: two young men with no women at their sides, grim despite their fine dress, shoulders facing her yet their eyes looking everywhere but.

Ramón grabbed her arm and pulled her close. "Now tell me, Miss O'Neil," he whispered into her ear, "who is on the side of right and good? The USSR, who set you free? Or the United States, who wants to silence you for the sake of power and profit? Who has Cuba's best interests at heart?"

Karen turned her head toward him. "Let go of me."

He released her arm. "I do wish you luck, Miss O'Neil. I truly do."

As fast as her stupid shoes would allow, Karen moved away from her pursuers and into the noisy crowd. The party sprawled across the entire ground floor of the hotel, so Karen ducked into another ballroom, where a lively band blared upbeat jazz. She needed to find Pierce and Isabel; their carefully laid plans hadn't accounted for the CIA crashing the party.

She stopped a blond man walking past her and asked him for the time.

He gave her a smile he probably imagined was charming but instead was mostly lecherous. "It's not quite midnight yet, sweetheart, but we don't have to wait if you want a kiss right now."

"Ugh, no," Karen said. "I need to know the actual time. Does your watch work, or is it as useless as that wedding ring?"

Dumbfounded, he gaped at her a moment, then checked his watch. "Ten after nine."

"Great," she replied. "Enjoy the party."

She needed to get to the service elevator where they were supposed to intercept Magnus. The others would meet her there, if they were able. And if not, she'd grab Magnus by herself; she wasn't going to leave here without him. There was only one way in and out of the ballroom, so she slowly inched nearer, always keeping a few other guests between her and the exit in case she needed to duck out of sight. Sure enough, just as she was about to make her move, her would-be captors appeared in the doorway, only about fifteen feet away.

"Hell," she muttered under her breath as she turned her face away. She could make herself invisible, or could try, though with all the light sources in this room, it would be tricky. But then she'd be stuck in place, and that wouldn't help her get to Magnus. She could throw the agents across the room or out the giant windows along the front of the hotel, but that too would probably draw just the sort of attention she was trying to avoid. But if she had to choose between causing a scene and being escorted out of the party to some CIA holding facility . . .

"At some point, you are going to have to explain why you are constantly running from every sour-faced man in Havana." The voice came from just behind her and almost made Karen jump out of her skin. She spun to find Sandra Saint smirking at her, one hand on a cocked hip. Her dress shimmered with gold sequins that sparkled with the slightest movement. Her eyes were shadowed in blue, and her bright red lips matched her perfectly polished nails. The room's gravity seemed to be centered on her.

"Sandra, I—" Karen began.

"Not now," Sandra said. "But I think I've more than earned that magic lesson." She gave Karen a playful wink, then gathered her waiting entourage of similarly glamorous beauties and made for the ballroom door. "Gentlemen!" she called out as she approached the CIA agents. All eyes turned as she walked. She was in her native element, a lioness stalking the savanna. "You two are just too handsome to be standing here all alone. I won't have it. I simply won't!"

As the agents struggled to make the appropriate introductions, Karen slipped out beside them, as invisible as any magic might have made her.

And she ran right into the barrel chest of Rabin's driver, the one who had picked her up as she made her escape from the Magnus facility.

"Miss O'Neil," he said. He held out her shawl, retrieved from coat check. "Mr. Rabin would like a word."

The elevator rumbled all the way to the top of El Paraíso. Her escorts said nothing to her, instead just stared straight ahead with their hands crossed in front. When the doors opened this time, the air was far colder than she remembered. Her shawl did little against the whipping wind. She hugged her arms to her chest and stepped out into the night.

Something's wrong. This wasn't the agreement.

Rabin was waiting. She didn't see Isabel. The blazing spotlights danced along the haze behind him as she approached.

"You're missing your party," she said.

"There'll always be another one," Rabin replied. His face was, as ever, unreadable.

Panic prickled the back of her neck. Had her magic recovered enough to help her if this went badly? She glanced over her shoulder; Rabin's men had fanned out behind her. They hadn't done that last time.

"Why am I here, Mr. Rabin?"

It wasn't Rabin who answered. "I asked for you," Magnus said as he appeared smiling from the darkness. The great white shadow of Solomon loomed in his wake. "There's been a change in plans."

THIRTY-FOUR

M r. Magnus," Karen said. "And here I thought I was going to have to track you down. How thoughtful of you to save me the effort. And I see you brought your favorite toy. Should I smash it like I did your others?"

"Oh, I don't think that will be necessary, Miss O'Neil," Magnus said.

"It's no trouble," Karen said. Her magic began to crackle at her fingertips. Then behind her, she heard the unmistakable sound of a half dozen pistols being cocked.

"You're quite talented, no doubt," Magnus said, coming to stand next to Rabin. "But can you really stop all those bullets and Solomon at the same time? I think not. So let's not make this messy."

To Rabin, Karen demanded, "What do you think Isabel is going to do when she finds out what you've done? Make a scene in your fancy restaurant? Throw wine in your face?" She laughed. "I think she'll show you what your entrails look like. Maybe even what they taste like."

"Don't blame him, Miss O'Neil," Magnus said. "I merely explained to our host here that the situation has changed, and it is all thanks to you. I really was starting to wonder if we would ever bring this project to a successful launch, but then you came along. I can't thank you enough for your contribution."

"He's lying," Karen said. Transference was impossible, and even if it weren't, it wasn't going to be discovered by some nonmagical snake oil salesman like John Magnus. "You have no reason to trust him."

"I don't trust anybody," Rabin said finally. "But I like what he's selling."

Rabin's men had closed in around her. When the wind died down, she could hear them breathing. The soft voice of her magic began to whisper again, surprising her; it had been silent since her ordeal at the research facility. *They are going to cage you again. They are going to hurt you,* it said. *You can feel the heat in their blood, the hearts pumping in their chests.* And she could. There were five of them—no, six. Her magic wrapped around them, seeped inside, and she knew in an instant that she could crush their hearts like a vise. They would die gasping before they could fire a single shot. Then she could deal with Solomon, before starting on Magnus and that ignorant fool Rabin.

She rolled this thought around on her tongue for a long moment—too long—before she cast it aside. She wouldn't go without a fight, but if she let her magic free like that, she'd never get it back.

But in that moment of hesitation, she didn't notice the goon coming up behind her until it was too late and she felt the iron collar hang heavily around her neck.

"I had my boys make that one especially for you," he said. "They warned me that pain magic this strong is probably fatal, but then again, they didn't think anyone could break free of the last one like you did."

Karen's skin crawled as the cold metal touched it. The hateful magic was waiting inside the collar, begging her to unleash it. "Do you think I need my magic to stop you, Mr. Magnus?" she asked in a voice icy with rage.

"Enough of this," Rabin snapped. He flicked a hand at his men, and two of them moved away from Karen and flanked Magnus instead. "You've got the girl like you wanted. Now, we're all going to take a little drive to your facility so you can show me the fruit of my many investments."

"Oh, no," Magnus said quickly. "That's simply not possible."

Rabin's eyes narrowed. "You told me you had successfully transferred magic ability."

"And we have, I assure you."

"Then I want to see it. Now."

Magnus started to take a step back, but Rabin's men blocked him. "It's just that the process isn't exactly perfected yet. I wouldn't want you to see the gift before it is wrapped with a bow, that's all."

Rabin sighed. "You don't take me seriously, John."

"Morris, please," Magnus said. Despite her current circumstances, Karen allowed herself a smirk at the fear that colored his voice. "There's no need to be hasty. I just need a little more time. My boys need a little more time. With Miss O'Neil here, we can unlock the rest of the puzzle, I promise. You won't be disappointed."

"Too late for that," Rabin said. He checked his watch. "I'm missing my party. If you need more time, John, take more time."

"Thank you, thank—"

"But you still need something to remind you how to talk to your betters." He nodded to the goon nearest to Magnus. "Break his fingers."

Magnus shouted an ineffectual protest that was cut short by a sickening crack. He fell to his knees. He cradled his hand where his fingers were twisted at an unnatural angle. Karen had to look away.

The next moments were something of a blur. Karen turned back just as Solomon lurched to its master's defense. The construct's huge hands came out of the rooftop shadows and closed around the goon's head. And squeezed.

Bullets began to fly. Solomon did not slow. It brought its fist down on another man's shoulder with a pulverizing thud; he crumpled in a heap. A third tried to run, but the construct was faster, catching the man by the foot. Solomon lifted the man up, then swung him by his leg and smashed him into the ground. Then did it again. And again, until the man dangled limp from its grasp like a broken doll.

"What are you waiting for?" Rabin demanded of his remaining men. "Kill the damn thing!" They leveled their guns and fired, but Solomon did not seem to notice.

"Move," someone growled in Karen's ear. It was Magnus. She felt a pistol pressed into her ribs. He dragged her back toward the service elevator as the remaining goons emptied their guns at Solomon. When they were inside, Magnus shouted a command at the construct, and it came charging through the enemy like a bull, knocking men aside with swipes of its long arms, and then stooped into the elevator. A few final bullets whined off the doors as they slid closed, but Solomon shielded Karen and Magnus with its broad back.

"Do you realize what you've just done?" Karen asked as Magnus mashed the button for the ground floor with his elbow.

"Shut up," he snapped. Pain had stripped away all the smiles and charisma; he looked like a completely different man now, a very troubled one.

"They are going to kill you."

"I said shut up."

"If you tell me where those kids are, maybe I can help—"

"This is all your fault, you stupid girl, and if you think for one second that I won't—"

The elevator had only gone down a single floor, but it was slowing to a stop. "What did you do?" Magnus demanded as the doors popped open. Two people stood on the other side of the doors: Pierce and Isabel. Magnus was about to confront them when Pierce grabbed both Magnus and Karen and then yanked them out of the elevator. Solomon began to unfold its impossibly long arms, but Isabel was faster. She hissed the final words of her spell and there was a strange metallic twang; the elevator jolted and then fell, vanishing into the darkness of the shaft.

"Get this off me," Karen said to Isabel as she pulled on the foul collar. Isabel fingered the metal, spoke a few words to dispel the lock, and unclasped it. Karen slid it into her purse.

Pierce disarmed the prisoner and pushed him against the wall to check for any other surprises hidden in his tuxedo. "Good evening, Mr. Magnus," Pierce said cheerily. "Nice of you to join us."

"And you didn't think we would need plan B," Isabel said to Karen.

Karen was intensely grateful she'd decided to immediately tell Isabel everything about the "deal" with Rabin. She'd finally chosen the right person to trust. "How'd you know he'd betray us?"

"Morris is a good man, but this pig," she said as she kicked Magnus in the leg with her high-heeled shoe, "was offering him the only thing he would call priceless. Morris would kill his own mother for magic." She ran a fingernail across Magnus's cheek, leaving a long red mark. "Tell me," she said, swearing at him exquisitely in Spanish, "where is my sister?"

Magnus clutched his bruise-blackened fingers to his chest and said nothing. Isabel snarled a word Karen did not recognize, and her hand erupted in green fire.

"Isabel," Karen said sharply. "Not here. We don't have time."

Flames and fear danced in Magnus's eyes as Isabel held her hand up to his face. "I won't take long."

"Isabel . . ."

Isabel reluctantly dismissed her magic. "If anything has happened to Graciela," she said to Magnus, "you will beg me to kill you."

"The elevator's out and there's a lot of stairs between here and the bottom," Pierce said as he shoved Magnus toward the stairwell. "I think we'd best get moving."

Karen and Isabel quickly removed their shoes and took to the stairs on bare feet. Pierce followed with Magnus, his gun pressed into the small of Magnus's back. Despite a few setbacks, they still had a chance to pull this off, but only if they weren't caught in the open by Rabin's men. The Mob boss was sure to be on the warpath now. And if the Mob got ahold of Magnus, Karen was certain there wouldn't be enough of the man left to interrogate.

Sweating and winded, they finally reached the ground floor. Joaquin should be waiting for them in the rear garage. They just had to make it through a few service corridors without drawing too much attention. A couple of waiters were visible at the far end of the hallway, but they were too busy balancing huge trays of empty glassware to notice the sudden intrusion of a few bedraggled guests.

"Make a sound," Pierce whispered in Magnus's ear, "and I will put a large hole in your kneecap. Understood? Good. We're ready," he added to Karen with a grin.

They moved as quickly as they dared. They could hear the buzz of the adjacent ballroom and the distant beat of a bass drum through the walls. On the other side, the metallic bustle of the kitchens. Voices everywhere.

"Almost there," Pierce said as the doors to the garage appeared ahead.

Just before they reached them, a side door swung open. A few men hurried into the corridor and then through another door that led into the ballroom. They weren't dressed like waiters or partygoers, but rather in drab olive green. More came through a moment later, eyes down, carrying a large canvas sack. The last to disappear into the ballroom was smaller than the rest, slight of figure, with long black hair tied up under a cloth hat. And a pink scar on her face.

Karen stopped. "Isabel . . ."

"I saw her," Isabel said. Her voice sounded hollow. *Elisa.*

"What is she doing?"

Isabel's mouth drew tight. "Something very stupid."

Karen grabbed Isabel's arm as the Yoruba magician made to follow Elisa into the ballroom. "Isabel, we have to get Magnus out of here."

"No one tells me how many of my children I am allowed to save," Isabel said, pulling her arm away. Without another word, she ran after Elisa.

"Get him to the car," Karen said to Pierce, pointing to the garage. She ignored his quizzical look and made for the ballroom door. Elisa had saved her from the rebels, even if Ramón had helped. Karen couldn't just leave her and Isabel behind. As the door opened, sound and heat washed over them as the partiers carried on laughing and dancing, oblivious to the rooftop gunfire or the crushed elevator.

"Do you see—" Karen started to ask, but never got to finish, not before a massive explosion filled the ballroom with fire and chaos.

THIRTY-FIVE

Even this late, the Magnus Special Projects Laboratory shone like a lighthouse against the black backdrop of the ocean as Meredith drove into the secure parking lot. Magnus had his teams working around the clock now, first to clean up after Karen's escape, then to capitalize on the breakthrough her magic allowed, and finally to stop everything from unraveling before their eyes when those breakthroughs proved too radical. They didn't realize something even worse was about to arrive.

Of course, neither did Meredith until it was almost too late. She cursed herself under her breath as she slammed her car door and started toward the main entrance. It had been a spectacular failure of mission protocol that had almost cost her everything. As it was, she had a couple of hours, maybe less. The bombs might already be going off in Havana.

"Welcome back," the guard at the door said with a smirk as she entered. "Forget something?"

Meredith smiled back. The gesture took some effort. "I was just about to enjoy my evening when the boss called," she said, rolling her eyes dramatically. "Suddenly he needs half a dozen things that can't wait for the New Year."

"Tell me about it. We're pulling double shifts, on a holiday no less," the guard said, shaking his head. He pointed at the leather briefcase in Meredith's hand. "That for the boss?"

She held it up. "One of his many," she said. "I think he bought one in every color."

"Probably costs more than we make in a year."

"You don't even want to know," she said. "I'd rather lose an arm than get a scratch on it." Meredith glanced down the darkened hallways. "Big crowd on-site tonight?"

"Bunch of white coats in the Transference lab," the guard said. "Some colossal mess up there, I hear. A few still on cleanup duty."

"And security?" she asked innocently.

"Sage let a few of us go and celebrate," the guard said, annoyed. "But I drew the short straw, so here I am, making sure nothing weird gets up and wanders out of the facility."

"Is Sage celebrating?"

"No way," said the guard. "He's around here somewhere, cracking skulls if anyone dozes off or spends too long taking a piss." He suddenly remembered who he was talking to and stammered an apology for his crassness. Meredith smiled and touched the man's hand gently and told him to think nothing of it. The man blushed. Even when you are on a tight schedule, it always pays to keep the security detail on your side.

She left the guard and started up the stairs. The disaster brewing in the Transference labs would be helpful, as it would draw attention away from the rest of the facility. With any luck, they wouldn't know what she'd done until it was too late, if even then. Soon, they'd have much bigger problems to deal with than Mr. Magnus's missing secretary.

It only took her a few minutes to remove the recording devices from Magnus's office. She doubted they'd find much in the ashes after tonight was over, but she wasn't going to take any chances.

Besides, the recent tapes she'd made were worth every miserable day in this humid prison. She set the briefcase down on Magnus's desk and clicked it open. The interior had been specially designed for this extraction; there were compartments for the tapes and the recording equipment, along with five square cutouts waiting to be filled. She quickly fitted the equipment into place and snapped it shut.

Meredith took one last look around the office: marble, gold, crystal. Expensive, tasteless artwork on the walls. She paused a moment in front of the huge windows overlooking the sea. From here, she could see the small pier Magnus had insisted upon installing, with his silver-white yacht moored at the end. Such vile opulence. Magnus deserved everything that was coming to him. Yes, the reckoning was finally here; she exhaled a deep sigh of relief, perhaps the first and only peaceful breath she'd had since arriving in Cuba.

Not long now.

Back down on the second floor, she could hear the flurry of activity going on in the makeshift Transference lab. Someone was shouting; Meredith couldn't make out the words. She moved briskly past and wished her shoes could be quieter on the tile floor. She wasn't important enough to draw too much attention, but she didn't have time for questions. But just as she was about to turn the corner, a door swung open in front of her and she stumbled back.

"Oh, I didn't see you." It was Duane Kellogg. Gray stubble covered his sallow cheeks, and his voice was flat.

"How are the tests going?" she asked gently.

"Oh, it's . . ." He sighed. "It's a nightmare."

A muffled scream came through the walls from somewhere nearby. Kellogg didn't even seem to notice.

"It was all just too fast." His glassy eyes stared right through her. "If we had just had more time to prepare, do more analysis, study the results, maybe we could have . . ." He didn't seem to have the strength to finish.

She was about to leave him to his demons when he looked up suddenly. "Is Mr. Magnus back? Does he have the magician?"

"No," Meredith said apologetically. "But I'm sure he'll return soon."

"Yes," Kellogg said, deflating. "I'm sure he will."

Another scream filled the hallway, followed by more shouting. "I'll let you return to your work," Meredith said. Kellogg nodded and seemed to immediately forget she was there. She left him and hurried along the corridor to the Containment storage room.

Ignoring the overhead lighting, she switched on a lamp at a single workstation, then froze as she heard voices outside in the hallway. A moment later, they faded. She found what she was looking for on the far side of the room: a massive black chest reinforced with steel and locked with a padlock the size of her fist. It had taken her months to figure out where the keys were kept, then another two weeks to find out which facility personnel had the necessary access. In the end, getting a copy of the key had been disappointingly simple; the threat of Mr. Magnus's displeasure had proven a powerful motivator for the overworked and underpaid staff. She took out the key and slid it into the lock. A perfect fit.

Meredith unhooked the padlock and tossed it aside. She set her briefcase down beside the chest and clicked it open. The lid on the chest was heavy, but eventually she managed to lift it. Her objective lay inside: five black animas, three of which pulsed softly with stored magic. Two were dark, unfilled.

"You shouldn't be here."

She spun at the voice. Alexander Sage stood in the doorway. Like a fool, she'd turned her back too long and hadn't heard him come in.

"You startled me," she said, a hand pressed dramatically to her heart. "I was just—"

Sage took a step toward her. "You shouldn't be here. This is a restricted area."

"Well, Mr. Sage, as I was trying to explain—"

The security chief lifted his hand; he was holding one of those Aktzin totems the security teams used to incapacitate troublemakers. His face was blank: no anger, no pleasure, just the dead-eyed resolve of a man who would do his duty without flinching.

"Wait just a minute," Meredith said, her tone sharpening. She was Mr. Magnus's private secretary, after all, not some common criminal. "You can't just barge in here and point that thing at me." She raised one hand toward Sage, while the other inched slowly toward her open briefcase. "You could hurt someone."

"Don't move," he commanded as his eyes switched meaningfully to her briefcase. He took another step and kept the totem high. "If you move even one—"

Meredith did not give him a chance to finish. She dove to the desk with the lamp and yanked the cord from the wall, plunging the room into near-complete darkness. A moment later, a burst of hot white light blasted into the back wall as Sage summoned the totem's magic. Meredith felt the lightning crackle on her skin as she dove out of the way and ducked behind a table.

"I've had my eye on you," Sage said into the dark. "I knew something was wrong here. Reports getting misfiled, keys going missing. And who could move around this facility completely unnoticed?"

He was moving, hunting. She couldn't see him, but his voice gave him away. He'd positioned himself between her and the briefcase, where her pistol was hidden. In a moment, he'd realize he could call for help and she'd be finished. But a moment was all she needed, and her pistol wasn't her only weapon.

"Who do you work for?" His boots squeaked on the floor. "The Commies? Those mobsters Magnus thinks are his friends?"

She slipped off her shoes; bare feet would be faster, quieter. Then she felt along the hem of her skirt for the slightly loosened threads. As she pulled them out, she retrieved the long, thin needle that had been hidden there and very carefully removed the protective sheath.

"Doesn't matter," Sage said. He was coming closer. "Whoever it is, they'll never find you. Not after we're done with you. Not after we—"

Meredith moved in behind him and drove the needle straight into his neck. He shouted in pain and spun around, sending another bolt of lightning across the room. Beakers shattered and the wall smoldered, but Meredith had already moved out of the way.

The light, however, had revealed her location; Sage came at her hard and fast. She dodged, but a fist connected with her shoulder and knocked her back into a hard table. Sage swung again, a glancing blow on her skull. This time she dropped to the ground and rolled under the table, out of his blind reach.

"What is . . . ?" She heard Sage slapping at his neck. His breathing was already rasping. He tried to call out for help, but his voice was gone. He knocked over a chair as he fell.

Meredith approached carefully. As he wheezed, she pried the totem from his hand and tossed it aside.

"Don't worry," she whispered. "The poison is quick. It'll be over soon."

"N . . . no," Sage managed to say, but then his muscles began to seize up and his jaw clenched shut. Tremors kicked the heels of his boots against the tile floor.

"You shouldn't be too hard on yourself," she said as she stood. "Everyone in this building will be dead soon anyway. You're just going a little early."

Meredith ignored Sage's final sounds. Instead she found another light and returned to the chest. The cubes waited.

With her objective secure, she locked her briefcase and recovered her painful high-heeled shoes. Sage gave a soft moan from somewhere in the back of the room. Meredith turned off the light, crossed to the door, and left him in the dark.

She started for the stairs that led to the lower basement. Only one last thing to do.

THIRTY-SIX

The grand ballroom at El Paraíso burned. Smoke and screaming replaced music and dancing. Well-dressed bodies were strewn across the floor like rubble. One wall, near the buffet, was gone, replaced by a shattered hole. Another was engulfed in flames. The glass windows had exploded outward. The doors had been blown off their hinges. And somewhere out front, over the cries and shouts, Karen heard the insistent tap of machine-gun fire.

She pushed herself up to her knees. The blast had knocked her down; she didn't see Isabel anywhere. Her head throbbed inside and out. When she touched a hand to her scalp, it came away smeared with blood.

As she got to her feet, one voice cut through the din: a primal scream. Isabel's.

Karen found her near the black crater the bomb had left in the dance floor. In her arms, she held the ruined form of Elisa.

"You stupid, stupid girl," Isabel was saying as she held Elisa's head to her chest. Tears ran down her cheeks and mixed with sweat and blood. Elisa's eyes were still open, though her eyelids fluttered and her breaths came in short, agonizing gasps. Her clothes were torn and dark with blood; underneath, Karen could see scorched and gashed flesh.

"It went . . . off . . . too soon . . . ," Elisa managed to say as her body spasmed.

Karen looked around for signs of Elisa's coconspirators, but the ballroom was mostly empty now, except for the wounded. The other rebels either had been too close to the explosion or had already run off to continue the spread of terror. The gunfire outside had only gotten worse.

"This is revolution?" Isabel demanded. She spoke into Elisa's dark hair, but really to no one. She had a handful of Elisa's tattered clothes in each fist. "This is what is supposed to save Cuba? No. To hell with all of them."

Karen knelt beside them and felt the girl's pulse: weak, fading. Isabel was imploring her in English, Spanish, and some other language. Elisa tried to stay awake, tried to respond, but each time, the effort drained what little reserves she had left. Soon even Isabel's voice had little effect.

They never should have let her go back to the rebels. If she had stayed at the orphanage, none of this would have happened. If only . . . But Karen knew these thoughts were worthless. She hadn't known Elisa well, but she doubted the headstrong girl who'd plucked her from the rebel camp could have been contained, even by Isabel. Young as she was—too young for a fate like this—she was ready to find her own way, carve her own life out of what the world had given her. And besides, it was too late now for whatever they might have done.

Isabel had told Karen that magic was power, but what good was any of it in a moment like this? *If you want to heal someone, call a doctor; you want to kill someone, call a magician.* That's how the old saying went. But Karen knew it wasn't as simple as that. She'd saved Jim in Berlin, closed his wounds with sheer force of will. It was a moment she'd dreamed about all her life: proving magic was more than a weapon. But when Jim was dying, she had all the power beyond the breach to draw on. Limitless magical energy. Even if she could focus her magic on Elisa's broken body, she'd never have enough power on her own to . . .

"Isabel," Karen said, grabbing her shoulder. Isabel refused to look at her. "Isabel, listen to me. I might be able to save her."

Tear-hot eyes snapped up. "Do not play games with me."

"I'm serious." Karen looked back toward the door they'd entered through. It was a mess, but they could still get through. "I need you to get to Joaquin's car, in the garage."

"I'm not leaving her."

"Isabel, listen to me." Karen pulled her away from Elisa. "This is her only chance. I need my satchel. Go, now!"

Isabel glared at Karen, then looked at the dying girl. She was up in an instant, sprinting across the ballroom on bare feet that ignored the fire and rubble. A moment later, she disappeared into the service corridor.

Stay with me. Karen picked up Elisa's hand and squeezed. The girl's eyes were just slits now. *Fight for it, Elisa.*

Karen exhaled. The chaos around her dimmed. She focused only on Elisa's faint pulse and the nearly inaudible breath that struggled past her dry lips. She remembered Jim in a similar state: the blood blossoming on his shirtfront, the terror of death in his eyes. And the magic that had saved him. She called on that now, the trapped-up power that she'd hidden away inside, the untrustworthy whisper that haunted her, the weapon she'd wielded without thought at the expense of many.

You're going to kill her. The voice of her doubts was never far. *And the others too. Like that poor man in the bookstore, like the researchers in the lab, like Maria. You couldn't save them; you can't save her.*

Her magic wrapped around Elisa like a bandage. Karen could

feel the unnatural rawness of her wounds, the wrongness of cracked bone. And in the deep distance, she could sense Elisa's spark of life receding; there was barely any glow left. Karen reached for it, blew into it, tried to draw heat from cold embers. But for all her magic's fierce potency, it was nothing against such damage. Flesh stayed torn, body unmended.

Then Isabel was there, clutching Karen's battered leather satchel. "Is she . . . ?"

"Not yet." Karen pulled the bag open and found what she was looking for: a soft velvet pouch, tied up with a string. She untied it and dumped the black anima into the palm of her hand.

"What is that for?"

She remembered how to do it, how it felt to draw together flesh and skin; it was the sort of feeling that stuck with you. But she couldn't do it alone. She needed to draw on something else, something immensely strong. Something like a soul. "Power," Karen said.

I'm sorry, Maria, but I hope you understand.

The cube gleamed. The flames reflected orange and gold on its surface. Such a small thing, but full of so much power. With her magic still around Elisa, Karen plunged into the anima. It was like diving into the ocean—no, like leaping into the endless sky. Karen's magic surged. It came so strong and so quickly that she almost lost control of it; how can you direct the flow of a tidal wave?

In her mind she saw the streets of Auttenberg, felt them break beneath the weight of her passing, heard the endless void beyond the breach calling to her. Something waited for her there, out of reach, out of sight. Something unspeakable. These were just memories, but didn't have to be. With the energy she drew from the anima, she could reach out and tear open the veil between worlds and feast on unimaginable power. It would be so easy . . .

But that was not all Karen saw. She also saw a fearless girl releasing her from her rebel captors. She saw moonlight in that girl's eyes as she ranted about Communism and disgusting men. And she saw brightly colored candies wrapped in paper.

Elisa stirred. Karen did not dare to look down, not until the work was done. She focused everything she had, everything Maria gave to her. All other voices and unwelcome memories, she shoved aside. *Will it be enough?* The anima burned like a flare in her hand, but she ignored the pain as well. *Focus.* That was all that mattered. *Focus on Elisa.*

It was Isabel's gasp that finally broke Karen's concentration, but by then, it was done. Every muscle in Elisa's body tensed and she gulped for air like she'd been drowning. She curled up around herself, held her arms to her chest, and cried. Isabel wrapped her up and buried her face in the girl's neck.

Karen sat back. It had worked. Somehow, she'd pulled her back together. Her clothes were still tattered, but the skin underneath was unmarred. Even the scar on her face had faded. The ballroom still burned—the air was still thick with smoke—but the disaster was not complete. All around, she could hear cries of others wounded, could see blood on tuxedo lapels and sequins. Maybe she should have used her power on one of them, someone who hadn't come to this place with men with violent hearts and a bomb that went off too early. But there was no time to dwell on that now, not with Isabel and Elisa sobbing in each other's arms.

Thank you, Maria, Karen thought. The anima had gone dark, full dark. The last whisper of Maria's magic had gone out. *You didn't deserve this, but thank you.*

"Isabel," Karen said. "We need to get Magnus out of here." But then Pierce was in front of her. His crisp white shirt was dark with soot and his face dotted with red gashes.

"Karen, can you hear me?" he was saying, though it took a long time for the sounds to become words in her head.

"What . . . what is it?"

"We have to go, now."

Karen's stomach lurched. "Where's Magnus?"

"The explosion collapsed the wall. I got knocked off my feet and . . ."

Isabel noticed Pierce then. "What happened? Where is he?"

"He escaped," Pierce said. There was an unexpected fury in his eyes. "The rebels are killing people out there. We need to go."

"They can burn this whole island down," Isabel said, "but I'm not letting Magnus escape. Not until he tells me where my sister is."

"If a revolution has begun," Karen said over the echo of gunfire, "there's only one place Magnus will go to be safe. We've got to get to our car."

The service elevator was a smoking ruin of bent metal. Its impact had sent the heavy steel doors of the hotel basement flying. No one was there to see the damage; the lavish gala upstairs had drawn all personnel away. In fact, over the roar of the guests and the thrum of the music—and the chaos that came next—the ill-fated elevator was not even noticed.

Nothing moved inside the smashed prison of impossible angles and twisted metal. Of course, nothing could have survived such a fall. Nothing natural at least. Sparks crackled from severed wires. A small fire had started, using whatever it could find for fuel.

And then the rubble began to shift as a great pale hand pushed its way free.

THIRTY-SEVEN

They drove through Havana's burning streets as fast as Joaquin dared go. Military trucks were already descending upon the city; soldiers ran down deserted sidewalks, rifles high. More explosions rocked the city as revolution ignited. Even with the windows up, the air smelled of gunpowder.

Karen and Isabel changed out of their once-glamorous dresses in the back of the car. They did not know what would await them at the Magnus Special Projects Laboratory, but knew they'd best be prepared for a fight. Their only hope was that they could reach the facility before Magnus had too much time to mount a defense. If he slipped through their fingers again, there wouldn't be another chance, not with columns of smoke rising over Havana.

Isabel had refused to let Elisa go, and the girl did not argue. She huddled in her seat, her knees pulled up to her chest, uncharacteristically silent. Karen doubted her dreams of a new Cuba had included being torn apart by a faulty bomb.

Then they saw the facility at the end of the dirt road. Lights were on in nearly every window, despite the late hour. When they neared, Pierce directed Joaquin to pull off the road and switch off the headlights. They rumbled to a stop, hidden from view.

"We need the element of surprise," he explained.

"I think we lost that when we nabbed him off that elevator," Karen said.

"So we should just kick in his front door and explain to his security team that we just want a nice chat with the boss?"

"Yes," Isabel said. "Enough waiting."

Pierce turned around from the front seat. Karen could see the lines on his face in the silver moonlight. "We've got one gun and some magic. Based on what Karen saw when she was a guest here, they've got an army. At best, we're hoping half of them are off getting drunk for New Year's, but somehow, I doubt it. That still leaves half an army against three of us."

"Do you have a plan besides talking?" Isabel demanded.

A yellow burst of headlights filled the road they had just abandoned. Three black sedans hurtled past, kicking up dust and gravel in their wake. The cars drove right up to the main entrance and parked in a line in front of the big glass doors.

"It's Morris," Isabel whispered.

Men in dark suits poured out of the cars, armed with rifles and shotguns. A Magnus security guard came out to greet them, a hand cautiously on the pistol at his hip. He didn't make it five feet before the shooting started.

"What are they doing?"

"Taking what they're owed," Isabel said, "before they lose their free rein in Cuba."

Morris Rabin stepped out of the third car. He wasn't armed, but he didn't need to be; two goons with sleek machine guns immediately fell into line beside him. He buttoned his jacket, stepped over the murdered guard, and followed his men into the facility.

"If they get to Magnus first, they'll kill him," Karen said.

"Eventually," Isabel added.

"If he dies, we may never find those kids."

"We still need a plan," Pierce said.

Isabel threw open her door. She said something soft to Elisa, then stepped out. "You can talk. But I'm going to save my sister." Joaquin spoke in Spanish and Isabel thanked him. He would stay and keep Elisa safe.

Pierce looked to Karen as she made to follow Isabel. His face was grim. "Karen . . ."

"What do you want me to say?" she demanded.

"There's probably another way," he said. "Magnus dies, fine. I won't miss him. But we don't have to go in there and risk everything on the hope that he'll be kind enough to tell us where those kids are."

Karen stared at the imposing building. She hadn't forgotten her last visit. She hadn't forgotten what they were risking by returning. "Yes," she said, "we do."

They caught up with Isabel as she was about to enter. The front doors were shattered; broken glass popped under their feet like peanut shells. The shooting continued unabated inside: the tap of rifles, the pop of pistols, the boom of shotguns.

"Where do you think Magnus has run off to?" Isabel asked.

Karen shook her head. "I didn't get much of an official tour." The inside foyer was empty, save for a few bullet-ridden bodies sprawled out on the polished floor. Posters lined the walls, warning about intruders, spies, and Communists. They didn't say anything about vengeful mobsters. "But if I were a rich coward like Magnus, my office would be at the very top."

The mobsters seemed to have the same idea; the path to the main stairwell was strewn with bullet holes and dead Magnus security guards. They moved slowly, careful not to get caught in the crossfire. Pierce had one hand on his locus, the other on his pistol. Isabel fingered the beads at her neck. And Karen teased out the magic she feared but knew she would need.

As they reached the stairs, they heard someone running with the unmistakable clack of high heels. A moment later, Magnus's blond secretary came charging toward them, clutching a leather briefcase. Her perfect hair was a mess, her makeup askew, and there was blood on her blouse. Surprised by the sudden appearance of Karen and her companions, she nearly fell until Pierce caught her.

"It's alright," Pierce said as he helped her back upright. "You're safe now. We're the good guys."

Karen didn't have time to warn him. Meredith grabbed his wrist and wrenched his gun from his grasp. Pierce gave a shout of pain but could only stare dumbfounded as the cold-eyed secretary pointed his own pistol in his face.

"Thanks," Meredith said. "I feel very safe now."

"Awfully late to be at work," Karen said.

"No rest for the wicked," Meredith replied as she switched the gun between the three of them.

"Interesting night," Karen said.

"You don't know the half of it," Meredith said.

Karen nodded to the briefcase. "That doesn't match your outfit."

"Get out of my way."

Karen breathed out. And then the pistol was in her hand. Meredith looked at her empty fingers, then to Karen, and then laughed. It was a brittle sound. "You know, I've always hated magic."

"Let's see what's in the briefcase."

"I don't think so," Meredith said. "I think you've got enough to worry about without bothering yourselves with me." Punctuating her words, sounds of gunfire and screams echoed down the stairwell.

"If you think I'm going to let you—"

Meredith gave an exasperated sigh, as though she were a teacher dealing with disobedient pupils. "You're here to find out where those kids are, right? If you let me go, I'll tell you where they're keeping them."

That stopped Karen cold. "You told me before that only Magnus knew."

"I lied."

"How am I supposed to—"

"Karen," Meredith said, "we don't have a lot of time. Let me walk out that door and I'll tell you where to find the address. Don't, and you can try your luck with Magnus."

Karen looked to Isabel, who said nothing, but her opinion was written clearly in the anguish that drew her lips tight and dug lines around her eyes.

"Fine. Tell me."

Meredith pointed up. "Magnus's office. Top floor, on the right. Big doors, can't miss it. You'll see my desk inside. In my Rolodex, look under the name Lincoln. You'll find the kids there."

"What?" Isabel demanded. "Forget all that. Tell us now."

"I don't remember," Meredith said. "And besides, I don't need you following me. Now, a deal's a deal. Let me go."

She could see that Isabel wanted to object, but Karen had lost interest in stopping the spy. That's not why they'd come. "Get out of here," Karen said. "Now."

"A pleasure," Meredith said. "If it were me, I would hurry. I don't think this place is going to survive the night. Oh, and a bit of advice: don't poke around on the second floor."

They mounted the stairs as more bullets flew overhead. When they reached the second floor, they saw the source of the noise: an intense gunfight had broken out between the Magnus security team and Rabin's mobsters. Some of the goons were facedown on the stairwell, but the security guards seemed to be losing ground. Ricochets whined all around them.

"We'll find another way!" Karen said, running to a door. The others followed as a shotgun blast smacked the wall just beside them.

They hurried along the corridor away from the carnage. It was empty and quiet save for the echoes of conflict behind them and a muted hum coming from somewhere nearby. There had to be another stairwell or an elevator they could use to get around the battle lines. If Meredith had told the truth—which Karen doubted—they didn't even need Magnus to cooperate. They just needed to get to his office without getting shot by one faction or the other.

Karen was so intent on finding another path upward that it took her a long moment to realize the hum they were hearing was in fact a scream.

"What is that?" Pierce asked.

"It doesn't matter," Isabel said. "We have to get upstairs."

But Karen had stopped, her hand pressed to her head, which had just started to ache. Something was wrong here, something she couldn't identify. It gripped her, dull and foul, like a rotting tooth. And whatever it was, it was familiar.

"Karen," Isabel said, "we have to keep going."

"Those goons could storm in here at any moment," Pierce added.

Karen was barely listening. It was close. Just beyond these walls. Waiting for her. No, calling for her. The voice was clear now, louder than the guns or the screaming or the concerns of her companions. She knew it; of course she knew it. It had whispered to her every day of her life. It had shouted at her in Auttenberg. She opened the door to the lab and stepped into hell.

It was a large room, with cabinets and tables along the walls and a great emptied expanse in the middle. It looked much like the lab that they had kept her in when they drained her magic, and probably like a dozen others in the facility. Interchangeable.

Or, at least, it had been. Now half of the room had been cordoned off by a flickering magical barrier, not unlike the Wall that had once divided Berlin. Intricate runes had been hastily carved into the floor; chalk writing apparently hadn't been permanent enough. The overhead lights were dim or dark. The room smelled of smoke and sweat, and some of the tile floor was badly scorched. In one corner, there was a dark puddle that looked frighteningly like blood. Nearby, a sheet had been draped over what appeared to be a prone body. Several of the tall cabinets had been smashed, as if something of immense size had fallen into them. Broken glass was scattered on the floor, but no one seemed to notice. A knot of haggard men in white coats huddled around a table piled with yellowed scrolls, leather-bound tomes, and three-ring binders. They looked up dumbly as Karen entered, too exhausted to be terrified.

But Karen ignored the researchers. Instead her eyes were fixed on what lay beyond the barrier they'd erected. She approached with measured steps, hoping she was wrong about what she saw.

"What have you done?" she asked when she neared it.

There were ten or so people on the other side. A few were older, some young. Mostly men, but there were a couple of women in cotton skirts and colorful blouses. They all stood apart from one another, barely moving, like a garden of lifelike statues, all carved into poses of utter agony.

One man was near the barrier. He was sitting with his back to Karen. He'd tossed aside his jacket and tie, but otherwise was dressed like any other man going to work: white collared shirt, brown slacks, scuffed leather shoes. Karen knelt. She thought she could hear the man weeping. She put her hand on the barrier; the magic crackled like dry leaves. The man turned slowly around. His sightless eyes searched in vain for her: wide, frantic, pleading. His mouth hung open absently, like his jaw could no longer be bothered to stay shut. His voice rasped, torn raw by endless screaming.

But it was his skin that made Karen sick to her stomach. Bloodless gashes crisscrossed his ruined face and hands like a cracked oil painting. At first, she thought he might have done it to himself, and looked for signs of a weapon, but then she realized he hadn't been cut; the wounds were created from within, as something forced its way to the surface. A darkness lay within the gashes; not exposed muscle, but a black empty void that mocked life, defied existence.

A void Karen had seen once before, beyond the breach in Auttenberg.

"Please . . . ," the man whispered with a broken voice, "let me die."

THIRTY-EIGHT

The other subjects-turned-prisoners were in the same dire state: bodies bursting with stolen, wild magic. The Magnus magicians had done the impossible; they'd actually transferred her magic into others. But the test subjects weren't ready. If she could barely hold her magic at bay, how could they expect those born without the gift to do any better? But this was far worse than she could have ever imagined. They hadn't just inflicted magic they couldn't control on these poor people; they'd opened the path to oblivion, the ravenous nothingness from whence all magic came.

The test subjects started to turn toward her, pulled from whatever communal reverie they'd been experiencing. They called out to her, some begging, some angry. They wanted to be released, or to call their families, or just for the pain to stop.

A portly man with a graying tonsure of hair threw himself at the barrier, only to be knocked back with a loud bang by the impact. He struggled to his feet. The horrible gashes bisected his face and snaked across his body. He screamed and lunged again. And again.

"Karen," Pierce said from the doorway. "We have to go."

"No," she replied without taking her eyes from the researchers. "If we don't stop this, saving those kids won't matter. Nothing will."

One of the researchers, ostensibly the leader of the shell-shocked group, elbowed his way to the front to stare at Karen. "It's you," he said softly. He pointed at the woeful test subjects. "This is your magic. Please, tell us how to stop it."

"What did you do to these people?" Karen demanded.

The man stammered for a moment, but eventually was able to force himself to form coherent sentences. "We've been trying to transfer magical ability into a nonmagical host for months now. It never worked. I was starting to believe that it wasn't possible, until . . ."

"Until you stole magic from me," Karen finished.

The man, whose stained white coat was embroidered with the name Kellogg, nodded. "But it wasn't only your magic. We had a breakthrough. Well, of a sort. We found some notes from one of our magicians who recently left. At first, they seemed odd, not like any other incantations I've seen, but we dug deeper and then we saw the genius behind them. That is what we used to transfer your magic."

Karen's skin was cold. "Show me."

The researchers scrambled to find what she requested. They were long past the point where they would challenge her authority. She could see it in their hollow eyes: they'd watched people die in this room and were afraid they were next.

Kellogg thrust a handful of pages at her. They were filled with a steady scrawl. Words in four—no, five—languages, plus diagrams that followed no obvious structure or school of magical instruction Karen was familiar with. And yet, Karen knew exactly where these pages had been copied from.

Gerald's note to her had said: *You have no reason to help me, not after what I've done. I should never have taken it.* Karen hadn't understood and hadn't had a chance to ask him what he meant. When he left the OMRD, he had seemed somewhat ashamed, but she'd believed he felt bad about leaving her with their research unfinished. But now she realized it was something else. The pages Kellogg handed her were in Gerald's handwriting; after seeing it on so many lab reports, she'd know it anywhere. But the words, the images, the spells, she knew them all intimately. Because she had written them.

Concerning that which must never come to pass . . .

She kept the book secure in her satchel now, but hadn't always been so careful. For a time, it sat in an unlocked drawer in her desk at the OMRD. She didn't even know how long it sat there, as she had little memory of ever writing it in those fevered months after Auttenberg. But apparently it had been there long enough to draw the attention of her curious colleague, who had copied down some of the inexplicable magic for later reference. And now here it was, staring back at her like an epitaph.

"Is that . . . gunfire?" Kellogg asked absently as the sounds of battle drifted into the lab.

"Forget about that." Karen held up Gerald's notes. "This is the spell you cast to transfer the magic?"

"We had to make some changes, but it provided the framework."

An inhuman roar snapped their attention back to the contained test subjects. The man who had been throwing himself at the barrier was on his knees, head in hands. Darkness was pouring out of the tears in his body; his flesh could no longer hold back the tide. The others recoiled from him as even his voice was consumed by the expanding void. The magic seethed like heat; Karen could feel it even through the barrier. The ground beneath him buckled. The barrier wavered.

Karen pulled open her satchel. She'd never even considered using the magic in the book; this magic wasn't meant to be wielded by sane hands. The book was a morbid test: How depraved was mankind truly? Enough to destroy everything in the pursuit of power? Twice over now, she had her answer. But she knew the words in the book, and she knew they—like all magic—could be bent to the will of the caster.

She flipped open the book and found the pages Gerald had copied. It was all there, if you had eyes to see. If they used these spells to create this nightmare, maybe she could use them to undo it.

"What is that?" Kellogg asked, trying to look into the book.

"Get out of my way," Karen said.

Beyond the barrier, things had taken a turn. Other test subjects were screaming now; the magic was surging. The tide was coming in.

This is what you've been afraid of all this time, she thought. *This is what your magic looks like: dark, monstrous, and out of control.*

But maybe Isabel was right. Maybe relinquishing it wasn't the right answer either. Not in a world like this, with men like John Magnus and Morris Rabin. And now, seeing her magic in the wild, she realized that she was the only one capable of keeping it in check.

She closed her eyes. The words of the book came to her in flashes, inspiration from a place beyond human understanding. But that was what all magic was, an elemental force ignorantly channeled by fools. Using any magic was little more than a guess: an estimation, a calculation of risks and rewards. A roll of the cosmic dice.

The room rocked and the barrier's magic failed. One of the test subjects, a woman in a pink dress and white pearls, ran out of their confinement and grabbed the nearest researcher with bloody, nail-polished hands.

"Make it stop!" the woman demanded. The black emptiness was coming out of her mouth now, and her eyes. The researcher's lab coat smoked where her hands touched him. "You have to make it stop!"

"We . . . we're trying," the researcher stammered as he tried to pull away. Then he burst into flame.

The researcher roared in pain and surprise. He grabbed at his clothing and tried to pull it free, but the fire just grew hotter and stronger. His colleagues stared at him in mute, useless horror, but then Pierce's quick magic doused the flames. The man crumpled and smoldered. Isabel knocked the shocked woman back, but the other test subjects took her place, unstable magic seething in their eyes.

Focus, Karen. Those familiar words, her ever-present incantation. *Focus.*

The rampaging magic was hers, was *her.* So despite her ignorance and her fear, despite the horrible knowledge that this power was no friend to its host or this world, despite the pain she'd caused and the lives she'd taken, despite it all, this magic belonged to her. It had to come when she called it. And so she did.

The test subjects reached for her with crooked fingers.

Her magic was waiting for her. All around, the lab was alight with heat and energy and power. The void was there too, a dark shadow cast along the wall.

One of the test subjects charged, but crashed into a wall Pierce summoned.

The void spoke to her, like it had in Auttenberg, but Karen was beyond listening. If her life as a struggling female magician had taught her anything, it was what voices to ignore.

Behind her, researchers tried to flee the room, but the door apparently wouldn't open.

She closed her will around her errant magic like a fist.

More screams, shouting. Pierce calling her name. Isabel swearing in Spanish and Yoruba.

Now.

The magic came back to her in a flood. She tore it out of their failing bodies, excised like a cancer. She didn't know what damage it would do to them or if they even could be saved. But she had to bring her magic to heel; she *had* to close the breach. It was terrifying to see the wave of magic coming, but it couldn't hurt her; it had to obey her. Her lips tugged up into a grin.

And then it was over. The lab fell silent. A few of the subjects stirred; some lay still. The dark wounds on their bodies slowly closed. The researchers cowered, muted by forces they did not understand. In the middle of it all, Karen stood. Her magic filled her and demanded release, but she held it back. Because *she* was in control.

"Karen," she heard Pierce say, "what in the hell was that?"

She slid the book back into her bag. "I'll explain later," she said. She sighed. The strain of what she'd just done radiated pain across her shoulder blades and forehead. Blood dripped from her nose, but she smeared it away with the back of her hand. "Or actually, I probably won't. Isabel . . ."

Isabel was already moving. She grabbed up the researchers' copies of the transference spell—and most of their other notes besides—and a moment later, they were engulfed in emerald flame. For good measure, she did the same to an entire bookshelf of binders and notebooks.

Karen approached the man named Kellogg. He sat on the floor with his back to the wall, eyes staring into nothing. "Are there other copies of Gerald's notes? Or the spells you derived from them?"

"No," he said in an empty voice.

"Why should I believe you?" Karen asked.

His eyes focused on hers. He looked like he thought Karen was mad. "Do you really think I ever want to see magic like that again?"

Karen took the broken man at his word. All around, the lab

smoked and burned. It looked more like a battlefield than a research facility. She joined her companions and reluctantly took Pierce's offered arm.

"Come on," she said, breathing sharply against the pain. "We've got to get upstairs."

In the darkness outside of the facility, just beyond the reach of the light, the tattooed man waited. The road he had walked was longer and stranger than he had expected, but it had not been walked in vain. Though Karen had again and again come close to death, his mission to disaster, she had prevailed. So far.

And now she had proven his suspicions correct and validated both his patience and his faithfulness. The book had returned. And she had it.

By the time they found another stairwell and worked their way to the fourth floor, the battle had gone silent. Somehow, this was more unnerving than the constant gunfire. The hallway leading toward the CEO's office was dark, and though they tried to be quiet, their footsteps echoed back to them like explosions.

They found the first body facedown in the middle of the hallway. It was one of Rabin's men. His gun lay a few inches from his still fingers. His head was turned to the side; his eyes were open but glazing over. The next fallen mobster wasn't far. He was curled over in a fetal position, surrounded with cooling blood.

"Looks like they ran into tougher resistance," Pierce said.

Karen stared down the hallway, where she could see another body. "They ran into something, alright."

Then Isabel was at her shoulder. She was staring at the third

fallen man, who was crumpled against a door marked ACCOUNTING/
FINANCE. His chest was bright with blood. The ground around him
was slick with it.

"Morris," she whispered.

The Mob boss's eyes fluttered as the women approached; he
wasn't gone yet. When he saw Isabel, he tried to speak, but only
strangled sounds came out. His brilliantly white teeth were
stained red.

Isabel knelt in front of him. She put a hand on his cheek; his
head lolled into her palm.

"Mi hermanita," she said. Her nails dug into the skin of his
face. "You let him take my sister, you bastard."

Rabin began coughing; it was the closest he could come to
speech. Blood and spit ran down his chin.

"Don't trouble yourself with apologies," Isabel said. "Save your
strength. I want you to take a very long time to die." She stood and
left him there. A weak hand reached for her, but soon fell back to
the floor.

"His wound. That doesn't look like a gunshot," Pierce said softly
to Karen.

A scream from up ahead broke the silence. A shotgun went off.

"Shoot it!" a voice yelled.

"Up there!"

And then more screaming.

Karen took the final corner slowly. The hallway opened up to
an expansive reception area. The words MAGNUS INNOVATIONS
were written in block letters on one wall just above a massive portrait of John Magnus, CEO. There were leather chairs for guests to
wait in and a large desk in front of double oak doors that led to the
inner sanctum. Meredith's desk. But rummaging for the recep-
tionist's Rolodex would have to wait, as they were not alone.

Four of Rabin's men were still standing; the rest lay in morbid disarray around the room. Their blood coated the floors and stained the artwork hanging on the walls. The survivors had their backs to each other and their guns up, pointing them at every shadow in terrified desperation.

"Where did it go?"

"Did you hear something?"

"What happened to the boss?"

"Forget him. Let's get the hell out of here."

"I'm telling you, I heard something."

"What's—"

A pale white blur leapt out of the shadows. One of the goons screamed and was thrown across the room. He crashed into the far wall, just below Magnus's smiling visage. The others tried to run; they didn't get far. They were cut down, cut apart, without firing another shot. And standing over their lacerated bodies was the unnatural shape of the Lamb.

THIRTY-NINE

In the bright light of the reception area, Karen could get a better look at the monstrous construct. It was certainly spiderlike, with long curved legs sprouting at random from a compact body, but to compare it to any living creature seemed inappropriate. It had no face, no head; she wasn't even sure if it had a front or back, or just moved in any direction it pleased. Its thin legs—far more than just eight—ended in flat blades like spearheads that carved deep scratches in the polished floor. Like the other constructs, it made no sound of its own and moved with a strange aquatic grace even as it tore the final mobsters apart.

Meredith. She'd set this thing free, and then sent them up here to die. Karen had been a fool to trust her. Now she just had to hope she hadn't lied about everything.

She was about to reach for her magic when she saw Isabel walking out into the open.

"Isabel," Karen whispered. "What are you doing?"

The Lamb tensed; it had noticed Isabel's approach. Blood dripped from its raised feet.

"Isabel!"

"What is she doing?" Pierce demanded. He had his gun out,

but seemed to understand that it would have no effect on something like this.

Isabel raised a hand to the creature and said a word that made Karen's stomach drop and heart stop. "Graciela."

The Lamb didn't move.

"Isabel," Karen called from the false safety of the hallway. "You don't know that's her. She could still be alive! We can still—"

"I know my sister," Isabel said sharply over her shoulder. "I know the shape of her magic. I know the feel of her in a room." Her voice was breaking. "I'd know her anywhere, even here."

The Lamb retreated a few steps. Its deadly feet clicked on the floor like chisels.

"Graciela, it's me," Isabel said. "Tu hermana."

"I don't think it recognizes you," Karen said. She inched out into the room. She didn't want to get any closer to that thing, but needed to be near Isabel to protect her, if the need arose. Pierce reluctantly followed.

Isabel ignored Karen's pleas. "Hermanita, escúchame, por favor. I'm so sorry they did this to you, that I let them do this. I failed you."

The Lamb thrashed. It spun, its legs snapping. Karen froze, but it didn't appear to be advancing on Isabel. Was something of Graciela still in there? Had the Magnus magicians failed in completely wiping her personality before implanting her into their foul weapon?

Then it stopped.

"Isa . . . Isabel . . ." The voice seemed to come from everywhere. It bounced off the walls and echoed inside Karen's ears. It sounded only vaguely human, like the speaker had a mouthful of broken glass. But Isabel must have heard enough of her sister lost in there, because her body was rocked by a sob.

"Mi hermanita, mi amor," Isabel said. She held out a hand to the construct. The anima at its heart was glowing blue, the light muted as it filtered through its claylike skin. "Graciela," Isabel said. Karen never knew what she was going to say next. Suddenly the Lamb plunged one of its bladed feet into Isabel's stomach.

"No!" Karen screamed. She hurtled her magic at the construct. It hit with a glancing blow; the Lamb reared back and skittered toward the far side of the room. Karen ran to Isabel, who had fallen to her knees, her hands pressed hard against the wound.

"She's gone," Isabel whispered. Tears ran down her cheeks.

"Stay here," Karen said. "I'll stop that thing."

"I'm fine," Isabel managed to say through clenched teeth. "I had a shield up, but she went right through it."

Karen examined the wound for as long as she dared take her eyes from the enraged construct. "That looks deep enough to me. Stay down."

"No. I can't leave her," Isabel said, taking a sharp breath, swallowing her tears. "Not like this."

The Lamb was moving again, circling them. "I don't think we're going to have much of a choice," Karen said. The reception area was large, too large; it gave the Lamb too much room to maneuver. They'd been able to defeat two of these things back at the orphanage, but while those constructs were strong, they hadn't been that fast. But the Lamb was created as a tool of war and could strike like lightning.

"Karen," Pierce said from behind her, "do we have a plan?"

She let her magic loose in her veins. It flooded her body like a drug. "Don't die."

The Lamb charged, a clacking storm of voiceless rage. Karen quickly wrapped magic around her and Isabel and rolled to the side. She heard Isabel swear in sudden pain as her wound was wrenched, but Karen had no other choice. When the Lamb realized it had missed them, it changed direction and came again, but then Pierce shouted something, and a slick of black ice formed underneath its feet. The Lamb lost balance and tumbled into a heap of legs.

"Move!" Pierce called out.

Thanks for the advice, Karen thought as she got to her feet. *Because my plan was to just lie there and hope it forgot about me.*

Her magic was ready. Eager. There was no time to be creative about it; instead she gathered it up as a surge of kinetic force and then let it fly.

But the Lamb was quicker than she expected. The magic crashed into the wall as the construct scrambled out of the way. It lunged at Karen. Blades cut the air above her head as she ducked, then slashed the ground as she dove aside. It was on her in the blink of an eye, but then was gone in a flash of green fire as Isabel knocked it back, one hand outstretched, the other still clutching her stomach.

Furious, the Lamb turned its attention to Isabel. Its legs struck at her like scorpion tails, but Isabel was too fast, despite her wound. With the creature distracted, Karen summoned her magic again, but just before she released it, one of the Lamb's legs sliced at her. The tip of the spearlike foot dragged along her shoulder; ugly hot pain blinded her as blood soaked the arm of her shirt.

Pierce came at it again. More frigid magic burned the air, but the Lamb barely seemed to notice the frost forming on its legs. Isabel redoubled her attack from the opposite side, pulling the creature's attention in both directions at once.

Karen gritted her teeth. There'd be plenty of time for pain later. But as she got back to her feet, the double oak doors leading to Magnus's office opened, and there stood Magnus himself. His hair was mussed and his tuxedo was stained; he looked like he'd seen a ghost. The great CEO of Magnus Innovations took one terrified look at the carnage that was still unfolding in his reception area and ran for the hallway.

Forget him. If we don't kill this thing now, it won't matter if he escapes or not.

But when Pierce noticed Magnus, he suddenly broke off his assault on the Lamb. "Magnus!" he called out.

"Don't worry about him," Karen shot back.

The Lamb, free from one angle of attack, turned its full force on Isabel. Isabel had just enough time to bring up a bubble of shielding energy as two deadly legs came down. Her magic cracked under the astonishing pressure, but didn't fail.

Karen ripped the oak doors from their hinges and sent them flying through the air like bullets. They hit the Lamb hard and pinned it to the wall. Magnus's portrait fell facedown. A second later, the Lamb broke free. One of its legs dangled, the clay cracked nearly all the way through. Karen tried to bring the doors up again, but the Lamb's blades lashed out and splintered the wood into kindling.

"Pierce! We need your help here!"

Karen heard the inquisitor swear under his breath as Magnus reached the hallway and disappeared. *Come on, Pierce, focus on the task at hand.* After a pause, Pierce let the coward go and turned back to the Lamb. His voice was hard with anger as he shouted out his next incantation. Inquisitors weren't known for possessing the most complex or nuanced magic, but they knew magical combat better than most. The full force of his spell hit the Lamb on its damaged leg. The cracks widened, but it had no other obvious effect.

How do we hurt this damn thing? A snap from its deadly claws sent Pierce sprawling. Isabel was clearly hurting. The Lamb advanced on Karen, legs tearing up the floor.

Karen backed away, through the shattered doorway and into Magnus's recently abandoned office. His massive desk sat in the center of the room. Behind it loomed huge windows overlooking the dark ocean. There was an open wall safe to the right of the door, its contents spilled out onto the floor. Magnus had apparently packed in haste.

As she went, Karen jammed a hand into her satchel and came up with a silver sphere, about the size of a golf ball, inlaid with Germanic runes. Her previous research into the bag's enchanted items had made it clear that this one was dangerous. The runes she recognized were explosive, and the ones she didn't know certainly looked menacing.

"Here goes nothing," she whispered as her magic lit up the markings. Motioning for her allies to stay clear, she threw the metal sphere at the Lamb.

And the sphere exploded.

The force of the blast took Karen off her feet and threw her backward. The huge windows behind her were blown apart, and she had to scramble to keep from falling through them out into the blackness beyond. She heard a ringing in her ears and the sound of the ocean crashing on the rocks below. She blinked away stars in her eyes and looked for the Lamb.

It had been thrown against the office wall, but it was already uncoiling its legs and rising. But it hadn't escaped unscathed; its damaged leg had been snapped off.

"Graciela!" Isabel, standing in the office doorway, pulled the construct's attention away from Karen. The Lamb was enraged now, a creature of pure brutal fury.

Isabel evaded the Lamb's attack with the help of Pierce, but Karen knew their luck would run out. One mistake, and they'd join the dead mobsters in an instant. They needed something more to break through the creature's defenses, do some real damage. Her magical grenade had nearly killed her but had barely wounded the monster.

But now she had an idea.

"Hey!" she shouted at the monster. She sent a burst of magic its way; it hit with a solid thump, enough to get the Lamb's attention. "Over here. You want to fight? Fight with me."

The Lamb obliged. It crossed the room in a rush, its legs moving so fast it was hard to tell them apart. The two foremost snapped up, ready to come down on Karen like serpent fangs, but just before it could strike, Magnus's massive desk crashed into it from the side. The heavy wood desk broke apart on impact, but the force was enough to knock the Lamb down, buried for a brief moment.

That moment was all Karen needed. Her magic reached out and found the Lamb's severed leg. With all the might she had left, Karen sent it through the air like a javelin, right at the Lamb's glowing heart.

It hit. The hardened ceramic blade gouged into the construct's clay skin, exposing the anima within. But then the blade snapped and clattered to the floor, useless. The Lamb scattered the remains of the desk and leapt to its feet.

"It didn't even slow it down," Pierce shouted. "Karen, it's coming for you!"

So helpful, Karen thought as she watched the Lamb charging at her. *Now if you would kindly shut up while I save the day . . .*

She ignored Pierce. She ignored the deadly blades that were coming closer with every breath. She ignored the crashing ocean waves behind her and the dead men at her feet and the pain in her arm and the blood she felt dripping from her nose. She ignored everything and focused on the blue light escaping from the crack in the Lamb's chest. Her whole world shrank down to one small cube, bursting with magic and a little girl's stolen soul.

The Lamb was almost on her.

Graciela, Karen thought. *You're free.*

Then her magic ripped the anima out of the Lamb in a shower of broken clay.

FORTY

The Lamb dropped like a marionette with cut strings. The empty husk came to a stop inches from where Karen stood. A black cube, gone dark, hovered in the air where the creature had just stood. The room was silent.

Isabel's face was creased with pain, but she still came over to where the anima floated, and took it in both hands. As she pulled it to her chest, she whispered, "Thank you."

Karen wanted to collapse, but they had to find that address.

"I'm going after Magnus," Pierce announced as he headed for the door.

"We don't need him," Karen said. Meredith had set them up to face the Lamb, but for some reason Karen believed she hadn't been lying about her Rolodex.

"I won't let him get away. He needs to be brought to justice." Then he was gone.

Isabel slid to the ground, and Karen ran over to her. Her eyes were closed and she was breathing strained breaths through her nostrils.

"How bad is it?" Karen asked.

Isabel lifted her hand away from the wound. It was a few inches long and oozing dark blood. "It will make a fine scar to remind me of my failure," Isabel said softly. Her other hand was clutched tightly around Graciela's anima.

"You can't blame yourself, Isabel. You didn't do this," Karen said, but even as she said them, the words felt inadequate. This was not the sort of loss that could be wiped away with a few moments' reflection and some facile sentiments.

"Your shoulder," Isabel said, "looks worse than my stomach."

Karen was doing her best to forget her bleeding shoulder. As long as she didn't look at it, she wouldn't have to acknowledge how much it hurt. "We'll compare scars when this is done," she said with a pained laugh.

She left Isabel with a torn bit of cloth to press into her wound and started rummaging through what was left of Meredith's desk. Useless bits of paper were strewn around the floor: budgets and letters and memos, crumpled and tinted with blood. She found a gold cigarette case and a smashed telephone and a cracked family photograph. Karen held the picture up and wondered if the smiling people in it were related to Meredith at all. She doubted it. And then, under the collapsed sides of a desk drawer, she saw a black metal Rolodex.

"I found it," she said to Isabel, who grunted in reply.

Karen flipped through the cards until she reached "L." Doubt hit her like a punch in the gut. If Meredith had lied, and Magnus escaped . . .

She clicked the Rolodex again and saw the card marked LIN-COLN. It had an address in Havana. Karen ripped it out of the binder just as she realized her satchel was gone.

Her eyes frantically scanned the room. There were bodies and debris, but no sign of her bag. Then she heard the waves again out the broken windows. *The explosion.*

It must have thrown her satchel out with the shattered glass.

"Did you find the address?" Isabel asked in a pained voice.

"Yes," Karen said, distracted. It would still be there. It had to be. She'd go down to the water's edge and find her bag. And the book. "Yes. I got it. Let's get out of here."

The tattooed man stirred from his place in the shadows. It was calling to him. Just as it always found its way back into the world, it would find its way into his hands. The book wanted its power used by those who truly understood its purpose.

He smelled the salt spray of the water and smiled.

Isabel and Karen limped down the four flights of stairs. They saw no one, heard no one. About halfway down, they started to smell smoke. A little farther down, they saw the flicker of flames. Someone had set the laboratories on fire. They descended as quickly as their injuries would allow, wincing at every step.

When they made it to the facility's lobby, they nearly stumbled over a body in a white coat. It took Karen a moment to realize who it was: Kellogg, the lead researcher in the Transference lab. He'd been shot once in the head. Another body lay nearby. There was more smoke coming from the lower levels. They pushed forward, out the shattered front doors.

"Leave me," Isabel said, pulling away from Karen's helping arm. "I can make it the rest of the way. Get him, before he gets away."

From Magnus's lofty office, Karen had seen a pier in the bay behind the research facility. A massive boat was moored there. Lights blazed on its deck as it prepared to set sail. Pierce might have tried to follow Magnus, but if he didn't know about the boat, Magnus might still escape capture. If he got away now, something told Karen that he'd be a hard man to prosecute.

"Pierce will get him," Karen said.

"Pierce is a fool," Isabel said. "And I can take care of myself. Go."

Karen left her and made her way around the facility in the dark. Smoke was coming out of some of the windows now as orange flames pulsed behind the glass. The whole place would be engulfed soon enough, taking its secrets with it. She held her arm close to her body as she went; her shoulder was hot with pain from the Lamb's slash. But despite the wound and her fatigue, she pressed on. Someone had to pay for all of this.

The path ahead opened up as she neared the pier. She could smell the ocean's spray and hear the rumble of the yacht's engines; good, it hadn't left yet. *Time to face the music, Magnus.*

Then she heard voices. She ducked low and crept in alongside the pier, hidden in the shadows. She saw Pierce standing with his back to her. She almost called out to him, but then saw he had his gun raised. John Magnus stood on the pier a few feet away, his hands up.

"We warned you, Magnus," Pierce was saying. "The Thistle and Bough are not to be ignored."

The Thistle and Bough? Karen had never heard the name before.

Magnus laughed. "Is that what this is all about?"

"We told you that you could keep selling your little gewgaws as long as you wanted," Pierce said. "But you just had to have more."

"I don't take orders from the Thistle and Bough," Magnus said. "I've got friends in Congress, in the CIA, the damn White House."

"We've allies of our own, Mr. Magnus."

Who the hell is Daniel Pierce?

Magnus ignored him. "You come in and ruin my legitimate business. A business with significant investors, let me assure you. And once I tell my friends about the trouble you've caused me here, they will bury you and your bosses."

Pierce cocked his pistol. "I don't think that's how this is going to turn out."

Magnus snorted. "You're not going to kill me."

"We warned you," Pierce said again.

"Pierce." Karen stepped onto the wooden planks of the pier. "What are you doing?"

"Karen." He sighed. He didn't turn or lower his pistol. "I'd consider it a professional courtesy if you'd just walk away."

"I can't do that," she said. "Put down the gun."

"And here I thought she was working for you," Magnus said. "Though your group isn't really known for its female members."

"What is the Thistle and Bough?" Karen asked. "What is this all about?"

"It doesn't concern you," Pierce snapped.

"It does if I say it does," Karen replied.

Pierce laughed; Karen could see his shoulders shaking. "You're talented, I'll give you that," he said scornfully. "They warned me, once you butted your way into this mess. 'Don't underestimate her,' they said. What did they call you? Oh, yes. 'Dangerous and unpredictable.' They had no idea how right they were."

"Who warned you?"

"I've never seen a magician who can do what you do," Pierce said. "How you handled that monster up there . . . wow. You could have made quite the inquisitor."

"So then you know you are no match for me," Karen said. She wasn't sure she believed it, not with her bleeding arm and exhausted body. After all, Pierce was trained exclusively to bring rogue magicians to heel.

"This piece of garbage isn't worth it, Karen," Pierce said. "Think of your future. True, you were a disruption to our plans at first, but you've proven to be an invaluable help in bringing Magnus down. The people I work for will be very grateful."

"If I let you kill him."

"If you don't get in the way of a necessary cleansing."

Over Pierce's shoulder, Karen could see Magnus's face. His bravado had faltered; the reality of staring down that pistol barrel had finally set in. His skin had gone sickly and his eyes wide, like a cornered animal.

"You of all people should appreciate what I'm here to do, Karen," Pierce said. "You have a remarkable gift. Your magic makes you special, makes you powerful. And this buffoon in a fancy suit was going to take that and give it away to the highest bidder. Magic belongs in the hands of the chosen, the pure; you have to see that."

Karen's thoughts raced back over her time with Pierce. Every memory was cast in a new, unsettling light. "I'm going to ask you one question," she said. "I'd appreciate you answering truthfully, if that's something you're capable of." She shifted her weight forward. "Gerald. Who killed him?"

Pierce's gun fired. Magnus fell.

With frightening speed and casual grace, Pierce spun and leveled the smoking pistol at Karen. Fear hit Karen with unexpected force. She'd known Pierce was good, that he'd been trained at this sort of thing, but he'd killed so easily, moved so fast. And now his gun was pointed at her heart.

"*You* killed him."

"What's done is done," Pierce said. His gaze was as cold as steel, his grip on the gun just as steady. "Long before you got involved, I was tasked with ending Magnus's transference program and eliminating everyone involved. Gerald may have been your friend, but he was also one of the lead magicians working on this project. Without his contribution, none of this would have been possible."

"That doesn't give you the right to be his executioner."

"You'd be surprised. Now, we can resolve this peaceably, or another way. You tell me which you prefer."

Though she'd done it before, Karen didn't think she had the

strength to stop a bullet, not after her fight with the Lamb. She had even odds that she could take Pierce's gun before he could get a shot off, but what then? Another battle, another dead body? Was it better to stand down and bring Pierce to justice once they'd returned to the US? But what had he just said? *We've allies of our own.*

Karen was tired of death. Magnus Innovations had already brought too much of it into the world, and she had no interest in adding to their tally. She exhaled, exhausted and hurting, and started to walk away.

"Karen, I can't just let you—"

She didn't see the great misshapen figure until it was already upon her, then hurtling past. The pier groaned under its weight as huge, twisted feet pounded against the wood. Pierce shouted in alarm as the broken form of Solomon charged him. He fired his gun, but the bullets didn't stop the construct any more than the fall through the elevator shaft had. Before Pierce could speak any words of magic, one of Solomon's massive hands closed around his neck. Pierce gave a strangled cry; then there was a pop, and his limbs fell slack.

Its master's death avenged, the broken creature tossed Pierce's limp body into the surf and then turned on Karen. It had not escaped unscathed from the elevator; one arm was mangled beyond repair, and one leg grotesquely bent. Its faceless head hung at a strange angle, like that of a man dangling from a hangman's noose. Its pale skin was cracked, chipped, and scorched. But despite its injuries, its power source still burned brightly in its chest, and it came at Karen with the same unwavering intensity as it had at Pierce.

Running backward, Karen fled the pier as the construct came. As she hit the sand, she lashed out with her magic and blasted the wooden boards apart. Solomon disappeared for an instant into the black water, but then reappeared a moment later, cutting through the waves toward the beach, barely slowed by the ocean's pull.

Karen tried to use her magic on Solomon's anima like she had on the Lamb's, but it was still too protected in its chest. She gathered up the water and threw it at the construct like a giant club. Solomon stumbled on its broken leg, but then kept coming. Karen ran farther up the beach, but even Solomon's lopsided stride was much faster than any she could muster. It kicked up gouts of sand as it stomped toward her. The moonlight shone white on its alien shape. Karen planted her feet and reached deep and pulled together what little magical energy she had left, for one final blow.

But she never had to deliver it. As Solomon raised its one working hand like a hammer, it was caught midstride by an emerald inferno. Karen turned to see Isabel standing a few feet behind her. The fire burned the air around her so brightly that Karen could hardly look at her. She'd seen Isabel summon this magic before, against the constructs at the orphanage and against the Lamb, but this was different somehow: hotter, stronger, fiercer. It had barely slowed the other constructs, but now the force of it was enough to knock Solomon back into the ocean. The water vaporized around the column of green fire.

And then Karen saw why Isabel's magic had gained such unexpected strength: in her outstretched hand, she held Graciela's anima.

First Maria, now Graciela, Karen thought.

But it was already done, and Graciela's anima was spent. Solomon writhed against the assault, but it could not withstand magic like this, a soul's final magic. Its clay skin bubbled. It reached for Isabel, but that great killing hand melted in the flames. A moment later, all that was left of the construct was its black heart, which dropped into the ocean and vanished.

FORTY-ONE

Joaquin's car pulled up to the address written on the card labeled LINCOLN. It was a small house just outside of Havana. A few lights were on inside. Two black sedans were parked in the driveway.

An American man answered the door. He had a gun in his hand, held down at his side. Waiting for him on the doorstep were three women, grim-faced and spattered with blood. He never understood what happened next. Suddenly, his gun was missing. As he gaped at his inexplicably empty hand, some unknown force smashed his head into the wall behind him and he blacked out.

Another man came running at the sound, but stumbled as a strange fatigue overtook him, forcing him down like a heavy wool blanket. The last thing he saw before he fell asleep was the mocking smile of the youngest of the three women, her hand touching her beaded necklace, her lips deftly forming the words of a spell even as she grinned at him.

There were two more men posted to the house. They lasted no longer than the others.

In a back room barred and locked from the outside, the three women found what they had come for. There were eight children in all, with dirty clothes and tear-streaked cheeks. When they saw who had come for them, they cried and laughed and cheered. The smallest child ran up to one of the women, an American with a bloody shoulder, and wrapped her arms around her legs. When the woman knelt down, the little girl handed her a matted, filthy stuffed bear the light tan color of a yam.

R amón waited. After all these years, it was something he was quite experienced at. He did not mind waiting, even as Cuba burned all around him. The revolution was gaining ground, in truth faster than he had expected. The Cuban military had mounted a response, but they hadn't been ready for the intensity of the opposition. They had believed their own propaganda and were expecting to fight against inexperienced students and ignorant farmers. Instead they were facing zealots. Now Ramón's sources told him that Batista was in the process of fleeing the country. The Cuban government was no more. And so, he waited.

But despite his patience, the delay did not sit well with him. Their orders had been prearranged and explicit. If Cuba was going to fall, so be it, but they could not allow valuable intelligence to be lost in the chaos. There would be time to evaluate new political realities with a Communist state so close to the Americans, and there would be opportunity to consider what they had gleaned from the revolutionaries and from the capitalists who had been using Havana as their own lawless paradise. There would be time for all of this, but only if they made it out. And she was running late.

If he returned without her, the gray-haired man would not be pleased. As much as he cared about the overthrow of Cuba's corrupt government, Ramón was certain he was more interested in what she had stolen from the now-destroyed Magnus Innovations. He checked his watch again. He had a little time left.

So he waited.

M eredith checked her rearview mirror for the hundredth time. She didn't think she was being followed, but that meant little. Her instructors had been adamant: this was the most dangerous part of any mission, when you felt so close to success that you let down your guard just for a moment. That is when disaster would strike.

She glanced over at the briefcase next to her. She'd risked everything for this mission. She'd given up more than a year of her life for it. But if she played her cards right, it would all be worth it.

Havana was in an uproar. Their government was gone, fled in the night. Now the streets were full of the curious throng, all waiting for the arrival of their new masters. What would Cuba make of Communism? Meredith thought of breadlines and starving children. Maybe Cuba could perfect what Russia could not. Maybe Cuba would prove at last that it could be done.

Not for the first time, she felt something resembling regret. Magnus deserved his fate, and she hoped the monster they kept locked in the basement had torn him apart slowly. But she wondered if she should have warned Karen before sending her to her likely death. The magician had proven useful, after all, and was no friend of men like Magnus. But the mission had come first; the mission always came first.

She checked the mirror again. Almost there.

R amón heard the car before he saw it. He rose from his seat and walked out to the road to meet it. He'd heard a flurry of gunshots nearby only moments earlier, but he hadn't been able to tell if they were a celebration or an assault. Either way, he was ready to return to more civilized society. The car stopped, and a gaunt man with a faded hat stepped out.

"No sign of her?" Ramón asked in Spanish.

Joaquin shook his head.

"And what of your American friends?"

Joaquin took off his hat and ran a hand over his balding scalp. "I'm sure they are halfway to Florida by now."

"Do you think they suspected you?"

"Karen, no," Joaquin said. "She is an impressive woman, but not a spy. Too singularly focused. Misses the details going on around her."

"What about your old friend Arthur?"

Joaquin shrugged. "Arthur suspects everyone. I would guess that he knew what he was doing when he asked for my help. This time, the Soviets were not his enemies."

The gunfire returned, a rapid snare-drum pop a few blocks away. It was followed by indistinct shouting and the sound of breaking glass. Ramón thought of Spain and the chaos of revolution. "What do you think of your country now?" he asked Joaquin. "What becomes of Cuba?"

Joaquin stared off in the direction of the noise. His guarded eyes revealed nothing of his thoughts but hinted at some unspeakable sadness. Though he was a valuable agent, he had not requested extraction, despite the recent events. Ramón could understand.

"Cuba has survived worse," Joaquin said.

"It may survive, but will you still recognize it?"

For a time, it seemed that perhaps Joaquin was not going to respond. Ramón did not blame him; there was little use in predicting the future. But then he put his hat back on and turned away from the sounds of battle.

"Cuba is Cuba," he said. Nothing else needed to be said while they waited for the wayward agent.

Meredith parked her car. The windshield was nearly opaque with a scrim of dust as the sky overhead refused to rain. She grabbed the briefcase in one hand and the door handle in the other.

Think of the mission, her training told her. *See it done, no matter the cost.* She'd done it all, exactly as had been required. The intrusion of the Americans had been unexpected—not to mention the sudden arrival of the revolutionaries—but she had persisted. They would be proud. They would be grateful. But she was no longer certain that was enough.

The road had run out. *Time to decide.*

For so long, there had been no decision to make. But everything was different now, with Magnus's facility burned to the ground. She alone had something of great value to one side or the other. Before, she'd been in a loveless, arranged betrothal. But now she had suitors. Or at least a tempting dowry.

She pulled her cigarette case from her purse. It was nothing special, just tarnished brass. But she'd carried it with her this entire journey, all the way to this final moment. She opened it. Inside were a handful of sweet Cuban cigarettes. And one other, one she had kept since Moscow. She pulled it out and held it up. A Belomorkanal, from the Uritsky Tobacco Factory in Leningrad. She must have smoked hundreds of these but it looked so strange to her now, like a relic from another life.

She put it to her lips and lit it. It was strong, too strong. The smoke burned inside her mouth. The taste brought back so many memories. Outside her car window, she could see the streets of Moscow. Snow fell vengefully from a black sky. The people hid their grim faces in coats and scarves and scowls. She saw the endless colorless buildings, the railway tracks that vanished into shadow, the work camps, the barbed wire. Above it all, she saw the

steady eyes of the gray-haired man: unyielding, unblinking, unforgiving.

Ramón had asked her if she was satisfied with the choices she'd
made, the sacrifices she'd made. Hardly.

Deep down, she knew she'd already made her decision. She
couldn't go back. That wasn't her world anymore. It had nothing to
offer her. She didn't fool herself; there was no promise of a brighter
tomorrow in a new land, only a faint hope. She tightened her grip
on the briefcase. She hoped she would find somewhere warm.

She got out of the car and walked purposefully toward the
building. The place was bustling. Men and women with serious
faces and hungover eyes ran about like ants in a flooding anthill.
Their world had been turned upside down overnight; there wouldn't
be many New Year's celebrations at the CIA operating base in
Havana, not this year. No one stopped her until she reached the
reception desk.

"Can I help you?" the woman behind the desk asked her skeptically.

"Yes," Meredith said. "I'm here to see Lloyd Ellis."

"Do you have an appointment?"

"No," she said unapologetically. She set the briefcase down on
the desk, scattering a few papers. "I have something better."

FORTY-TWO

They told her the airplane was scheduled to leave in ten minutes; that had been two hours ago. Karen wasn't surprised by the delay, not with smoke still rising over Havana. Things had changed in a way no one could describe, not yet. On-time flights were just one of many sacrifices Cuba would have to make before something like normalcy returned, if it ever would.

"Don't worry about me," Isabel had told her when they'd parted. Joaquin had taken them to the orphanage, and the nuns had summoned a doctor to look at her wounds. Elisa had refused to leave her side. "You Americans have enough to worry about on your own. Leave Cuba's troubles to Cuba."

"You saved my life on the beach," Karen had said.

"How many times did I save you, but I just get credit for the once?" Isabel had asked in feigned disgust.

Karen had taken her hand and squeezed it. "Thank you."

"De nada," Isabel had said; her smile overpowered the pain in her eyes.

Finally they allowed passengers onto the airplane. The friendly stewardesses offered her lipsticked smiles as she boarded, despite their constricted waists and tall heels. Cuba might be falling apart, but Pan Am still required perfect makeup. Priorities. Karen managed a weak nod in their direction. She'd just settled into her seat and closed her eyes when someone nudged her uninjured shoulder. "That seat taken?" asked a gruff voice.

Karen looked up. "Arthur?"

The old CIA chief looked sallow and exhausted, with greasy skin and bulging sacks under his eyes. But he managed a grin all the same.

As the airplane leveled out and turned north, Arthur asked her how she'd found her holiday abroad.

"Enlightening," she replied. "How did you get them to let you out?"

Arthur chuckled to himself. "They were glad to see the back of me. I've never been a good houseguest." When she pressed him further, all he would add was, "It might be hard to believe, but I still have a friend or two in the Agency, and what they lack in number they make up for in belligerence."

Over the brilliant blue Atlantic, Karen told him what had happened since his capture at the hotel. He didn't interrupt or ask any questions, just grunted at a few details and generally looked unwell. Even the complimentary scotch the stewardess brought him did little to brighten his mood.

"That," he said when Karen and his drink were done, "sounds like a damn fine mess."

"Couldn't have said it better myself," she replied.

"I never liked that Pierce."

Karen winced. She'd have a lot to explain when she returned to the OMRD, but the betrayal and death of a decorated agent of Public Inquiry would undoubtedly be the hardest. "He said he was working for 'the Thistle and Bough.' You ever heard of them?"

Arthur shook his head. "Sounds like magician nonsense to me."

Yes, it does. What sort of group could infiltrate the OMRD and escape the notice of the CIA? She wasn't sure she wanted to find out. But it wasn't only Pierce's mysterious allegiance that bothered her; she still hadn't figured out the motivations of the strange tattooed man who had saved her in the Miami airport. She'd left that part out of her story to Arthur; it wouldn't make it into any report she wrote, either. How long had he been watching her without her knowledge? And what did he want from her?

"Karen," Arthur said as the airplane began its descent, "you have a remarkable talent for stirring up trouble wherever you go. I think you might be the most unlucky person I've ever met. And maybe the toughest."

"What did they do to you, Arthur?" Karen asked. "They've made you soft."

"Oh, no," he said. "Those scared little boys had nothing on me. It's the memories and regrets that got to me. And that drink." He clinked the glass and the stewardess refilled it.

"I couldn't have done all this without you."

"Feel free to forget that during your deposition."

"Arthur who?"

"That's my girl," he said with a snort. "I'm sorry you couldn't save Maria."

A pang struck her chest. *Memories and regrets,* Arthur had said. "She was gone before I ever stepped foot in Cuba," Karen said, "but that doesn't make me feel any better. Someone should have been there to help her."

"You can't save them all."

She knew he was right, just like she knew that was no excuse.

"What will you do when you get back to DC?" he asked.

"Face the music," she answered.

"Hopefully it's a tune you can dance to."

Karen thought of a little stuffed bear hopping from one chubby leg to the other, one arm nearly falling off, and of the cheer of onlookers as it promenaded across a dusty classroom table. "I think I'll be alright."

The director's office looked much the same. Karen had to keep reminding herself she'd only been away a short while; most people in the building hadn't even gotten around to taking their Christmas decorations down. And yet it seemed like a lifetime ago that she opened up Gerald's box and pulled out that small black cube.

She'd been in his office for less than five minutes, but Director Whitacre had already told her at least half a dozen times just how happy he was to have her back. "You were missed, my dear," he said with a broad smile as he took his place in the chair across from her. "It just wasn't the same here without you."

Karen nodded to the file in his hand. "You've had a chance to read my report, sir?"

Whitacre looked at the pages with surprise, as if he'd forgotten he was holding them. That smile never faded; it reminded Karen too much of John Magnus. "Yes, yes I have," he said. "Thank you for taking the time to write all this up. Seems like things have taken a rough turn down there in Cuba. Hope the boys over there in the State Department can sort that one out for Uncle Sam."

"And you reviewed the section on Agent Pierce?"

Lines appeared unbidden across the director's forehead, and the wattage of his smile seemed to dim. "I did, Karen," he said. "I did. Actually, that's why I asked you to meet with me today."

"Good," Karen replied. "Because I have a lot of questions myself, sir."

"Questions," Whitacre repeated, like it was a word he hadn't heard before. "Yes, lots of questions and too few answers. Never the way I want to end an investigation. Very unsatisfying, like a book without an ending."

"The investigation doesn't have to end, sir."

Whitacre tapped the document on his knee. "John Magnus has gone to meet his maker. His company is in turmoil, their stock price has dropped like the mercury in January. These 'transference' experiments seem to have been thwarted, thanks to your intervention. What is there possibly left to investigate?"

Karen held up her fingers to enumerate a list. "Who was Pierce working for? How did they know about the experiments before we did? Why did they order Magnus killed? What other secrets are they hiding?" She paused and let her words hang in the air. "Should I go on?"

The look on the director's face showed that he hadn't meant for his question to be answered. He set the document aside and folded his hands. "Karen, I think it is in the best interests of the OMRD if we leave some of these outlandish questions unanswered."

"You mean unasked."

"I mean that we need to show some discretion here."

"You want me to rewrite my report?"

He shook his head emphatically. "No, no. Your report is excellent. I just want you to take it and read it again, really read all of it, and ask yourself if there aren't any parts that might be better if they were . . . revised." The smile came on again, full strength. "Could you do that for me?"

Karen stared at the director and tried to remember what it was like when Dr. Haupt sat in his place. She had wanted to believe the best of him too.

"That's an interesting ring, sir," Karen said, pointing to his right hand. "I'd never noticed it before."

Whitacre blinked and touched the gold ring absently, turning the face away from Karen's view, but not before she noticed the crest that was stamped on it. She'd originally thought it was a class ring of some sort, but she knew of no university with that particular symbol: a spiky flower crossed over a crooked stick. A thistle and a bough.

"Actually, sir," Karen said, "I think my report is already as accurate as I can make it. I don't think any further revisions will be necessary."

Whitacre's eyes fell and he exhaled a long blast of breath from his nose. "Very well. If that's your answer, then I'm afraid there's nothing else I can do." He reached into his jacket and took out a single sheet of paper, and set it on the small table between the chairs.

Karen didn't need to read the words; she'd written them after all:

> *Dear Director Whitacre,*
>
> *Please accept my resignation from the Office of Magical Research and Deployment, effective immediately.*
>
> > *Sincerely,*
> > *Karen O'Neil*
> > *Head Researcher, Department of Theoretical Magic*

"Where did you get this?" she demanded. "This was locked in my desk."

"I'm not any happier about it than you are, my dear," he said, his voice heavy with regret. "But if you've decided that you no longer have a place here at the OMRD, I will not stand in your way."

We've allies of our own.

"We'll always be grateful for the work you've done for us,"

Director Whitacre said. "And we do wish you luck, wherever your future path leads."

The air in her apartment was cold and stale. A gray winter rain slashed the windows; she could hear a drip ticking away somewhere. She didn't bother turning on a light, but instead sat at her lonely table in the dark.

The OMRD was the only place she'd ever considered working. When Dr. Haupt had invited her to join right after school, it hadn't felt real. Could she truly spend the rest of her life researching new and unexplored magic? No, it turned out; apparently she could not.

Her life had been her research. She'd stay in her lab all night, if they let her. Magic was an unconquered and unending frontier, a new world where she could make her mark forever. With her research, she could prove it was more than fire and flash; it was as complex as the human soul, and just as infinite.

But what good had she ever done there? What good had she actually done for this world while she was searching out new ones? She'd spent the years since Auttenberg hiding in a lab that looked remarkably like those in Magnus's facility while people like Gerald and Maria were suffering, dying. It was only when she took off the lab coat and went out into the world—the messy world full of magic she didn't understand or trust—that she did anything worth remembering.

When she finally flipped on a light, she noticed a stack of packages in one corner: Christmas gifts she'd never bothered to wrap, let alone deliver. Had she even told her sister not to expect her for Christmas dinner? Or for New Year's?

The rain showed no sign of letting up, but it wasn't late yet, a small perk of abruptly losing one's job. She could probably make it to Helen's before they sat down for supper. Her sister would pretend to be put out because Karen didn't call ahead, but secretly would love nothing more than to set another place at the table. Martha would cheer, especially at the thought of an unexpected surge of Christmas presents. Karen would have to endure her sister's judgmental gaze at her bruises and the bandages on her shoulder, but maybe that was a small price to pay.

She'd need a new job, maybe a change of scenery. What options were there for a magician who'd made powerful enemies in Washington and Moscow? A smile crept onto her lips as she remembered the woman she'd met in Havana, Sandra Saint. What was the name of her movie again? *The Magician's Curse*. Sounded about right. Maybe they'd need a consultant with real-world experience. She wondered what the weather was like in Hollywood this time of year.

She gathered up the gifts, stuck on a few bows as appropriate, and made for the door. But as she was about to walk out, her eyes fell on her satchel. Ehle's satchel.

The leather was scratched and scuffed. It had taken her nearly half an hour to find it among the rocks below Magnus's office. It was still crusted with ocean salt.

"Did you find it?" Isabel had called out to her in the dark.

Karen's fingers were shaking as she retrieved it from among the black seaweed. Her heart had been in her throat; she hadn't been able to breathe.

"I found it," she called back. The name—and the memories—had come back to her as soon as she'd touched it: *Erwin Ehle*. A German magician, talented in enchantments, haunted by regrets. She'd followed him into Auttenberg, and when they'd done what they came to do, he'd stepped into the breach, hoping to be forgotten. And he had been, by everyone but Karen. She didn't know what that meant, but doubted it was good.

Splashed by ocean spray, battered, bleeding, and cold, she had reached for the flap reluctantly. The weight of the bag felt wrong, like it had been hollowed out. It wasn't possible. She had exhaled and flipped the bag open, hoping, praying, begging. She'd reached inside.

The book was gone.

Photo by Kimberly Goodwater

W. L. GOODWATER is the author of the Cold War Magic series. He lives on the California coast with his wife, kids, and cats. When he's not writing books, he's usually reading them. Or thinking about them. Or just staring lovingly at them. His wife might like books even more than he does, and she finds his vain attempts to organize their bookshelves endearing; they are a perfect couple.

Ready to find
your next great read?

Let us help.

Visit prh.com/nextread